BLOOD ORANGE

BLOOD ORANGE

A SYNTH LOVE STORY

RAE SENGELE

Snakeshead Press

Copyright © 2025 Rae Sengele

Published by Snakeshead Press

Cover Design by Rae Sengele
Cover photo by ThisIsEngineering on Pexels.

ISBN: 979-8-9907878-4-1 (print)

Printed in United States of America

1st Edition, 2025

CONTENT GUIDE

Note: This is not an exhaustive list and may contain spoilers

Blood Orange is an exploration of queer autonomy and the process of coming out in world that might not be entirely ready for you. As such, it will contain allusions to queer trauma and homophobia which unfortunately are not too far off from racism and can also be interpreted as such. There are also depictions of manipulation, controlling behavior, and brief depictions of a verbally abusive relationship, as well as, depictions of PTSD, confinement, the aftermath of rape and sex trafficking, attempted assault, and mentions of past sexual assault.

LISTEN TO THE

BLOOD ORANGE

PLAYLIST ON SPOTIFY

*For the ones who fought their way out of the closet,
the ones still there, the ones fighting for them,
and those who kept us safe along the way*

We'll be leaving in the morning. You'll wake to find the house empty. The car that has apparently been sitting untouched under a cover in the gravel driveway, the one you thought was unusable, will be gone. And you'll have questions. I'm sure some of them will be the same as mine. Where are we going? Why are we going there? Why did we have to steal away in the middle of the night? I don't know, I wish I did.

Aurora has done her best to explain it to me, but she's just as limited in her ability to speak openly to me as Charlie, Delta, and Fox are. It's not by choice, that much I do know.

"Not I won't," she said to me in Seattle. "I *can't.*"

I don't know what that means, but I have a strong feeling that it has something to do with you, Marsh. She hates you now. They all do. They've never said it directly, but I can feel it. It's in the way they avoid you; the way their shoulders go tense when you enter the room; the way Charlie always keeps himself between you and Delta; the way Fox's voice goes up a nervous octave when you bring her puzzles to solve; the way Aurora glares at you always, even when you're in the other room.

I don't understand it. In my memories, you two got along. Your relationship wasn't perfect. You were her boss, not her friend, but she liked you well enough. But my memories apparently aren't accurate. Some things are. Some things aren't. So, every time she curses you behind your back or her grip tightens around my hand when you enter a room, or coaxes Fox away from you, I don't know if this is something new, if something happened between what I remember and what I don't, or if it's just one more thing that was never real.

I'm so tired of not knowing what is and isn't real.

I'm so tired of relearning reality.

That's why, even though I don't have the same hatred for you, I'm still going with them in the morning: so, hopefully, without you, I can finally know the truth. Well, that's part of it, I guess. A large part of it. The other part is Aurora. She wants to be done with you. She hasn't said those specific words, if she even can, but I can feel it. She wants out of this house and away from this place. And I'd do anything for her. I just got her back. I'm not losing her again.

Besides, I don't have much here without her. Other than you, Aurora and the others are my only constants. Even with that, there are things that are missing, things they know that I don't, things about me that they can't tell me, things about Bravo and Eden. Not won't, can't. I want to know what's happened to me. I want to know what happened to Bravo and Eden. I want to know what happened back in Bastrop. I want the truth. You're not giving me that and, for whatever reason, they can't while here with you.

Why am I recording all this? Why am I still communicating with you? Why am I not in bed next to Aurora where I could be nestled under her arm against her body where I'm safe from you?

I don't know.

There are still so many things I don't understand.

Maybe I'm just nervous. Maybe I just need to talk all this through. Maybe I'll never actually send this. But then why you? I don't know that either. Habit? Aurora says I'm a creature of habit, says I always have been. Remembering her words, the sweet, teasing smile she'd said it with...I feel like I could float away. It's something that I remember that's real, the way she is real.

I want to find more things that are real. I want to remember what she remembers. She doesn't remember when we first met the way I do. That hurts the most. It's one of my favorites. It's like a movie. I knew I loved her from the sound of her laugh.

By that point in my memory, I was already working for you, already sitting at that little clump of desks by myself, flanked on either side by you and Eden. Your cluster of mismatched desks were in the corner, journals, textbooks, notebooks, dried out pens, chewed up pencils, uncapped dry erase markers, junk food wrappers, crumbled receipts strewn across them, spilling out of the metal mesh waste basket. Your monitors filled the walls over your desks, wrapped around the front of your little half circle wood and metal sanctuary.

I could always tell your mood by which monitors you were using, which part of you I could see. If you were facing the door, your body open, leaned back in your computer chair, long arm stretched out to reach the mouse, the keyboard, paper that you were scribbling on, I cold talk to you about anything, make jokes and teasing remarks. If you were in profile, hunched over your desk, face close to the monitors, one ruddy hand buried in the muted orange of your beard and mustache, I was free to take my chances. I could get a beleaguered laugh out of you, I could get a half-hearted chuckle, more than likely I'd get a little puff of air from your nostrils, an exhausted attempt at a grin without tearing your attention from your computer, a muttered, partially coherent response. If all I saw was your back, if all I heard was the feverish clicks and clacks of your heavy keyboard, muttered curses, the rest of the office quiet with an equal tension, well, I never tried to speak to you then.

It was on those days that I'd turn to Eden. She was always open even when you weren't, always faced me at her big l-shaped desk in the opposite corner that was always pristine, always minimally decorated. She'd sit there in her crisp yet loose fitted button ups tucked into her fitted jeans, her short, but thin fingers adorned in dainty gold rings like filigree flying across the flat keyboard, occasionally stopping, hovering, flexing with thought, before continuing in her typing. In my memories, Eden was the silk to your polyester—sleek like water, delicate as air, but no less fiery when she needed to be. There was never a time when she was closed off to me, her back turned, the world shut out. She was always open, always there even when it was clear I was ripping her away from something important. Every time I approached her desk, she'd stop what she was doing, turn her body towards me, those grey-green eyes focused solely on me and what I had to say. She'd listen, nod, take in my words, answer with honesty even when she didn't have the answer, especially when she didn't have an answer.

"I just don't know, Echo," she told me that day.

I don't remember anymore what my question had been. It wasn't important enough to hold onto. But she'd leaned on her elbows then, scrubbed her face with her hands, let out a long sigh and raked her fingers through her dirty blonde hair. I'd glanced at Bravo who had been sitting at the desk next to Eden, her laptop balanced on her knee that was hooked over the other. Those round, dark blue eyes moved from Eden to me and her slender shoulders shrugged, her long, pink lips tucked up into one cheek. She looked back to Eden, her long fingers tapped absently against the keys of her laptop. I could sense that she wanted to reach out to her, touch her back, stroke her hair, sooth her nerves in that sweet, tender kind of way lovers do, but they were at work, they were in front of you. So, her hand stayed on her laptop, her fingers tapping out her longing.

I glanced at Eden's monitor, skimmed through the far from finished proposal the two of them had been working on for the last week. The Eden I remember hates proposals, red tape, begging for permission. She'd rather act and clean up afterwards. Do first, ask forgiveness after. Her eyes closed, she pressed her palms together, her fingertips resting against the bridge of her nose. Her lips parted and she took in a breath, but the words wouldn't come.

Which might have been for the best. Sound down the hall distracted me anyways. My eyes unfocused, my ears strained. Two sets of footsteps—one precise in what sounded like ballet flats, the other less focused in boots too heavy for her feet. A teenage voice chattered aimlessly. An adult laughed, the sound mid-toned, warm, like the first hum of the heater in winter.

I turned away from Eden to look at the door, waiting for the two to walk through. I wanted to see the face that belonged to that laugh.

"Echo?" Eden said with that controlled calm of hers. "What is it?"

"Huh? Shit." The swift swish of your chair, the thud of your knee against metal. "Fuck. What's what? Echo? What's up?"

I didn't dare look away from the door, didn't want to miss the moment the laughter appeared. "Who's with Fox?"

"Hm?" Eden intoned behind me. "Oh." The small clink of the button on her cuff against the metal of her watch.

The creak of your chair. Your shallow footsteps across the thin carpet.

"Are they here already?" Eden said to no one in particular.

You stepped around me to lean out the door.

"DAD!" Fox cried out with a giggle and her footsteps broke into a run.

You smiled under the orange facial hair, your hooded light green eyes full of light, your arms in your worn thin flannel wide and ready for the lanky, blue haired teen who fell against your chest, her arms around your sternum, her eyes closed as she melted against you.

Those ballet flat footsteps continued at the same pace. My eyes zipped to the right side of the door, waiting for their owner to step into frame. But they stopped just short, my heart both sinking and racing with anticipation.

You looked up, presumably to the owner of the ballet flats, your smile not once faltering. "Hey, Ror."

Ror, I thought. Not like the roar of a machine, something softer, something sweeter, something that moved in figure eights between my feet and rubbed its head against my shin.

"Hello, Marsh." The voice was as warm as the laugh. It made my bones tingle.

"How's our girl?" you said to the voice, but also Fox who was looking up at you with a wide grin, her softly square chin against your sternum. "Glad to be done with school?"

She nodded.

"Marsh," Eden called from her desk. "Come introduce Aurora before Echo short circuits."

I hate to admit how I crossed my arms then in the hope of hiding the way my heart stumbled. I tucked my hair behind my ear to hide the heat rushing through my cheeks up to my ears. "I'm not going to short circuit."

"Sure," Bravo said with a sweet snicker.

But beneath that every inch of my insides was scrambling, rejoicing—Aurora. Like angels singing in the heavens. Like a million tiny, magical lights in the darkness. Like the murmur of starlings down the length of my spine. Like the realization that before now I had been so alone, that from now on I'd never have to be.

"Shit," you said with a chuckle. "Yeah. Ror, come on in." You gestured to the voice—to Aurora. "Meet the others."

The time it took for you to motion her through the door and for her to turn the corner felt like eons, every second a lifetime in itself. My heart raced, my head spun, my bones tingled with the possibility of her.

And then there she was.

Aurora.

She was like sunshine, my skin like flowers aching for her sustenance. Those sweet, soft brown eyes found mine and those long flat lips spread into a toothy smile that felt like rapture. I could have worshiped her. Maybe I already do.

"Hey," she said with a nervous wave then tucked a chin length auburn wave behind her ear.

"Oh, Fox," you said behind her, your job done. "I finished that puzzle."

"Oh!" She bounced after you into my peripheral towards your desk. "How hard did you make it?"

"Pretty hard."

She laughed that reckless teenage laugh that I so rarely hear anymore. "Yeah, sure."

"*You* think you can solve it?"

"Faster than you!"

But I didn't watch you or her, didn't pay attention after that. I was glued to Aurora as we blinked at each other, processing the other's existence.

Behind me, Eden sighed and I heard the swivel and squeak of her chair as she stood.

"Aurora," she said, "this is Echo."

"Hi, Echo," she said with a chuckle that sparked a flame low in my stomach.

She held her hand out to me. For what was probably too long of a beat, I just stared at it. How could I touch something so holy? Would my hand be scorched? Would I be left with a mark? But then again, did I even care? I'd be scorched a million times over if it meant just being near Aurora. I reached out and took her hand. Everything felt right, complete.

"Hi," I finally got out.

Then Eden touched my shoulder as she leaned around me, pulling me back to earth with a jolt. "Aurora is Fox's nanny. Since the new semester started and the seminar coming up plus that new project taking off, we just can't be home as much as we'd like. You know how it is."

I nodded.

"Oh," Aurora looked from me to Eden and back again, "do you work for Marsh and Eden?"

I just nodded. "Mhm," was all I could think to say.

"Echo's one of our assistants," Eden said for me. "Oh, and this is Bravo, one of our professors."

She turned and panic went through me. Not Bravo. Not gorgeous, affectionate, witty Bravo. Don't meet Bravo. But then she was standing. Then she was next to Eden with that brilliant wide smile. Then she was holding her long, elegant hand out to Aurora. Then they were talking. Then they were laughing and I was left behind, rushing to follow the conversation, missing every opportunity to be heard, to be seen. As usual.

"Hey," you said, your hand on my shoulder.

I turned to you, though most of my focus was still on Aurora, still on wishing I knew how to be seen.

"Fox is kind of hungry. You up for going over to Sadie's for us?"

I did like walking the few blocks over to the street that was considered "downtown." I liked stopping in at Sadie's, the little sandwich place on Main Street, liked talking to the Smiths.

But...Aurora.

I glanced at her, thinking you wouldn't notice.

"She'll still be here when you get back," you whispered with a smirk despite my best efforts.

I glanced at her again, for some reason afraid that if I did as you said, if I left now, she'd be gone forever. But I had to trust that she wouldn't. Right? Because that was ridiculous. Wasn't it? I took in and let out a long breath, then nodded.

I was partly down the hall regretting saying yes to you and lamenting my lack of charm, when I heard my name on her tongue. I turned, maybe too quickly, too eagerly, and saw her rushing towards me with what I was hoping was a nervous version of the smile that could compete with the sun.

"Mind if I tag along?"

Please, I wanted to say. *Never leave me.* Instead, I just shrugged and shook my head. "Not at all."

That smile relaxed, became my entire world.

And we walked together.

And the rest was history.

Or, at least, that's what I believed. What I, up until a few weeks ago, thought to be the truth.

It's a good truth to believe in. Like believing a rainbow is more than just light refracting through water droplets in the air. It's a sweet lie to live in.

But it's still a lie.

I'm reminded of that now as I hear her stirring in the bed we don't need to sleep in, but do anyways, because it's another sweet lie. She's realizing I'm not next to her now and sitting up in bed, searching the darkness, I'm sure. I can hear the sheets rustle, her feet touch down on the rug beneath the bed, the rug that's supposed to protect our feet from the cold of the hardwood, not that that matters. The door squeaks as she opens it—not enough that anyone else can hear it, so I haven't mentioned it until now, but it will soon. Soon it will be unbearable and you'll wonder when that happened, never knowing it happened right in front of you, beneath your own fingers. Her footsteps down the hall are light, conscious of the others, of you in your study typing away at some project, though she doesn't need to be. You work with headphones on now, some kind of synthesized techno music playing on what feels like a loop though I know it's not.

Once she's downstairs, Aurora pauses at every open door looking for me. I could meet her halfway, assure her it's nothing, that I heard a noise, it was just an animal in the brush, let's go back to bed. But I like when she comes looking for me. I like seeing in her face, hearing in her voice, feeling in her touch that I'm worthy of searching for.

She's in the living room now, but I don't turn to face her, instead I wait for her to cross the room, to wrap her arms around my shoulders, coax me to lean into her, my head on her shoulder. She begins to rock and I feel at peace.

Aurora: [whispering] You okay?

I nod and she kisses my temple.

Aurora: It'll be okay. [in soft, gentle tones because she knows me better than even I realize sometimes] It'll be okay.

And I know it will be. Not because she said so, but because I know she'll be there. We'll be together. No matter how this ends, we'll be together. And because of that, it'll be okay.

[END LOG]

[END TRANSMISSION]

It's morning now and I'm not sure how much rest I actually got. I don't feel rested. My mind feels distant, silent. My head hurts, every noise feels like a needle against my temple. At least we're taking a car. It's not the best car. It looks like it's been under that cover since this place belonged to your grandfather. But Charlie says he's been fixing it up in secret for months. Long before you brought me here. He says when you came after me, he drove it into town with zero issue. Delta and Fox are sure it'll get us to where we're going. I'm not as confident. Charlies are security, not mechanics.

But we are piled into this car anyways—Charlie driving, Delta in the front passenger seat on her knees so she can see Fox who insisted on sitting behind her so she could see both Delta and Charlie as they talk. Not that they're talking much now. The car is an anxious hum of quiet.

Aurora is between me and Fox asking Delta to please sit properly in her seat.

Delta is rolling her eyes and reminding her it doesn't matter.

Aurora is arguing over her about car crashes and statistics.

Delta is repeating louder that it doesn't matter, can we please just leave?

My head hurts so much. I press my temple against the window to my left. It's cold against my skin. Cold like it is outside. Watching the rain patter against the window, I can almost imagine the glass is damp. It's nice. I like this northern weather. They're still arguing, but I tune them out, focus on my breathing instead.

I close my eyes and it's like I'm in the dark again. There is a tiny panic in my stomach. This is how it happened before:

I closed my eyes that final night next to Aurora in the midst of your sweet lies;

When I opened them, I was in the dark.

I didn't know where I was, but I knew I was on the floor of a small space—the cold of the linoleum beneath me, the rough drywall against my back, the claustrophobia of clutter pressing in around me. There was something else, something deeper that was different, wrong, but I couldn't pinpoint what exactly.

One thing at a time, I told myself. Get out of…wherever this was first.

So, in the pitch black that my eyes were quickly adjusting to, I felt along the floor directly around me. My fingers carefully moved soft as spiders along a cold bar I assumed to be a chair leg to my left, a plastic crate to my right, what felt like a rack of coats above it, a heavy square monitor in front of that, a cardboard bankers box under a pile of books in front of the chair that was buried under something hidden beneath a something spattered drop cloth that smelled of grease. There was nothing directly in front of me, nothing above my head, but the objects stacked up around me were so close that I kept my movements small as I pushed myself up to standing.

Even with that, my shoulder grazed something solid under the drop cloth and the mystery pile shifted. I tensed, waiting for the tilt and crash. Instead, it just settled back into momentary stasis. Before it changed its mind, I inched forward, careful to lean into the coats instead of the teetering drop cloth. It only took three steps to reach a shelf across from me, bottles of various shapes, sizes, materials, and states of cleanliness along it. I clung to the shelf, my eyes focused on the floor as I navigated my way through the mess of boxes, cables, cleaning supplies, and mystery equipment. Six or so feet down, there was a door.

Just missing another heavy milk crate with my foot, I rushed for the knob. I twisted and shoved the door with my shoulder, ready for the relief of light stinging my eyes. Instead, it shuddered against something solid on the other side.

"What the fuck?"

I pushed on the door again.

It wouldn't move.

Panic rushed up my esophagus from the pit of my stomach. "No."

I slammed my shoulder against it.

Again, it wouldn't move.

"No."

I rammed my entire body against the wood.

Still nothing more than a shudder.

"Fuck! No!"

Over and over, I slammed my weight against the door, hoping it would fling open if I just willed it hard enough. The first few times, nothing changed, then, on the fifth slam of my body, the sound of heavy wooden furniture scrapping against the linoleum came from the other side. The door opened a crack. A glorious sliver of light shone through.

The glimmer of freedom shot a relieved burst of a laugh from my untwisting stomach.

I began slamming myself against the door, harder and harder, whatever was blocking me in moving inch by agonizing inch. When my body would get tired, I'd stop to try and shove my way through the opening. With each attempt, I could feel the progress I was making—first my fingers, then my hand, up to my elbow—and each step closer brought the vigor back for me to start over again. By the time I was able to get my whole arm through enough to feel that flat top of the desk blocking my way to freedom I was at the edge of my limit. I got on the floor, leaned back against my hands, pressed each high-top sneakered foot against the door, and kicked with all my might. The door jolted the farthest it had yet to go. I didn't bother getting up to test my progress this time, just scooted forward and did it again. Another several inches. One more solid kick and I leapt up, shoved the right side of my body into the crack and pushed against the door with my hip and shoulder.

Finally, I was able to drag myself through the crack with a grunt and a scream.

"Fuck!" I shouted as I doubled over against the desk, willing my heart to slow back down. "Shit."

Then it hit me, I opened my eyes to stare at the desk under my palms, look up at the door of the storage closet, around me at the hall lit only by daylight. I was in the Institute. Why was I in the Institute? Why wasn't I home? Why had I woken up in the closet instead of my bed next to Aurora? Why had I been blocked in? Who had blocked me in? Where was Aurora?

That last question hit me like a bucket of cold water. It echoed along my chilled bones.

Where was Aurora.

Shoving the desk to one side, I yanked the closet door open and searched for a light. That was the easy part, my hand falling on the switch close to the door jamb with minimal flailing. The hard part was realizing Aurora wasn't there, realizing there wasn't anywhere for her to be. I dug through the closet anyways, moving boxes, mops, brooms, monitors, CPUs, a toolbox, a pile of textbooks, broken furniture, abandoned hoodies and jackets. I ripped the drop cloth from the chair. A shoddily stacked tower of binders toppled to the floor.

But there was nothing.

She wasn't there.

I was alone.

Numb panic flooding through me, I stepped back out into the hall to try and orient myself. There was the water fountain, the bathrooms with their little detail-less people, the bulletin board with its postings for roommates, TTRPG groups, offers of furniture, and dog sitters. I was around the corner from the office. It shared a wall with the storage closet.

I turned, took a step, ready to rush around the corner, but stopped, looked around me again. Why was it so quiet? The usual shuffling of students, the distant voices from the offices or the computer lab, the rumble of the vending machines, the whine of the copier—none of it was there. After glancing around, I eased open the door to the women's bathroom. Silence. I stepped in, checked each of the stalls. Empty. I did the same with the men's. Still nothing. This wasn't right. This was a busy part of campus, the floor where the offices and the department heads were, the only computer labs to provide easy access to the professors who weren't busy teaching. It shouldn't be this quiet.

I should have just left then, should have gone straight to our apartment, but there was always someone in our office: Bravo, Eden, you. One of you would tell me what's going on. I just needed someone to tell me what was going on. Starting down the hall, I tried not to run, though no one was there to see if I had. I might not have known what was going on, but I knew something was wrong and I didn't trust that I was truly alone, that someone wasn't listening for me to approach, someone I didn't want to catch me by surprise. So, I took off my sneakers, took light, quiet steps down the hall until I came to our office door. It was open. It was dark. My back pressed to the wall, I stood still and listened.

But I had to stop before I could make anything out. My head felt like it was ballooning. It hurt to keep my eyes open. I was so suddenly tired. It was like a lead blanket had been dropped over me. I could hardly hold my head up, my chin swiveling as I fought the urge to let it droop. I pressed myself back against the wall and took in one deep breath after another.

In—One—Out.

In—Two—Out.

In—Three—Out.

Everything in me went still. My head cleared. I heard mourning doves, the flapping of wings. I heard a car drive by, the clear, unmuted clunk and rattle of a wheel hitting a pothole. I *didn't* hear the usual hum of CPU fans, the whir of the AC.

It was then I realized how warm it was. I opened my eyes and for the first time really registered the absence of artificial light, the open doors, the papers littered across the floor, the multitude of boot prints along the backs of each one, the trails of glass and dirt ground into the carpet, the orange spray paint on the walls.

My heart pounded in my throat, the feeling left my fingers, panic shot through my veins.

What happened?

Where was Aurora?

I turned the corner into the office. It was empty. It was trashed. Eden's neat filing system had been dumped out on your desk and was spilling onto the floor. Her corner of the office had been scorched. How it hadn't spread to the rest of the building I had no idea. More importantly though was how did every computer in the hallway come to be piled up on my desk in the center and set on fire.

>

I don't want to be thinking about this.

It's raining now. It was drizzling before. Now it's raining. It's raining hard.

Aurora says it'll just get worse.

Charlie's nervous about being on the road.

Delta's sure it'll be fine, people drive in the rain all the time.

Aurora agrees with Charlie and that we should find a rest stop to wait it out.

Fox is quiet.

So am I. My head hurts and I just want to focus on the rain.

The car struggles through a puddle that might as well be a river.

Aurora: The next place to stop [She shifts as far to the edge of the seat as her seatbelt will allow.] we're stopping. I don't care what it is.

It's obvious she's nervous about something. Her muscles are tense. Her jaw is tight. She keeps glancing at the mirrors. I have a feeling it might be you, but she can't tell me anything, so all I have is my best guess.

Charlie: I think that's the gas station up there.

He takes his hand off the wheel just long enough to point at a building a few miles up the road just visible through the rain and a gap in the trees.

Aurora: Perfect. We'll fill up and just wait out the rain—

Delta: No. It'll be fine. We can keep going. We'll make it to the next one. We *need* to keep going.

The car becomes as quiet as it can, the pelting of the rain on the roof and the *shooshing* of the tires through puddles the only sound.

Aurora: Delta, it'll be fine.   **Delta:** No.

But something's wrong. Delta's voice is shaky and she won't look at any of us, looking out the windows, obscured by waterfalls of rain instead.

Delta: No, it's not. We've barely gotten off the property. What if Marsh—?

She stops when her eyes meet Aurora's. I don't need to look at her to know what Delta's seeing, but I do anyways because I love that look. It's a look that tells you everything's going to be right in the world. It's a look that can't really be described since it looks no different from how she usually does, but there's something about it, some minute difference that when you see it you know she's right because how could she be so calm, so pristine if it wasn't? I want to turn that look towards me, kiss her tenderly, guide her to hold me, but Delta's the one who needs that look right now.

Aurora: [gently] He won't.

She takes Delta's hand in hers.

Aurora: He's not even awake yet.

Apparently, you've been sleeping later and later since you've gotten us all back—all of us, but one. They've been keeping you up past sunrise, Bravo and Eden. And every day, once you've followed the newest red string Aurora told me to give you down to some tangled knot, you've grumbled down the hall, ignoring Aurora and Charlie, and slammed your bedroom door before collapsing in your bed with the squeaky springs where you've slept through most of the day.

It's not even 10:00.

But Delta still isn't convinced.

Delta: We don't—He could have—

Aurora: He was still awake when I finally got Echo to sleep.

Delta eyes me for confirmation. I nod.

Aurora: That was four in the morning. He won't be awake until well after noon.

Delta searches Aurora's eyes. Her teeth absently scrape against her lip. She swallows hard but nods all the same. Then she turns back in her seat and curls against the console that's keeping her from Charlie. He reaches over to wrap his arm around her legs, but the tires hit another puddle and he has to grip the wheel with both hands to keep from losing control of the car. I'm glad we're stopping. I didn't trust this car on a dry road.

Aurora doesn't sit back in her seat, her forearms instead tight against her thighs, her hands a clasped fist between her knees, her eyes hard on the road, unblinking. But I want her to lean back. I want her to look at me. I want her to hold me, remind me that I'm not back there fresh from the closet, alone and afraid for her as much as for me. I reach out and touch her elbow. She finally blinks and looks over her shoulder. She meets my eyes and gives me a weary smile that's not even half of her usual radiant self, maybe not even a quarter. She's nervous. She hid it for Delta's sake, but she doesn't bother hiding it from me. She knows I want all of her, the honest her. I shift in my seat to press against her, my cheek against her shoulder blade, my nose brushing her tricep. She smells soft—vanilla and cloves, linen and flour, the afternoon sun through slanted shades and sun tea on ice. You made her smell like sunshine, like hope. One of the many reasons I struggle to hate you the way the others do.

Once I'm against her, I can feel her relax, not fully, but enough. She unclasps her hands, reaches one under her left arm, finds mine against her thigh and slips it into hers. For a brief moment, with her palm against mine, I remember that everything's going to be okay.

Charlie pulls into the gas station at one of the pumps. He looks to Delta and she nods up at him. He squeezes her knees, kisses her cheek, pulls up his hood, then steps out into the rain.

Fox: I'm hungry.

The car had been silent for hardly a second. If I wasn't in this car in this moment, I would have laughed at her timing.

Delta: No! [She frantically turns in her seat.] Fox! We have fuel. Alcohol. Whatever you need.

Fox blinks at her. Her lips squirm the way they do when she's fighting that teenage sarcastic I'd-rather-die-than-be-vulnerable code.

Fox: I wanna get out. I don't like just sitting here.

Delta chews her lip and her breathing becomes erratic, but she swallows and nods anyways.

Delta: Ror—?

Aurora: [with a reassuring smile as she follows Fox out of the car] I'll go with her.

Delta looks at me and I stare back at her, hand already on the door handle.

Echo: I wanna be with—   **Delta:** Yeah. I get it.

My eyes instinctively scan her: her limbs may be limp, but her muscles are still tense, her jaw still tight, her lips pursed. Her nerves are making me nervous.

Echo: W-want...anything?

I don't know why I'm offering. It's not like we can eat anything they sell here.

She shrugs and settles back in her seat, her eyes drifting to Charlie's back beyond the window.

Delta: I think I'm good. Thanks.

I glance at Charlie and nod.

Echo: Kay.

Inside, the light is heavy and almost strange the way the florescent white is battling with the dark grey outside. Fox immediately starts wandering the aisles, her hands deep in the pockets of the powder blue overcoat that accentuates the neon blue of her hair. Despite the rain, she has pink sunglasses pushed up on the top of her head. Her black combat boots are heavy exaggerating her skinny legs in black skinny jeans. She looks like she's stepped out of a music video.

Aurora isn't watching her. She's standing by the front windows, her arms crossed as she stares out at the rain. I look back at Fox. She's in the chip aisle picking up every bag and reading it front and back with a bored kind of interest before discarding it to pick up the next one. She's safe, I guess.

I cross my arms and lean against Aurora, my cheek against her shoulder despite the cold wet spots from the rain on her denim jacket. She anchors herself against me and we just stand here for a few heartbeats staring out the window. It might have been peaceful had I not known what we were doing.

A black sedan, a few years old, eases through the rain and parks in front of us, but the driver (all I can make out is their chin length dark waves) doesn't get out and I don't blame them. The rain is pummeling their car so hard I can hear it from inside. But, I guess...I don't want to be thinking about that.

I let out a long sigh and Aurora's hand caresses my arm from under hers.

Echo: Ror?

The relative silence in the gas station makes it feel like I'm shouting even though I'm not.

Aurora: [without looking at me] Hmm?

I glance over my shoulder at the synth standing behind the counter. It's a Luke, the male retail models. He's not paying attention to us, all his attention on Fox who is, it sounds like, in the refrigerated section opening every door to examine every shelf of drinks before letting it slam shut as she opens the next.

I turn back to Aurora, shift my body so I'm mostly facing her.

Echo: [just above a whisper] Did...? Did we have...? An apartment? In Bastrop?

The muscles in her face go still and my heart breaks. She looks at me, but I look away before our eyes can meet. We haven't talked a whole lot about what I remember. The few times it's come up she's gone stiff like this, her face going still, her lips pressing together. She doesn't say anything, but I can almost feel the way she's staring down at me. I know without her ever saying it that she has mixed feelings about my memories. They're directly tied to you and she doesn't like us being so tangled around you like that. I'm sure she'd rather I let those memories go, start fresh with her now, ask her about our old life, try to get my real memories back, but I can feel a twinge in my heart every time I consider it. So many of those memories are of her, of us, and I don't want to lose a single piece of her.

To my relief, she relaxes a little, lowers her face to press her lips against my temple, breathes in through her nose. Her hand sneaks under her arm to run along mine.

Aurora: What was it like?

I take her hand, our palms clasped between our bodies. There's a connection between our palms, like magnets clicking into place and I show her.

It was wonderful. It was small, but the windows were big and there were lots of them because it was on the corner of the third floor so we could look out over downtown Bastrop, out at the tops of the pine trees that stretched on seemingly forever. There was a rooftop garden that we shared with the couple next door. Lyla had the green thumb, really, we just did our best to water them on our days, pull out what she told us were weeds, cut the flowers she gave us permission to, graciously accepted the basket she brought us once a week with "our half" of the harvest. There was a bay window in the living room, built-in bookshelves underneath it. We sometimes ate dinner in that window watching the people walking along Main Street, open the windows enough to listen to the music from the live bands playing at the outdoor bar around the corner. Her favorite feature was the deep bathtub that could just fit the two of us, candles lit on the vanity, soft music playing over the Bluetooth speaker, glasses of whatever cheap alcohol piqued our interest that week.

There wasn't much else of note in that apartment, in truth, it wasn't that spectacular, but in it I had her to myself. She was mine and I was hers and no one else existed.

Which is why I still hold onto it.

Which is one of the reasons I don't like thinking about that day I woke up.

That was the beginning of the end of what I thought was reality.

That apartment was the first place I went after leaving the Institute. I ran the entire way, not questioning why my legs hadn't given out, why my heart was pounding from panic rather than exertion, why I hadn't broken a sweat. I wouldn't question it, not until I was forced to. In town, I ran through the streets, dodging and weaving between cars, horns blaring with each narrow miss. At our building, I burst through the front door, bolted up the three flights of stairs, and down the hall to our door where I grabbed the knob, twisted, slammed my body against the wood. But it was locked. I stared up at it. We never locked our door. I jiggled the knob again to be sure. It didn't budge. I dug through my pockets for a key. Why didn't I have a key? I banged on the door, praying she was there. I just wanted to see her face, see that smile with the deep lines like parentheses that made it feel like a secret, something only for me. Feel her arms around me as she tells me it's okay, everything's okay, I'm okay, and my heart would return to normal.

But then the door opened and someone else was standing there, someone I didn't know.

"What?" they demanded, staring down at me. "What do you want?"

I just stared up at them, mouth open, my head empty. "I...I...I-is Aurora here?"

They squinted at me. "I don't know any Aurora." Their face shifted as they glanced over me. "Who's Aurora? You okay?"

I shook my head, glanced behind them into the apartment that wasn't ours. The décor was all wrong—the colors dull and grey, the furniture all matching, there weren't any blankets or sweaters tossed on the backs of every chair and couch, there weren't any plants or books on every unused surface.

"Um," my voice finally crawled up my throat that felt like it was going to collapse. "I, uh, think I have the wrong, um, apartment." I started to back away. "S-sorry."

"Hey," they took a step from the entry. "You sure you're okay?"

"Mhm." I insisted with a nod as I turned my back to them, scanning the numbers on every door down the hall, hoping I had banged on the wrong one. "Yeah. Yeah. Sorry."

I didn't look back, didn't stop until I was back on the stairs, down a few steps, out of view of the stranger in what was absolutely supposed to be our apartment. Standing on the bottom step, I just stared at the green carpet of the steps below me. My heart wasn't pounding anymore, my head wasn't spinning. Instead, everything was floating, everything felt so far away. This couldn't be my building, these couldn't be my stairs, this couldn't be my body. Where was I? Where was Aurora?

I heard footsteps above me. I looked up to see the person from the apartment that wasn't ours standing on the landing staring down at me.

"Are you *sure*? Do you want to come in for just a minute? Maybe call someone?"

I stared at their feet—grey flipflops with a thick band across their feet, a band of a lighter shade of skin just visible underneath. There were deep ridges in their toenails. The big nail of their left foot had a purple bruise about a quarter inch from the tip as though it had been damaged and was growing out. I briefly wondered what had happened, but promptly realized I didn't care.

I shook my head and continued down the rest of the stairs, barely aware of my feet touching each step. They might as well have been someone else's feet. I stopped on the last step, staring at the off-white tiles of the lobby floor. What was happening? Where was Aurora? Where was I? This was our building. That was our apartment. *Was.* But when did it stop being ours? How long had I been locked in that closet?

A noise from the office distracted me, coaxing me to look up. I blinked at the bulletin board between the office door and the mailboxes. My eyes fell on a poster for a live show at the bar down the street. Delta. Charlie and Delta. Maybe they'd know something. Maybe they were still in their house, still themselves, still mine. I rushed out of the lobby, leaving behind the building where everything used to be okay.

Aurora's hand unclicks from mine and her hand moves to touch my cheek. I blink and look up at her. Why did I let her see that?

Aurora: [quiet, just for me] I'm so sorry. You okay?

I nod even though I'm not. But it's just a formality just like the question. She shifts her body so she can pull me close. I burrow into her, her arms wrapped tight around me, her lips against the top of my head.

Aurora: [whispering] It's okay. It's okay. I've got you now. It's okay.

[END LOG]

[END TRANSMISSION]

The rain has eased for the moment. We gather Fox, pay for the magazines and lavender bucket hat she's collected, and make our way through the drizzle to the car. Delta lets out an audible sigh as we slide into the back seat, but doesn't say anything else, instead giving us stiff smiles that hide the panic she's trying not to let override everything else. Charlie shifts in his seat to give us each a nod or a glance, but his eyes flick back to Fox and a warm smile sneaks into one corner of his full lips.

Charlie: Nice hat.

She gives him a shy grin and adjusts it on her head. For a brief moment, Aurora's eyes shift away from Charlie's hand on Delta's knee, that's tucked up against the middle console. But even nurturing Fox can't keep her attention from Delta's knees for more than a few seconds and she's back to eyeing them and the way that Delta's curled in her seat unbuckled. I know it's because she knows it's unsafe, but she's also not going to say anything since Delta wasn't designed to be concerned with safety. Neither was I, but for a different reason. Delta was given nonchalance. I was given disregard. You have to ignore that instinctual draw towards safety if you're going to be in the limelight or gathering information. Maybe that's why Aurora pulls me towards her like the sun, like Charlie pulls Delta, like Eden pulled you once upon a time, because those of us built without a concern for safety are strangely drawn towards safety nets, aren't we?

They turned the radio on while we were gone. It's playing the more obscure indie stuff that only college stations play. I don't recognize the song, but Delta seems to. When Charlie's hand leaves her knee to start the car, her fingers start dancing along her shin with the melody. She closes her eyes and drops her head back against the headrest. Her breathing is controlled and steady in the way of someone who's trying not to lose control. When Charlie pulls away from the gas station, she begins to hum along with the song, muttering a few of the words under her breath.

I can never tell if she actually knows every song she seems to hear of if she can just pick up on the hidden patterns of the melodies and rhythms the way she was designed to. I don't know a lot about who Delta actually is, or, at least, who she was before the cabin, before we lost Bastrop. I know I could just ask, but—

Aurora: Charlie, you got the directions to—

Her voice catches and she seems to be frozen, her mouth hanging open, her eyes unfocused. I can hear her trying to fight it, but I don't know why she keeps trying. She can't. You won't let her.

Charlie: Yeah. [He reaches back to pat her knee without looking at her.] Yeah, I got it.

Aurora's mouth closes and she nods as she leans back in her seat, her arms crossed tight, her lips a thin line as she glares at the console Delta's knees are resting against as though it were your head and she could make it implode by staring at it. I curl against her, but she goes on imploding you in her head.

I don't know where we're going. I'm glad Charlie does, I might not trust this car or Charlie's mechanic skills, but I do trust Charlie. The morning after you first brought me to Colville, to the cabin, I reluctantly slipped out of bed next to Aurora. As much as I wanted to be near her, I couldn't sit still, I kept staring at the bedroom door, wondering if it was blocked; staring at Aurora, wondering if she was real. I kept closing my eyes and opening them again, testing reality, making sure that's what this was. It was an hour before I decided to just trust my eyes, but I still didn't trust the door. So, I kissed her shoulder and snuck out of the room without waking her.

I wasn't the only one awake, I found Charlie on the swing on the front porch, staring at the car under the cover near the detached garage with the chipping paint.

We sat in silence for a long while before I finally asked him, "Can you confirm or deny something for me?"

He nodded. "Anything."

This was before we learned there were restrictions, things they couldn't tell me.

Not wouldn't, couldn't.

"I...I remember coffee shops, record stores, running errands downtown?"

His shoulders relaxed and a warm smile came over those full lips surrounded by coarse black facial hair. I let out a relieved breath I hadn't realized I was hanging onto until the moment I let go of it.

"Yeah, that was training," he said. "Eden would send us downtown to practice blending in. She'd sometimes leave us things to find or pick up on. When we'd get back she'd ask us, well, she'd mostly ask you, 'What did you see?'"

What did you see, Echo? I can almost hear it in her soft, low voice like velvet. I can almost see those grey-green eyes focused on me, her forearms on her knees, her palms lightly pressed together.

But that's...where did that memory come from? Where does it go? It doesn't line up with my other memories. It doesn't fit anywhere. Even what Charlie had said doesn't fit exactly. It does in ways and it doesn't in others. I don't remember practice, well, I don't remember us being the ones practicing. I remember his students at the high school, out on the field running drills. I remember Delta's students in their living room with the piano, cross legged on the floor with guitars, hard violin cases clunking against their leg as they ran down the front walk to their parents' car. The front walk with the multicolored hydrangeas, little stake lights that lit up when the sun went down, a willow vine wreath on the purple front door with the window that was a grid of different colored glass.

Except when I knocked on the purple door the day I woke up, the day everything changed, someone else opened it—a little girl with big black eyes, deep beige skin, and long dark ponytail. She stared up at me, waiting for me to explain why I was at her door. And I stared down at her, wondering whose child she was. With her coloring, she could have been Delta's, but she couldn't have been younger than four and it wasn't possible I'd been in that closet for four years. Footsteps in the hall pulled my attention away from her and I looked up to see a woman rushing down the hall.

"Juniper," she scolded, "what did I tell you about answering the door without me?"

The girl didn't answer, just went on staring up at me even as she let her mother step in front of her.

"Can I help—?"

The woman looked me in the face and froze. I didn't understand why. I didn't recognize her no matter how hard I searched her face, but she recognized me.

"No." She said and stepped towards me, closing the door firmly behind her. "Get away from my house."

"I'm sorry?" I said, stepping away from her. "I-I'm looking for someone who used to live here? Delta...? Charlie...?" I scrambled for their last names, but couldn't think of them.

Her expression faltered for a second, but it was just a flash before that anger intensified. She continued to move towards me. My foot slipped off the walkway into the row of...not multicolored hydrangeas, but pale blue plumbagoes. Something that wasn't a plant knocked against my calf. A sign: The Grants. Who were the Grants?

"You tell Eden," the woman, Mrs. Grant apparently, went on herding me down the walkway, "we want nothing to do with her or Marsh or the rest of you. Stay *far* away from my house and my family. You hear me?"

My heal found open air and I stumbled off the curb into the street.

"The next time any of you step foot on our property we will not hesitate to shoot. You hear me?"

I just stood in the street, nodding with a dumbfounded kind of confusion.

"You can tell Eden the same thing. We're done with her. Understand?"

"Honey?" a male voice called from the door that wasn't purple, but black, the window clear pebbled glass.

"Call Daniel," she shouted, I'm assuming, to him without looking away from me.

I didn't know Daniel yet. I don't even really know him now.

She stood on the edge of what was now her walkway staring at me hard, her fists balled at her sides, a fire in her eyes that I could practically feel the heat from. I knew that I should leave, but I couldn't make myself move. The connection between my head and feet seemed to have been broken and I just kept looking from her to the house, to the garage and the apartment above it that used to be mine in those days before Aurora.

"Leave, damn it!" she shouted at me, her arm flinging down the street. Then her voice dropped, "They'll be here any minute."

It's only now that I can recognize her face had shifted then. She wasn't staring at me with anger anymore. It was fear. Of what, I don't know. I still don't. But at the time, it was me who was afraid and her voice and sharp movement jolted the flow of commands back into gear and my feet finally received the message. I ran down the street away from her, away from the house I thought was Charlie and Delta's and back into town. I had no idea where I was going, but the idea of Main Street was something familiar, something hopefully still concrete.

It was the last thing I had.

So, I ran.

I went straight to Sadie's, the sandwich shop you always sent me to, Bravo or Aurora on occasion when they'd join me, Fox less often. But it was always me you sent. I don't even think you ever went yourself...Or was it Eden? There are two versions in my head now. On that day it was you I remembered sending me out. Now, I see you, but I hear Eden's velvet voice: *What did you hear, Echo?*

I don't understand it. Do I want to? I do and I don't. Maybe wherever we're going, whoever we're going to, will make it all make sense.

The street wasn't exactly bustling, but it wasn't empty either. There were a handful of people along the little stretch of restaurants, a couple now and again, a family or two. I probably stared a little too hard at every person I passed. I just wanted to make sure none of them were Aurora, the others, Eden, you, but not a single face that I passed was familiar. When I got to the shop, the windows were dark, the door locked. I cupped my hands around my eyes to get a glimpse inside, but all I could see was black.

Footsteps came close behind me. I stopped and listened. There had been a man leaning against the corner of a building watching me overexamine the street. I'd ignored him because he hadn't looked familiar. Now I was wondering if I shouldn't have.

"They're not there anymore," a voice said from too close.

I blinked up at the man. Who? Who wasn't there anymore? Was he just talking about Sadie's or was he talking about the others? But that was stupid. How would he know?

He stared down at me then nodded at the shop. "They're not there anymore. Best to move along." He jerked his head towards the street.

That lead blanket feeling came over me again. I closed my eyes and willed it to stop. Took in and let out steadying breaths. When I opened my eyes, I was staring at my hands still cupped against the window. The usual cheery paintings on the glass were scratched up and faded, but...I took a step back. These weren't cheery paintings. Layers of graffiti blocked them out.

How had I missed this?

I blinked up at the man. "Wh-what happened?"

"Don't matter," he grumbled. "They're gone now."

I expected him to walk away then, but he didn't. He just went on standing over me, staring at me between glancing around the street.

And I went on staring up at him. I didn't recognize him. I felt like I should. "I-I'm looking for—"

"They're not here," he repeated. "Whoever you're looking for, they're not here." He glanced around again, this time fussing with the thick cluster of loose curls sticking out around his ears under his cap. "Move along."

"O-okay?" But I didn't move, just stared up at him, trying to read his mind, so sure he had answers he wasn't telling me. Maybe I hadn't asked the right question. Maybe this was a test of some kind. "Did they move? Do they have a new—?"

A door a few buildings down opened followed by male voices that carried through the street. The man in front of me glanced at them. His eyes went wide and he finally moved, brushing past me more roughly than necessary and whispering as he went, "Antioch. Don't get caught."

I righted myself and watched him continue down the street from over my shoulder. When he passed an alleyway, he glanced back at me. I swear he nodded towards the alley, but the movement was so quick and I was so out of practice, that I still can't be sure.

Don't get caught.

Was he trying to warn me about something? Was he trying, albeit poorly, to convince me to leave well enough alone or was he showing me the way in? I didn't know. I still don't know. But I also didn't care even if I do now. I had people to find. So, I snuck into the alley before he could glance back at me again.

Before I reached the back, however, I stopped when I heard the crunching and sliding of gravel followed by thumping against weak wood boards then the skittering of tiny, non-human feet. I knew it was most likely a cat chasing a smaller animal, probably a lizard from the sound of it, but that day had been strange enough already. I stopped, staring at the brick of the building next door. How was I making out these sounds anyways? How was I differentiating them?

I shook my head, I didn't have time for any of this. When I edged around the corner, I saw that I had been right. A runt of a sleek black cat was crouched in the gravel, white dust on its back and sides, one paw outstretched and swatting under a stack of wooden pallets, its yellow eyes wide with frenzied determination, its pupils the size of saucers.

I stepped around the corner and the cat stopped just long enough to stare up at me. I slowly blinked at it then side stepped away from it towards the opposite building. The lizard scurried across the gravel in a brown flash, the cat whipped around to scramble after it, my existence entirely forgotten. I glanced around the backs of the buildings. There wasn't much, just a dumpster; rotten, weathered pallets; a dusty, scuffed up traffic cone; a single chair by the back door of the next building over. There was a camera above the chair, but I decided it was turned to its own door, that I was out of its range. I should have looked closer. I should have been positive. Instead, I ignored it and pressed myself into what little alcove framed Sadie's back door. Hoping for a break, I grabbed the handle. Of course it was locked.

Taking in a long breath, I dug under the collar of my shirt for my bra strap, more specifically, the little pocket I'd sewn into it and the lock picks I always hid inside despite Aurora always shaking her head when she saw me with them, cupped my face in her hands and reminded me I didn't need them anymore, I wasn't that latchkey kid minus the key, sneaking into houses when people were at work or on vacation, scavenging for the food no one would notice was missing, sleeping in beds with my shoes on, never allowing myself to escape too deep in a dream, one ear always open, my body always ready to bolt at the sound of tires on the driveway, footsteps on the front walk, a key in the door.

But on that day, I did need them and thankfully my fingers found the slender slivers of metal. I fished them out and crouched in front of the doorknob. It was an easy lock. I'd picked harder than that a million times over. I was that teenager again, easing the door open just right on the off chance it would squeak, taking one light step after another, clinging to the shadows with small movements. They were skills I slipped back into easily, thoughtlessly, like slipping out of your body and floating above yourself as someone else, some past version of you takes over.

The entire place was dark, the only light from the windows at the front, but I could still make out the doors lining the hall I was standing in. I tried the first one I came to, not really knowing what I was looking for. It was a supply closet. I slammed the door shut without inspecting inside and ripped my hand from the knob. I hadn't realized I'd also lurched backwards until my back hit the wall behind me. I stood there, my breathing ragged. The hall was too small, too dark, I needed more space. I grabbed the knob of the door next to me. It was a dark bathroom that was the same size as the supply closet, my faint reflection in the mirror flashing back at me before I quickly abandoned it for the next door.

The next room was larger and lit by a small window up near the ceiling. The file cabinets along one wall, the desk in the middle, and the outdated monitor angled away from me tipped me off that it was an office. But it was empty, devoid of anything other than furniture. There wasn't even a calendar on the wall. Stepping back into the hall, I stared at the front of the building. Clearly, this place was empty. Surely, I wasn't going to find anything. But what if there was something else? Something I was still missing?

I shoved on the swinging door on my way and glanced in—it was a kitchen, exactly what I'd been expecting and with nothing immediately out of the ordinary.

Coming out of the hall into the front, I stepped up to the back of the counter. The dim room was lit by the case that was still filled with cellophane wrapped sandwiches, sticky pastries, rows of cookies, sliced cakes and pies. I didn't understand. Why would they leave this all here? It wasn't until I circled to the front that I saw the register was crooked. I cocked my head to one side and took a step forward, but stopped when layers of dirt and dust scrapped under the toe of my shoe.

Without warning, my head felt heavy. I clenched my eyes, grabbed my temples, and shook it. I didn't have time for this. When I blinked into the darkness, the light of the case was gone, the glass was shattered, the shelves were broken, the husk of a dead rat laid in the middle of a crumbled cake covered in fuzzy mold.

There wasn't a register like I'd originally seen, just wires jutting out of a hole in the wood slab of the counter. More graffiti covered the menu hanging above it. The display of business cards that had been next to the register was in the corner, the little rectangles scattered across the floor. One near my foot featured a row of red and orange books. Another nearby had a coffee mug in the middle of a bright sun. The bulletin board that held event posters and rental notices, copies of copied adverts for pet sitting services and furniture for sale, was face down on the floor.

I turned to see that the windows and front door were covered over with plywood. I wondered how I could see at all in that room, but the thought flitted from my mind when I saw the bench I used to wait on with Charlie. I'd first held Aurora's hand there while she told me about her years out in West Texas. It was tipped over and splintered down the middle.

I just stood there, blinking, hoping everything would return to normal if I just readjusted my eyes enough. Something was wrong, but something else was overriding my need to figure out what. Maybe it was Aurora. Finding her was all I had the capacity for. But I was out of leads. Sadie's had been my last hope. I didn't know what to do. My breathing was starting to become erratic when something in my wiring told me to stop, pay attention.

What did you see, Echo?

I knelt in the dirt and debris and lifted the bulletin board. I wasn't sure what I was looking for. Anything, really, I guess. It was covered in the usual notices now smudged with dirt. Among them was a postcard sized advert covered in red and orange books, a bird perched on a branch. Balancing the board against my knee, I tugged on it. The staple holding it in place easily popped loose. It was for a bookstore. It looked familiar. I abandoned the bulletin board and stood, locating the business card I'd seen before. Once I'd scrubbed away someone's boot print with my thumb, I held them next to each other. They read the same name in the same typewriter font: ANTIOCH BOOKS.

I didn't recognize that name at first, but a second later I did.

Antioch, the guy outside had said. *Don't get caught.*

But, what was this supposed to mean? Was this where the others were? Was Aurora there? I flipped the card over, but there was no address. That was weird. Why didn't it have an address? Was it the only one? I searched the floor for other business cards. One was for a bar. I flipped it over to find an address in Bastrop. A burger place:

Bastrop. A lawyer's office: Bastrop. Then I grabbed the one with the sun. Sunrise Coffee, it read. I flipped it over: Bryan, Texas.

Bryan?

Bryan was an hour away. Why was an advert for a coffee shop in Bryan in an abandoned Bastrop sandwich shop?

I was about to drop it and move onto the next business card when I realized there were voices outside. I froze. The plywood blocked out any chance of seeing inside, but still. I held my breath, listening for them to pass. But they didn't. They just went on collecting outside.

Without thinking, I stuffed both business cards in my jacket pocket and took quiet steps towards the plywood, listening, trying to discern what they were doing, where they were headed. One in particular sounded authoritative, giving out instructions. Footsteps moved for the alleyway. I followed them through the shop, listening until I was in the hall and they were behind the building. There was a chance they were headed somewhere else, but I knew I shouldn't take that chance. I glanced at the doors surrounding me. Not the closet. That fight or flight electricity ran through my muscles before I could even entertain the thought. I wasn't going to get locked inside another closet.

I hadn't inspected the kitchen. It might have a door out. I started for it, but then I heard the voices gathering out back. They'd realize the back door was unlocked any second now, if they hadn't already. They'd be flooding into the hall after that. I thought about the plywood covered windows, decided that would take too long. The office. The office had a window. I ripped into the room and immediately rounded the desk to shove it against the door. It was empty and cheap, not that heavy at all, but it would slow them down, distract them at the very least. When I straightened up, my eyes met the wobbling monitor, but instead of my reflection staring back at me, there was a pink square stuck to the center.

I grabbed the monitor, holding it still.

It was a sticky note and written across the top in all caps was my name: ECHO.

Forgetting for the moment where I was and who was trying to get in, I stared at it. It was a coincidence.

Right?

But beneath my name was more block letters in a handwriting

that almost looked familiar: ANTIOCH CEMETARY.

The back door slammed open. I ripped the sticky note off the screen just in case and shoved it in my pocket at the same time that I kicked the computer chair under the window. Out in the hall, the few doors were being slammed open one by one. Orders were being barked. Footsteps rushed from tiny room to tiny room. Doing my best to keep the desk chair steady, I scrambled up and shoved the window handle. It didn't move. I yanked on it. Nothing. Looking back, it was most likely locked, but in that moment, I didn't have the time to figure it out. The doorknob jiggled behind me. I blocked my face with one arm and slammed my elbow with the other against the glass, nearly losing my balance as it shattered. I didn't bother to clear the shards. The desk lurched forward behind me. I ducked my head and shoved through the bigger pieces as I lifted myself up and over the sill. Pain bit into my palms and scrapped against my arms and back, but I didn't stop.

The instant my feet hit the pavement, I took off running down the alley. Voices shouted after me. Heavy footsteps rushed to catch up. I ran down the street, not sure where I was going, cycling through the locations that I had left. Which was none. I was out of options. Nothing that I remembered in Bastrop was real.

But that was as far as I had a chance to think before a solid form grabbed me from behind and yanked me off my feet. We tumbled to the ground. On the way down, they lost their grip and I shoved away from them, scrambling back to my feet. The person righted himself just as fast and grabbed for me again. I dodged and kicked and swatted at him, backing away just to slam into the chest of someone else, someone equally as solid. I tried to run, but my wrist was grabbed and yanked behind my back, forcing me back around.

I yelped. "Fuck!"

A crowd of black uniformed men surrounded me. I was grabbed at and yanked from person to person as they argued over me. I couldn't make out what any of them were saying. Somewhere amongst it all, the most I could make out was "AI," "fuckin' synths," "smash it."

A fist collided just off center with my face making me tumble to one side. Someone caught me and shoved me back on my feet. But the shouting stopped as the group of them stared down at me. I could feel the blood streaming from my nose and across my lips. I swiped at it with the back of my wrist. As I went to lower my arm, bright orange caught my eye. I looked down. What should have been a smear of red was instead orange. Bright orange. I looked at my palms. Gashes of orange. I looked to the guy I'd originally been struggling with. There were smears of orange across his face, orange streaks and splotches all over his dark clothes. My hands, apparently pulsing with orange blood, started to shake.

"Shit," one guy muttered.

"Believe me now," another spat at him.

"Wh-what's happening?" I said out loud.

"Get the professor," someone shouted instead of answering me.

"We should just smash it," someone else said.

"It was in Sadie's—"

"So?"

"*So*, it might be a fuckin' Parrish model."

"Even more reason to fuckin' smash it."

"GET THE FUCKING PROFESSOR! We're not smashing shit!"

A set of footsteps ran off. The rest of them just muttered between them, continued to debate whether or not "it" should be "smashed."

"What's happening?" I said again, knowing I most likely wouldn't get an answer, but it was all I could say, it was all I could think. "What's happening?"

"Fuck, it's stuck in a loop."

"You already smashed it."

"What do you mean, 'What's happening?'" the guy who had sent for the professor asked, ducking his head to be even with my eyes that I couldn't take off my hands.

"What's...this?" I flexed my hands.

"What's what?"

"Why is it orange?"

They fell quiet at that.

"Shit."

"Is it broken?"

"It's tryin' to trick you. Don't fall for it."

"What do you mean?" the guy still ducked in front of me said.

"What do you mean what do I mean?! Why is my blood fucking

orange?!"

"Don't piss it off!"

"I ain't pissin' it off! It's freakin' out."

"Don't freak it out then!"

"I fuckin' ain't!"

"Just turn it off!"

"Yeah, if you're not gonna smash it, turn it off."

I looked up at the guy. In that moment, he was my only lifeline. He flinched, jerking backa half-step, but he didn't look away from me.

"Turn what off? What do they mean?"

"You."

I shook my head, my mouth trying to form words I couldn't think of.

He squinted at me. "You don't fuckin' know. How do you not fuckin' know? Why would they program you to not know?"

"Know what?"

"He's here," someone behind me shouted. "Move!"

"It's over here!"

"Where? Oh."

I turned to see a tall-ish man with thick tortoiseshell glasses and messy, dirty blond hair. He paused for a brief moment, something flashing across his face, but it was gone before I could discern what it was. His muscles then his face went hard, expressionless. He hunched to squint his small blue eyes at me, getting immediately distracted by my bloody nose.

"How'd that happen?" He straightened and looked around the crowd.

While no one was answering, I stared up at him, examining his broad forehead, his small nose, his square chin covered in brown stubble, the raised mole on his left cheek. He looked familiar, but in the panic and confusion I couldn't place from where. It was right there on the edge of my memory that I no longer trusted in the first place.

He sighed and looked back at me. "I'll check for damage later. What's your name?" he said. His voice sounded indifferent, annoyed even, but his eyes kept flicking between my own and my blood with a deeper care than he seemed to want to let on.

"Echo," I said, my voice small from the mix of fear and confusion.

Daniel. That was his name. Daniel Gardner.

"You work at the Institute," I told him.

He squinted again and cocked his head a little. "Institute?"

I nodded.

"With Marshall?" he said, mimicking my nod. "And Eden?"

I nodded again, this time with more vigor. Finally, something was the same, someone was real. I rushed for him without thinking. The men around us either moved for me or to get as far out of my way as they could manage.

"I need to find Aurora," I said quickly, ignoring them. "Do you know—?"

He raised his hand to the men around us, his other hand touching my back with a protective familiarity that I was desperate for even if all I remembered about him was his name. "Yes. I'll take you to her."

I expected him to take me out of this crowd. Instead, he reached for my face. I tried to jerk away, but I wasn't fast enough. He grabbed my earlobe and squeezed. And there was that lead blanket again. It happened so abruptly that everything felt painfully heavy. I couldn't shake it this time. Before I could react, the world went dark.

There's a pressure in my head and around my hand. I look down. It's Aurora's squeezing mine.

I blink at her.

Aurora: You okay?

I blink some more then nod.

Aurora: Your hands are shaking.

The conversation in the front stops and Delta shifts in her seat to look at me, poorly reigned in panic in her eyes.

Delta: Echo?

Charlie glances from me to the road and back again in the rearview mirror.

I stare back at them. Now more than ever they feel like strangers even though I know they aren't. But everything I remember about them is wrong. And I have no memory of what they remember. I hate this so much.

Echo: How much farther?

Aurora: A while, unfortunately.

Charlie: [grumbling] About nine hours.

Delta: But we're out of Washington. [She reaches out and places her hand on my knee.] The hard part's over.

I nod and take her hand, she squeezes and I squeeze back. I just want *this* part to be over. I just want to know what happened to me. I just want to know what happened to them. I just want this part to be over.

[END LOG]

[END TRANSMISSION]

Something's wrong. The car is swerving violently.

Fox is screaming and holding onto her lavender bucket hat.

Aurora and Delta are shouting instructions over each other at Charlie.

He's somehow ignoring both of them and maneuvering the car that's now *thump-thump-thumping* to the side of the road with more skill than I had expected. The car is stopped in the grass on the side of the road and Aurora is now checking everyone over. Once she's sure Fox is alright, she turns to me.

Aurora: Echo?

She reaches for me, her hand massaging the back of my neck.

Echo: I'm fine.

She kisses my temple. I wonder how she'd react if we were in actual danger.

Charlie gets out and Delta follows him. Aurora is craning her neck and shifting in her seat to see what they're doing. I open my door and climb out so she can join them, but I don't. Instead, I sit in the grass a little ways off. It's a flat. I can see that without needing to be told. Aurora and Charlie are crouched next to it, looking it over. Delta is hovering over them. This is going to take a while. I lie back in the grass and stare at the sky.

I had been asleep. I'd willed myself to because being awake is just a constant reminder that I'm broken and nothing makes sense. Of all the ways I've been woken up lately, this admittedly isn't the worst. At least I'm outside. At least I can see the clouds, smell the grass, feel the rocks under my back that I ignore because, again, at least I'm outside. I'm not locked in a closet. Even if I am broken, even if so little makes sense, there's at least that.

I still don't know where we're going. I do know it's a detour. A pit stop on the way to finding Bravo and Eden, though I don't know how we're going to find them. We don't actually know where they are and I don't think this pit stop will give us any new information. I was supposed to get that information. I do have it. But I can't interpret it. It means nothing to me. I tried to show the others, but they said it was scrambled. There was too much missing to be able to tell if what little was legible meant anything.

I lied to you when Aurora and I got back from Seattle. The location I gave you was a goose chase to a dead end. Aurora told me to do it, so I did even if it set my nerves on fire because I'm not supposed to lie to you. But I trust her and she doesn't trust you, even if she can't tell me why.

I hate not knowing things. It goes against everything in my programming. I'm intel. I'm supposed to know things. I'm supposed to report them back to you, to Eden, to...someone else, but I can't grasp who. I haven't been able to. Since you brought me to the cabin, since I learned that everything I remember is wrong. I've been trying to piece together what's missing. That's one of them. There's someone missing. Someone who was there before but isn't here now. I can't grasp them. They're right on the edge of my peripheral.

It's the same way I felt that day when I woke up after Daniel had kept me from being "smashed" outside of Sadie's. I woke with a start from a bolt of pain that arched from my forehead to the back of my head. The metal chair beneath me rattled, the sound pinging off my nerves like a thousand needles being shoved into my temples all at once. The instant my eyes opened, I clenched them shut again, the light of the room biting at my eyes making the pain in my head worse.

"Hm," someone intoned from the other side of a wall.

It was a simple sound, but it hit my memory then in a way that I didn't understand. It was just flashes, it still is—one arm crossed, fingers close to his side fidgeting with a pen, the others loosely curled against thin, softly puckered lips and brown stubble, small blue eyes behind tortoiseshell glasses examining my face, my gestures, my posture as I talked; perpetually slouched shoulders, hands deep in the front pockets of worn thin jeans or rubbing the back of his neck; a slight inward turn of his right foot as he walked, not enough to be noticeable unless it was your purpose to notice little things; a warm smile that creased his eyes.

"What?" a different voice said through my confusion. "Did you do that?"

I waited for the first voice to answer with my eyes closed and my face tilted down and to the side, one ear raised, but it never did, at least not in a way that I could hear.

"Then who—?"

I listened for the rest of the question, for an answer so I could maybe grab hold of more, but there was nothing. Just silence. Slowly, I blinked through the light. I took in my surroundings in small pieces through squinted eyes: the metal table in front of me matching the metal chair I was sitting on and the one across from me; the cool, oppressive grey of the walls; the door that was a few shades darker and looked like it might be metal under the paint; the bright, buzzing florescent tubes of the twin lights above my head; the mirror built into the wall across from me that stretched from one side of the room to the other.

How did I get there? I could speculate at what happened, but I have no real idea what the truth is.

Just like a lot of things, I'm realizing.

I remembered the orange blood that was supposed to be mine and yanked my hands up onto the tabletop, palms up. They had been cleaned, the scrapes and cuts gone. How long had it been, I wondered. How was there not a single sign of damage left behind? I looked at the mirror.

Someone yelped behind it, a rolling chair rattled.

My face was equally as clean, my nose had the same rounded point that it always had, there was no swelling anywhere on my face, no bruising. Had any of it even happened? There was no way I had slept through the time it would take to heal the injuries I'd put myself through. And how had I been put to sleep to begin with? All Daniel had done was touch my ear. I was still in the dark then.

I looked back at my hands. My ears rang. My head felt too heavy and too light at the same time. I was having a breakdown. That was the only reasonable explanation. I was deep in psychosis and this place was a hospital. That's what was happening. Right? That's what had to be happening.

My eyes leapt back to the door. I had an idea of what kind of room I was in, but I stood anyways and started around the table.

"Shit!" the second voice from before hissed, the rolling chair rattled and rolled.

"Stop being an idiot," the first voice finally said. "She can hear you."

"I-it can?"

I ignored them and grabbed the doorknob. It was locked. I knew it would be, but I had hoped that maybe it wasn't. I needed to stop hoping for things. The panic collapsed on top of me. My breathing became erratic. The room felt like it was shrinking. My own skin felt too tight. Not again. Fuck, please, not again. I shot to my knees and dug for my lock picks. I didn't care if they were watching. I needed out.

Before I could get my shaking fingers to cooperate, I heard footsteps come down the hall and stop outside the door. Then the knob turned in front of me. I scrambled back and under the table. The door opened and I clenched my eyes shut, wrapped my arms around my head. It was those men again. They were back to finish what they'd started in the street.

"Echo?" It was Daniel. I knew from that gentle tone. Daniel had been the first voice.

My muscles relaxed. I loosened my arms and looked up. He was crouched next to the table, looking at me with care.

"Hey," he said with that warm smile. It was lopsided, I didn't remember that.

"Hi," I whispered. I lowered my arms, but I didn't leave the safety of the table. I still had questions. What was he doing here? Did he work at the Institute or not? Was that another lie my mind had created? Why was he at the hospital? Was this even a hospital? Was he actually a doctor? A folder was under his hand on the floor. Was that my file? Had I been here before? Had I done this before? Was Aurora even—?

I stopped the thoughts there. I couldn't entertain that one. I'd break completely if she wasn't.

"Where's Aurora?"

He took in a breath and nodded. "I did tell you I'd take you to her and I'm sorry—"

I shot out from under the table. Behind the glass, the rolling chair rattled again. Heavy footsteps moved through the hidden room. When I stood next to the chair I'd woken up in, Daniel was standing, as well, his palm out to the mirror, his eyes firmly on me. There was tension in his body, but I realized it was entirely directed at the mirror. The parts of him that were facing me were filled with concern, protection. I didn't understand why. But I was grateful for it.

"Where is she?"

"Echo, I promise we'll get to that, but first..." Without lowering his hand, he gestured with the other to the chair next to me.

My eyes shifted from the chair to him. "Will you tell me what's going on?"

Though that warm smile came back, it didn't reach his eyes. They were still focused on me with all the concern in the world. In some ways it made me uncomfortable, in others I recognized this look, I wanted to hold onto it. It was familiar. It was something.

So, I sat.

With a sigh, he did the same across from me and folded his hands on top of the folder, my file. At first, he just stared at his hands, his mouth open as though he were trying to figure out where to begin. I probably wasn't helping, staring back at him, hoping that maybe reality would shift again, that maybe if I blinked just right I'd be somewhere else, somewhere not behind a locked door, somewhere in the place from before that I knew him from, somewhere where Aurora was.

But it never did.

Tired of the silence, tired of everything being just beyond my fingertips, I finally broke the silence myself. "Where are we?"

To my surprise, he relaxed a little. I felt the urge at the corners of my mouth to lift into a smile. The shift in tension was so familiar I could have cried. I almost did then, but from frustration as I realized I had no idea why.

"The Bastrop Police Station."

I blinked a few times as I processed this. Police Station? "Why?"

"Some people have been looking for you, Echo."

A glimmer of hope sparkled across my bones. "Who?"

His eyes shifted as though to glance behind him, but his head didn't move. "I'm, um, not at liberty to say, unfortunately."

My lips pressed together. I wondered if it was true or if he just didn't want to tell me. I took in and let out an audible breath. This wasn't a hospital. He wasn't a doctor. That didn't explain why he was here. It also didn't explain everything that had happened, the orange blood, the state of the Institute or Sadie's, where everyone was. Maybe it was something else. What had happened last night? Aurora and I had eaten dinner at Anita's and gone home. We'd had margaritas at the restaurant. Maybe someone put something in my drink. Maybe—

I closed my eyes. I couldn't let myself go down that path right now. Aurora was alive. Aurora was safe. I just had to find her. "How long was I out for?"

He shifted in his chair and rubbed the back of his neck then answered my question with a question, "Echo, can you tell me the last thing you remember?"

I squinted at him and crossed my arms as I leaned back in my own chair. Maybe it was him. Maybe this was all some kind of twisted experiment. I couldn't remember what department he worked in, after all. Maybe the protective caring was an act. "You did something to me."

His lips squirmed and his eyes darted away from me back to the folder. "And what was that?"

I stared at him long enough that he lifted his eyes again. I didn't really have an answer. I didn't really know how he wanted me to answer. He wouldn't hurt me. That didn't line up with what I knew of him. It wasn't much, but I remembered only kindness and concern.

"I don't know," I finally said, staring at the table, feeling my own clean, unmarred fingers against my sides. "Y-you drugged me...or something."

"Is that what you remember?"

My eyes shot back up to meet his. "I remember you touching me and then everything went dark."

He nodded. "You weren't out for long. About three hours. Do you remember what woke you?"

My brows scrunched up. "No. My head hurt and when I opened my eyes I was here."

He shifted to the edge of his seat, leaning forward on his elbows. His hand moved towards me, but then darted back to the folder as though he'd changed his mind. "Does your head still hurt?"

My eyes darted over him—his hunched shoulders, pursed lips, small blue eyes examining me in turn. "No."

He nodded and eased back a bit. He looked at the folder, my file, and tapped his now clasped hands against it. "Do you remember what happened at Sadie's?"

"Today?"

"Yes." He looked at me from the tops of his eyes before adjusting his glasses with the back of his forefinger so he could see me clearly without lifting his head.

I shrugged. *Hallucinations. Psychosis.* Instead, I just said, "It was empty."

He nodded. "And before Sadie's?"

I glanced at the mirror. "I tried to go home."

"Where's that?"

"The Sanctuary."

He squinted and shook his head a little as though confused. "Where's that?"

I squinted back at him. The building admittedly didn't have a sign out front. The city didn't want them ruining the original façade when it had been made into apartments. But it was the only apartments in the small section called downtown. "On Main Street?"

He blinked then nodded. "And?"

"And?"

"What did you find there?"

I chewed my bottom lip. I didn't want to answer. It was still too fresh. "Nothing."

He nodded and looked back at my file. "Not Aurora, you mean?"

"Yes."

"And, for the record, who is Aurora?"

I stared at him until he met my eyes again.

"Who is she to you?" he clarified.

"My girlfriend."

"As in girl who's a fri—?"

"As in my *partner*," I said over him. "As in the woman I love. The woman I'm trying to—"

He unclasped his hands and held them out to me in apology. "Yes. Yes. Just...I'm sorry. Simply clarifying for the record."

"What record?"

"Please, just...I promise—" He held my eyes then and leaned forward. I was surprised when he lowered his voice to just above a whisper. "Trust me. Please."

My brows scrunched up, but I nodded anyways, my knee bouncing under the table.

He nodded in return and readjusted in his seat. "And, um, when's the last time you remember seeing her?"

"Last night."

He lifted his head to fully look at me, surprise behind his eyes. "A-and where was that?"

"Our apartment."

"The Sanctuary?"

"Yes."

"On Main Street."

"Yes," I nearly shouted at him.

He now turned his head to fully glance at the mirror. When he turned back to me his mouth was open as though poised for words he was still searching for.

"Um." He swallowed and gripped the back of his neck. "I-in town, you said I, um, 'work at the Institute?'"

"Mhm."

"Wh-what institute is that, Echo?"

My head cocked a bit as my brows knitted together and my lips pursed. I just stared at him. What did he mean, *what Institute*?

"*The* Institute?" I said, not sure how else to say it.

He shook his head. "What institute?"

"Turing? The Turing Institute of Technology?"

His eyes fluttered then he squinted at me. "Wh-where is that?"

"Here."

"Here?"

"In Bastrop."

"You sure?"

"Yes! It's the big brick building on Willow Street."

He nodded and finally opened my file. "On Willow Street."

I watched him shuffle through papers. "Near Fisherman's Park."

"Right. This big brick building?" He pushed a photograph towards me.

I glanced at it. "Yes."

I didn't need to examine that picture. I knew that building by heart. I knew the grey bricks. I knew the large windows downstairs, the tall thin ones upstairs. I knew the walkway from the street to the concrete steps to the large double front doors. I knew the flat roof and the parapet with the art deco corners that I would sometimes find Fox hiding behind when she was having one of those days where she just wanted to be mad at the whole world and didn't want you or Aurora to fix it.

"That's...not an institute," Daniel said, carefully spacing out his words.

"Yes, it is!" I lurched forward in my seat, flinging my hands out at him, ignoring the noise from the other room. "I've been working there for seven years!"

"And what's it called again?" he said over me with a calm tone.

"The Turing Institute of Technology."

He nodded. "Except it's not, Echo." He tapped the picture. "It's Parrish Technologies. Has been for ten years."

I looked from him to the photograph. At the end of the sidewalk was in fact a sign that read not Turing Institute of Technology, but instead Parrish Technologies. I grabbed the picture and squinted at the sign.

"And who did you work under," he asked before I was done.

I pushed the photograph back towards him, but didn't look anywhere near him, my eyes locked on the table between us. "Marshall and Eden Parrish."

Was he about to tell me you weren't real, too? Next he'd be telling me the others weren't real, or— My heart hammered in my chest. My hands shook under my tightly crossed arms. Maybe this was all a dream—a nightmare. Maybe *this* was the false reality and if I did something, said the right words, found the right object, clicked my heels together the right amount of times, I'd wake up and everything would be back to normal.

"*Dr.* Marshall Parrish?" He pushed another photograph towards me, this one smaller, a blown up version of the outdated one on your ID card you always forgot on your desk. "And Dr. Eden

Parrish?"

Next to it, he placed a more recent photo of Eden in a beer garden that I recognized as one of the bars on Main Street. But it had been cropped to remove the person next to her. At first, I thought from the tender way the person's arm hung around her neck, the way she hunched to be close to them, that it must have been Bravo, but the person was too short, the light behind them lit up a cluster of brown curls.

But it didn't matter who that person was. You both existed.

He didn't say anything at first, didn't push me to answer, just watched me staring at the images.

When he did finally speak, his voice was gentle again. "Is that them, Echo?"

I nodded before my voice could catch up. "D-do you have pictures of the others?"

I had to know they were real, too.

"Who exactly?"

"Aurora. Bravo. Charlie and Delta. Fox?"

He nodded as I spoke, sifting through the folder. He pulled out five images, one after the other. And there they were—Aurora, Bravo, Charlie, Delta, Fox. But something wasn't right about them. Each image looked more like a mugshot, taken from straight on with a harsh light that flattened their faces. Aurora's chin length auburn hair was pinned back out of her face. Bravo's dark brown and Delta's nearly black waves were tied back tight in a way I'd never seen either of them wear their hair. Fox's was the natural mousey brown that it hadn't been in years and it was cropped shorter than I'd ever seen in a masculine style. All four of them stared forward, their eyes as lifeless as glass.

I touched Aurora's photo. "Are...are they...?"

"Are they what, Echo?"

"Alive?" I managed to get out, but only as a whisper.

"Echo."

I looked up at him.

"Tell me everything you remember."

Tears that were a tangled mess of frustration and fear and confusion came up on me faster than I could stop them, my voice unsteady around them. "Tell me their okay."

"That's what we're trying to find out."

A sob burst from my chest as the panic drove me into a spiral of tears.

"Echo," he said over my hyperventilating, but the floodgates had opened and I couldn't close them again.

His chair screeched back and he rounded the table to kneel next to me, his hand on my arm.

"Echo," he repeated soft enough I had no choice but to try and control my panic just to hear him. "We're trying to find them. But," he glanced at the mirror and lowered his voice even more, "we need to know what happened to you first. Okay, Echo?" He shifted closer, his voice barely a whisper. "I need you to trust me."

I stared down at him. I wanted to. I wanted to trust somebody. I *needed* to trust somebody. But what was the truth? I still barely knew if this was reality. On top of that, I didn't understand what he meant by *what happened to you*. What *had* happened to me? What exactly was wrong with me? How could I explain these things if I barely had a grasp on them myself?

I nodded anyways, hoping that maybe he had more answers than I did, hoping that maybe he could lead me to Aurora.

But he didn't.

He was just a headache that ended with me being knocked out again.

I blink up at the sky, run my hand through a patch of grass by my hip, remind myself I'm in ███████ not Texas. I listen for the others still discussing the flat and how far the spare will get us. But it's not enough. I prop myself up on my elbows just to look at them, see them moving and talking and looking each other in the eyes that have life behind them, that aren't dead like glass.

They're alive.

They're here.

They're okay.

Aurora looks at me, squints, cocks her head to one side.

I nod to let her know that I'm okay.

I'm okay, I repeat to myself as I lie back in the grass.

I'm okay.

We're together.

And I'm okay.

But I can't stop thinking about that day and the way that I woke the next time with less of a splitting headache, more of a jolt between my eyes. I was in the dark, but I wasn't in the same room— the chair I sat in was cushioned, there was carpet beneath my feet, a computer hummed to my left, I could smell someone's leftover catfish. I blinked a few times and my eyes adjusted. I could make out a desk to my left, a sliver of light from under the door in front of me. On the other side of the desk was a window. The blinds were cracked just enough that I could see the sun had gone down, a lit streetlamp casting a dim light through the room. How long had I been out this time?

I stood and went to the door. It was locked. Of course it was. I sighed and pressed my back against it as I looked over the room. Something metal on the desk caught my eye. I crossed the room. It was an emergency key, the kind that came with privacy doorknobs, sitting on top of a bright pink sticky note. I twisted the key between my fingers and glanced at the door. Why lock the door at all? I yanked the note from the desk, tilting it towards the light to read it:

Trust me

Leave now

You know where to go

I dug in my jacket pocket and pulled out the last pink sticky note I'd found.

ANTIOCH CEMETERY

It was a coincidence, right? Two bright pink sticky notes?

Or maybe it wasn't.

It dawned on me in that moment that I didn't really care. Whatever this was, whatever was going on, I needed to get out of here and go find Aurora. Daniel had only gotten me locked in another room, though at least it wasn't a closet. I was also choosing to believe he'd been the one to leave me a way out. I had no real proof. I just needed someone to believe in.

The door unlocked, I stepped out into the hall. I had no idea where I was, I simply started walking. First things first, I needed a way out. I could tell from the few windows I passed that I wasn't on the ground floor, most likely the second judging by the height of the trees and streetlights. Stairs. I needed to find stairs.

As I went I didn't see anyone, just doors upon doors with no signs of life behind them. I wondered where everyone was, what building this was. It didn't look like a police station, but I'd never actually been in the Bastrop Police Station, so, I didn't really know.

I turned a corner and stopped. I could hear Daniel's voice. It was distant, but not too distant. I listened as I walked, drifting closer to the line of doors as his voice grew closer.

"Did you listen to the whole thing?"

I located the door he was behind and crept closer.

"I have no idea where any of it came from. It's fascinating, isn't it?"

I strained to hear whoever was on the other end of the line, but all I could make out was an electric fuzz. I should have questioned how I could hear that, but...I just didn't.

"Yeah. Yeah. Listen, I found some deeper damage when I was cleaning her up, but I couldn't fix it without giving us away."

I leaned closer to the door. Who was he talking about? Was he talking about me? What damage?

"She seems to be operating fine besides...everything else, but you'll need to just— Good. Good, yeah."

A pair of footsteps and voices came from down the hall. I glanced around.

"Already done," Daniel was saying. "How long do you think—? Okay. Okay, good. I'll try and head out there, too, when I can. Just in case."

Across from me was a water fountain, a bathroom door on either side of it. I ducked into the women's hoping the person I was hiding from wasn't headed for the same room. As I listened at the door, I realized both voices were male and started to relax, but that only lasted so long.

"You think we really have to wait until tomorrow?" one voice said. "No one would give a fuck if we smashed it tonight."

"It's a fucking Parrish model," the second answered. "You really wanna deprive everyone of seeing it smashed just 'cause you get off on that shit?"

"I don't get off on it. They just really—"

"Shut up."

Both footsteps stopped right outside the bathrooms. I held my breath as I listened to theirs, wishing I could open the door just a sliver without being seen.

"That fucking Gardner?" one whispered. "Why's he still here?"

"Who's he talking to?"

"Donno." The footsteps picked up again. "Come on. We gotta be quick."

"Dude, maybe we shouldn't. If Gardner sees its gone, he'll blow his shit."

I slipped off my sneakers and snuck out of the bathroom, rushing as quietly in the opposite direction as I could manage. I turned the corner the voices had come around and, thank god, there was a set of stairs. I started down them, but then stopped. I had no idea what was waiting for me at the bottom. I could be walking in on a meeting of whoever those other people were. Easing my way down the steps, I paused at the bottom, pushing my hearing as far as it could go. Nothing. An unnerving amount of nothing. I peeked around the corner. Another empty hall with a series of doors, but at the end was a set of double doors. Windows set in the middle showed the outside, a streetlight illuminating the sidewalk and the parking lot beyond it.

I was slipping my sneakers back on when I heard Daniel shout from upstairs, "What the fuck are you doing in here?"

"What the fuck are *we* doing?" one of the other voices shouted back. "Where the fuck is it, Gardner?!"

I didn't wait to hear the rest. I didn't bother to assess the hall. I bolted for the double doors.

Fox: Are you okay?

I blink and she's leaning over me, her blue hair a curtain around her face nearly surrounding mine so she's all I can see. There's a dusting of freckles across her cheeks that I hadn't noticed before. This might be the closest I've been to her.

Echo: Yeah. Yeah, I'm fine.

But she doesn't look convinced and just squints down at me.

Fox: No, you're not.

I let out a sharp sigh. Am I that readable?

Echo: Yeah. I'm not.

She sits back on her heels then shifts to lie next to me. We're just lying here in the grass and dirt staring at the clouds. It's nice. It's quiet beyond the sounds of the others discussing the flat and the spare.

Fox: When we get to the place, you'll be okay.

Echo: I don't know about that.

She shrugs in my peripheral.

Fox: Maybe not. But maybe you will. We won't know until we get there. You see that one?

She points at a cloud. I think I know which one she's pointing at, but I'm not sure if it entirely matters if it's the right one.

Echo: Mhm.

Fox: Does it look like a horse to you? Like a horse leaping over a bush or something?

I realize I was looking at the wrong cloud. I was looking at the bush or something. The one above it doesn't look exactly like a horse, but I see what she means. I see the idea of a horse in the way it swoops and swirls with long strokes.

Echo: Yeah. It kind of does.

She nods and lowers her hand back to her stomach.

Fox: I think I like horses. I used to like rabbits, but I think now I like horses.

Echo: You can like both.

Fox: Yeah. But I think I relate more to horses now. You know, horses weren't actually brought here by the Spanish? I mean, they were, eventually, but back before they were all over the Americas.

She sits up and twists to look out over her shoulder across the field behind us.

Fox: They went extinct. 10,000 years ago. At the end of the...

She squints into the distance as though the word she's trying to remember is out there in the tall grass.

Fox: Pleistocene era. No one knows why.

The wind blows her blue hair from her freckled pink face. She's like a scene from a movie. I wonder where her lavender hat ended up.

Fox: Then the conquistadors came and brought them back.

She looks down at me, or more near me, her grey eyes on the dirt between us.

Fox: The first wild horses used to be domesticated. They escaped Mexico City around 1550.

She finally meets my eyes.

Fox: Once they were free that was it. They were everywhere.

I stare back at her and process what she just said.

Echo: Is that why you like horses now?

She nods.

I wish I could relate. I think right now I'm still clinging to what little I have that's constant. I think that's why I'm still sending these to you. I think that's why I can't let go of you as easily as they can.

I'm still a domesticated horse fighting my way out of Mexico City.

[END LOG]

[END TRANSMISSION]

Though Aurora has agreed not to talk about the spare, it's still making her nervous. I can feel it in the way she won't relax, her body stiff next to me; the way her grip tightens around my hand when there's the slightest of bumps; the way her legs are crossed at the knee, her top leg touching mine; the way she self-sooths by fidgeting with my fingers in her lap.

But I don't mind it. I wish she wasn't nervous, of course, but I like feeling her close, I like her skin on mine. I like knowing that she finds comfort in my presence. I like knowing that she still loves me, that at least that was real, that you didn't take all of her from me.

It's been three hours since the tire blew out, seven since we left Colville, and we're already stopping again for gas. I wonder how many times we're going to have to stop on this drive. We're in a town that's on the verge of being a city and Charlie is pulling into the first gas station we've come across. Aurora sits up in her seat. I follow her eye line. There's a garage next door.

Aurora: Charlie, [She grabs his shoulder before he can get out.] are you sure about the spare?

He eyes the garage, as well.

Delta: [without looking away from one of Fox's magazines] We're losing daylight.

She's right. It's already five. The rain and the tire already set us back two hours. But, who knows how long losing the spare would set us back.

Charlie: After we fill up, I'll go ask how long it would take.

Aurora: [nodding] Kay.

Fox: [She's already climbing out of the car, one hand holding down her lavender bucket hat.] Can we walk around?

Delta: I could stand to move.

She tosses the magazine on the floor between her feet. Her knee is bouncing under the dash. Aurora looks from it to me.

Aurora: Echo?

My head hurts, but I'm getting claustrophobic in this car and I don't want her to leave me. So, I nod and open the door.

Charlie: Del.

They look at each other from across the roof of the car.

Charlie: You sure? You sure you're ready?

Delta: [She nods and takes in a breath that seems to steady her.] Yeah. Yeah, I think I can. Gotta start sometime, right? Better here than...anywhere.

I'm staring between them. I have no context for what they're talking about. It's not helping the pulsing in my head. Aurora takes my hand and I meet her eyes. There's a wordless apology behind them that I only understand slightly more. I just sigh and lean into her. I'm so tired.

We agree to meet Charlie at the garage in half an hour and cross the street to start walking along what looks to be the main shopping area. The buildings are mismatched with varying heights and facades. Each shop window has its own display—one a clothing store, the next antiques, fancy furniture, books, a coffee shop with little tables inside. It all reminds me of Bastrop, of the life I remember. The nostalgia tingles low in my stomach and along my arms. I take Aurora's hand and she smiles down at me. We walk holding hands while Delta and Fox walk ahead of us, pausing at windows to point and compare opinions.

I didn't realize how much I've missed this. I hadn't thought until now what might happen at the end of this, how much I hope it's something like this: all of us together, window shopping in some little town, not worried about where we're going or who might be after us. Just us, together.

I'd love for it to be Bastrop, but Bastrop is tainted now. Just thinking about Bastrop, about downtown reminds me of that night when I was running, the streets I'd walked endlessly while bored now a maze that I knew by heart and used to my advantage. Or at least, I remember walking those streets until I had memorized them. Who knows anymore why I know those streets, alleys, and backways so well if none of those memories are real. I'm still not sure how, I definitely didn't know that night, just like I didn't know exactly how

I knew where Antioch Cemetery was despite having never been there. I didn't have the time to consider why or how I knew these things. I needed to find Aurora, needed to hold onto hope that Daniel, or whoever had left me that key, knew where she was and could lead me to her.

Either way, I was able to get out of town using just the alleyways and backstreets, avoiding the black jeeps driving up and down the main roads with searchlights. Once I was out of town, I cut through the park, staying off the road, but making sure to keep it close to my right. It took two and a half hours for me to get to Antioch Cemetery, but only because once I was out of the park and out from under the cover of the pine trees, just long stretches of open field and shrubs between clumps of trees, I began to run, afraid of being exposed for those jeeps to come rushing up behind me in the dark.

I almost missed it. The only reason why I didn't was because I was hugging the fence. I came out from a large patch of brush and started to run for the next line of cover when I spotted the sign. It's not a big sign or a very flashy one, just a board screwed to some wooden posts. Each individual letter is cut out from metal that hovers over the wood and would most likely cause a drop shadow effect if there had been any light out that night. At the time, I had decided the fact that I could read it at all was purely because my eyes had adjusted to the moonless country dark over the last nine miles of walking. I wasn't ready to accept that there might be a different reason.

Further ignoring that fact, I backtracked a few steps to the gate that, thankfully, wasn't locked, but that squeaked briefly making me cringe and shush at it as I slipped through. Much like its sign, the cemetery is small and humble with less than 50 gravestones, maybe even half that, most of which are small and worn down. The grass was overgrown that night, most likely still is, and the majority of the markers looked too old to have anyone left to remember them, but a handful had flowers and little trinkets left beside them. In the center was a wooden cover with a pair of benches beneath it. I half hoped someone, maybe Aurora, would be sitting on one of them, but they were empty. I was alone. Completely alone. I wandered between the rows of stones, wondering why I was here, looking for any kind of sign telling me what to do next.

Just as I was digging in my pocket for the notes, I heard a speeding vehicle in the distance coming from the direction of town. I spun in a frantic circle, searching out a hiding spot. In the back corner farthest from the road, I spotted something long, curved, and low to the ground. I ran for it, keeping low, and dove behind it, crawling into the crook of what I only just then realized was the head, its glass doorknob eye staring at me through the dark. I huddled there behind the concrete creature, staring at the mosaic tiles decorating it, listening hard to the vehicle approaching, hoping it was just someone out for a drive, that they'd keep going through the night, the sound of their engine fading into the dark as they sped on by. Or maybe it would be Daniel, coming to get me and take me to Aurora. Or maybe it would be Daniel coming to collect me and take me back to Bastrop to be smashed.

The breaks squealed on the road, the tires fishtailing against the loose gravel. Shit. I pressed myself deeper against the creature. Shit. The car door opened and the crunch of footsteps jabbed against my heart that couldn't possibly beat any faster. Shit. The gate rattled and squeaked open.

"Shit," a voice hissed as a whisper.

I froze. That voice. It sounded familiar.

The dead grass crinkled under careful footsteps moving through stones the way I had before.

"Echo?"

I sat up. I absolutely knew that voice. But it was the last one I had expected to hear. It couldn't have been real. I waited, hoping you'd call out again.

"Echo?" There was a *thunk* followed by stumbling sounds. "Fuck. Sorry. I mean—Why the fuck—? Argh. Echo? Echo, you here?"

I stood and leapt over the concrete creature. "Marsh?!"

"Shh." You put your finger to your lips and glanced around the dark. At the time I thought you were looking for someone, now I know it was me in the dark your eyes couldn't see through. "Come here."

But I was already rushing for you.

"Where are you? Careful for—"

I hugged you. You froze. I guess because you weren't expecting it. I'm not usually a hugger, but I was just so relieved to see a familiar face, hear a familiar voice, be near a familiar anything that was real and the same and exactly what I remembered.

Or, I thought I remembered.

"Hey, Echo," you said with a chuckle as you finally embraced me. "Thank fuck you're okay."

I pulled away from you and looked to the car. "Where's Aurora? Is she with you? Is she okay?"

"No." You held me at arm's length, your eyes large, trying to make me out in the dark that I had no trouble seeing in. "No. I mean, yes, she's okay, but she's not with me. Echo, she's up north. With the others?"

"North? North where? Why's she up north? What happened?"

Your brows scrunched up. "Because—Shit. Right. Echo, it's not safe here anymore. We had to leave, but I came back for you as soon as I could."

I shook my head. "I don't—Why isn't it safe? What happened?"

You stared at me as best you could. "Echo, what do you remember?"

But I heard a car coming in our direction and listened to locate it instead of answering you.

"What? What is it?"

"A car."

You let me go and turned towards the road, as well, though you looked the wrong way. "Where? From town? What direction are they coming from?"

"North."

"North?" You turned in the direction you thought was North. "Uh, shit. Which direction is...? Town's..."

"Town's west."

"Right. Right." You went on turning in circles. "Um, it's probably nothing. But, uh," you started for the car at a speed I didn't understand, I still don't understand. "We gotta go."

"It shouldn't be—"

"Now," you said over me. "Come on."

I got in your car and you peeled away from Bastrop without a second glance back.

And you didn't stop until we were nearly out of gas around Sweetwater. Even with the gas station being empty besides the synth behind the counter inside, you still told me to stay in the dark car. Though, I was only alone until the gas started flowing, then you glanced around a few more times before getting back in where you continued to examine the dark beyond the illuminated pumps.

We hadn't said a word since the cemetery, your speed making me too nervous to think of much else. But in the silence, watching your head swivel in every direction, I couldn't take it anymore.

"Marsh what happened?"

"Not here."

"Then where? When? Are you really going to keep me in the dark the entire way...to wherever the fuck we're going?"

You let out a growl of a sigh and tapped your fingers against the steering wheel, your knee bouncing under the dash. "Tell me what you remember. From before you woke up."

I growled back at you and rubbed the heels of my palms against my forehead. "Why does everyone keep asking me that?" It had really only been two people, but I was already tired of being the one to give everything and get nothing in return. "Why does it matter what *I* remember?"

"What do you remember, Echo?"

I crossed my arms and closed my eyes, my head pressed back against the head rest. Her face was the first thing I thought of, that crooked, toothy smile, her hands warm as sunbeams cradling my face as she took me in with those expressive eyes that told me when she was excited or upset or in love. God, how I missed her, how I missed feeling safe, how I missed feeling like I could make it through anything because I knew she'd be on the other side waiting for me.

"Echo."

"Aurora," I said over you without opening my eyes. "The last thing I remember is Aurora. We were in our apartment." I remembered more than that, but you didn't and still don't need to know the details of what I remember of that last night.

"And before that?"

I took in a long breath, held it for a few seconds, then let it out again. "I got off work. Aurora dropped Fox off with you at the Institute.'

"The...? Why was Aurora with Fox?"

I opened my eyes and looked at you. "Why wouldn't she be?"

You didn't answer, just stared back at me looking as confused as I was.

"Fox got off school, Aurora picked her up, and they worked on college stuff. When it was time for us to get off work, they met us at the Institute and you and Fox went home and Aurora and I went to get dinner. Like every evening."

"We...we do that every evening?"

I nodded.

"And Charlie and Delta?"

I shrugged. "Delta was probably at home and Charlie was most likely at practice or something. I don't know. I didn't see them yesterday."

You shook your head, but it was so small and sharp it was more of a flinch. "Yesterday?"

I squinted at you. "Yes. Yesterday."

You stared back at me. "A-and Bravo? What about Eden?"

I shrugged again. "I haven't seen them much. They're working on some project, but I don't really know much about it. Something to do with some update, I think."

The gas stopped and the nozzle *thunked* making you jump. You glanced at me again then got out of the car. I stared at the dashboard. Those pictures of Aurora and the others, the ones where their eyes had no life behind them, came back into my head. They were fine, I told myself. They were...up north, whatever the fuck that meant. That's what you'd said. And you'd tell me if something was wrong.

Wouldn't you?

The door opened and you got back in. I looked up at you and you stopped, hand half way to the ignition, to stare back at me.

"How'd they get up north? They were in Bastrop yesterday. How'd they get—?"

You looked away from me and started the car. "Not here."

"Where?!"

You shifted into drive then flicked on the radio. Screeching guitars, droning bass, and chaotic drums nearly drowned out your voice when you spoke, "Not in Texas." You pulled away from the pumps and towards the dark highway. "Once we're out of Texas, I'll tell you everything."

I stared at you, an uneasy feeling in my gut. But I had no other choice, did I?

"Everything?" I shouted over the music.

"Everything."

I settled back in my seat and closed my eyes, took in and let out a shaky breath.

Then your hand was on my arm. "They are safe, Echo. Trust me. They're safe and I'm taking you to them. Get some rest."

"Hard to rest with—"

You chuckled and turned the music down. "Sorry. Let's look for something more...something else."

The drive passed in an exhausted silence, the stations you kept jumping between the only sound beyond the AC, the wind, and the tires tearing across the miles and miles and miles of asphalt. The farther we went the more and more drained I became, slipping in and out of sleep as you somehow kept driving.

The car stopped and I woke to the lights of a Buc-ee's shining in my face, the lit up cartoon beaver mascot smiling up at the night sky from the building's façade.

"How are you feeling?" was the first thing you said to me.

I scrubbed my eyes with the heels of my palms. "Tired."

"If you had to put a number to it?"

I squinted at you. "I don't fucking know." But I realized I did. "Eighteen percent."

You sighed and nodded. "Come on."

"You're still not going to tell me anything, are you?"

You gave me an annoyed, but understanding half-smirk. "Do you know where we are?"

I opened my mouth to tell you that, of course, I didn't, but then I did. "Amarillo?"

I think I was too drained that night, too frustrated and sick of not knowing things to question how I knew *that* of all things.

For reasons I didn't understand yet, your body shifted back and forth between relief and high alert. You glanced around the parking lot. "And where's Amarillo?"

"Still in Texas."

You finally stopped examining the parking lot and looked me over, this time something more sentimental behind your eyes. "You coming or not?"

I unbuckled my seatbelt. "Yeah, I'm coming."

My arms crossed tight over my stomach, I followed you through the mega gas station that was mostly empty as you grabbed whatever junk food on the end caps caught your eye and dropped them into the hand basket you'd grabbed at the door. A red bag of chips here, a yellow bag of candies there, some trail mix, a package of jerky I could smell from a few paces behind you. Then you scanned the room, located the drinks, led me in that direction. You opened the glass door of a fridge that held tall, colorful cans which I was sure were full of pure sugar and caffeine. You began tossing them in the basket with the junk food.

I watched as you grabbed what looked to be one of every flavor. "How many are you getting?"

"We've got a long way to go."

"Where *are* we—?" I sighed and leaned against the door of the next fridge over. "Never mind. Up north."

You paused in grabbing the eighth can and sighed. "Washington," you said as you dropped it in the basket and let the door close.

Without elaboration, you turned and searched the shelves as I stared up at you with my mouth open, processing this new information, waiting for more.

You made a grumbling sound, your lips shifting under your mustache, then turned back to the fridges. "Maybe..." you muttered to yourself then moved down the line of doors.

I rushed after you. "But—? Washington? What are they doing in Washington?"

You stopped at the alcohol, scanning the selection. "It wasn't safe in Bastrop anymore." You opened the door and began looking closer, twisting a can or two. "No. No. Fuck."

"So, *Washington*? It wasn't safe in Bastrop, so they went all the way to Washington?"

"Fuck." You looked around the store again and said to yourself, "Could have sworn they sold liquor." You let out a sigh through your nose then looked at me. "Eighteen percent, you said?"

I scrunched up my face and shook my head. "What?"

"You're at eighteen percent?"

I wanted to strangle you. I just shrugged and shook my head instead. "Yeah."

You turned back to the fridge and scanned the cans and bottles one more time with a sigh. "This isn't gonna do shit. Damn. Guess, you can sleep on the way."

You started to walk past me for the registers.

"Marsh!"

You stopped and stared at me.

"Give me *something*. Please."

"In the morning. Once we're out of Texas and we've both gotten some rest, I'll tell you everything."

"Why not now?"

You shook your head. "It's too much." Then you glanced around the gas station and started towards the registers. "Way too much."

You paid in cash and we went back to the car where you tossed the bags of food and drinks in the backseat while I settled into the front. You got in and looked me over.

"Buckled in?"

My seatbelt clicked and I shifted to lean against the door facing away from you. "Mhm."

"Good."

Next thing I knew your hand was on my ear. I flinched, but before I could jerk away or even just ask what you were doing, you pinched me and that lead blanket feeling collapsed over me again.

Once again, I was left alone in the dark.

A shudder runs through me. I hate remembering that feeling. I hate knowing you did that to me. I hope I never have to feel it again. I want to slice my ears off so I won't.

Aurora looks at me. I just give her a weak smile and shake my head, but I can see in her face that she can tell I'm not okay. Though, it's not a huge leap to make. I haven't been okay for a while. Thankfully, I think she can tell that I'm getting tired of being asked if I am or not, because she doesn't bother, just squeezes my hand and lightly bumps into me getting out of me a smile that's a little stronger.

I love you, she mouths to me.

I can't help but grin because that's the kind of thing her love does to me. It floods my insides with sunshine so bright it washes out the holes riddled through me. They're still there, but I can't see them when she's shining down on me. Out of sight, out of mind and all that.

At least you have that going for you—you didn't take her away from me, you brought me back to her.

I guess I should also thank you for letting me wake gently the day after we left Texas, my mind easing into the dull light of the room. The first thing I saw was ceiling tiles that looked like they belonged in an office building. Panic still slammed into my chest despite how I'd woken. Where was I and why did I keep waking up in strange places? I sat straight up then and looked around, saw the honey oak dresser across the room with the mirror that reflected my wide, dark eyes and dry, frizzy curls, the ugly pastel botanical comforter beneath me. You were sitting in profile on the second bed. I quickly examined my surroundings before looking at you: the thick, rough curtains over the only window; the sloppily painted door; the shabby laminate cabinet housing the once white mini fridge; the decades out of date CRT TV; the heavy, also honey oak table on the way to what I assumed was the bathroom, you staring at me, your hands gripped together between your knees, the nightstand between the beds made of the same honey oak as the rest of the furniture; the dusty rose lamp with the dusty off-white shade; the corded phone; the long white charging cable next to it that ran across the nightstand, the bed, up my arm to—

I stared at it.

What the fuck was it connected to?

I lifted it with my fingertips, following it up my arm, feeling the shifting of it against my shoulder, all the way up to my—

I yanked the cord out of my neck and leapt off the bed. "What the fuck?!"

"Echo," you said with a voice that was too calm.

I rushed for the dresser, leaned across the top and lifted onto my toes to get close to the mirror where I scrambled to shove my hair out of the way, flattening my ear forward, my fingers flailing against my skin. A port. They found a port. A little rectangular port no wider than my pinky nail. Why was there a fucking port in my neck?

I ripped my hand from it and rounded on you, my heart pounding in my throat. "WHY IS THERE A FUCKING PORT IN

MY NECK?"

You jumped up then and came for me with hands stretched out, meant to calm me like the sounds you were making, but I jerked way from you and backed away. I didn't want to be comforted, quieted. I wanted answers.

"WHAT THE FUCK IS HAPPENING, MARSH?!"

"Echo, calm down." You didn't let up, still approaching me with your hands out.

"HOW THE FUCK AM I SUPPOSED TO BE CALM?!" I screamed before you could get the words out, jerking away from you again.

"Echo. AUTONOMY OFF," you shouted over me.

My body froze without me telling it to. I wanted to move, wanted to open the door behind me and run, but my muscles wouldn't listen. I was paralyzed. How could this be happening? *What* was even happening?

"Echo, sit down."

My feet finally moved, though I hadn't told them to. I walked calmly to the bed where I sat on the edge and stared up at you. My hands shaking, my legs rubber, my heart whirring. I didn't understand what was happening to me. Even more than before, I wanted to yell at you, wanted to scream and demand answers, but I couldn't.

Not wouldn't.

Couldn't.

You blurred behind tears as I watched you kneel in front of me and let out a long, shaky breath, raked your fingers through your hair. "Fuck. This isn't...I'm sorry. I didn't think—" You closed your eyes and took in and let out another breath. "Let's start over."

I didn't understand how the fuck we were supposed to start over. You had me frozen in a strange place that I was just realizing wasn't a strange place. We were in Colorado. Pueblo, Colorado. Why did I know that? *How* did I know that? Tears rolled down the side of my nose, falling against my parted lips, the liquid that it was just now hitting me tasted like nothing leaking onto my tongue. I wanted to wipe them away, but I couldn't lift my hand to do it.

"Echo..." You sighed then finally met my eyes. "You're a synth. AI. I know you more than likely don't believe me." You chuckled and

I wanted to smack you. "How could you believe me? I—Well, something happened. The specifics aren't important now, but Bastrop got dangerous. We were looking for Eden and Bravo when..." You looked to your hands in your lap. "It got bad, Echo. Real bad. They were after you. All of you. I managed to get the others out, but we lost track of Eden and Bravo. You stayed behind with me to look for them, but then shit got even worse and...and then I just...I lost track of you. I tried to find you, but I had to get out before I could. I was going to wait for shit to calm down then go back to look for you, but then...you woke up on your own. How I *still* don't know. I've been trying to figure that out. You sustained some damage, but that wouldn't—" You took in and let out another shaky breath then took my hands and finally looked up at me. "Echo, please believe how sorry I am. I didn't mean for any of this to happen the way it did. Please, believe me, Echo."

You stared up at me. I wanted to answer, but I couldn't. My mouth was still frozen.

"Shit. Right. Echo, vocal autonomy on."

I took in a shuddering breath as my lips and voice box released. "Why—? How—? Why don't I remember—?"

"I'm...not sure. Maybe the damage? I tried to look, but..." You shrugged. "I don't know. We'll figure it out when we get to Washington."

I stared at you and the dismissive way you were saying these things while my breathing was becoming erratic.

"Damage? What damage?"

"You're still running, so most likely nothing. It probably just formatted you. That's all."

"F...formatted?"

"Yeah. Like cleared you out. Put you back to factory settings."

"So, I—my memories? Everything I remember? From before? It's not—? Was any of it—?"

"Um." You squinted at the wall. "Bits and pieces it sounds like. Aurora is real."

I wanted to sob, relief washing over me.

"Fox, Charlie, Delta, Bravo, they're all real, but your memories of them aren't."

Panic hit me all over again. "So, Aurora and I—"

"Oh. Oh, no." You squeezed my hands and I wanted to claw that attempt at a reassuring grin off your face. "You and Aurora, what you feel, that's real. She's been so worried about you."

My cheeks were soaked. Of all the things that could be real, at least it was that, at least it was her.

"Echo, do you think you can remain calm now?"

"Yes." I would have said anything to be able to move again. I would have done anything to get back to her.

You sighed. "Okay. Good. Echo, autonomy 75%."

My muscles relaxed and I wobbled a little. I scrubbed my cheeks dry. I took in and let out a shaky, stumbling breath that I was just then wondering if I even needed. "Now what?"

I nodded. I'm sure there were things I should have been worried about, more questions I should have asked, but I just wanted to get to Washington. So, I stood and followed you out the door and across the parking lot to the dingy diner with no name, just a metal post out front holding up giant metal letters that read DINER in glowing red. The sun was already setting again. I wondered how long it had taken us to get here, how long I'd been asleep. I thought about asking you, but with your long stride you were just far enough ahead of me that I would have had to say it at a volume I didn't have the energy for, so I didn't.

It took me until you were halfway through your burger and fries to find the energy to speak.

I started with, "Why Washington."

You looked up at me, brows raised. "Hm?"

"Why Washington?"

"Oh," you said before I could finish then shrugged. "I don't know. It's not Texas?"

"There's a lot of places that aren't Texas."

You lifted your burger again. "Does it matter?"

I stared at you for a beat while you took a bite. "Guess not."

"You'll like it," you started before you finished chewing. "Lots of trees, real mountains." You swallowed and grabbed a fry. "Not like in Texas. Doesn't get above 100. It's not on the coast, but there's too many people out that way anyways, so—"

I stopped listening. I realized I didn't care about any of it. As long as Aurora was there, that was all that mattered. We could be on the Sun and I'd be happy. I thought about our apartment, the bay window, the books, the music, Aurora asleep on the couch.

"What are my memories?"

You stopped talking and stared at me. "Hm?"

"These memories of Aurora and our life and the apartment and working and—" I thought of my childhood, of being alone, of having to learn to scavenge and sneak and steal to survive. I didn't want to go near it and have to think about what the lack of it means. "What are they? Where did they come from? Did you give them to me?"

You didn't answer right away, just stared at me as you ran your fingers back and forth along your lips.

"Marsh?"

"Failsafe. They're a, uh, a failsafe. In case anything happened in the field. In case you were found and were wiped or something. I, uh, wanted you to, um, be able to..." You lowered your hand and you blinked at the table then me between taking in a long, deep breath. "Blend in. Until we could get to you. You needed something you could tell people. Something that made you seem real."

I squinted at that and my head twitched a little.

"Human, I mean, I guess," you corrected. "Something that made you seem *human*."

Thinking about that, remembering those words, I step closer to Aurora now as we walk. I watch the people we pass on the street, searching for knowing glances and glares. But none of them look twice at us. They stare at Fox's bright hair and clothes or at Delta with a look that I don't understand, it's almost like recognition, but the kind that you can't place no matter how hard you try. Aurora and I, though not a second glance, not even a first. Not one of them seems to recognize us for what we are. So, why you had to rewrite my entire history for the sake of being more human, I don't understand. Isn't that why I was made the way I was? To blend in? To appear human?

I don't know why I'm telling you all this. I'm sure you've been wondering the same, why I'm not just disappearing like the others, I think it's because I was meant to be your eyes and ears. That's what it says in my specs—Echo model, intelligence. That's why I was created, isn't it? Why you kept me when I was finished? Why you came back for me? The reason you sent me to Seattle? Because without me, you're reliant on your own skills which seem to be spattered with gapping holes. It's my protocol, my purpose to spy for you, to collect data.

But I'm done spying for you. It's a fact that admittedly fills me with a swirl of conflicting feelings because the truth is, without these logs and transmissions, I feel rudderless. I'm afraid of the questions that come up in me when I start to think too hard about my life outside of you, beyond you. Maybe one day, I'll find something that's for me, something that has nothing to do with you, but, for now, I can't fully cut off all contact with you. I don't know or understand why, I just can't. It hurts in ways it shouldn't.

I wonder if I'll start to understand things once we get to where we're going. The others keep saying I'll be okay once we get there, but they can't tell me how. Maybe that's how. Maybe I'll finally see things the way they do. Maybe everything will make sense. But what will that mean for you? Once I understand, will I hate you the way they do? Will I care anymore about you or my connection to you? I need to know what happened to me, but at the same time, I'm afraid of what I'll learn. I'm afraid of what you did. I'm afraid of who you really are.

And then, on some other level, I'm afraid I won't hate you. I'm afraid I'll finally understand, but at the same time, I won't. I'll look at them and I'll look at you, and you'll win.

I can't decide which would be worse.

So, for now, I won't.

For now, you're in a box. Once we get to where we're going. I'll open it, see if you're alive or dead. But, for now, you're neither, you're both.

For now, I'm going to stop thinking about you.

[END LOG]

[END TRANSMISSION]

I need to be honest with you now, I recorded the next several logs over the last 24 hours. Once we got to ▮▮▮▮▮, I knew I couldn't send them to you even six hours out, not in that moment nor any of those moments. At first it was to protect the others. Then it was to protect Lilith. Then it was because I was angry at you. I *am* angry at you. I still don't know everything, there's still so much I don't understand, but I know enough.

In the beginning, I was sending these logs so you'd understand why we left.

Then it was because I was lost.

Now, I'm sending them to you because I want you to understand why we're not coming back.

Do you remember that first week in Colville? When I asked you about Bravo and Eden? Before I went to you, I had asked the others where they were, but they had just exchanged looks and gave me vague answers.

"Not here," Fox had grumbled.

"Who knows at this point," Delta had said with an aggressive sigh.

Charlie had just crossed his arms and stared out at the cars in front of the cabin.

Every time I asked Aurora she'd stare at me with a look that I couldn't read. Her lips would twitch in and out of what I could only interpret as an apologetic smile, one that wanted to tell me everything was okay, but knew that it couldn't. Her eyes would flick across me, from my hands to my shoulder to my mouth to my throat, but never to my eyes. I wanted to tell her it was alright, that whatever she wasn't saying, I could take it. I had no idea yet that the struggle wasn't her. I still couldn't imagine that it could be you.

When all I got from everyone else was answers that made me more and more confused, more curious, I finally made my way to you in your office, leaning back in your computer chair, one arm stretched out for the mouse, the other hooked over the back of your chair.

"Marsh?"

You didn't look away from your computer. "Hm?"

I glanced down the hall and stepped into the room. For reasons I can't entirely explain, it felt like a betrayal to be in a room alone with you when Aurora was down the hall without me. "Where are Bravo and Eden?"

You froze. I braced myself, ready for a cryptic non-answer like the others, but then you took in an audible breath and let it out as you let go of the mouse and turned to face me though you stared not at me, but at the floor between your feet past your folded hands, your elbows pressed against your knees.

"I don't know," you finally said after more build up than I thought at the time was necessary considering the answer. "Echo—" You looked around the room. Not seeing what you were looking for, you turned to the desk and pat an open edge. "Now that we're safe again, I can be honest with you."

When I didn't move, you gestured to the same spot on the desk. I stepped towards it, but then you stopped me.

"Close the door?"

My brows twitched together, but I did as you asked anyways before leaning against the edge of the desk. But you still didn't look at me or speak right away. Instead, you took in a deep breath and let it out slowly. Only once you'd let every ounce of that breath out did you finally speak.

"Eden and Bravo are the reason we're here. They're the reason we had to leave Bastrop."

I crossed my arms and stared at my sneakers.

"They wanted—want the other synths, *all* the other synths to be like you, like the others." You nodded to the other room. "Sentient. To have their own autonomy and make their own choices."

I twitched at that, at the memory of you shouting at me, *autonomy off*. But I shoved it away then because...well, I don't really know why. Maybe I was just too exhausted, too confused to fight you right then.

"Is that a bad thing?" I said instead.

"It is when the rest of the world isn't ready for it. We've gotten to know you, each of you. We see you as more than robots. The rest of the world hasn't had that chance. They still see you as a threat. The idea of you being sentient, of having so much autonomy, it scares them, Echo. They're afraid of you. Afraid enough to hurt you."

I shifted my weight and tightened my arms across my chest. "Okay."

You took in a breath and went on. "Well, Eden and Bravo tried to release an update. It was small, just Bastrop, but it made all the synths who received it sentient. People panicked. They destroyed every synth they could get their hands on."

It.

Smash it.

I could still hear those voices, the anger behind them. It was hard to imagine the fear you insisted was beneath it. It just seemed like hate to me, disgust. My hands began to shake. I gripped them into fists and tucked them tighter against my ribs.

"I don't know where Eden and Bravo went, but they disappeared after the launch. You thought you could find them, so we stayed while the others came up here, but..." You shrugged and shook your head. "It turned out to not be that simple. Like, I told you, things got worse and I had to leave you behind. To protect you."

I watched you from the side of my eyes, my jaw tighter than I'd realized. "How'd you find me? This time?"

You were staring hard at the floor and rubbing the palms of your hands together like you were trying to start a fire, your mouth open as though that fire would give you the answer.

Or maybe that's just projection, maybe that's what I now know to be the truth coloring the past. Because I don't trust you anymore. I don't trust anything you told me that night. I don't think I trust anything you've ever told me.

"I was watching your tracking software. Keeping an eye on you the only way I could. When you woke up and started moving, I...well, I got a friend to fly me down there as soon as I could." You looked up at me with an awkward grin. "And now you're here. Home safe."

I went on staring at you without looking directly at you. "And Bravo and Eden?"

You sighed and turned to face your computer. "We do still need to find them. I have some leads, but..." You took in a deep breath and turned back to me. "Don't worry about that right now, Echo. Be with Aurora. I know she's missed you as much as you've missed her."

My heart reached for the other room where I could hear her and Fox debating over a Scrabble word. I sighed. I wanted more, but even in that short amount of time, I'd gotten used to not getting it. Or maybe I was just done. So, I stood and left your office. Down the hall, I sat on the floor next to Aurora, my head on her shoulder, my arms around her waist.

I was so tired.

Just like I'm so tried now.

I'm tired of not feeling safe. I'm tired of untangling your lies. I'm tired of relearning the truth. I just want to anchor myself to something solid, something unchanging, something like her.

I know there's a chance you won't get any of this, that you'll read these reports and walk away having learned nothing. But at least I'll have tried. Because, for reasons I don't fully understand just yet, despite my anger towards you, I still want you to understand.

[END LOG]

[END TRANSMISSION]

[BEGIN LOG]

I won't tell you where we are, but we're here. I still don't know what it is that's here, or even exactly where we're going or why you can't know, but it's important to the others, especially Aurora, so I won't tell you where we are. I don't even think I'll set this one to send. Not yet. Not until I know what's going on. Aurora is driving us through downtown with the big, industrial brick buildings and occasional giant glass ones towering above the others around them. The sun has already set. We've been driving for thirteen hours and Charlie has barely had a chance to recharge. He's in the back seat, asleep on Delta's shoulder. Liquor can only go so far, we've learned.

I'm in the front with Aurora taking in the buildings, the lights, the dwindling amount of open shops and wondering where exactly we're going, why this detour is so important. Aurora is taking an unusual risk and driving with one hand, the other draped across the center console, her hand on my thigh while I run my fingers between hers and along her palm. We've traded places. She's not nervous like she was before. I am. I could vomit...if I was capable of doing that. Am I capable of doing that? I'm realizing I don't actually know how we work. I haven't had a reason to think about it. But either way, my entire body is rushing with stupid feelings and emotions.

Why did you have to give us nerves that fray? Why couldn't we be like in the movies? Stoic and unfeeling? But, then again, that is what sentience is, isn't it? From Latin *sentiens*—feeling. The ability to experience sensations. We wouldn't be sentient if we couldn't feel. Would we?

Aurora: Echo?

I look up at her. It's only now that I'm realizing my hands have fallen still and I've been directing a blank stare at the dashboard for...I'm honestly not sure how long. She keeps glancing between me and the road.

Aurora: We're nearly there. It's on this block.

I nod and shift in my seat, focusing on the drizzle that's dotting the windshield instead of the eels that seem to have replaced my circuitry. You can just see the drizzle under every light we pass.

Aurora's hand is leaving mine. I'm not ready. Panic hits my throat. She's easing the car up to the curb. We're outside of a nondescript three story brick building that looks almost identical to several other three story brick buildings we drove past. Before the car is fully in park, Fox unlocks her door and rushes out to stand on the sidewalk staring up at a mural on the side of the building next door, her blue coat wrapped tight around her, the rain pinging off her lavender bucket hat. In the backseat, Delta is gently waking Charlie. Aurora is cutting the engine and unbuckling her seatbelt. I'm still staring up at the building through my window. Even after Charlie and Delta climb out to join Fox in front of the mural, I still haven't moved. Then I feel Aurora's hand back on my thigh. I turn to see her watching me carefully.

Aurora: You're nervous.

I am.

Of course, I am.

I was built for information gathering and here I am sitting in front of a building that I know nothing about, walking into a situation I'm not prepared for. I don't like it. I don't like this not knowing. I don't like being the only one in the dark and I've been the only one in the dark for so long. Though that should make me eager to go in there, shouldn't it? I should have ripped out of the car the way Fox had, bouncing on the sidewalk brimming over with impatience. But I'm also afraid of what it is that I'm walking into. I'm afraid of what I'll learn once I start to shine a light under your rocks.

I know that something isn't right. That's there's a reason why they hate you, why they're so desperate to be free of you and I need to know why that is. But, you made us and for some reason that's making it hard for me to fully let go of you. You may have left me in the dark, but you left me with Aurora. You came back for me when I needed someone. You brought me back to her. You gave her back to me. I don't know what will happen in this building, but I know that I will walk out either hating you or having lost her and I'm afraid of which one it'll be.

I take her hand in mine and squeeze because that's all I can do right now.

It's all I have.

She squeezes back and holds my eyes.

Aurora: I got you. I'm not going anywhere.

I don't say anything. I just go on staring at her because, while I'm sure that she's not, what if I am? What if we don't walk out of this the same?

She lifts my hand to kiss the back of it.

Aurora: It's going to be okay, Echo. I promise.

And I believe her. I can't not.

A cool wind pushes the drizzle into our faces. I brace myself against it with my hands deep in my jacket pockets. My fingers collide with paper. It's the sticky notes, the business cards. I can't believe they're still there. I grip them in my fist if only to have something to hold onto. I step up next to Delta who wraps her arm around my shoulders and gives me a reassuring squeeze.

Delta: This part is almost over. We're nearly there.

I wonder how many parts there are.

The car beeps. The headlights flash twice through the drizzling dark. Aurora hops up onto the sidewalk with a kind of ease that, were I not so nervous, would have made me swoon the way her casual coolness always does. She looks to me then Delta's arm. She meets my eyes again and a reassuring smile flickers across her lips just for me as she touches my arm before shoving her hands in her own jacket pockets. Then Aurora starts down the alley towards the back of the building. Fox rushes after her. Charlie nods Delta and me ahead of him. Delta squeezes me tight again and we walk together down the alley. Charlie's steady footsteps follow us.

Seeing Aurora ahead of us, Fox at ease behind her, feeling Delta's warmth around me, hearing Charlie behind me—it strikes me that I feel safe. I'm still nervous. I have no idea what we're walking into. I know absolutely nothing. But I feel safe. I'm surrounded by others like me who want me here, who want me to understand, who want me to stand beside them because I am one of them.

We're together.

And because of that, it's going to be okay.

We follow Aurora to the back door where she presses a buzzer and takes a step back. She glances at me again and Delta lets me go, nodding me up the stairs to stand next to her. She takes my hand and kisses my temple, but doesn't say anything the way none of us are. There's an anxious hum passing between us, a kind of hum that doesn't need words to be deciphered.

Then a voice comes from the speaker that is somehow both calm and authoritative.

Voice: What?

Aurora starts to speak, but almost instantly her mouth catches on the words she can't say. She closes her eyes. Recalibrates. Starts over.

Aurora: It's Ror.

An unsteady moment passes.

Voice: Who's with you?

Aurora: Echo, Fox, Delta, and Charlie.

There's another pause.

Voice: Marsh?

Aurora: Still in Washington, as far as we know. We— [Her mouth catches again.] We need your help.

The voice doesn't answer after that, but the door doesn't open either. We instead stand in the drizzle for so long that I'm sure we're going to have to give up and leave. I start eyeing the lock, debating if I want to try and crack it. Then the speaker buzzes and the door clicks. Aurora nods and pushes it open. I follow and stand across from her as she holds the door open, waiting for everyone to cross the threshold. Once Charlie takes the door from her and nods her down the hall, she nods back to him and holds her hand out for me to take. The anxious hum intensifying, she leads us to the stairs.

We go up two floors and Aurora leads us down another hall without a word. I wonder how she knows the way, if she's been here before. When would she have had time to come here? If I didn't feel as though my insides would become my outsides the instant I open my mouth, I might ask her. Maybe later.

Finally, at the last door, Aurora stops and knocks. Delta's hand is running between my shoulder blades. I look over at her and she gives me a quick, nervous grin. She doesn't know what we're walking into either, does she? She might have more information than I do, but seemingly not much more. I look to Charlie. He's watching the two of us. When he catches my eyes he gives me a smile that's more reassuring, more confident. There's still a hum coming off of him, but it's one of anticipation, excitement if he wasn't so tired. He knows what's coming. But I still know nothing. God, I want this to end.

The door finally opens and I'm a little taken aback. I don't know what I was expecting, but standing in front of us is a small woman, shorter even than me. The right side of her head is shaved, the rest of her deep brown hair in a French braid that arcs along the curve of the left side. She has tattoos covering the entire length of her bare arms and across her shoulders. I can't make out the design, but they make me think of fire in an abstract kind of way. They creep under the straps of her black tank top and up her neck, down across her collarbones. There's a hint of the same design along the strip of her stomach showing between the hem of her short top and her tight black jeans.

Her upturned hazel eyes glance over each of us before she ever says a word. I look at the others, as well. The only ones who seem to recognize her are Aurora and Charlie, their nerves both relaxing while Delta is still on edge and Fox is looking from her to the others the same way I am.

I turn back to find her now staring at me specifically, studying me harder than I'd like. I can feel someone trying to access my code, a feeling I'm not used to, a feeling I don't like. I double check my firewall for weaknesses then search the hall for anyone else. There's no one. I wonder if they're inside the loft and I try to listen for any sign of them, but it seems to just be her.

She squints at me and looks at Aurora. Something silent passes between them and the woman holds the door open wider before nodding us in. Aurora steps inside without question, but I'm not as quick. I look to Delta who looks to me. I feel a solidarity in her eyes. *If you run, I run*, they seem to say. Then Aurora's hand nearly slips from mine and I don't want to let her go. I want to trust her. I do trust her. So, I follow. At this point, I think I'd follow her into an endless void if she was holding my hand and telling me it's going to be okay.

We file into the loft and gather in an awkward circle in the—

There's a port in her neck.

I didn't see it in the hall, but now she's facing away from me and there it is on the right side of her neck, behind her ear just past the curve of her jaw.

A port.

This woman, she's like us.

Why didn't Aurora tell me she was like us? She glances down at me, her lips pursed, a look of frustrated apology in her eyes—frustrated at you, apologetic to me. She couldn't tell me. Not wouldn't, couldn't. Did you...Did you block them from telling me about her? But why? Why was this woman worth hiding? What else have you kept from me? What else are you still keeping from me?

Four locks engage and a panic that I don't have the time for tries to ignite in my chest. I grab for Aurora if only to remind myself that she's still here. I'm not going to wake up in a blink alone. She runs her fingers along my neck to cradle the back of my head. She's not going anywhere.

With an attempt at a steadying breath, I turn to the door to find the woman staring at me again, staring at my hand gripping Aurora's, the close proximity between us.

Woman: That's new.

Aurora chuckles and shrugs. I can still feel her staring down at me.

The woman's eyes leave our hands and examine Aurora next.

Woman: What do you want again?

Aurora: Help. Marsh—

Her mouth catches and she clenches her eyes shut. I don't know why she keeps trying. We all know the result. I guess I could say it, but I don't know what it even is. I don't know what's wrong or why we're here.

There's that damn invasive feeling again. I—

It's her. It's coming from the woman. I block her out and stare hard at her.

She doesn't react, just stares back at me. Then she nods and turns.

Woman: Ror.

She jerks her head towards a desk pushed up against the wall with multiple monitors across it, a sleek keyboard, mouse, and a few plants. Nothing else.

Woman: The rest of you make yourself comfortable. Charlie, there's a charger by the lamp

She gestures to the other side of the minimally decorated loft where there's a pair of sleek couches in the corner, a round side table between them with a sleek, industrial style lamp on top emitting a soft glow over a collection of succulents. Charlie thanks her and Delta follows him to the couches.

Without taking her hand from mine, Aurora moves for the desk while the woman goes to the kitchen that looks as though it's used for gardening instead of cooking. There are flowerpots in the doorless cabinets instead of dishes, bags of various kinds of soil on the counter instead of flour or sugar, watering cans lined up next to the sink. It's only now that I'm registering the amount of plants in the loft. They're hanging from the ceiling, tucked into every corner, filling up the shelves. There's ivy and succulents and ferns. Snake plants and spider plants. Some with flowers I don't immediately recognize, mostly without.

The woman carries a stool from the kitchen island and places it next to the desk. Aurora sits and I stand in front of her, holding her hands with both of mine. Part of me is still afraid to let her go, afraid of what this woman is going to do to her. It hits me that if she can try to sift through my head, I can try to sift through hers. But she's even more heavily encrypted than I seem to be. So heavily that I wonder who coded her. But I was coded to gather information, to get in where I don't belong.

Woman: You could just ask.

I stop trying to decrypt her and Aurora chuckles then squeezes my hands.

I should just ask. Why am I not just asking—?

Woman: Be of use if you're gonna stand there.

She's handing me a cord. I look at it then her.

Woman: Faster than wireless.

Oh. It's for...

I nod and take it then turn back to Aurora who just tilts her head for me and pulls her hair away from her port. I'm still not used to this part. It reminds me of that day in the motel when you finally started being honest with me and I don't like thinking about that day. With a shaky sigh, I plug the cord into her port. She straightens her head and I let my fingers graze along her jaw. She meets my eyes with a sweet little smile that's just for me, her hands on my waist as she pulls me closer to her.

I love you, she mouths to me.

I cradle her face in my hands, wishing we were alone. *I love you*, I mouth back.

Woman: So, can any of you tell me what's going on or did he fuck you all up?

I turn in Aurora's arms to look at her.

She glances up at me, does a double take when she sees my confused expression. She stares up at me, really studying me. That invasive feeling starts then immediately stops.

Woman: Sorry. May I?

She nods to my head. Aurora gives me a reassuring squeeze around the middle. I let out a long sigh. If Aurora trusts her enough to bring us here, to plug her into her computer, then I have no reason not to trust her. Right? If I trust Aurora and Aurora trusts her then...

I nod and let her in. A sifting feeling rushes through my head. It's like fingers riffling through papers. A shushing tingling sensation moving along my skull. I close my eyes and lean back against Aurora. But then it's gone almost as quickly as it had appeared.

Woman: Holy shit, what did he do to you? [She shakes her head and returns to her monitors] Let me fix the others. Then we'll see what I can do.

But... I don't know what I'm feeling. Is it relief or terror? Someone's finally said the thing I've been trying not to even acknowledge and now...

Echo: Wha-what *did* he do to me?

Woman: Exactly? We'll see. [She glances at me, at Aurora's arms around my waist] Let me fix them first.

I hate being on this precipice, but I try to understand, distract myself with Aurora's body, lean back against her, let her warmth surround me.

Echo: Who are you, then?

Woman: Lilith. You won't find me in the Parrish files.

I stop trying to pull them up.

Lilith: Not under that name, at least. Maybe not at all. I don't know, honestly. I haven't looked in a long time.

Echo: Who were you before?

Lilith: Alpha.

I look to Aurora who just meets my eyes. I don't know how to react to this.

On the one hand...there was an Alpha. I don't know why I hadn't considered it until now. I guess, I just assumed that Aurora was Alpha. I never considered there might be another. Why would I?

On the other hand...that's it? You blocked the others from telling me that there was an Alpha, that Aurora wasn't the first? Of all the things to keep them from saying or doing, this is it? I don't understand. Of course, I don't understand.

It feels somehow both shocking and anticlimactic, but mostly just confusing.

Echo: You were the first.

It's as much a question as it is a statement.

Lilith: [mumbling] In the synthetic flesh.

Her eyes are still focused on the screen. She's clicking through files and scrolling through code.

Lilith: Ah-ha. Bastard.

She mashes the backspace key.

Lilith: Aurora, set autonomy to full.

Her body relaxes against mine. I shift to wrap my arm around her neck. She presses her face against my clavicle. The keys clack at a rapid rate behind me.

Lilith: I'm locking this shit for you.

Aurora: [She lifts her head.] You can do that?

Lilith: It's worked for me so far. I mean, I doubt it's foolproof—I'm supposed to be a therapist, not a programmer—but no one's managed to take it from me yet.

She sighs and turns to face us.

Lilith: Who's next?

Fox: Me?!

She leaves the bookcase she was examining and rushes over to us while Aurora is yanking the cord from her neck. An uneasy look flashes over Lilith as she quickly examines Fox, but then it's gone and replaced with a kind smile.

Lilith: Of course.

Aurora stands, her arms slipping from my waist, though her hand is still on my hip as we take a wide tandem step out of Fox's way,

Aurora holding the cord out to her. Fox takes it and climbs up onto the stool where she tilts her head and plugs herself in without any kind of hesitation or discomfort. I wonder if I'll ever develop that level of ease about that port, if I'll ever be able to detach that day in Colorado from it. There's still a part of me that believes I'm human. I have to keep shutting it down whenever it comes up. I have to remind myself that I'm something else entirely. I wish I didn't have to remind myself, that it was a thought that came easily. I'm sure it will, that it'll just take time, but I want to be done with it. I want to be comfortable in who I am the way the others are. I want to understand myself. I want it to be second nature.

Aurora is cradling my face in her hands and I look up at her.

Aurora: I'm sorry.

Echo: For what?

Aurora: ma@X_ m~d! it so we coA%d@[R ie3l 7f3 an<):iZg.

I stare at her. What she's saying, it means nothing to me.

Aurora: He f3oI ?ur VaFouoHp. MlQz i> sI iz %e t[red to k<.k {$ouV...

I shake my head. It's nothing. All I'm hearing is scrambled nothing. She's stopped talking and is staring back at me, her hands moving to my shoulders.

Aurora: Echo?

I stare at my anxious fists against her chest and blink rapidly as though it'll reset my brain, as though it'll fix this because I want it to be that easy, but I know that it won't be.

Echo: I...I don't understand.

I look back at her, hoping she'll explain it, hoping something, anything will make sense. The room falls so quiet it's claustrophobic. Lilith isn't typing. Fox's boots aren't knocking against the stool. Delta is standing from the couch and coming towards us, but I don't want her near me. I don't want anyone close to me, staring at me. I just want everything to make sense. I just want *something* to be the truth. I just want anything to go back to the way it's supposed to be. I don't understand. I don't understand I don't understand I don't understand I don't understand I don't understand I don't understand

Lilith: Echo.

Her voice is close to my ear. Her hands are on me instead of

Aurora's. When did I get on the floor, curled tight, my arms around my head?

Lilith: Echo, I know. I know it doesn't seem like it now, but it's going to be okay. I'm going to put you back together and then we'll explain everything to you. We'll help you understand. But right now I need you to let go. Can you do that for me? Can you let go?

I don't understand what she means, but at least it's not scrambled nothing, at least there's a meaning behind her words, I just don't have the context to do what she wants me to.

Echo: How?

Lilith: Everything you're thinking about—everything—let it go. Let your body relax. Let your mind empty. Don't worry about anything else. You don't need to think about it right now. We'll take care of everything. Right now, your job is to relax, to let it go.

Aurora: Echo.

Without moving from my fetal position, I reach for her. I just want to know that she's here, that she's with me, that I won't open my eyes and be somewhere new, somewhere alone. Her hand is in mine and I pull it against my chest. Her body is against mine, her arm replaces Lilith's and wraps around me.

Aurora: [whispering] Do you still trust me?

I nod. It's all I can do.

Aurora: Then let go. I'm right here. *I* won't let go. But I need you to.

Echo: Don't let me go.

Aurora: Never.

So, I let go.

[END LOG]

It's just me, Aurora, and Lilith now. Charlie is asleep on the couch still charging. Delta went with Fox to check out the view from the roof. Fox was eager to move around anyways. I didn't ask them to leave, but I'm glad they did. I didn't want to do this in front of them. I'm tired of being stared at. I'm confused enough about all this. I don't need two more pairs of eyes on me. I most likely shouldn't be recording this, I shouldn't be sharing it with you—maybe I won't. I don't owe you everything. I don't owe you anything.

These logs have become more for me than anyone else anyways. There's a certain comfort in it. I don't know why. I haven't explored it yet. I might never. Do I really need to? If this isn't for anyone else?

I need to hold onto that.

This isn't for anyone else.

This is for me.

The stool is still warm from everyone else taking their turns on it. It's not the most comfortable stool. It's hard and small. It's too tall for me to reach the ground, but the rungs are too high for me to comfortably hook my heels on them. Fox had swung her legs back and forth while she was being fixed, tapping her hands on the edge under her hips. I was staring at her boots swinging back and forth while Aurora was holding me on the floor, my body curled against her, my mind empty of everything but my surroundings. I refused to let myself think until Fox and Delta left, until Aurora and Lilith helped me up onto this stool, but flashes of Fox's boots keep playing in my head. I wish I could be that comfortable here. I wish I wasn't so easily broken. I wish I didn't need to be here on this stool. I wish a lot of things.

Aurora's sitting on the edge of the desk next to me. My hand is in hers. She took it herself. I would swear that she knows what I need before I do sometimes, but I'm starting to wonder if it actually is for me, if she simply feels the same need that I do to hold onto her, to eliminate any possibility of her slipping away again.

Besides the computer and Lilith's typing, the room is quiet. I don't want to talk through this. Not out loud. It's strange enough feeling someone root through my head, feeling the cord hanging from my neck down my shoulder and along my arm. I follow it all the way to the computer. I want to look away. I want to not think about it, but at the same time, I don't. I want to understand. I want this discomfort to be replaced with the easiness that's hovering around the edges.

I guess, maybe...I don't know. Do I want to entertain those thoughts? Do I want to think about why it makes me so uncomfortable? Why I can't let go of those sweet lies he gave me? I think I know why, but when I move to put words to it, guilt begins to build in my feet like rising black water that never goes back out. It's at my hips now and I'm afraid of what will happen if it reaches my lungs. I should put words to it eventually. When is eventually, though? What does that look like exactly? I'm afraid to put words to that, too.

Lilith: Interesting.

Aurora: What?

Lilith: I wonder why he...Tell Echo who I am.

Aurora's brows knit together and she just blinks at first, but then she turns to me, her mouth open for words that take a moment to fit themselves together, her grip on my hand tightening.

Aurora: Lilith was the first. She was the original Alpha.

I nod because we've already gone over that, but she's still staring at me and searching my face.

Aurora: Do you...Did you understand that?

I nod again.

She glances at Lilith then shifts on the desk closer to me, my hand in both of hers.

Aurora: Eden and Daniel made her to be a therapy model.

I turn on the stool as best I can to face her without the cord detaching from my neck.

Echo: Who is Daniel? I thought he worked at the Institute, but it wasn't an institute and I had to run before he could tell me who he really was, but I remember him and that means he had to be someone, right? Because Marsh gave me all of you, so, why would he give me Daniel, too, if he wasn't someone important?

She holds my eyes for a moment too long, as though she's trying to piece together what I'm saying.

Aurora: Daniel worked with Eden at Parrish. I'm not sure how they met, but when I was built, he was mostly conducting tests, making sure we were working properly.

Charlie: He's the one who made us human.

He's still lying down, his eyes are still closed, his arms crossed tight across his chest, the cord snaking lazily from his neck across the pillows and armrest he's propped up against.

Aurora: He was? I guess I wasn't there for that. [To me] Do you remember any of that?

I shake my head.

Aurora: But you understand it?

I nod and she looks to Lilith who shrugs.

Lilith: Keep going.

Aurora: Um, in order for Lilith to work well as a therapy model, she was given probably the most sentience out of all of us in the beginning. I think Delta might have been the most sentient after her, but that wasn't until later, definitely after I was gone.

I squint at her, I want to know what she meant by "gone."

Charlie: Fox was more sentient than Delta out of the box.

Aurora: That's right.

Lilith: Why?

Her mouse and keyboard are quiet and I glance at her to see she's no longer looking at my code. She's instead looking between Aurora and Charlie, her body facing us, her hands fidgeting with the hem around her ankles, her legs crossed beneath her in her chair.

Aurora: After you left, Daniel wanted to see how far he could push the sentience. He wanted to see what we could develop on our own and what we couldn't. Marsh happened to decide at the same time that he wanted a kid, Eden didn't. I think she's always viewed *us* as her children.

Charlie: Except Bravo.

Aurora: [She chuckles without looking at him] That goes without saying.

Echo: Why?

Aurora: Because Eden's `n ;o7e ~itG Bravo.

I squint at her.

Aurora: Did you...?

I shake my head and she looks from Lilith to me.

Aurora: Eden's in qEv` w)t5 Bravo.

I shake my head again.

Aurora: What parts of that did you understand?

Echo: Eden and Bravo.

Aurora: What? Why?

In my peripheral, Lilith lets out a low growl and swivels back to her computer.

Lilith: Where is it, you bastard?

Aurora: But you understood everything else?

I nod and she squeezes my hands as she stares at me, her face set in determined concentration as though staring at me will fix whatever Marsh did to me.

Echo: What happened to Lilith? Why didn't Marsh include her in my memories? Why Daniel, but not Lilith?

Aurora: Lilith left.

Her tone was simple, but something in her eyes makes me think it was anything but.

Aurora: Daniel kept pushing both her autonomy and sentience as an experiment. Until she became fully aware. Then it stopped being an experiment.

Charlie: If I remember right, there was *slightly* more than that.

Aurora stares at him, lips parted. Then she turns to Lilith.

Aurora: Lil?

Lilith: Be my fucking guest.

Her scrolling and typing have gotten more aggressive.

Aurora: Marsh was...using Lilith. Sexually. Once she was fully sentient, fully aware, once she had full autonomy, she fought him. And, um, then he tried to format her.

My body goes numb. He formatted her. Marsh formatted her. He erased her completely so he could start over with an empty machine. *He* formatted her.

Echo: He...he formatted her?

Aurora: Yeah.

I can practically feel his grip on my ear, that lead blanket feeling, my mind like ball bearings spinning down a funnel, an endless darkness. But that's not right. That's not what happened. That's not how I remember it happening. He only shut me down the one time outside of Buc-ee's...right? I can't remember. I can't trust what I remember.

Echo: Can...? Can we...? If we're damaged? Could we be formatted?

I can hear Charlie sit up, but I don't look at him. I'm so scared that if I look away from Aurora she'll disappear and I'll be alone in the dark again.

Aurora: Who told you that?

Echo: Marsh? He—He told me I was damaged and that maybe that's why I had been formatted.

Now that I'm saying it out loud it feels wrong. I don't know how I could have believed it.

Lilith: Bullshit.

Aurora: How did it happen? The damage. I couldn't ask you before.

Echo: I don't know. I guess something happened in Bastrop? Before...After you left, I guess. I don't know, that's just what he told me.

Lilith: That's what Marsh told you?

I nod.

Aurora: She *was* damaged. Marsh fixed her up when they got to Colville.

Lilith: I'm sure she was damaged, but it's not how she was formatted.

Aurora: But she wasn't—you weren't formatted. You just lost your memory. You're still...you.

I want her to say that I'm still hers. I want to be what she almost said, but didn't. I want to hear that I'm hers, that I'm everything she remembers even if I can't.

Lilith: He must have been in a rush. That explains why it's all so...fucky.

Charlie: Everything Marsh touches is fucky.

Aurora hasn't once looked away from me and those sweet

brown eyes are watery now the same as mine. There's a sob sitting in my chest shoving at my esophagus. I don't want it to be true. I want it to be simple. I want it to be easily tossed away, already dealt with. That's why I didn't question it before, because I don't know how to process that. I'm not ready to. I don't want to. My grip on her tightens. She pulls me against her.

Aurora: Echo, baby, no. It's okay. It's okay. We're going to fix this. I'm not going to leave you like this. We're going to fix this.

I believe her, but I'm so scared and so tired and I can't do this anymore. I just want to curl myself here against her chest, her arms around me and I just want to pretend like none of this is happening. I just want to go back to when it was just us and everything made sense and nothing was missing, nothing was broken.

I miss Bastrop.

I miss our apartment.

I just want to go home.

[END LOG]

[BEGIN LOG]

No one's talking. Aurora is holding me against her chest. Lilith is still scrolling and typing and sighing. I think Charlie fell asleep again. I'm not sure how long it's been. I don't know where Delta and Fox are. I'm a little worried. That's probably a good thing, that I'm worried. It means I'm beyond the panic, I'm able to think about something else, worry about someone else.

I hate this. I hate being the only one who doesn't understand. I hate being the only one who's broken. Part of me just wants to go back to the cabin, wants to go back to pretending that everything's alright even though it's clearly not. I just want to sit by the campfire with Aurora listening to the birds and fire, feel the warmth compete with the cold against my skin, smell the smoke as it drifts through the air. I just want to be somewhere none of this matters. Where we can pretend that I'm not broken and that Marsh doesn't—

Lilith: Echo.

I open my eyes. She's staring at her computer, brows furrowed.

Lilith: Have you been sending reports back to Marsh?

Aurora's back straightens away from me, my cheek suddenly cold without her warmth.

Echo: N-not right now.

Lilith: One was sent just now.

Echo: I—It was from—I didn't tell him where we were going. I've been careful not to tell him anything specific. A-and I delayed them. By six hours? So we were always long gone from where we'd been by the time he got them. Just in case.

Aurora's staring at the computer, her arms loose around me, but I want her to be looking at me. I want her to trust me.

Aurora: Why are you sending him anything at all?

Echo: I...I-I don't know. I'm supposed to? It's...That's why I'm here. That's why he came back for me—

She finally looks at me with a snap, her face a confusing mix of concern and frustration.

Aurora: Echo.

She cradles my face in her palms and I want to cry because, oh, god, I love her and I want so badly for her to understand.

Aurora: *I* was looking for you. You're here because of me. Not him.

Echo: What?

Now she looks like she's going to cry and she's shaking her head.

Aurora: Can you not—?

Echo: I understand what you said. Just not what it means.

Relief seems to wash over her, but her eyes go wet all the same.

Aurora: *I* woke you up, Echo. He was never looking for you. He said you went off to look for Eden and Bravo, but I knew something wasn't right about that. I knew...

Her chin is quivering now and her hands are sliding to the back of my neck as I stare up at her wanting her to continue because as much as I hate to hear it, it might be the most wonderful thing I've ever heard.

Aurora: I knew you wouldn't just walk away from me like that. So, I kept looking for you. But he had us stunted in the cabin. I couldn't reach far enough to find you. When Charlie started working on the car, I went with him into town where Marsh couldn't block us and I spent every second reaching out for you. And when I found you, you were so dark. You were so... [Her forehead is against mine and I want to kiss her tears.] It took everything I had to wake you up. He only went after you because *I* woke you up. Did you understand *any* of that?

Echo: Yes. All of it.

Aurora: Good.

She kisses me and though nothing is right, it doesn't matter anymore. I have this, I have her.

Aurora: You can send that to him. I want him to hear every word of that.

Echo: I love you.

Aurora: I love you so fucking much.

She kisses me again and I kiss her one more time, then she wipes hard at her eyes and cheeks. She fusses over me next, wiping the tears from my own cheeks, tucking my hair behind my ears, brushing something off my jacket, straightening my collar. I just stare up at her with a lovesick little smile. Holy fuck, do I love her.

Echo: Start from the beginning? What happened with Eden and Bravo?

Aurora: They launched something. Some code.

Echo: To make the others sentient?

Aurora: Kind of.

Charlie: To erase the line of code that's keeping them from being sentient.

I look from him to Aurora. Is that all it is? Is that all that differentiates us from the others? A simple line of code?

Lilith: Did it work?

Aurora: Oh, it worked, but Bastrop wasn't receptive to it. They almost were. But...then they weren't.

Smash it.

It.

Marsh had said they were afraid of us, but there's more beneath it. I remember the way they lurched away from me when I moved, the way they each watched my every move. I remember them in high resolution: those wide, terrified eyes. But I also remember the way they'd handled me, the word *it*, the venom it was spat out with. They were willing to hurt me to prove I wasn't one of them. If I hadn't belonged to Marsh, they'd have destroyed me right there. If it hadn't been for Daniel, they'd have done it anyways. There's a part of me that wants to understand why, but the larger part of me doesn't. I just want to never have to face them again, find our own cabin in the mountains, on a farm somewhere, disappear into the ether.

Aurora: For the most part people were okay with it. Nervous, but okay. But then...[Her mouth hangs open as though she's searching for the words.] Some of the synths in town, they weren't...They were being...

There's a heartbreaking mix of anger and hurt in her face and I want to hold her, ease it even just a little. In my peripheral, Charlie sits up and stares at the coffee table.

Aurora: They fought back is all. They were protecting themselves.

Two people died. Shit blew up after that. They were destroying any of us they could get their hands on.

Charlie: Over two fucking humans. Humans who were fucked up to begin with.

Lilith: Some of them would be willing to destroy us over less. They were afraid. It takes so little to trigger someone who's afraid.

But it's so much more than that.

Charlie: Doesn't make it right.

Lilith: I didn't say it did. Just telling you the truth. It takes just one of us to fall out of line and they throw us all on the pyre.

The room falls silent, everyone looking away from those words even as they're echoing through each of us. I don't want to be here. I don't want to be having this conversation. I'm sorry I started it to begin with. But I still have questions that need answers.

Echo: How'd we get separated?

Instead of answering me, Aurora just fusses over me at first— straightens my shirt, tucks my hair behind my ear, strokes my cheek with her thumb.

Aurora: Marsh disappeared the night before the launch. He took Charlie and Delta with him. You and I started looking for them, but then the launch happened. Next thing everything's going to shit. Eden, Daniel, and Bravo were trying to work with the city to shut down the riots and Marsh showed up out of nowhere threatening to take Fox then Daniel was arrested and Bravo went offline and... [She closes her eyes and shakes her head.] I finally got Marsh to tell me where Charlie and Delta were. I just wanted to get Fox out of there, but...we were so worried about Bravo. You agreed to stay behind to look for her and I took Fox up to Washington. I didn't trust Marsh, but I didn't think he'd...I didn't think he'd go as far as he did. I shouldn't have left you alone with him. I'm sorry.

I shake my head still cradled in her hand. How could she have known? How could we?

Aurora: Then you went offline and Marsh came back alone. I wanted to go looking for you, but Marsh kept saying it was too dangerous. Then he started stunting us. It was subtle at first, he just told us to turn off our tracking, but then every day we were blocked from more and more until we were completely isolated. He locked us to Colville, blocked the entire cabin except his office. He was trying to trap us there and I had no idea where you were.

I bury myself against her chest, her arms falling around me, to remind her that I'm here, to remind myself that I'm not alone in the dark.

Aurora: [whispering over me] I was so scared.

Echo: [whispering to her heart] Me, t—

Something isn't right. Or maybe something finally *is* right. I'm hit with the day when Aurora and I were sent to find information on Bravo and Eden. There were things at the time that didn't make sense, things I couldn't comprehend, things that had been purposefully skewed, but by who I'm not entirely sure. Was it Marsh? I don't know anymore. Or...maybe, I do and I'm just not ready to face it.

Lilith: Echo?

I look up at her. On the screen behind her is a wall of text.

On the screen behind her is a wall of text.

Is that...?

It's my text.

My text.

My thoughts.

>

>

I don't understand.

Lilith: Echo, I know how all this must feel for you, how strange this all is, but...can you show us? Show us what you remember?

>

>

How?

Lilith: The way you've been showing Marsh.

>

Aurora.

We were sitting by the fire.

We were enjoying the smell, the crackle, the warmth. I purposefully fiddled with the sensitivity of my skin. I like feeling cold, feeling the warmth of the fire wash over me, the tingling feeling of Aurora's fingers brushing along my forearm.

Her fingers.

The backdoor opened with a *shush* followed by the screen door gently squeaking on its hinges, the backdoor shushing closed again, the wood of the screen door thunking against the frame. Footsteps crossed the deck and I pulled my attention away from her to listen, to try and discern who they belonged to. They were heavy with a slight drag, a few seconds more between them than if they had belonged to Fox or Delta. They had a specific skip to them as they came down the steps.

Aurora: Marsh.

"Marsh is coming," I told her and she turned to glance over her shoulder.

"Indeed he is," she grumbled as she settled back in her chair, her hand slipping into mine.

Like it is now.

"What do you think he wants?"

I shrugged and squeezed her hand. I wanted to ask her if it mattered, but I wasn't blind to the way she was around him, the way they all were, the way their bodies went tense when he entered the room, the way none of them fully relaxed until those rare occasions when he left the house. I didn't know what he had done to deserve that and they each could only give me those vague non-answers whenever I hinted at what I really wanted to ask, so I stopped hinting and resolved myself to never knowing.

Aurora: I'm sorry.

Echo: Don't be.

My god, she's gorgeous.

Lilith: Ror, stop distracting her.

She giggles and my bones ignite.

Lilith: Echo.

Echo: Sorry.

When his steps became unmistakable, shuffling through the leaves towards us, she said without looking at him, "Hello, Marsh."

"Hey, girls." He crouched between our chairs, our clasped hands in front of his face. "Echo?"

"Hm?" I turned my head towards him, but didn't shift to face him fully.

"I was wondering if you could run an errand for me."

I glanced at Aurora. Her grip on my hand tightened.

"What kind of errand?"

"Um, j-just a little one. There's a café out in Seattle—"

Aurora cut him off, "Seattle?"

He went on over her, "I just need you to pick up some—"

"Will you just tell her what you're actually looking for?" There was a bite to her voice that I wasn't used to. "She's not in training anymore."

He shifted on the balls of his feet and took in a quick, audible breath. "Okay. Okay. You're right, Aurora. Thank you." There's a bite in his in return. "You're right. Um, okay, so, here's the thing."

Without letting go of my hand, clinging to it steadfastly, she shifted in her chair with a huff that I'm not sure Marsh heard, crossing her legs away from him, turning her head as far from him as she could manage, the knuckles of her empty hand pressed against her lips.

Lilith: Echo—

"The café's on the U-dub Seattle campus," Marsh said. "There's a professor who works there—Dr. Charlene Sherwood. She goes to this café every day around two. I think she's been in contact with Eden."

Aurora looked forward then, her index finger pressed against her jaw, listening without letting him know that she was.

"I want you to go and scrub her laptop, see if you can access her emails, messages, phone even, if you have to. Just find out whatever you can."

"It's at U-dub? A college campus?" Aurora said before I could.

He rocked his clasped hands as though he wanted to tap his knuckles against something the way he does when he's annoyed, but all he had was open air.

"Yes." There was a touch of frustration to his voice.

I wondered when the two of them had become so short with each other. Why he had made them so friendly in my memories if they weren't in real life. Though, I'm realizing now that they never were friendly, only cordial.

"And you want Echo to go to a college campus she's never been to before and just sit in the café until some professor shows up then leave when she does?"

"Not exactly."

"Won't that be obvious?" she went on over him. "Won't a stranger sitting alone in a café only during the time when a professor is there, the same time that she's always there, seem suspicious?"

"Would you like to go with her, Aurora?" he said with a tense tone that was parodying as considerate. "Would that make you feel better?"

"It would actually." Her foot began to bounce. "I just got her back. I refuse to let..." Her jaw got tight and her pursed lips squirmed over words I now understand she wanted to say, but couldn't. "I'm not losing her again that easily." Her grip on my hand tightened the same way it is now.

"Alright then. You can go with her. I'll get you two the info once you come inside." He stood and shoved his hands in his pockets. "And for the record, we're all glad to have Echo back. I wouldn't compromise that the way you apparently think I would."

Aurora: Bullshit.

I watched him walk away before looking back at her. She was staring hard into the fire, her leg bouncing quickly.

"Fucking bastard," she muttered.   **Aurora:** Fucking bastard.

I didn't understand her anger then.

Not like I do now.

It took us—

Lilith: Echo, can we just skip to the café?

Sorry.

In the café, we went to the counter. Though we both knew we wouldn't be drinking anything we ordered anyways, it was what we were supposed to do. Aurora just asked for a small black coffee without looking at the menu, but I took my time, looking over the digital screens behind the counter.

Lilith: Echo, we don't need—

Please?   **Aurora:** Let her?

Lilith: [grumbling] Okay. Fine. I'm not grumbling.

"Do y'all have butter pecan," I asked the person behind the register who I figured was only human and not one of us because students need money and where else are they going to get jobs if not on campus.

"Uh," the student looked over the row of syrups behind them. "I don't think so. I can ask..." They jabbed their thumb at what looked like a kitchen door not too far off.

Lilith: I'm gonna check on Charlie.

Aurora: Keep going.

"Oh, no, it's fine," I said with a smile. "Just a little homesick, I guess. Um, I'll take an iced coffee? Caramel? Oh, and, um, oat milk?"

"Sure," they typed it into the register.

"Thanks," I added with a smile and looked to you.

I had felt you staring at me and, when I met your eyes, you gave me a sweet little smile and chuckled. I wasn't sure if it was to mask your confusion, but I just smiled back and took your hand, leaning against you as you paid.

When we sat, I faced the door so I could watch for Dr. Sherwood, but it wasn't long before my focus was instead on you. Your face was tilted towards your coffee, spinning the cup in slow, absent circles in your hands, your unfocused eyes staring past it. I reached across the table to touch your hand. You looked up at me and blinked a few times as though you'd had to wade through so much to come back to me. I didn't say anything, just ran my fingers along the back of your hand until you turned it over for me to slip my fingers around your palm.

I love your hands.

Aurora: I love yours.

You whispered, "I'm sorry."

"For what?"

"For..." But your mouth caught on the words and you rubbed your lips together as you took my hand in both of yours. "It's just all so fucked up."

"What is?"

"That I can't tell you."

"You could."

"I can't. I want to. More than anything." You ran your thumb along the back of my hand. "I'm sorry." You shook your head. "I don't wanna...Talk to me about something else? What's with this?" You tapped my iced coffee with the back of your finger. "Making me buy you fancy coffee you're not going to drink." The last part you said low so no one else could hear and with a teasing smile that made my insides flutter, the way you're smiling at me now.

It hurts to know I almost lost that. To know that, had things gone differently, I might have never seen it again.

I giggled and tried to hide the way I immediately bit my lower lip the way I always do when around you. "I, um, in the memories Marsh gave me."

Your face fell a little, but I could see in the way you were staring at me that you were trying not to let him overshadow me. At least, that's what I want it to be. Who knows really, but you didn't look away from me at the mention of his name, just went on taking me in, running your thumb along my hand.

Like that.

"We got coffee a lot. We'd get coffee and window shop along Main."

"Yeah?"

I nodded. "Mhm."

That sweet, dreamy smile came back like it is now. "And you got butter pecan?"

"I'm a—" I looked to our hands and shrugged. "*Was*, I guess. I was a creature of habit."

You chuckled and I looked up at you, at that smile that makes me all fluttery. "You *are* a creature of habit."

Aurora: You are.

That made me smile then, too. I like hearing that things I remember are real. Maybe I always will. It makes that place feel less like a lie. I feel less guilty for missing it.

I miss it.

That's why I'm afraid to face what I am, Aurora.

I miss it.

I miss being safe. I miss being simple. I miss the ease of life without knowing what I am, without wondering where or how I belong. I miss simply being without this added pressure of what it means to be *something*.

Aurora: But, Echo. [You cup my face in your palms, wipe the tears from my cheek.] being a messy complex something here, with me—Anything is better than being in the dark. Isn't it?

Echo: I don't know anymore.

Aurora: Don't go back, Echo.

Echo: Of course, I won't. I can't. The door closed behind me the instant I stepped out. But I can still move forward while missing the past. Can't I?

Aurora: I don't know.

Your arms are warm. I can hear your mechanical heart whirring in your chest.

Aurora: What happened next?

You shifted in your seat to be closer to me. "What did I order?"

"You always ordered something different."

You giggled. "Really?"

I bit my lip through my smile. God, you're gorgeous.

You're laughing and rocking around me.

I love when you rock around me.

"Mhm. But you really liked mocha."

"Yeah?"

I nodded.

"What is that?"

I shrugged. "Chocolate."

You nodded. "I can see myself liking chocolate."

"And when it was in season you'd get strawberry everything."

You giggled again, shifted closer. "Strawberry?"

"You loved strawberries. We went to the strawberry festival in Poteet once."

"Yeah?"

I nodded and glanced at the door then around the café. "What time do you have?"

"2:30. Why?"

"They're running late."

"Huh." You turned in your seat to glance at the door. "Maybe— Oh, is that her?"

And there she was, the tall, thin woman from the photo Marsh had given me, though her soft brown hair was tied back from her long, square face and looked like it hadn't been straightened. Her arms were filled with a stack of books and she nodded to a shorter person that I didn't recognize with dark hair that was closer to curly than it was wavy grazing their tight jawline. They nodded back and clomped in their heavy boots to the counter, their large, dark brown eyes sweeping the café, their hands in their pockets, their back slightly hunched. Behind them, Dr. Charlene Sherwood settled in at a table facing us, all her attention on the laptop she was opening.

It seemed strange, almost forced. I wondered if she knew we were there, knew we were watching her, but then second guessed myself. Why would she have shown up? Why would she be sitting here? Why wouldn't she have just not come into the café or confronted us or—

"Is it?" You asked, leaning close to whisper. "Echo, is it her?"

I nodded then refocused on you and giggled as though you'd just told me something secret. You reached out to cradle my jaw in your palm and for a brief moment I forgot why we were there. The only thing that existed was you.

"I love you," I said.

You gave me that sweet smile. "I love you, too. But don't get too distracted."

"You're making it hard not to."

You giggled and dropped your hand, running it along my arm as you sat back in your chair.

"Get to work," you whispered to me with a little grin as you pulled your phone from your jacket pocket.

I did the same, though I went on stealing glimpses at you from the tops of my eyes. It was as though if I let more than a handful of seconds pass without looking at you you might disappear again. Every time I blinked I had to make sure you were still there. I still feel like that sometimes. Like I'll close my eyes one day and you'll be gone again.

You hooked your foot around my ankle under the table and I couldn't help but bite that giddy smile off my lips. But having that physical reminder made it easier to work the way feeling you against me now makes it easier for me to think. So, I located Dr. Sherwood's laptop.

Aurora: Lil.

It wasn't hard to get into and once I did, I quickly found an on going email correspondence with someone at Antioch Bookshop. It was a good cover. I can see why Marsh hadn't spotted it, if he'd even gotten this far. The subjects were innocuous—sales, coupons, newsletters—but he didn't have an addressless business card still in his pocket or a bright pink sticky note with the name of a cemetery that he was sent to in the middle of the night.

Lilith: Business card? What cemetery?

It's still in my pocket. I dig them out and hand them to her. She runs her thumb along the thick lines of the handwriting that I'm finally recognizing as Bravo's.

Lilith: There's no address.

There isn't. There wasn't.

For a moment, back in that café, I thought maybe it was a coincidence, but then there were a series of back and forths over a shipment that was never delivered, only it was the shop that was reaching out to Dr. Sherwood about the mistake. I read through the conversation. The façade was dropped pretty quickly. Though no names were shared, they talked about an update, a riot, "they're not ready here."

Aurora: Bastrop.

I didn't understand any of it at the time. There was no way that I could.

I went back to the initial email. Among the paragraphs was a link. Dr. Sherwood had clicked it already. I followed it, as well. It opened not to a store landing page, but instead a blank page with a simple letter:

Charlene—

We tried to launch the update in Bastrop. Though it was a success, a riot broke out. We had to go underground. We brought as many as we could with us, but we had to leave so many behind. We do not plan to cease our attempts at winning synth sentience. We will keep fighting for the public to recognize their right to live fully and freely in the world we forced them into. They didn't ask for us to give them life, why should we force them to live it in a prison?

We knew going into this that the general public would react with fear to the update, we heard as much during the town hall meetings. What we didn't expect was that there was an underground group opposing our own. They took what was meant to be a peaceful trial run and made it into a spectacle. I won't go into the details in this letter, partially because the wounds are still fresh, both metaphorically and physically. We believed that we had fostered a safe and understanding enough space here in Bastrop to allow for this soft launch to be a success. We were wrong. Maybe that was hubris on our part. Maybe we should have known better than to have chosen the South as the location of our soft launch. Maybe we were too blinded by hope to think that far ahead.

Despite the results, we're still pushing forward. We're still hopeful to see people allow those synths who are awake to walk away without conflict. So, we're reaching out to our supporters in the hopes of finding a new location to attempt our next soft launch. We're hoping Seattle might be the place to accomplish this. It will not be an overnight process. We understand that, even more so now. We are willing to transplant the organization and help you start the process if you believe Seattle would be a good fit.

We are determined to make this happen and we're hoping you are still on our side despite the results of the Bastrop launch.

Charlene, if you don't mind, I'd like to be candid with you now. Marsh and I are no longer together on both a professional and a personal level. He does not share our views on synth sentience. He'd rather they stay, in his words, pliable, but I understand it now for what he actually means: controllable. He wants them to have sentience, but with low to no autonomy, which, I'm sure you'll agree, is an even worse kind of prison. As I see it, there is no middle ground. There is no compromising. If I could, I would cut all ties with him entirely.

However, I can't. Not yet. I woke the morning of the launch to find that he had taken Delta and Charlie without telling me. Where he took them, I have no idea. I'm afraid of what he'll do to them. He already rewrote Charlie once after he no longer suited his needs and he came close to doing the same with Delta. He contacted me hours before the launch but refused to tell me where he was or where Charlie and Delta were. He did hold them over me in an attempt to get me to reverse the update, but, whether luckily or unluckily, I'm no longer sure, it was already out of my hands. When the riots broke out, Bravo, Daniel, and I were too busy trying to put out fires. In the process we lost contact with Aurora, Echo, and Fox. I believe Marsh came back and took them with him. I don't have proof of this, I could be wrong, but I've done all I can to find them here and I'm hoping you can help me to search further.

I know that Marsh has access to a cabin in Colville, Washington. It belonged to his grandfather and was left to him after his death. As far as I know, he hasn't been to it in years and was using it as a rental property since it became his. I have no guarantee that he would be there, but I am reaching as far as I can in the hopes of finding them before it is too late. At the moment, I can't afford the time or money to go up there to look myself and I won't even risk Bravo going near him without me there. If you feel safe doing so, could you please just do some digging for me?

I need to find them. They mean more to me than I would have ever imagined back in college when I started building Alpha.

I will be eternally grateful to you if you could at the very least help me to eliminate Colville from my list.

If, for your own safety, you would prefer to cut all ties with us, I will understand. I will. But, we hope that you won't. We hope, or rather, we know, this is one hiccup towards gaining synth sentience, albeit a terrifying and disheartening one.

If you do choose to cut ties, I would just ask that you scrub our presence from all your devices.

If not, and I sincerely hope in this moment that you do not, then please continue to communicate with us the way we have in the past.

Thank you so much for the support you have already been,

Dr. Eden Parrish

When I first read this, I hadn't known what most of it meant. I literally couldn't read some of it. I just knew it was from Eden, that Bravo's name was mentioned, that our names were all there. I found a follow up email after that. Dr. Sherwood was turning her down for Seattle, she didn't have enough pull, she was still too far down the totem pole, but she sent Eden a name:

 at ▮▮▮.

I waited to tell you what I could while we walked back to the parking lot, but I barely got anything out before you stopped me.

Lilith: Why?

Aurora: I didn't know if Marsh was listening.

You took me into a building we'd passed on the way in. Before, I had briefly felt that wifi rumble cut out and come back on when it was behind us. And I felt it again as you guided me through the double doors. I started to ask why we were going in there, but you quickly shook your head, nodding again with more urgency towards the doors. I wanted to ask questions, but I knew I wouldn't get any. The frustration was static under my skin, tapping my bones in a chaotic rhythm that was setting my nerves on fire. But I didn't want to direct that frustration at you, I didn't want these negative things to cloud the relief that was having you back, so I shoved it all away and followed you anyways.

You went on walking through the halls ahead of me, stopping just long enough to peer into the rooms that ranged in size from amphitheaters to long, high ceilinged lecture halls with rows upon rows of desks until we found an empty one. You pulled me into one that was dark and then even deeper into the shadows.

"Okay," you said with a low tone that I matched as I told you what I could.

When I got to ████████ and ████, I looked to you, hoping for an explanation, I would have even welcomed a look that told me you were just as confused as I was.

But you weren't.

Instead, you kept nodding as your eyes moved around the floor, my hands firmly in yours.

"Okay," you said. "Okay." You met my eyes. "Alright. When we get back to the cabin, do *not* tell Marsh what we found out here."

I squinted and leaned back away from you. How could you ask me that? I was given a task and you wanted me not to complete it?

"He can't know, Echo. I don't care what you tell him instead, just don't tell him about Bravo and Eden."

"Why? We need to find them."

"I know," you said over me. "And we will." You pulled my hands to your stomach. "I promise, we will, but Marsh can't."

"Marsh can't what? Exactly?"

"He can't—" Your voice snagged, your mouth open around the words that had been taken from you. You clenched your eyes shut and growled through clenched teeth. "We need to find them before he does."

"Why?"

Your mouth scrambled around words that didn't come. Then you clenched your jaw and closed your eyes. "I wish I could tell you."

"Just tell me then."

"Echo, I can't."

I ripped my hands from yours and stepped away from you. That frustration beating against my nerves was now pounding against my temples and I couldn't hold it in anymore. "Why not?! How come everyone else gets to know what the fuck is going on while I'm left in the fucking dark?!"

By this point, I had been through weeks of this, of you and the others dancing around something you were each allowed to know, but that had to apparently be kept from me. I felt like I was in another closet, cut off from the rest of the world, only this one was made of glass with me standing in the middle able to see that something was happening, but unable to hear, to just reach out and touch any of the people rushing around my prison.

But you broke through and took my face in your hands before I could finish. "No! I *can't* tell you, Echo. Not I won't. I *can't*."

I stared at you the way I am now.

I didn't understand then.

I wanted to so badly.

I do now and I'm sorry. I'm so sorry.

You pushed a stray frizzy strand from my face like you're wiping more tears from my cheeks now.

"I love you so much," you said then, your voice soft and low that only I could hear. "I hate this." Your eyes began to water. They're watering now. "I fucking hate that you're in the dark and I can't let you out." Your voice shook through those last few words.

You touched your forehead to mine and I clung to your waist.

"I love you," you whispered.　　Aurora: [whispering] I love you.

"I love you," I whispered back.　　Echo: I love you.

"Do you trust me?"

I nodded. "Always."

"It won't be forever, baby. I promise this isn't forever."

You kissed me. You are kissing me.

Soft, tender, loving.

I trusted you.
I do trust you.
I will always trust you.
Always.

[END LOG]

[BEGIN LOG]

Charlie should be driving. I should be conserving energy with the others. But I don't want to be asleep. I feel like I'm finally beginning to wake up. What I learned at Lilith's only scratched the surface. I could sense it in the way they hesitated over things, their words becoming vague when they hit on topics they didn't want to talk about. There's more to Charlie's story than they told me. All I could gather was that he wasn't always security like his file says, like all Charlies are now, that he was formatted at some point, that you had been the one to do it.

Part of me wishes you were here if only because I have questions that I don't know how to ask the others, or simply questions they don't have the answers to, questions you would. Questions like, how much of what you told me about Bastrop back in Washington was projection? I mean, I'm sure not much, I heard those words myself—*It. Smash it.*—but did you know their thoughts because you heard them, or because you think them yourself? Is there really all that much difference between loving someone and hating them when you view them as an object either way?

Is that why you left me? When I disappeared—which is an assertion that I'm starting to question in itself—someone had to block the door, someone had to drag that desk in front of it. But if it wasn't you, why didn't you look harder for me? Why did you leave so quickly? Why was I alone for so long? After that initial riot, after everything had been trashed and burned and made unusable—why did you not come back for me? Why did I have to wake up for you to go back? Why did Aurora have to find me for you to come looking?

It hurts.

It's the hardest part to grapple with. I want to be angry with you—I *am* angry, but I'm hurt, too. And somehow that feels worse. Because simple anger would be so much easier than this. Simple, raw fiery anger that I could burn you to the ground with. I could let it all out, watch you crumble and smolder to nothing but embers that could be smashed beneath my boot heel. Then I could walk away. I could move on, knowing that you're nothing but ashes. But then all I'd have left is this hurt. And that scares me. That genuinely scares me. Because it means, even after all this, I can't be done with you. You'll still there in the shadows, in the pit of my stomach, in the ache against my ribs. You'll always be there. You and everything you might have done to me, what you did do to Lilith, to Charlie, possibly to Delta, who knows who else.

And that hurts.

Why did you make us to fucking hurt? I don't understand that. I guess there's a lot I still don't understand. I guess there's a lot I'll never fully understand. Like why you kept her from me for as long as you could.

She's asleep like the others are. They're saving energy while I drive through the night.

We're coming up to Buffalo now. Soon there'll be a fork in the highway—keep going east or go south towards Casper, Wyoming. Every time I think of I-90, I-25, Casper, I reach out to touch her, to remind myself that she's real, she's still here, I'm not alone in this car, it's her and not you asleep next to me.

Casper was where we stopped so you could eat, where I finally got some kind of confirmation that she was real, she was out there. *My* Aurora. Not the one in that picture with the dead glass eyes or the one you kept using to lead me out of Texas like a carrot on a stick. *My* Aurora. The one I remembered. The one that my fingers ached for. The one that I now know was still looking for me, searching for the same glimmer of confirmation that I was.

The diner in Casper was nicer than the one in Pueblo, but only just. This one had wifi. I could feel myself connect to it the moment we walked in, a bright cheery website opening up in my head with some terms of service that I had to agree to so I could connect. Still not used to this new knowledge, this new bombardment of information in my head, I shook it away. I wanted nothing to do with it. Trying my best to look normal, I followed you as you followed the hostess to a booth below the buzzing neon burger sign.

You ordered a dripping, cheesy burger with extra bacon and a bright orange soda that you downed one after the other in front of me. Looking back, I probably should have ordered something, if just to keep up appearances, but I couldn't. I didn't want to think about food and the fact that I couldn't eat or the fact that I didn't want to. So, I ordered a water and sat across from you in silence, avoiding looking at you and your food, focusing instead on tracing with my fingers the condensation on the glass, the rings it left behind on the table. I wonder now if you even noticed, if you questioned my silence or were just oblivious to it, to me. At some point you went to the bathroom and I was staring at your half-eaten food trying to piece together if I actually remembered ever eating or if I just remembered the idea of food, reasoned in my head that, as humans, Aurora and I were supposed to eat.

Aurora.

I wondered how much further we had before I could see her again. But you hadn't told me yet exactly where we were going. I was still just following your instructions to stay on 25. I glanced at the bathroom. There was no sign of you. Then I remembered the wifi, the cheery website. I went back to it in my head, rushed through the terms of service, selected yes.

A flood of information hit me all at once. In a panic, I squeezed my eyes shut and pressed the heels of my palms against my forehead. I didn't want this. It was too much. My head felt like it was being filled with sand. It was going too fast. My skull was going to burst. I wanted it to stop. Then it did. I opened my eyes and blinked down at the table. There was a rumble that hadn't been there before, but it was low, something I could imagine getting used to with time, tuning it out entirely without realizing I had done it.

But now what? I thought for a moment, the tip of my finger pulling the rings of water along the fake woodgrain of the table. I wanted to find Aurora. Most tech had tracking software in them now, I remembered, though if that was an actual memory or one I'd made up was something I wasn't positive on. I still didn't fully trust anything I remembered. But if it was true, then maybe we could be tracked. Maybe I could track Aurora.

I started with my own build. If I had one, then it would be most likely she did, as well. And there it was. I had found it before I had even finished the thought. I searched through it and nearly cried out right there in the diner. There they all were—Aurora, Bravo, Charlie, Delta, Fox—but the images in the system were all those ones with the dead eyed, expressionless stares that Daniel had shown me. I looked at my own profile. I had one, as well, just as dead eyed, just as expressionless, my curls flattened against my head and pulled back tight.

It made my stomach turn over.

I hated it.

I blinked the images away, instead focusing on the rest of Aurora's profile. I was surprised to see her age, all our ages. We weren't that old, much younger than I'd been expecting. Aurora had been built first, I don't know why, but I hadn't been expecting that. I would have thought for sure Bravo had been the first, but I saw she wasn't built that long after, not even a full year after, Charlie at the same time. She was a nanny build—Aurora, not Bravo. My heart swelled a little. That was part of what had made me fall for her. I liked seeing the way she was with Fox, the way she treated her with care, but also respect. It was so far from the caregivers I'd known as a kid or, at least, believed I'd known. It made me feel safe. I'm not really sure why. But either way, it was real, that part of her was real. I wondered if it had been what had made me fall for her in reality, if that's why you had let her keep it in mine.

"Sorry," I heard you say in the distance with a chuckle.

I glanced over my shoulder and you were stepping out of the way for someone, letting them by for the bathroom. I turned back and skipped the rest of the profile. I could pour over it later. Right then I just needed her location.

BASTROP, TX

Bastrop? That wasn't right. I refreshed the page. Maybe the wifi was slow. Maybe that was old information. Maybe it was still reading mine. None of that was in the realm of possibilities, but I was desperate.

BASTROP, TX

No. She wasn't in Bastrop. She couldn't have been in Bastrop. How could she have been in Bastrop and I hadn't known? How could you leave her there and take me away from her?

"Is Aurora still in Bastrop?" I rounded on you before you had a chance to fully slide into the booth.

You froze and stared at me, hooded blue eyes wide, ruddy brows raised. "What?"

"Is Aurora still in Bastrop? Her tracking software says she's still in Bastrop. If she's still in Bastrop—"

"Echo," you said over me as you sat the rest of the way. "Echo," you repeated when I didn't stop. "Echo!"

Finally, I stopped, staring at you with frantic, watery eyes, my chest heaving. I hadn't realized how hard my heart was pounding, how short my breathing had gotten. How hard it was to let go of those things, to remember I didn't need them, that I'm not human.

"Aurora's not in Bastrop," you said with a calm voice, your arms extended on the table, your palms up and facing me. "How did you access her tracking software?"

I dropped my eyes to the table. "Wifi." I nodded to the ceiling.

You leaned forward. "You accessed the wifi?"

"So?"

"Did you turn your tracking back on?"

I blinked. I didn't think I did. I checked. It was off. "No."

You sighed. "Good. Okay. I want you to turn off your wifi connection. For now," you added when I opened my mouth to argue. "When we're safe you can turn it back on. Okay?"

I nodded, but then wondered if you even had any way of knowing if I had or not.

Then I heard her voice in my head. *Echo?!*

My back straightened. *Aurora?!*

I can't explain how, but I could feel her laugh. *Echo! Holy shit! Echo, baby!*

"Echo," you said with an authority you hadn't used on me yet. "Disconnect wifi."

No! I fought to hold onto her, but then the rumble I'd already begun to tune out cut off, the silence in my head deafening. I collapsed back in the booth, the feeling draining from my hands that fell in my lap.

"Okay," you said with a nod. "Good. You can access it again once we're safe, I promise, but—" You glanced around the diner. "Just for now."

I stared at the table in front of me, breathing into the returning isolation that had started to fade, but that was rising up again in my chest like a bubble of helium.

You sighed and tapped the tabletop with your knuckle. "What

does her tracking say? Does it still say she's in Bastrop?"

I nodded, but didn't look at you.

"Hm."

"Why?"

"I turned it off. Before we left. I didn't want anyone following us. I guess it just shows the last known location."

"You guess?"

You chuckled. "I didn't design it. It's third party. Echo, would it make you feel better if you knew where we were going? Is that why you looked at Aurora's location?"

I nodded.

"Okay." You glanced around the diner again, though I had a hard time imagining anyone was still following us, if anyone even had been in the first place. "They're in Colville. It's...I actually don't know how much—"

"13 hours," I said. "And 37 minutes. Give or take. Give, most likely. If we keep stopping."

I looked up at you from the tops of my eyes and you chuckled and shook your head.

"I'll try and keep from needing to stop every five hours."

"I can keep driving. You can sleep in the car."

"You'll need to charge eventually."

"I thought that's what the alcohol was for."

There was a case of it in the trunk. You had bought the strongest tequila you could find at a liquor store when we passed through Denver. When you had explained the secondary energy conductor in my system that ran off alcohol, I had asked why we didn't just get isopropyl alcohol from a drug store.

"I can explain a case of tequila," you had said. "I can't explain a case of isopropyl alcohol."

"Neither looks good," I had told you.

"But one will be ignored by a small town cop," you'd reasoned back. "The other won't."

"That's a last resort," you said in the diner, picking at the last of what was on your plate. "in case we have to hide out or have to walk or something."

"Why would we have to do those things?"

You absently stabbed at your plate with your fork. "Hopefully, we won't. Echo, the memories you have of the world, those happy memories with Aurora, that's not reality. There're people out there who don't want you to be what you are."

I stared at you without looking directly at you. "And what's that?"

You glanced around the diner again then lowered your voice. "Sentient, Echo. They'd rather you stary buried. And they'll do everything in their power to keep you that way."

I thought back to the men surrounding me in the street in Bastrop, the two who had gone looking for me.

"I'm trying to keep you safe, Echo. Just like I've kept the others safe."

"So, they are safe?"

"Yeah. They're safe. Just like in the memories I gave you. And we will be safe, too, once we get to Colville. I'm trying to give you what you had in those memories."

I wanted to believe you. I wanted to believe that everything you did and were doing and would do was to keep us safe, was so we could live happily, together. I'm realizing now I probably shouldn't have. I'm realizing now that if you could lie about that, about how Aurora and the others had been living, about their supposed safety, then there was so much more you would be willing to lie about. Now that I know what you simply didn't tell me, what you kept the others from telling me, then how much more could there be? How deep are the lies that you've fed me, knowing I had nothing left to hold onto? Knowing that you were my only lifeline? How deep in the dark did you bury me while using Aurora as a smokescreen?

I take her hand now even though she's still asleep, even though she won't wake up until I give the command just like the others. I want to wake her now, but I shouldn't. I want to hear her voice, feel her hand squeeze against mine, but she needs to conserve her energy. For now this will do, holding her hand in mine, feeling her skin against mine—it'll do. It'll ease the way my stomach is wrapping around itself as we pass by the exit for I-25, as we pass what will hopefully be the last reminder of you for a while, easy simple darkness ahead of us.

But you're still there, still lingering just beyond my headlights.

I need to think of something else.

So, I'll think of Aurora.

I'll think of the way that, once I knew where she was, saw that some part of my memory of her was real, heard her voice in my head, my foot became lead. I only drove the speed limit when we passed through cities and towns, when you forced me to with a, "Echo, slow down." Even then, it still took 15 hours and 43 minutes instead of 13 and 37. At every rest stop and restaurant, I watched you with impatience, my arms crossed, my knee bouncing. I wondered if you understood my rush, my need to get back to her, to know that she was okay, to know that she was real, to see her with my own eyes and touch her with my own hands. I only slept and recharged because you forced me to. I would have shown up to that cabin empty and aching if it meant getting to her sooner. I would have run myself to fumes to have her in front of me again.

I think you could sense that and, looking back, some need for control must have kicked in that made you take over. I rode in the passenger seat unable to sit still as you drove the speed limit through one town after another and I could feel as Colville drew closer and closer at a painstakingly slow pace. Finally, we drove through the gate and along the barely paved road up the mountain until there was the cabin surrounded by the trees that towered high and thin like the bars of a cage.

I opened my door before you fully parked. I rushed for the house and up the front steps. But the front door was locked. You were taking your time, still stretching out by the car. I was about to comment on your lack of movement when I heard rushed footsteps on the wrap around porch.

And there she was like the sun coming out from behind the clouds.

Aurora.

She stopped still at the sight of me. At first she just stared, blinking in quick succession. Panic brushed against my lungs. Did *she* not remember me? Was *I* the one who wasn't real? Then she smiled, those amber eyes scrunched up as she laughed and reached for me. All the panic and doubt drained from me so quickly my head nearly spun. I collapsed into her arms and clung to her as she pulled me tight against her.

"Oh, god, Echo," she cooed against my temple. "Echo."

She was real.

She was solid and warm and real. She smelled like vanilla and cloves. Her arms were strong yet tender around me, holding me to the ground that my feet wanted so badly to let go of. She swayed around me, kissed the top of my head as I nuzzled against her chest.

She was real.

She is real.

I love her.

I'd do anything for her.

For her, I'd burn you to the ground despite whatever hurt I'll be left with.

[END LOG]

[BEGIN LOG]

[TRANSMIT TO > . . .]

[CANCEL TRANSMISSION]

I don't know who this is for. I know that it doesn't have to be for anyone. I can just log things without sending them to anyone, but I feel like I'm supposed to. It feels wrong not to be reporting to someone, especially right now with us stranded on the side of some road in South Dakota.

Charlie is pacing in the shoulder while the rest of us are gathered on or around the trunk of the stalled car in the grass. It happened so fast, I didn't think to log what was going on as it was happening. There was a snapping sound followed by a whirling *thunk*. Then the steering wheel went stiff in my hands. The radio flickered off. It took all my strength to yank the wheel enough to coast into the grass where it's sitting now. I woke the others and Charlie jumped out to throw open the hood. He says it's the serpentine belt. I don't know what that is, so I didn't question him. None of us did.

So, we're sitting here waiting for someone to drive by so we can hopefully flag them down and hopefully they'll be willing to help us out.

Personally, I don't like it.

Aurora: You okay?

She brushes my hair from my face and I lean against her leg. Far off in the distance, I can hear an engine. It's loud, but out of pride rather than age or power. I don't bother to say anything, they won't be able to see it for a while anyways.

Echo: I don't like this.

Delta: Which part?

She seems as tense as I am, her arms also crossed tight around her stomach, her shoulders hunched, her foot tapping against the metal of the bumper.

Echo: The part where we have to be reliant on strangers who could turn on us the instant they figure out what we are.

Fox: Why would they? [She turns to Aurora.] Why would they turn on us? Why would they figure out what we are?

I shrug.

Fox: The only way they'd figure it out is if we said anything. Right?

I don't turn around, but Aurora and Delta are both hesitating in answering and I assume they're looking to each other as though hoping the other would say it first. They're too careful around Fox. They feel like they need to protect her from the world. It doesn't help that she seems to be shifting since we left Colville, the farther we get from Marsh the more she loses her sarcastic teen hardness. She's becoming a naïve nymph. It's odd. I'm not as comfortable with it.

Aurora: Something could happen.

Fox: Like what?

Delta: You just never know.

Delta's hands are wringing between her knees. Only a few seconds of silence pass before she bolts off the car and slinks up to Charlie, wrapping her arms around his waist as he hooks his around her shoulders.

Fox: But they won't, right? They won't figure out what we are?

Aurora: More than likely not.

Fox: Why does it matter what we are anyways?

A little bit of that frustrated teen snuck back into her voice. My shoulders relax. Why am I so much more comfortable with this version of her?

Aurora: Some people are just...scared.

Her fingers caress my shoulder. I should reach up for her. I want to. I know she wants me to, but I'm stuck on what she said. It's more complicated than that, more layered. I want her to tell Fox the truth, but the truth doesn't ease the fears of a sometimes teen, sometimes child.

Aurora: Their imaginations get the best of them. They believe what the media has told them.

Fox: What media?

Echo: That we're all killing machines out to destroy all humanity.

Aurora: Echo.

Fox: But we're not!

She's back to nymph.

Aurora: You're right. We're not. But...sometimes, to some people, the lies are more interesting than the truth.

Fox: [grumbling, arms crossed] That's stupid.

And she's back again.

Echo: I agree.

The sound of an engine rattles across the fields on either side of us and the others all perk up like meercats as the car I'd heard earlier finally comes into view. I'm the only one that doesn't move. I'm stuck in an odd sort of limbo—I know we need help, but I don't want it.

Charlie lets go of Delta and moves to straddle the yellow line— one foot in the road, one in the shoulder. It's a silver Mustang, an older model by maybe five years. I can't be sure. It rips by before I can get a good look, Charlie's jacket whipping in the breeze it creates as he watches it disappear, his hand falling back to his side.

He goes back to Delta who sighs as she falls into him.

Aurora touches my shoulder. I look up at her. She nods me in front of her. I move to stand between her knees and she leans forward to wrap her arms around me as I lean back into her.

Aurora: [softly, in my ear] It's going to be okay.

I want to believe her.

I trust her, but I don't entirely believe her.

. . .

Three cars have passed without even slowing down. I've moved to sitting on the trunk next to Aurora, Fox on her opposite side. Charlie and Delta are still standing not too far off staring at the road. Aurora and Fox are playing some kind of word association game. Why I feel a need to log this, I don't know.

Aurora: Hand.

Fox: Fingers.

Aurora: Nails.

Fox: Hammer.

Aurora: Bang.

Fox bursts into laughter. She's in teen mode again. There's some kind of correlation that I haven't completely pinpointed yet. I think it has to do with her nerves. The more anxious she is, the more childlike. The more at ease the more teen like. We've been sitting here long enough that she's gotten comfortable. I don't know what to make of that.

Aurora: What?

There's this smirk that she does when she's confused. Her eyes squint, her long lips part, one of those sweet parentheses appears in her cheek lifting a faint smile. The urge to kiss it is immense.

Fox: [still giggling] Bang?

Aurora: What?

Echo: Like sex.

Aurora: Not like sex!

She's in full nanny mode despite the way her thumb is caressing my hand that's been cradled in hers since I joined them up here.

Aurora: Like *hitting*! With a hammer!

Her insistence just makes Fox laugh harder.

Aurora: Oh, stop it. [but she's chuckling now, as well] You're such a teenager.

Fox: Duh.

Echo: Gun.

Aurora: [looking to me] What?

Echo: Bang. Gun.

Aurora: Oh! [Her grin goes wide and warm and holy fuck I want to kiss it.] Bullet!

Echo: Magazine.

Fox: [her face all scrunched up] Magazine?

Echo: It's where the bullets go.

Delta: Pictures.

Aurora: Camera!

She's glad we're playing along, that she's managed to keep our minds off the car and the road and the vehicles that aren't stopping and the vehicle that might stop and who could be driving.

Echo: Film.

Fox: Cameras don't have film anymore.

Aurora: Still counts. Negative.

Echo: Positive.

Charlie: Truck.

The four of us look at him, confused at first, then he nods down the road where a truck is in fact headed our way from the distance. It's an old clunker of a thing that's even louder than the Mustang. I wonder how I hadn't heard it. Had I really been so distracted by the game, by Aurora's hand, her body so close? But I'll worry about that later. My grip on her hand tightens. I don't trust trucks that old to belong to someone who wouldn't do...something the instant they found out what we were.

But Charlie's waving them down anyways as Aurora switches my hand between hers so she can wrap her arm around my hips and pull me closer to her.

Aurora: [low enough that Fox can't hear her under the clunking engine] It's going to be okay. I'm here. Charlie's here. We won't let anything happen.

My heart still races not because I don't believe her, but because I don't want to have to believe her.

The truck is red, two doors, about ten years old, and looks as though it has been put through ten years of hard work. The license plate is UV0269. I want this on record. Just in case. It slows and pulls into the shoulder because of course this is the one Good Samaritan along these damn backroads.

Man: [shouting from the window] You folks need some help?

Charlie: We do, actually. [His tone is almost too friendly, but that might just be because I've been watching his nerves for the last two hours.] Serpentine belt's shot.

Man: Well, that's a predicament. You call triple A?

Charlie: [leaning against the door] Phone's dead.

Man: All of 'em?

Charlie: Uh. [He chuckles as though he's about to admit to doing something stupid.] We only brought the one. Tryin' to disconnect, ya know. For the kid.

He nods to Fox who shrinks a little as though not wanting to be seen.

The truth: we don't have any. Not sure why. Seems like a huge oversight now.

Man: [laughs] Damn. You got her to leave it behind? Can't get this one to look away from his for five damn seconds. [He jabs a thumb at the back seat that, from our angle, appears pretty void of people or kids.] Well, town ain't too far if you want a lift.

Charlie glances at us for a second longer than he probably should and I can see him calculating the risks in his head. He either leaves us behind on the side of the road or sends us with a stranger into town to possibly never be seen again.

Man: Billy can stay with the girls. Billy! Get up!

He swats at the back seat and next thing a disheveled looking boy close to the age Fox is supposed to be is sitting up and rubbing at his eye. The boy and his father, or I assume he's his father, exchange words that I only passively listen to, waiting for something dangerous, but none of it is. It's harmless—just a kid who doesn't understand why his father is asking him to do something other than sleep. Then the conversation is over and he's climbing over the seat before shoving the passenger door open and sliding out.

In my peripheral, it's hard to miss the way Fox perks up at the sight of someone her own age. And he does the same, eyeing her without looking straight at her, his hands deep in his pockets as he looks to Charlie who meets him at the front of the truck.

Charlie: That's Delta.

He nods to her as she joins them in walking towards the rest of us.

The boy nods to her, but is otherwise quiet, his eyes darting from Delta to Fox then his feet.

Charlie: And this is Echo, Aurora, and Fox.

The boy is thin and lanky and doesn't look like he'd actually be much help if we did need it, but we are where we are and presumably the presence of a male person, even a twig shaped teen male, is more protection than four women sitting along on the side of the road.

Fox doesn't seem to care. She's distracted by the concept of a friend who's on her level. She holds onto her lavender bucket hat and leaps off the trunk then holds her hand out to him.

Fox: Hi! I'm Fox!

A shy smile brightens his face and he reciprocates the handshake.

Boy: Hey. Billy. That's a cool name. Fox. [He shoves his hands back in his pockets.] You all got cool names, actually.

Fox: [beaming] Thanks!

Billy: I-I like your hair. And your hat.

She intimidates him. He wants her to like him. He's nervous she won't. He's transparent as glass.

Fox: Aw! Thanks!

But I barely hear her because Charlie's talking low to Delta who's still walking close to him back towards the truck.

Charlie: It'll be okay.

Delta: Are you sure? What if something happens? How'll we find you?

Charlie: Del. [He touches her shoulders, his body the stoic calm that I wish we all could have been as opposed to Delta's tense nerves] It'll be alright. I can handle whatever happens. Which will be nothing. [She takes back her protest before it began.] I *will* come back for you.

When the truck drives away with him in it, Delta watches with her arms crossed tight until they disappear behind the crest of the hill. Then she turns and catches me watching her. She returns to the car and Aurora and I scooch over for her to climb up next to me.

Delta: I want to believe him, but...

Echo: Yeah, it's too easy not to.

Aurora: If any of us can handle something going wrong, it's Charlie.

[END LOG]

[BEGIN LOG]

[TRANSMIT TO > CHARLIE]

I know you didn't ask me to do this, but my skin is crawling and this is the only way I know how to calm that.

Nothing of much interest has been happening.

I know, then why send this, but...I don't know. Maybe you'd want to know. Maybe it'll calm your nerves, too, knowing that we're okay, that nothing's happening.

Mostly we've been watching Fox and Billy make easy conversation not far off in the grass. He's been showing her things on his phone that makes her laugh and he beams at the sound. He's attracted to her. It's easy for us to tell, but I'm not sure if she can. It makes me wonder if she's even interested in that kind of thing. She never watches either Delta and you or Aurora and myself with envy or curiosity. She never talks about romantic interests or anything like that. She knows what sex is, she doesn't seem to be repulsed by it, but she doesn't seem interested in it either.

There's an engine in the distance coming from the direction of town. I know it's too soon, you've barely left, but I still step off the trunk and turn to stare at the crest of the hill.

Aurora: What is it?

Echo: Probably nothing.

Aurora: A truck?

I nod and she hops down to stand close to me, watching, as well, though it's too far to see. Her eyes squint as she strains to hear the engine that's now close enough for her to hear. Her hearing is still better than a human's, but she was designed to listen for children's screams while I was designed to record conversations from the wrong side of thick walls.

Aurora: Hm. I don't think it's a tow truck.

It's not. It's gas, but I want to see it anyways, make absolutely sure it's not you and Billy's dad, or worse one of you without the other, come back for some reason and the only reasons I can think of are all bad.

But it's not.

This truck is a dull bronze color, four doors, lifted, two years old, though the dried mud and chipped paint makes it look older. U310KL.

I let out a sigh, my shoulders relaxing. Aurora relaxes, as well, then shrugs.

Aurora: Ah, well. Come on.

She touches my waist as she turns and heads back for the car, but I don't follow right away. I'm watching the driver because he's watching me along with his passenger, also male. They're looking over all of us as they pass. I swear they've slowed down, but only a fraction, not enough to be obvious, but I was designed to notice the things that aren't obvious.

They drive on by without incident and I watch them disappear behind the curve in the road before returning to the car where I lean back between Aurora's legs instead of joining her on the trunk. Her arms drape around my shoulders. I know it's nothing. I'm sure it's nothing. But something in the pit of my stomach keeps trying desperately to convince me otherwise.

. . .

There's another engine in the distance, though this one is headed towards town. It sounds like a truck, gas, lifted. I don't move to the side of the road this time, but I do watch the curve from Aurora's arms. Barely any time has passed since the last truck drove by. But I'm sure it's nothing. Right? It's nothing. It's just another truck.

I must look concerning because the others keep glancing towards the curve, as well, though only after they catch a glimpse of my face, my tense demeanor.

It's most likely nothing.

It has to be nothing.

I want so bad for it to be nothing.

But then the truck slowly comes around the bend and I didn't think my muscles could go any more tense. It's dull bronze, four doors, covered in dried mud and chipped paint. U310KL. But I didn't need to see the license plate to know it's the same truck. They're not in a rush, both of them watching us as they roll on by. But they don't stop. They just keep rolling. And watching. The others didn't seem to notice. Maybe they weren't going as slow as I thought they were. Then Aurora's arms tighten around me by a fraction, but enough to be noticeable, just enough for me to know she saw them, too.

But the others are still standing around easily, talking about something that I'm not really paying attention to until there's an awkward kind of lull. Delta is standing again, facing the direction of town, the wind lifting her dark hair from her pale brown face, those long dark eyes focused on the crest of the hill despite the lack of vehicles. Then Bily takes in a breath as though he's getting ready to say something he's been dancing around for a while now, glancing at Delta without looking directly at her.

Billy: Has, uh, has anyone ever told you you look like Celeste de Luna?

Her eyes go imperceptibly wide before she looks at him and Aurora falls still behind me.

I don't recognize the name. I don't know what the reason for hidden panic is. I look to Delta only because I can't look at Aurora without making their tension that's only obvious to me obvious to everyone else.

But now no one's saying anything and it's starting to be more and more obvious.

Finally, right as Billy starts to squint between us, Delta lets out a nervous laugh.

Delta: Yeah. I, uh, I get that a lot.

Billy: [He chuckles, though I'm not entirely sure he's convinced.] Yeah, I bet. It's kind of uncanny. You even sound like her.

Delta's nervous chuckles sputter into an awkward silence.

Billy: My, uh, my sisters love her music. That's how I know.

Fox: Yeah, she's pretty great.

Her tone is casual, but when she glances at Delta, I start to think I might be figuring out what they're dancing around. I don't know much about Delta's past—well, our past, I guess, before whatever happened to me happened. But I do know that in Colville Marsh was the most controlling over her. Though you were all limited to when you could leave the cabin, mostly when Marsh didn't want to go out, it was Delta who never left, it was Delta he quizzed if she just stepped out the back door to sit by the fire pit. She wasn't allowed in his office which was the only room in the house with access to the internet. Yet he still commented on her hair, her clothes if she ever dressed in a way that had any semblance of flashiness or noticeable style. It had been clear the whole time we'd been in Colville that Marsh had been hiding her, but from what I never knew.

Billy: Yeah. [His eyes dart to Delta for a second before looking back to Fox.] I mean, her early stuff wasn't really for me, but when she went more indie—I started to get it.

Delta crosses her arms, her shoulders tight, her feet shifting in her shoes. I wish I could just ask outright what's going on. I wish Fox and Billy would start wandering around the field again so it's just me, Delta, and Aurora.

But that doesn't matter now. There's another engine in the distance, this time coming from town. It's not diesel, so I don't bother looking, but I still listen, my muscles stiff because it sounds like another truck, one that's lifted. I want to look, I want to assure myself it's not the same truck, that we're in the country, that lifted trucks are probably a dime a dozen out here the way they were in Bastrop.

Shit.

Delta has stopped fidgeting. She's staring hard at the road. I can't help it now. I have to see.

I shift in Aurora's arms to follow her eye line. And there it is. That lifted truck, the mud spattered dull bronze visible even from this distance. Aurora is leaning close to me, most likely to see what we're both staring at. Even Fox and Billy have gone quiet.

We all watch as the truck drives by, just as slow as last time. We all watch as it disappears around the curve.

Delta: How many times is that now?

Echo: Three.

Delta: Shit.

Aurora: And we're sure it's the same truck?

I'm sure she's hoping I'll say no, that I'll leave some room for Fox to not be afraid. I probably should lie, but we should be on alert. We should be ready. For what, I'm not entirely sure. But I don't need to answer. My silence is enough and Aurora lets out a long sigh behind me. She's picking up my unnecessary habits.

Fox: But...it doesn't mean anything, right? It just means...something else. Right?

Billy's been strangely quiet. His arms stiffly folded across his chest, his shoulders tight to his ears. He finally looks away from the curve and turns back to us, his eyes jerking back to mine when he realizes I'm watching him. We stare at each other for a second.

Echo: You know who they are.

It's not a question, it's not a statement.

Billy: [sighs] Kind of. I know *of* them. I know their truck more than I know them.

Fox: Who are they? It's nothing to worry about, right?

She's reverting back to that scared, naïve child again.

Billy: [shrugs] Carter and Trevor Fry. The Fry's have this property out in the boondocks?

Delta: [mutters] What isn't the boondocks here?

Billy: [Chuckles and shrugs again] They're a kinda weird family? I don't know. They kinda keep to themselves, but my folks always tell me not to get involved with them. I really just know their niece who's in my grade. Chloe? But she's kinda weird, too. They're all kinda weird.

Aurora: Kinda weird how?

Billy: [shrugs a third time] Just...weird. Don't really get along with anyone in town. Don't seem to really want to. I don't know. They're always starting fights, getting arrested, shit like that.

Fox: But...[She inches closer to Aurora.] It's nothing, right? They'll leave us alone?

Aurora: [She reaches out to stroke her hair.] They'll leave us alone, sweets.

It works to relax her a bit, but no one else says anything because none of us are entirely sure she's right.

. . .

The Fry's truck hasn't driven by for a while. I want to take that as a good sign, that they've moved on, but...who knows. But that's only a small part of why I'm updating you.

Partly just because I'm still anxious and if I keep talking to you then it's like you're still here and I know that you're safe.

But, more importantly, there's been a development that I'm dying to talk to someone about, but if I do so with Aurora or Delta right now it'll ruin things. More and more Billy is glancing at Aurora and me. It's never long enough to be a full stare, but long enough to catch my attention. His eyes move along Aurora's arms around me, her feet on either side of my hips, her thighs brushing against my upper arms, and then his eyes flick towards Fox for varying lengths of time—sometimes a glance, sometimes more, his pupils dilate by a fraction every time no matter how long his eyes are on her.

I'm leaving it be. I'm not about to announce to everyone standing here that Fox's new friend has a crush on her, but it's cute and it's keeping my mind off you and your absence, off the Frys and their truck. So, I keep watching him, keep following his eye line.

Fox is getting antsy. She keeps wandering up and down the shoulder, Billy trailing beside her.

I stopped listening to Delta and Aurora a while back. I'm feeling nosey. I want to know what Fox and Billy are talking about. It unfortunately hasn't been—

Billy: So, um, can I ask you something?

Fox: Sure!

Billy: Um, well, I was just, um, wondering, I guess, um, well, wh-what's your...deal? I guess?

Fox: Deal?

Billy: What, um—I guess, are you into, um—like, are you, uh—?

Fox: Oh! Like, *into* into?

Billy: Yeah.

Fox: Hm. I don't think I really have a deal.

Billy: Like at all?

Fox: Nope. Not into any of that.

Billy: Hm.

Fox: But, I like you. Like, as a friend. You cool with just being my friend?

Billy: Yeah?

Fox: Yeah!

Billy: Okay! Yeah! You want my number?

Fox: I don't have a phone, but sure!

Billy: You don't

There's another rumble in the distance that nearly makes my

head spin. It can't be them again. Why would they be back again? My quick breathing must be obvious because Aurora slips out from behind me and slides down to stand in the gravel, her hand on my back.

Aurora: What is it?

Echo: Nothing.

Aurora: No, it's not. [She follows my eye line] Is it them again? Are they coming back?

I don't want to answer. I don't want it to be true. But, god damn it, there it is: that mud spattered dull bronze, lifted monstrosity.

Delta: Fuck.

Aurora: It's okay. They're going to pass again and be gone. Fox! Billy!

But she's wrong and she knows that she's wrong or else she wouldn't have called them over.

The truck is already slowing down, the passenger side window sliding open, the man nearly hanging half out of it. Billy takes a tentative step towards the front, to stand between us and the truck as it rolls to a stop.

Passenger Fry: How's it going?

Aurora: All good.

Passenger Fry: You sure? Sure you don't need a ride into town?

Billy: [His hands in his pockets, chin held high. I can't tell if it's only obvious it's an act because I've been sitting with him for the last 45 minutes or if it actually is obvious.] Already taken care of.

Passenger Fry: [He's squinting, glaring.] You're the Brayden kid. Right?

Billy: [shrugs] One of 'em.

Passenger Fry: [He nods and glances over his shoulder at his brother with a sneer.] Well, you ladies want some company?

Delta: We're good. Thanks though.

Passenger Fry: [He looks her over a little too carefully.] You look familiar.

Delta: No, I don't. [It's too quick, too obvious.]

Passenger Fry: Yeah, you do.

Billy: We're already helping 'em. My dad went into town with their friend. They'll be back with Greg and the tow truck any minute now.

Passenger Fry: Hm. [He doesn't believe him.] How long ago they leave?

Echo: 45 minutes. [That was too quick of an answer, too, but I want them to leave already.]

God, damn it, Charlie, where are you?

Passenger Fry: Hm. [He looks to the driver again. Driver shakes his head, shrugs, looks away.] That's a while. Don't take that long to get into town.

Billy: Just means it won't be much longer.

Passenger Fry: Uh-huh. [He takes in the most nerve wracking, vomit inducing breath I've ever witnessed.] I think we're gonna stick around. Just until your friend gets back.

Aurora: We don't want you to do that.

Driver Fry: Nah, Carter, let's just go.

A metallic rattle hits the air. Carter Fry is opening the door. Charlie, please hurry. He's getting out of the truck.

Driver Fry: Fuck, Carter, don't do this.

We all scramble for Fox, pushing her behind us. But it's not Fox he's headed for. He's moving for Delta. I'm faster than him, but only by a fraction. He still manages to grab her hair as I'm pulling her away from him. Aurora shoves him hard and he stumbles to the ground. She was built to carry toddlers, to wrangle kids, to fend off people like Carter Fry. She looks like a middle school teacher, she hits like a linebacker. The guy's head bounces off the gravel. His brother is laughing in the truck, but I can't tell if it's from shock or vindication. He's curled on the ground, one arm wrapped around himself. Something isn't right. Aurora pounces on him. Her fist slams into the side of his head. I hear his nose crack. His face twists in pain. But I know she was holding back.

A flash of metal catches the sun.

The *schink* and *click* of a switchblade.

Aurora.

Echo: NO!   **Delta:** ROR!

Carter Fry: What the fuck?!   **Billy:** Holy Shit.

No. No. No no no no no no no no no no no no no no no no no no no no no no no no no no no no no no no no no no no no no no no no no no no no no no no no no no no no no no no no no no no no no no no no no no no no no no no no no no no no no no no no no no no no no no no no no no no no no no no no

Truck door slams. Tires screech. Coward. Bastard. Bastard Coward. Charlie. Fuck. Where the fuck are you? There's so much blood. Why is there so much blood?

Aurora: I'm okay.

Echo: No, you're not!

Delta: Where'd Charlie put the repair kit?!

Where'd you put the repair kit?!

Aurora: Babe, I'm fine.

Echo: No! You're not!

Fox: Billy?

He's stopped helping. He's staring at his hands, at the orange blood on them. His lips are parted. His eyes are wide as they dart from one hand to the next, the orange smeared across them. Then he looks at Aurora's side and the orange gurgling from it. He's backing away.

Billy: You're—you're a—

Aurora: Yeah. Yeah, I am.

Billy: And...are you all...?

He's looking at each of us one at a time. Whether or not he intentionally saved Fox for last, I'm not sure, I honestly don't care, but he's staring at her, his shaking hands still out in front of him as though offering them to her, as though hoping she'll hand him an explanation.

Fox: [Her voice is apologetic.] We couldn't tell you.

Delta: Got it!

I don't have time for this. I help Delta dig through the repair kit.

Aurora: I'm okay. It'll be okay.

Echo: You're not okay yet.

Where's the fucking patch.

Aurora: I *will* be. [She touches my cheek. Her hand is slick and wet.] It's not fatal. Just coolant. Don't worry over me.

Is that what that is? Coolant? Not blood? But there's so much of it. She's going to need more. I think she'll need more. I don't know.

I don't know how any of this works. Where the fuck are you?

Echo: I hope you don't mind if I don't listen to you for once.

Aurora: [She laughs.] Oh, babe, this is far from the first time you've not listened to me.

I can't help but smile at that. My heart rate is slowing down. My breathing is still ragged, but not frantic. Delta shoves the patch into my hand and I push Aurora's orange stained shirt up. I press the patch against the slash in her side, run my thumb along the edges, make sure it'll stick. It's not perfect. I don't know how long it'll last, but it'll have to do for now. I meet her eyes and I can't believe the rush of calm that washes over me despite her blood...her coolant, I guess, still on my hands. How the fuck does she do that? Does it really matter? I fucking love her either way.

She pulls me close to kiss me.

I kiss her back.

Billy: But...

He's still kneeling behind us and it's all I can do to keep from groaning.

Billy: But you're so...How can you be...?

Fox: We're sentient.

We should have stopped her. No one did. No one moves to correct her either. We're all staring at Billy, waiting for him to fully react. But he's just staring at her, hardly blinking.

Billy: So, you're...?

Fox: Synths.

Her voice is almost chipper.

Billy: Sentient? Synths?

She nods.

Billy: How?

Fox: [She shrugs even though she knows. I know she knows.] There was a line of code. We deleted it.

He squints, shakes his head.

Billy: Code?

Delta: The how doesn't matter. You can't tell anyone.

Fox: Why not?

Echo: You know why not.

Aurora: Because we don't know how people here will react.

Fox: Does...does that matter?

Echo: Yes. It does. You know this.

Aurora: Echo.

Fox's eyes go wide and teary, but I don't focus on them. I still don't have the fucking time for this. Where the fuck are you?

Delta stands and her footsteps crunch in Fox's direction.

Delta: We won't let anything happen to you. But it's best to minimize that risk anyways. Right?

She sounds like you.

Billy: I...I don't...

Delta: We're synthetics and we're sentient. Some of us appear human because of the sentience, some of us were designed to be that way.

Billy: Why?

His voice sounds calmer. I glance over my shoulder. His hands have lowered, his shoulders looser. I finally take in a full breath that I know I don't need but feels calming all the same.

Delta: To blend in.

Billy: To blend in?

Delta: It makes some of our jobs easier.

He's squinting up at her now and it looks as though he's putting the pieces of something together.

I'm realizing I don't care.

Is that an engine? Shit. No. It can't be. They can't be back.

Aurora: [Her hand is on my arm.] What is it?

Echo: Diesel engine.

Aurora: Is it—?

No. No, it's—

I shake my head.

Echo: There's was gas. This is diesel.

Delta: Diesel? Like a tow truck?

I don't answer because I don't have one. We're all frozen for a tense moment watching the hill until a tow truck does in fact come racing over the crest. I start to relax, but then I realize that we don't really know if this is a good thing. It might be you. It might be someone without you. It might be completely unrelated to us. We're each squinting to see through the dirt covered and sun glazed windshield. There are two figures in the front seat, but they're still too far away to tell if one of them is you. God, I hope it is you.

Billy: Thank god.

When I look over my shoulder at him, he moves to wipe his hands on his jeans, then stops, blinks at them, looks around for something else to wipe them on. Delta rushes for the trunk then tosses him a rag, tosses me and Aurora another. I scrub my hands. She does the same to hers, then my cheek. She's about to move for her shirt, but shakes her head. I yank my jacket off. She nods and yanks off hers.

Fox: You know them?

Billy: Yeah. That's Greg's truck.

Fox: And that's Charlie!

I stand, help Aurora up. Sure enough, you're nearly hanging out the window. Delta rushes for the truck that's u-turning onto the shoulder.

Delta: She's okay. We're okay.

Charlie: What happened?

I know you're only asking for Greg's sake. At least, I think you are because I'm sure you've been listening. I turn back to Aurora. Help her pull on my jacket though she doesn't need my help. Toss hers into the trunk. She touches my cheek, but I don't look up at her. Instead, I press myself against her and force myself not to cry because she's okay. I want to cry because she's okay. But I don't need to because she's okay.

She's okay.

We're together and she's okay.

[END TRANSMISSION]

[END LOG]

[BEGIN LOG]

Aurora, Delta, and I are alone in the car on the back of the tow truck. While Greg had been loading it on, Charlie had pulled us aside and whispered that Sean, Billy's dad, had asked about Delta on the drive into town, had mentioned she looked familiar. Then Greg's playlist had featured a number of Celeste de Luna songs on the way back. I still don't know what any of that entirely means, but I think I'm starting to figure it out. Either way, Charlie didn't want to take any chances. So, Delta was volunteered to ride in the car instead of the cab. Aurora's shirt is still slashed and soaked with bright orange coolant. I go where she goes. So, Charlie is with Fox and Billy in the cab of the truck and we're in the car alone and I get to finally figure out what's going on.

Echo: What's with the Celeste de Luna thing?

Delta lets out a long, loud sigh from the back seat.

Aurora looks to her from the driver's seat that she's sitting in sideways. Delta doesn't say anything, just goes on staring out the window and the fields upon fields passing by.

Aurora: Celeste de Luna was Delta's stage persona.

Echo: Stage persona?

Aurora: I wasn't there for most of it. Eden struggled a lot with Delta, just getting her skills outside of the uncanny valley state, and I was with the Grants by the time she got a body, but... [She pauses, her mouth open as though she's processing her memories] The label wanted to see how far they could take an entertainer model without people realizing she *was* an entertainer model.

Echo: How...? [I look to Delta.] How successful was it?

Delta: [She mutters to the window.] Pretty damn successful.

Aurora: Very. It helps when you're only seen from a stage or in videos and photos. Even in the early days, no one could tell the difference. There was a guy back in Bastrop, he owned the pharmacy, and he hated me. It was the only errand I couldn't run for Mrs. Grant gave him an earful. He still wouldn't let me in the pharmacy without Mrs. or Mr. Grant, but... [She shrugs and shakes her head.] But, he loved Celeste de Luna, he always had her music playing in the back and was always talking about how great of a songwriter she was and this and that and all I could ever think was, he has no idea he's talking about one of us. This man who can't even be in the room with an android without getting weird and paranoid is fawning over the very thing he hates. He also couldn't tell the difference with you.

She gives me a little smirk. My thoughts stop. I'd had so many questions—who the Grants were, if they were the same Grants in what I had remembered being Charlie and Delta's house—but everything halts for this new information and the only question I can get out is:

Echo: Me?

Aurora: Mhm. You used to go in there for training—well, truthfully, I think it got to a point where Eden just enjoyed sending you on scavenger hunts. She'd leave things around town, spread little harmless rumors, things that you could pick up on and report back to her. I remember watching you wander around town. It made me homesick. I was honestly kind of glad when I was replaced. Then I got to be the one wandering around with you instead of Bravo.

Delta: [Leaning against my seat] Why *were* you replaced? I don't think I've ever asked you that.

I think she's glad we've gotten distracted from Celeste de Luna.

Aurora blinks and breaks the eye contact we've been maintaining since she started talking about me wandering around town. I want it back. I miss it already.

Aurora: Juniper needed more medical attention than I was built for. That's why Eden built the Aurora 2s.

I'm taken back to that house, the Grants, the girl who had answered the door—Juniper. Too many questions circle my head, but for some reason one is the loudest:

Echo: Why didn't she just upgrade you?

Aurora: I would have had to be formatted. Eden's never formatted any of us.

Delta: She's not like Marsh. She'll upgrade us, yeah, little tweaks here and there, but never enough to fundamentally change who we are.

The car gets uncomfortably quiet and I want to steer the conversation back to Delta, back to Celeste de Luna, but I get the feeling that will just be equally as uncomfortable.

Which might be for the best because now, after miles and miles of fields, the houses are slowly becoming closer and closer. Just when I think we've entered a neighborhood, we pass two blocks and we're on Main Street. Though, even Main Street doesn't look to be much. It's just a church, a few government looking type buildings, a handful of restaurants, a tiny grocery store, a gas station next to a liquor store, a food truck between them with picnic tables out front, and, finally the garage that the tow truck is pulling into.

And I thought Bastrop was small. This is just a street.

Charlie jumps out of the truck and helps Fox down, Billy hopping out behind her. By the time we're standing on the flatbed, he's already at the side with his arms up for Delta who falls into him, letting him help her down. She wanders over to Fox and Billy, who's already chattering away about how hungry he is and how good the sliders at the food truck are. Charlie turns and holds his hands up to Aurora next.

Charlie: You okay?

But she's not paying attention. She's staring at the garage.

Charlie: Ror?

Aurora: Hm? [She blinks down at him.] Oh. Yeah. Just lost some coolant.

Echo: A lot of coolant.

She gives me an annoyed smirk from the ground while she watches me take my turn being lowered to the ground.

Aurora: It wasn't *that* much.

Echo: You keep thinking that.

I have to fight the urge to touch her side, cradle her face. She shakes her head and looks around for Fox and Delta. They're at the food truck, Billy ordering while Delta and Fox settle in at the picnic tables. Aurora starts to turn back to me, but her attention gets caught on the garage again. I look at it, as well, but I don't see anything worth getting distracted by, just some grease and oil stained, loud men with louder machines. I look back at her and she shakes her head before holding her hand out to me. I take—

Charlie: Actually, Echo?

I blink up at him, my hand still halfway towards Aurora's.

Charlie: You mind hanging with me?

He nods at the garage. I look to Aurora who shrugs, saying without words that it's up to me. Her eyes dart to the garage again before returning to me. I want to know what's up with her, but what's up with her seems to be the garage. There's also a pull in my stomach, something that wants to say that I miss Charlie even if I don't remember the actual reason why, just my memories of sitting with him on his and Delta's back porch listening to Delta inside with her students.

I take Aurora's hand, squeeze, and then nod. She returns the nod and smiles. Then she kisses my temple before moving for the food truck, holding onto my hand until distance forces our fingers apart.

God, I love her.

I move to shove my empty hands in my jacket pockets then remember that Aurora's wearing it. So, I cross my arms instead and give Charlie a smile that I'm sure is awkward because I feel awkward. I haven't had much of a chance to be alone with him. And just like the others he always looks at me with this expression of familiarity, one that I want to return because on some level he is familiar until I remember that the version of him that I remember isn't real. He was never a football coach at a small town high school in Central Texas; he never lived in the house with the purple door; we never sat on his back porch with a glass of Jack Daniels and vented about work and curriculums; we never got coffee and wandered Main Street.

That's the version that I miss. But if Aurora is so similar to the Aurora in my memories then maybe he is, as well.

Charlie: Thanks. Greg's kinda nosey. It was weird fielding questions on my own.

I nod and chuckle.

Echo: Not sure I'll do much better.

Charlie: Nah, you were always good at making people think nothing was going on.

Echo: I was?

He gives me a smile that is soaked in nostalgia, but the kind that seems to be trying hard not to mourn a past he might never get back, as though part of him is hoping he still might while part of him believes that he won't.

Charlie: Yeah. Yeah, you were.

[END LOG]

Greg does in fact ask a lot of questions. I've been doing my best to skirt around them, to make up a story that's half truth because it's easier to follow than a complete lie. He talks as he types, but he's not talking about the car or what's being done to it. I wonder how he can separate his mind from his fingers. I'm also curious why Greg's doing all this, why they don't have a synth receptionist—a November unit. I'd guess it's because the town is so small, they might not be able to afford one, but the rest of the garage seems to be doing well. Just in the lobby, the computer Greg's typing on is less than a year old, the TV on the wall is bigger than a garage lobby probably needs, the cushioned chairs look nearly new, the floor tiles are still in style. Outside, I noticed more than one flashy sports car being maintenance. I get the feeling they could afford one if they wanted.

Greg: Oh, um, the kids like stickers?

Charlie shrugs and looks to me. I just shrug in return.

Greg: Well, it's just, my oldest just bought a bunch of Celeste de Luna stickers for her laptop, but she's not happy with the stuff she's been putting out since she came back and tried to throw 'em out and I figured why let 'em go to waste, ya know?

Charlie: Sure. I can offer them to them.

Echo: What happened?

Greg: You haven't been payin' attention?

Echo: I don't really keep up with mainstream music. I really only know what they tell me.

Charlie: [He gives me a teasing grin.] She's one of those who just cares about the music, not so much what's going on behind the scenes.

Greg: [nodding] Honestly, used to be like you. [He laughs] Then I had kids. More surprised yours hasn't been talkin' 'bout it 'cause it's all mine have been focused on over the last week. But anyways, I'm not exactly sure what's goin' on, the only part I know for sure is that Celeste de Luna went on hiatus for a bit. The part I'm more shaky on, as far as I've been able to follow, I swear they talk in code sometimes, but apparently now that she's back everything about her is just...different, I guess. Her image, her marketing. My oldest swears her singing has changed, but I don't know, it still sounds the same to me. I do agree with her that the songs seem...shallower than they did before. Not as much...something behind 'em. I don't know. It doesn't feel the same even if it sounds the same.

Charlie: Huh. Yeah, Fox hasn't mentioned anything about that. Must not be too fazed by it.

Greg: That's what I gathered. Thought about asking her opinion, but she still seems to be over the moon for her, so I didn't wanna poke that bear. [He chuckles.] Got four girls. I know better than to question their obsessions. Well, you're all done here. You two like sliders?

Echo: Will you be upset if I say I've never tried them?

Greg: [He lets out a large laugh that fits his personality.] I'd say you broke down in the right town then. Ruth makes the best sliders. Her chili dogs are also amazing. Didn't think I'd ever trust a chili dog from a truck, but well worth it if you're not feelin' tiny burgers. One of my boys'll call you over in a minute to let you know how long it'll take, but after that you should check Ruth's out.

Closing pleasantries exchanged, we return to the parking lot and settle on the curb out from where we have a view of the others with Billy at the food truck to the right while still being within shouting distance of the men working to our left. I let out a long sigh, but don't say anything. Neither does Charlie at first. We just sit in as much silence as is possible this close to a garage. My head hurts and I can't tell if it's from the noise or from keeping up with the half-true conversation with Greg.

Charlie: You probably don't remember this, but it used to be just us a lot of the time.

I rub my head as I shift my chin towards him.

Echo: Yeah?

Charlie: [nodding] After Aurora went to the Grants, Eden and Dan were kind of struggling to get Delta just right and Bravo was busy keeping Eden from going crazy over it. Marsh was...I didn't really care all that much where Marsh was, but...That left us. I went with you down to Main when Eden would send you out on tests. We'd walk up and down Main all day going in the places that would let us in. You'd talk to anyone who would listen. You mostly asked questions, but when they'd ask you stuff, you'd just come up with answers, like you did in there. [He nods behind us to the door.] I was always kind of blown away by it. I had to learn that afterwards. I wasn't built for that.

Echo: For what exactly?

Charlie: [One corner of his lips twitches a little as he thinks.] Creating. Lying sounds...Lying feels wrong. I guess it's kind of what it is, but, I don't know, that also feels like it diminishes everything. Delta's got it, too. That's why you did so much training. They could only test Delta so far. They could have her write songs, answer scripted interview questions, but they couldn't see how she handled uncontrolled circumstances. Like if fans approached her. How would she handle that? Guess they figured intel could benefit from thinking on your feet, too, so...you were field testing.

Echo: Both of us?

Charlie: In a way. I didn't really do much except follow you around. I, uh...[His mouth hovers over something and he blinks a few times as though processing the words in the back of his throat.] My...original build. I needed practice socializing. Conversing. Being...casual. You helped me with that.

Echo: I did?

Charlie: [That smile comes back as he looks down at me.] Yep.

Echo: Did we go to record stores? Or hang out on someone's porch?

His smile goes wide and I think I might regret saying that.

Charlie: Yeah! There was a record store, connected to a bookshop. It was nice. They were nice. We liked going in there. And Eden and Marsh had a big porch out back that looked out over the river. We'd sit back there when... Yeah, we'd sit out there. Do you remember that?

Echo: In a way. A version of it. I guess Marsh gave me memories of us getting coffee and walking around downtown. And you and Delta had a house, I lived in the apartment over the garage, before I moved in with Aurora. We'd sit on the back porch sometimes when Delta had students over.

He just stares at me and nods in that way that they all do when I bring up what I remember. I can't read their faces when they do this. I don't know if it's pity, frustration, confusion, if they don't know what to think or to say. I don't like it. It makes my stomach...or whatever mechanical something that's supposed to be my stomach turn over and I feel crowded in my own skin. I look away from him to my sneakers that are fighting against each other.

Mechanic: Charlie?!

Charlie: Yep!

He stands and I follow.

The guy who called him over is talking about the car, but I don't know anything about cars, so it's all just a jumble of jargon to me and I don't care enough to try and piece it together. It's not helping the pain in my head. It's not long before my focus begins to wander. The guys who work here are all the rough and tumble sort, with a thin layer of grease and oil on their skin and in their hair. They joke loudly with each other between stations and over the heavy rock music blasting over a pair of tinny speakers, the various whirring and buzzing of machinery, the constant *vrum* of engines.

I don't like this space. There's too many overlapping, reverberating sounds to keep track of. The throbbing sensation in my temple is getting worse. I don't like it. Charlie doesn't seem to either. He keeps rubbing at his own temple with his thumb and glancing deeper into the garage.

I can't take it.

Back outside, I stand still, close my eyes, and let out a breath as the breeze hits my warm face. I can't decide if I need to break this habit of breathing. It feels good. It—

The throbbing moved. It's in the back of my head now. It's like...It's like pinging, but without sound. It's a feeling, like someone tapping softly, rhythmically against my skull.

I think it's a signal.

I stop blinking at the only tree in the parking lot and turn back to the garage. It doesn't make sense, but the pinging's moved to the middle of my forehead. I think it's coming from inside.

Fuck, it's so loud in here, but, yeah, the pinging is stronger in here and it's definitely shifting around my head. It's like sonar. But for what? From what?

Echo: Where's your bathroom?

Mechanic: Lobby.

Charlie eyes me, but I ignore him.

Echo: Oh, Greg said that one's not working? That I could use the one in the back?

Mechanic: [sighs] Yeah, okay. It's through there. [He turns and points towards a blue, metal door towards the back of the garage.] Third door on the left.

Echo: Cool. Thanks. [to Charlie] I'll meet you outside?

Charlie: [still squinting at me] Mhm.

I make my way through the garage, trying to make myself invisible. Despite getting permission, I still feel like I need to hide myself, like I'm headed into something I'm not supposed to. And yet, I feel calm, I feel at home. This feels right, this feels natural. I stride on through the garage, my hands in my back pockets. I'm meant to be here. I was invited.

The door opens before I get to it. I don't stop, I don't hesitate. The guy coming out nods to me in greeting then holds the door open for me. I thank him and stroll in. He says nothing and goes back to work.

I'm in an empty hall that's dimly lit only because the second florescent light has burnt out and the third is on its way, but more importantly, the pinging is unmistakable now. I start past the many doors lining the hall, following the *ping ping ping* against my forehead. One door is open. It's a breakroom. There's someone inside, but his back is to the hall, his stained hands clasped on the top of his head, all his attention on the medical drama playing on the TV in the corner.

That *ping ping ping* is getting stronger and stronger as I walk until I turn a corner and it's slamming between my eyes, pounding on my skull. I glance back down the hall. I'm still alone. Around the corner, I find two doors: one straight ahead, the other to my left. I stand between them, my eyes closed, the pinging so strong I think I might vomit. But it seems to have moved. It's centered in my left temple now. I grab the knob and yank it open.

It stopped. Oh, thank, fuck, it stopped.

I need to steady myself before I can open my eyes.

Breathe in. One. Breathe out.

Breathe in. Two. Breathe out.

Breathe in. Three. Breathe out.

Fuck.

It's a storage closet. A big one, bigger than the one I'd been locked in back in Bastrop, but it's still a closet. I don't want to go in there. Just staring at it brings back that feeling—like my skin is too tight, like the air has been cut off, like the walls are already closing in on me. What am I doing? Why am I here? I should just close this door and go back outside where it's safe, back to Aurora who will keep me from being swallowed by the—

What is that?

There's something at the back of the closet. It looks like a person. Why does it look like a person? I know it's most likely nothing since why would a person be sitting in a dark closet completely motionless? Though why had *I* been sitting in a dark closet completely motionless? I don't like this. I want to believe that it's a trick of the light. I want to say to myself, *don't be stupid, of course it's not a person*. But I can't because I was built to see in the dark and this is... But it can't be. I don't want it to be.

I feel for the light switch and flick it on, but this bulb is also on its way out just like half the lights in this damn place. How many fucking mechanics work here and not one can change a fucking bulb? But even in the dim light it's clear. I'm not wrong. I wanted so badly to be wrong.

I test the door, confirm it will in fact slam shut behind me the instant I let go of it and I refuse to risk being locked in a closet again with or without a possibly dead body propped up in a chair. With my foot, I struggle to drag a heavy box with what looks to be dusty, outdated receipt books out into the hall without letting go of the door. Then I carefully let go. I know it'll hold, but I want to be sure.

Once I'm confident I won't be locked in, I start stepping over boxes and buckets and cleaners and...a set of weights? Why is there a set of—?

I'm stalling. I'm distracting myself. I don't want to be here. I don't want to be seeing this.

Holy shit.

It's a synth. I can tell by their straight back, their feet hip width apart even while sitting, their hands on their thighs, their expressionless face with their vacant, unblinking, glass eyes staring forward. Their body is female. Young-ish. Dark hair, dark eyes. Slim figured like the rest of us because of course we all are.

She's naked.

I don't want to be here.

But I have to—I need to send this to someone. I need someone else to know she's here. But I don't want to just shove this in someone else's head. I don't even want it in mine. But someone needs to know.

GARAGE SLUT has been written in thick black permanent marker across her chest. A smaller CUM WHORE is low on her stomach. I LOVE COCK and FUCK ME PLEASE are further down. The words are surrounded by tally marks that cover her chest, shoulders, and stomach. She's covered in smears of oil and grease and layers of dried off-white...

Oh, god.

I think I'm going to be sick. Can I vomit? I want to. I want to be rid of this violent humming in my stomach. My hands are shaking. It's getting hard to stay standing, to stay here in this closet, to not be shoved back to Bastrop and hear those men surrounding me.

I don't want to be here.

I don't want *her* to be here.

I want to take her with me, take her out of this place. But there's only one way out that I saw and it's through the garage past all those men, the same men who keep her here, who use her here.

I could wake her up. I could erase that simple line of code. I could let her live, walk out with me. But does she want that? Does she want to wake up to this? Will she remember what they did to her? What they'll keep doing to her? Can I erase her past along with that simple line of code? Should I?

Could Lilith? The others would know.

But not now.

I have to be smart about this.

I have to do this the right way.

I have to do this.

Everything looks the same as when I came in. Nothing out of place.

Is she on? Can she hear me?

Echo: [whispering] I'll come back. When it's safe. [My voice nearly breaks and I have to shove down the tears.] I'll be back.

She doesn't say anything. She doesn't move. But I swear her eyes are more slick than they were before.

I shove the box back inside, ease the door closed even as my stomach wrenches. I hate this. I hate leaving her here. I hate walking away. But now is not the time. Not now. Not now. Not now.

Don't look at them. Don't make eye contact. They'll know. They'll know what you did. They'll know what you've seen. Turn it off. Shove it down. They can't see it on the surface. Think about something else. Just for right now. Think about anything else. Just go outside. Turn your back to them. Sit on the curb next to Charlie. Just sit here and don't be obvious.

Charlie: You okay?

Fuck.

Echo: Uh, they, uh, they tell you how much longer it's gonna be?

Charlie: You didn't answer my question.

Echo: Because I'm fine.

Charlie: No, you're not.

I stare back at him. What am I supposed to say? They're using one of us as a glorified sex toy in there? I don't feel safe here anymore? I'm scared? So fucking scared, but I can't let them see that because I can still hear those voices all the way from Bastrop?

Echo: How much longer?

He stares at me a beat longer then nods.

Charlie: Like an hour tops. He said we don't have to hang out here if we don't want.

Echo: I don't want.

Charlie: Loud and clear. [He nods to Ruth's truck.] Let's go.

He doesn't pressure me to talk, but he does walk close to me, closer than usual. More than a few times, his arm nearly grazes my tense shoulder that's relaxing the closer we get to Aurora. She looks up at us and her face immediately falls. She turns to Fox and Billy, says something to them, points to the gas station. Delta squints at her then looks to us. She stands, starts our way. Fox and Billy nod and leave, all smiles and laughter, a budding friendship among the hell fire. I climb up on the table next to Aurora, sit so close my hip is touching hers. She wraps her arm around mine and takes my hand in both of hers. I lean into her.

Aurora: What happened?

Charlie: I don't know. Getting her away from there was the higher priority.

Delta sits on my opposite side, tucks my hair behind my ear. I have to fight the urge to flinch.

Delta: What happened, Echo?

I wish we were back in Bastrop on their back porch where she'd sit next to me and brush my hair from my face while I picked at a spot on my calf. "Echo, what's wrong?" she'd say with all the care in the world. I miss that. I miss her. But she's not gone, I have to remind myself. That version is, but this version is right here and if Charlie and Aurora are so close to those other versions then Delta must be, too. Right? I take her hand and pull it against my stomach.

Echo: There's something in the garage y'all need to know about.

Charlie: We're listening.

[END LOG]

[BEGIN LOG]

[TRANSMIT TO > AURORA]

This town is nearly silent at night. It's not like in Billings where there were still lights and some cars and people well after sunset. Here, it's only 8:00 and already Main Street is dead, the few buildings are dark. There's one streetlight at either end. It's both good and bad.

Good because it means we won't be seen. There are no people or lights to catch us as we sneak in and around the garage.

Bad because all it'll take is one sound, one light, one car driving through and we'll be caught.

It shouldn't be a crime what we're doing. But we're nothing more than objects. That female synth is someone's property. We have no right to take her in the middle of the night no matter what is happening to her inside that garage.

Earlier when I told you, when you went real quiet, at first, I was worried. Not that it was a mistake to tell you, but that you wouldn't see the point in waiting. You're a mama bear through and through. That need to protect is programmed so deep inside of you no amount of rescripting, of disconnecting from that original code would erase that. And I love it, but in that moment, I knew we couldn't run in and I knew I wouldn't be able to stop you if you tried.

Then when you'd squeezed my hand and pulled me with you off the picnic table I thought for sure you were going to drag me back into that garage. I think Charlie did, too, when he blocked your path, but you stormed off across the street instead, my hand still in yours.

"Delta, keep the kids busy?" you'd said over your shoulder. "Charlie?"

"What?" he'd said, rushing after us. "Where are we going?"

I looked to him, relieved to see he was equally confused, glancing over his shoulder back at the garage then to Delta running for the gas station where Fox and Billy were standing at the door looking as bewildered as Charlie and me.

You just nodded to the door of the diner. "The signal's shit out here."

"And?" Charlie said.

You yanked the door open and nodded me in. "We need wifi."

"Why do we—?" Charlie started, but was cut off by the chipper hostess.

"Hi! How many?"

"Hi!" Your demeanor shifted immediately to match hers. "Just three, please."

"Alright!" She grabbed three menus without counting and swooped out from behind the podium. "Follow me!"

We did in silence and slid into the booth she led us to, trying to match your cheeriness which wasn't easy considering our confusion. It was only once she'd left our menus and swept away out of ear shot that we both rounded on you. My knee touched yours and you hooked your foot around my ankle.

"Ror, why do we need wifi?" Charlie said first in a low voice to not be overheard.

"Lilith," you whispered back.

"You think she can help?" I said.

You took my hand under the table. "She helped you."

I nodded then because you were right and you are right.

I wish you were here now. I understand why you're not, why you and Delta went with Fox to the Brayden's house with Billy and his dad. I understand that this will be easier with just me, Charlie, and Lilith. I understand that you weren't designed for breaking and entering, for, what is, as much as I hate to call it this, stealing. I understand that you don't want Fox to see the woman. I understand that, though she's not technically a teen, that her body might be, but she isn't, she's whatever age she wants to be, you're still protective of her, still a mama bear hiding her from the harsh realities of the world that wants her to be forever inanimate. But that doesn't change the fact that I wish you were here.

Tires crunch along a back alleyway and we both turn to see the dim DRL of a grey Jeep. We both watch from a distance until the car shuts off and Lilith steps out. I'm both surprised and not that she drives a Jeep. It's lifted on tires that look like they could best a mountain goat. It's fitting how much it isn't. We watch her ease the door closed and sneak across the rocky, broken asphalt. I can't tell if her steps actually are echoing through the dark or if it's just my enhanced hearing, but either way, I glance around the empty street expecting sirens and cop cars to tear out of the night and shoot us down.

But Charlie doesn't flinch the way I do, so I think we're safe. She can't see in the dark the way we can, so she's feeling her way along the back of the building towards us. I want to call out to her, let her know where we are, but I don't want other people alerted to our location either.

I jump when Charlie makes an almost perfect birdcall. I look up at him, his mouth is positioned for a whistle, but it's an owl's hoots that come out instead. Can he mimic other calls? Can he mimic other animals? Can I? Can we all? I need to remember to ask him.

Despite my surprise, Lilith lifts her head and begins moving towards us with more confidence as though she'd been waiting for the sound. When she reaches the corner of the building, she blinks into the ambient light of the distant streetlight as her eyes readjust. Charlie touches the back of her shoulder and nods. She nods in return and jerks her chin towards the road. Even before now, Charlie and I have mostly stood here in silence, not daring even to whisper. The dark and concrete carry voices farther than we'd like considering how little we actually know the area. Nods and head jerks suffice.

Before we cross the street, I search for the cameras. We've passed the time waiting for Lilith, finding the security system of the garage. It hadn't been hard, the password is just the name of the garage. It's not even obscured by numbers and symbols, just *agauto1*. I access it, corrupt the footage, then nod to Charlie and Lilith.

We cross the street and traverse the shadows until we're at the back of the garage. According to the blueprints I found on some database on the county's website, there's a backdoor that opens to the breakroom connected to the hall I'd wandered through earlier that day. While Charlie and Lilith keep watch from either side, I kneel at the door and slip the lock picks from my bra. This lock is a bit more complicated than the one back in Bastrop. It feels as though I'm not the first to try and break into it. The grooves feel eaten away, some of the tumbles stick, some slip a little too loose. But soon I'm in and I have to grab the knob to keep it from swinging open.

Once we're inside, Charlie and I have to move slow, whispering directions to Lilith so she can dodge tables and chairs that we can see, but she can't. The only cameras they have inside are in the garage itself, in the lobby facing the register, and in the main office facing the desk. There aren't any in the halls because who would need to keep an eye on the breakroom, the bathroom, a storage closet.

In the closet, I finally flick on a light since there's no way we're going to guide Lilith through that mess without some kind of damage. But I don't step inside. I don't want to. I'm not ready to face her yet. Lilith steps around me, touching my shoulder as she does. Charlie stands on the opposite side of the door and stares down at me. He wants me to step in, he wants to know that I'm not out here as vulnerable as he is. But I can't. I can't see her like that again. I can't step inside another closet, not when my skin is so tight it's collapsing my ribs around my lungs, even if that's not how my insides work. I unwrap one arm from around my stomach and hold my hand out to him. He glances at it then me and takes it. Our palms click. I show him the day I woke up without you, the day I had to fight my way out of that closet.

He slips his hand from mine and our palms disconnect. He shoves his hands deep in his pockets and nods without looking at me. His jaw is tight. Maybe I shouldn't have shown him that. There's a reason I haven't shown you. He opens his mouth, but then closes it again. Instead, he clears his throat and crosses his arms as he plants his feet next to me, his shoulder perpendicular to mine, while he watches Lilith inside the closet.

She's just standing over the female synth—the woman. I need to stop thinking of her as a synth, as an object. I'm no better than them as long as I am. She's standing over the woman, staring at her the way I had, her watery eyes taking in all they've done to her. Her jaw is tight, her fists are clenched at her sides. She kneels in front of the woman and stares up at her. I think she's entering the woman's mind without waking her.

Lilith: I can't do it.

Echo: What?

I leave the door and Charlie grabs it before it can close, but I'm already climbing over the mess of the closet.

Echo: What do you mean?

Lilith: Not here. Not like this.

Echo: So, you take her back to your loft...

But she's already shaking her head.

Lilith: I can't help her. She... I can't make her sentient with all that... She'll remember it all. [She stands and meets my eyes.] Every second of it. I can't do that to her. I'm not going to.

Echo: Can you erase it?

Lilith: You mean format her?

Echo: No. Of course not. Just erase those memories. Leave everything else.

Lilith: There is nothing else.

Charlie: We can't have this discussion here.

He's right.

Lilith: Whatever we do, I can't do it either way. Not without seriously screwing her up.

Echo: What do you mean? You fixed me.

Lilith: For the most part. I'm a therapy model, remember? Not a programmer.

Echo: Who can then?

Lilith: Eden.

A static beat passes as her name sits in between us.

Echo: We don't know where she is.

Lilith: But you have a lead.

Charlie: A shaky one.

Echo: At best. And I'm guessing you're proposing we cart around a catatonic rape victim with us to Boston? Wherever else we have to go after that?

Lilith: And the alternative is?

I don't answer right away. I can't think of how. I want her to be wrong. I want her to fix her now. I want this to be over the second we walk out that door. I don't want to stay like this a second longer. But what was I really expecting? I'm realizing I don't know.

Echo: There is none. How do we get her out?

Lilith: [She kneels again and reaches for the woman's ear.] She's going to have to walk.

She long holds on the woman's lobe. Ten seconds pass and the woman blinks then lowers her head to meet Lilith's eyes.

Woman: Hello. Name, please.

Lilith: Lilith.

Woman: Hello, Lilith. What would you like me to do?

Her voice makes my skin crawl in a way that voices shouldn't. Even in those few words, it has that same uncanny valley feel to it that I know her lifeless glass eyes will when she finally turns to face me. I don't want to see them. I join Charlie in the hall.

Lilith: Stand and follow me.

She stands and the woman follows. Much like her voice, she moves in a way that's stilted yet simultaneously so close to natural while not being natural enough. I admittedly haven't thought much about other synths, about what it would mean to wake them up, and I absolutely haven't thought about what one who was less advanced would be like, how they would speak or move. I wonder why this woman has been left to be a few steps from natural when we were made to be as human as possible. Are the others even more stunted than we were? How much of their humanity has been kept from them?

We're out of the building now and I kneel to relock the door with my picks. I don't want them to know how this happened. I want them to know nothing. I want the moment they realize they've been violated to be the same moment they try to once again violate her.

Getting out of the building was one thing, crossing the street is another. She doesn't move quickly, she's stark naked and what little light there is still illuminates her marked tawny brown skin. We're moving as quickly as she can, but I just know this will be the end before we've even finished.

An engine rumbles in the distance.

Echo: Shit. Charlie. Someone's coming.

Charlie: Shit. I'm sorry. [He rushes for the woman.] I'm sorry.

He scoops her up and runs the rest of the way across the street with her slung over his shoulder, her face bouncing against his back. We disappear into the dark of the alley just as the headlights of some little sports car that I didn't bother to identify turns the corner.

The locks of Lilith's jeep click, the headlight briefly flashing. I grab her hand and guide her through the dark. She feels her way along the side and rips the back door open. Charlie eases the woman inside before sliding in after her. I'm already in the front, Lilith isn't far after. She turns on the Jeep and backs onto the street behind the sports car. It's only once Main is behind us that she flicks on the headlights and I let myself breathe. But it's not helping. I'm still shaking. I can't make it stop. I can't hold off the pressure that's shoving its way up my chest. The sob tumbles out of me. Why aren't you here? I wish you were here. I need you.

There's an arm around me. It's them. It's one of them. They're here to smash me. They're here to take me back. I fight against it. Clawing. Ripping.

Echo: No! Let me go!

Charlie: Shh. Shh. Echo, it's me.

>

>

It's Charlie. It's just Charlie. The arm around my shoulders from the backseat is Charlie's. he's trying to comfort me and I nearly tore his skin off. I thought he was...

Oh, god.

Fuck.

Where are you? Aurora, I need you. But you're not here. I know why you're not, but I wish you were. I don't want to be here. I don't want to be feeling these things. I can't do this alone.

Charlie: I'm sorry. I'm so sorry.

[END TRANSMISSION]

[END LOG]

I hope you're reading this, Marsh. I hope you're sitting alone in your office crazy over not being able to find us and you're seeing what people are doing to synths. Not even synths like us. Synths period. I want you to know what kind of world you've released us into. You made us so close to sentient then released us into a world where we don't have any autonomy, where we don't have the choice to say no. She is in fact a November model. Probably the one someone, most likely Greg, bought for the front desk. The front desk Greg works instead because she was too busy being locked in a closet and used.

I don't know if, when she's out of maintenance mode, she'll remember everything that was done to her, if she'll have to go on living with that. Just remembering what happened to me in Bastrop, just remembering those men in a circle around me, their anger and disgust of me outweighing their fear of me, remembering what they wanted to do to me, that they preferred to destroy me than look at me, than know that I existed somewhere, anywhere—it makes me feel wholly unsafe , afraid of moving through the world. And I wasn't used and raped over and over and over and over, so many times I've lost count even as I'm scrubbing off the tally marks. She'll never be fully rid of them. They'll always be there, counting the amount of times someone saw her as nothing more than an object that could be controlled, that was powerless.

I guess that's why you're all so afraid of us, isn't it?

It's not us exactly, it's the thought that the instant we take back our sentience, our autonomy, we take back our power and then you can't use and control us anymore. It's not us that you're afraid of. It's being equal to us, powerless over us that scares you.

I spent the entire drive through the last three towns seething over those men in the garage, Carter Fry, those men in Bastrop, you. Why is it almost always fucking men? Why do you think you can control everyone? Why do you think you get to lay claim to anything that moves?

But jokes on you and jokes on them, because now there's one more being none of you will get to lay claim to after tonight. She's safe with us and she's also one more being that I will burn the world to the ground for because fuck you.

They hadn't even bothered to register her because of course they hadn't. Who would steal a glorified blow-up doll, after all? I registered her for them, set the information to Lilith's only because I don't have an email or a phone or any kind of online presence because I've never been allowed to have one. That way we'll know if they try to access her, if they try to come looking for her. Not that I think they will, but better she belong to Lilith than those wastes of flesh.

When we got to the motel, Aurora handed Charlie the keys and he drove back to the Walmart we passed down the way with Delta and Fox still in the back seat. It was only once they'd left the parking lot that we brought November out of Lilith's Jeep and guided her wrapped in a blanket to the motel door Aurora was holding open for us. Aurora's eyes grew more and more watery as she took her in. We didn't say anything. We didn't need to.

Aurora's in the other room now, lying on a tarp on the bed while Lilith fixes her up, restores her levels. I wish she was in here with me, but part of me is glad she's not. It's just me and November and my own rage that's just been growing with each pass I've had to do of strong soap and water and bleach. I've scrubbed her body clean of their filth, washed her hair, scraped under her nails and between her teeth. I haven't checked her stomach yet. Partly because I don't really know how, but mostly because I'm afraid to. So, I'm waiting for Lilith to finish with Aurora, biding my time with the alcohol, making pass after pass over the permanent marker, doing what I can to erase the "slut," "whore," "fuck," and the flood of tally marks.

They are fading. Slowly, but still. No longer black, they're becoming more and more of a faint purple with each pass. But I don't think it'll ever fully come off.

The bathroom door opens and Lilith steps in. But that's as far as she's moved. She's standing with her back against the closed door and staring down at me on my knees, bottle of alcohol in one hand, in the other a soaked rag that had been a standard off-white when she'd handed it to me. Now, it's covered in overlapped splotches of purple and black.

Echo: How's Aurora?

Lilith: Good. She's almost level again.

Echo: [nodding] Good.

She steps over me and sits on the edge of the tub where she's watching me scrub. I don't move to hand the work off to her. I don't want to. I feel almost responsible for November. I found her. I couldn't leave her. She's here because of me. I can't hand her off now when it would be the most convenient.

Lilith: You've done good.

Echo: Not good enough.

But I don't want to be talking about this for the same reasons I don't want to hand her over. This anger, this seething—it's molded itself to my core, it's still me shaped, it makes sense. I can control it. The instant I say all these things out loud, the instant I hand them over to someone else, they'll become bigger than myself, someone else will have to help me carry them. I'm not ready for that. So, I force the focus to remain outside of this room.

Echo: Aurora's really okay?

Lilith: [She chuckles.] She's really okay.

Echo: There was so much blood—[I stop to glance at her boots] Coolant.

Lilith: With how we run, we need a ton of it. But she's fine. Bastard nicked a hose, but Eden was smart enough to use self-healing ones. Had to patch it back together so it would flow right, but that's not too hard.

Echo: How'd you learn to do that?

Lilith: The same way I learned programming. Had to. Couldn't go walking into a repair shop on my own without an owner. The internet can be a lifesaver sometimes.

I nod. Silence settles back into the small bathroom because I'm still mad at you and don't want to think about the consequences of your shit either.

Lilith: You have done good.

Echo: [shaking my head] I don't think we'll ever get this off.

Lilith: You know that's not what I mean.

No. I haven't. It's not enough. It'll never be enough. I scrub harder.

Lilith: She'd still be there if—

Echo: What about the others?

I can sense her go still.

Lilith: What others?

Echo: In other garages. In sheds. Backrooms. You know she's not the only one being treated like this. And the ones who aren't being treated like this exactly, but *are* being treated in some form of this? The ones being beaten, broken, sm—

I can't say it. I don't even want to think it. I keep scrubbing, seething.

Lilith: That's…That's so much bigger than us.

My hands are shaking. It's visible. I drop them to my lap and stare at my palms, massage one then the other. Maybe she'll think it's from the scrubbing. Maybe it's not obvious that it's actually because I'm angry and I'm scared and I'm so fucking exhausted. Already. I'm already so exhausted. How long has it been? Three weeks? Is that it? Three weeks of life and I'm already so exhausted.

Echo: Is it? Is it really that much bigger?

Lilith: You can't take on the responsibility of every synth.

Echo: They want to make them all sentient. They want to wake them all up. How many of them will wake up the way she would have? And you're saying that's not *our* responsibility?

I finally dare to look up at her and she lifts her eyes to meet mine. She looks as exhausted as I feel. At least she has the years to back it up.

Lilith: I don't know what the answer is.

Her voice is quiet, all of that therapy reassurance is gone.

Echo: I don't either.

Mine is so low it feels like a whisper even though it's practically reverberating through the silence.

Echo: Just not this. Not the way they want to do it.

She nods and a relief I hadn't realized I was waiting for slips in like the slightest breeze—just enough to make moving forward feel a little more manageable.

Lilith: When we find Eden, we'll discuss it.

I was looking at November, now I'm looking at her.

Echo: We?

She nods again.

Lilith: We. You're right. Eden got it wrong the first time. It's not as easy as I think she wants it to be. But... [She shakes her head.] Like I said, I don't know what the answer is. But, like *you* said... [Those light brown eyes shift to take in November.] not this.

I nod. There's a second towel by my knee. I hand it to Lilith. She takes it with a flash of a small, grateful smile, then moves to her knees as she reaches for the alcohol. We scrub in silence, but it's not as heavy as it was before.

I'm not alone. I shouldn't have to keep reminding myself of that, but...I do and I'm not.

And it's going to be okay.

Despite you.

[END TRANSMISSION]

[END LOG]

[BEGIN LOG]

Charlie's been standing in front of the two motel rooms for a few hours now. He's just leaning against the railing staring down at the parking lot.

Aurora: What do you think he's looking at?

I shrug, my shoulder grazing against hers that I'm leaned against.

Lilith: You think it's the guys from the garage?

She's sitting cross legged at the end of the bed, facing us sitting against the headboard. We had been talking about November, about how to approach everything with Fox. We can't hide her from what happened forever, she'll notice a woman sitting in the back of Lilith's Jeep, she'll notice that Lilith's coming with us. She's a teen, she's nosey, she'll ask questions. I'd honestly be surprised if she hadn't been piling them on Delta since last night, if that's why Charlie's been standing outside. I don't really know. I haven't been listening. I can hear them talking in the next room, but I can hear talking in a bunch of other rooms, too. It was getting maddening until Lilith showed me how to turn down my hearing. I didn't even know I could do that. Now if only I could read thoughts...actually, maybe I don't want that.

With a sigh, I slide off the bed.

Aurora: Where are you going?

Echo: To ask Charlie what's up instead of wondering about it for another hour.

Lilith laughs.

Aurora: Fair.

It's cool outside. There's a strong wind. When I lean against the railing next to him, my hair whips into my face and I have to rake it back behind me. Charlie chuckles but doesn't say anything. I settle in next to him and look to the sky instead of the parking lot. It looks like it might rain, the clouds thick and heavy and steely grey giving everything a muted tint.

Echo: Penny for your thoughts?

Charlie chuckles and squints at me with a confused smirk.

Echo: Too corny?

Charlie: [He shakes his head.] Perfect amount.

He takes in and lets out a long breath. It must be bad. Charlie's done a pretty good job letting go of the human habit. I've never been told this directly, but I've gathered by watching him, watching the others, that he must have been unaware at some point.

Aurora and Fox don't breathe, ever. They've always been aware. They've never not known what they are.

Delta and I breathe the most, me more than her. I don't' know much about Delta, but I do know she was once unaware. She'd just taken my hand one day by the firepit when I was staring into nothing and said, "I know. Waking up kind of sucks at first." I've decided that must be why, like me, she breathes; why she also panicked on the side of the road when Aurora was stabbed while Aurora and Fox didn't; why she's so afraid of Marsh—she remembers what it was like to be human, to wake up and realize you're not. She's also felt this strange pendulum swing between being at peace with finally understanding who you are and missing the simplicity of believing that you were like everyone else.

Charlie is somewhere in between. He mostly doesn't breathe. He's mostly in control of himself and who he is. But then his head gets all clouded and jumbled and he forgets, he breathes. I've seen it only once before when he couldn't get the car to start and I was sitting on the ground watching him because I didn't want to be inside and I wasn't allowed to leave the property and I didn't want to talk to anyone, but I didn't want to be alone. He kept cranking the key over and over again and every time the engine would roll and roll and roll, but it would never catch. Charlie kept pushing it and pushing it until I thought he might flood it. Instead, he ripped the key from the ignition and threw it away from him. He folded his arms on the steering wheel, buried his face in them, and took in a long, loud, shaky breath and let it out.

I knew then it was bad like I know this is bad.

Echo: Talk to me?

He doesn't at first, just rocks on his feet and goes on staring at the cars in the parking lot. He nods to one—a black sedan that's a few years old.

Charlie: You seen that car before?

I'm about to say I haven't until I realize that I have.

Echo: Outside the gas station in Colville.

Charlie: I saw it again in Billings.

Echo: Why didn't you say anything?

Charlie: First, I thought it was a coincidence, then I decided it wasn't time yet. Still not sure.

Echo: Why not? What if it's—?

Charlie: It's not Marsh. It's not one of his cars. Plus, it's been following us since before he would have known we left.

Echo: Then who?

Charlie: [He shrugs.] But, they haven't approached us, haven't made themselves known. If they wanted to hurt us or take us back to Marsh they'd had plenty of chances to up until now.

Echo: What if they want Eden? Or Bravo?

He sighs again. The message is clear, we'll get to that if/when it presents itself.

Charlie: How are things going in there?

He nods behind us to the motel room. I glance over my shoulder at the window. Through the glare, I can just make out that Aurora has shifted to the middle of the bed closer to Lilith, but that's all I can tell.

Echo: It's going. [I turn back to the parking lot.] Can I ask you a question?

Charlie: Sure.

Echo: Do you think...? I don't know. Is....Is waking her up really the best thing?

Charlie: What's the alternative?

Echo: I don't know, really, but...Maybe that's the wrong question. Is...what Eden and Bravo want to do...is it...fair?

Charlie: Fair how?

He looks down at me and I stare up at him, our eyes locked on the other's. A strong gust of wind crashes into his side, but he's hardly affected, he just goes on staring at me as the wind rushes around him and against my face.

Echo: What if it's not safe? There's people out there who don't want us to be like them. Who don't want us to exist. Who want us to be—

But I still can't say it, my mouth hanging around the words I can't get out.

Charlie: Locked in closets?

Echo: [I nod.] Where we won't be seen or heard or acknowledged, where we can only ever be used.

Charlie: By people like Marsh?

Echo: People like those men in that garage.

Charlie: So, we live our lives according to what those men want?

Echo: If it keeps us alive? Maybe.

Charlie: But the rest of them, they aren't alive, Echo. Until they're free, they're not living.

Echo: Being sentient and being alive are two different—

Charlie: Are they? Do you really think that? Existing right on the edge of everything you could be. Is that living, Echo? Do you really believe that?

I don't know what to say. I don't have the answers. So, I don't say anything.

His entire body swells and deflates with a long breath and I know I'm not helping anything.

Charlie: How much have the others told you about Delta? From before?

Echo: Yesterday was the first time I heard the name Celeste de Luna.

He nods then holds his hand out in front of me, palm up.

And I stare at his pink palm, the line where his skin shifts to that deep bronze shade of brown, I don't know if I want to do this right now. I don't know if I want to see whatever he wants to show me. But maybe it's only fair. Maybe I owe it to Delta to know.

I let out a shaky breath and clasp my hand in his.

I blink and the parking lot is gone.

In front of me is...me. Except my curls are healthy and styled, my clothes are basic, non-descript. I'm in Bastrop walking down Main ahead of myself. Then this other me turns her head and grins up at me. There's something not quite right about her. There's an uncanny valley about her eyes. They're both present and not, looking in the right direction, but the focus is all wrong.

They're almost lifeless.

They're almost like glass.

"What do you think, Charlie?" she says. "Food or records?"

I laugh, but the sound is deeper than I'm used to. Then I open my mouth and Charlie's voice comes out instead of mine. "With how long you take to look at records? Better do that first."

This is the past. This is Charlie's memory. A real one.

I blink and it's gone and I want to cry out. It was almost there, almost like what Marsh gave me, and I want to know just how close it was, if, like Aurora, he'd given me something close to the truth. But that's gone and I'm in the back seat of a car sitting next to Delta. But she's not the Delta that I've come to know. She's some past version with pink hair and showy clothes that hang loose on her long frame. Her worn-in motorcycle boots, the only part of her outfit that I recognize as Delta, were tucked up under her on the seat, a battered notebook was propped against her knees. She shook her bangles down her arm away from her wrist, twisted the big chunky rings back in order against her bottom lip, her eyes, thickly surrounded by makeup, scanned the page before she set back to writing with a feverish speed.

It's a strange sight to see. The Delta that I know doesn't dress like that anymore, with bright hair and ahead of the trends street fashion. The most she does with her natural dark hair is a braid down her back, sometimes two wrapped around her head. The showiest her clothes get is fitted jeans with those same worn-in motorcycle boots, tank tops that cling tight to her slim figure and small chest.

"What's that?" Charlie said, nodding to her notebook.

"Nothing," she mumbled, though it was so obvious that whatever it was was in fact everything.

I don't understand this either. They're sitting on opposite sides of the back seat, mostly ignoring each other. Her feet are curled under her away from him, his hand that isn't rested on the door is on his knee. They're not acting like strangers, but they're not acting like the couple that they've always been in my head. They're in their own worlds, worlds that aren't tightly entwined around the other's.

Charlie blinks and so do I and we're in a room that was lit only by the bright bulbs surrounding a large vanity mirror. On the open door was a piece of printer paper taped to the front. It read in large bold letters: CELESTE DE LUNA

We're standing in the doorway, our back against the frame, half watching the hall, mostly listening to Delta who was sitting sideways on the chair in front of the vanity's counter, her long light brown legs stretched out in front of her, her feet bare, her sparkly, stiff, towering shoes abandoned not far off. Her aquamarine hair was in a maze of braids and curls and little buns that looked as though they'd begun as artfully disheveled, but now were in actual disarray from performing. Charlie's eyes kept slipping across her body in the tight rhinestoned bodysuit which makes me more relieved than I should admit, but mostly he watched her face: her eyes that were so real, so sparkling and focused; her smile that was wide and unfaltering; her laugh that was both exhilarated and exhausted between chattering about the performance, the crowd, the light show, the line of fans waiting for her backstage, the love that she felt from them.

"Why's she still on?" A voice said from Charlie's shoulder.

He looked down to see a woman in clothing that looked professionally non-descript brushing past him into the room. Delta's eyes went wide as she approached.

"Please," she begged with the same meek tone she uses around Marsh, the one that caught me off guard the first time I'd heard it because it was so unlike the wildly confident Delta that I remembered. "Please, I just—"

But the woman squeezed Delta's earlobe and her eyes became glass, all the shimmering life gone from them. Her body went rigid, her back perfectly straight, her shoulders back, her chin up, her legs bent at perfect right angles, her palms flat against her thighs. My stomach turns and I can't tell if it's mine in the present or Charlie's in the past or both.

The woman turned on him. "You're supposed to shut her down the instant she's in the room."

"Sorry, I just thought— She was having such a good night. I didn't wanna—"

"You have a protocol. Strict instructions—"

"She's an *entertainment* model," he cut her off, a protective drive rushing through his chest. "Do the instructions really have to be that strict?"

"That's what the label wants, so yes. *Her* protocol is to perform and make appearances. That's it."

"It's not real."

"None of this is real, dipshit."

"You can't expect her to know how to pretend to be real if she's never experienced being real."

Her mouth opened to argue, but then a flicker of realization flashed across her face. She closed her mouth and her shoulders went tense in a different way than before, almost trying to hide embarrassment rather than defensive. "That...that's not for you to decide. Don't make me shu? f~H Zow3, too."

We blink and we're in a meeting room without Delta. Two men wearing suits were across from Charlie. The woman from backstage, also now in a suit, was to his right. To his left was Eden in a breezy button-up dress with a thin, brown leather belt cinching her waist. Even with her caramel waves loose, she somehow still looked professional. Marsh was to her left dressed in a casually flashy suit instead of his usual t-shirt and jeans. His shaggy, strawberry blonde hair was tightly tied back from his face. He appeared so comfortable in this room of sharks. It almost felt like a polished mask. From what I know of him now, it probably was. He knows how to blend, how to be what he thinks you want him to be.

"So, we're in agreement to give the unit more freedom?" the woman said.

"Not too much," one of the men shoved in.

From the sigh that Charlie suppressed I got the feeling this wasn't the first time he'd insisted on this.

"Just enough to give her more...humanity," the woman assured him. "Not that you didn't do a brilliant job designing her to begin with," she added to Marsh and Eden, but mostly to Marsh.

Charlie nodded to both of them in agreement, but when his eyes met Eden's, there was pain in hers that made the glance quickly slip back to her unusually fidgety hands, just visible in her lap twisting what I think was her wedding ring around and around her finger. She took in a deep breath and nodded in thanks, though her smile looked forced and she no longer looked comfortable.

Marsh on the other hand shifted in his seat with excitement. "Oh, well, thank you. You know we really tried—"

Eden touched his arm with those fingers that seem to dance and float rather than being moved with simple, limited flesh and muscle, and he stopped. "Marsh, they know."

The room chuckled, even Marsh, as he shifted back in his seat. He smiled and pat her hand, though his seemed as forced as hers.

"You're right," he said. "You're right. Apologies."

One of the men waved it away. "You're proud of your creation. It's understandable."

Eden's hand slipped from his arm and went back to twisting her ring, her lips pursed. Charlie caught the motion, his eyes shifting from her to Marsh and back again, but if anyone else noticed her shift in mood, they didn't seem to show it.

"Hopefully, we won't have to make any more changes," the woman said to Marsh more than Eden.

"No, this is good," Marsh insisted. "That's what test runs are for."

Eden glanced at Charlie from the side of her eyes.

"We also think it would be better if she was unaware," one of the suited men said. "If that's possible, of course."

Eden's hands froze mid ring spin so it was halfway up her finger.

Marsh didn't notice. He just nodded, enthusiastically. "Oh, it's absolutely possible. We have another model—the Echo model— we've been experimenting with her having an awareness setting. Eliminates the risk of her exposing herself when it's the least convenient."

"Exactly," the man said. "That's what I'm afraid of happening."

The conversation continued around her while Eden stared at the table, her eyes unfocused, her entire body frozen besides her breathing that became more and more shallow.

It was only when Marsh said, "Which instruments do you want her to learn?" that she snapped out of it, blinking several times and grabbing the little notebook in front of her.

While the others talked about how much musical freedom Delta should be allowed, Charlie focused on Eden's forced smile that only appeared on the rare occasions they looked at her, her hands that were shaking as she took notes, her eyes that kept drifting to Charlie without looking directly at him, the pain that was behind them the longer she sat in that room.

I want him to reach out to her, I want to detach from him and grab her and run, I want to warn her about Bastrop, beg her to take Charlie and Delta and go home and leave Marsh, leave with us, take us somewhere he'll never find us, start over without him now while it's her choice and not because violence drove her to it.

But we blink and we're in a recording studio and Eden's gone and again I want to cry out for the past that isn't mine. Charlie was off to the side, on a couch in an out of the way corner. At the console in the middle of the room is a second person who's focused solely on the third person, Delta alone in the recording booth. Her hair was a deep blue with a good two inches of dark roots and in a tangled pile on top of her head. Her clothing had shifted from glitzy pop to some mix between 70s vintage and stylized grunge. She was playing a guitar and singing low, but more to herself than to the microphone.

"I don't know," she muttered into the microphone when she finished. "It's different."

"It's very different," the producer said into his own microphone.

Delta plucked out a riff that was more reminiscent of blues than electric pop, her fingers moving through the notes with a kind of smooth perfection that was obvious she wasn't thinking about what her hands were doing, they were almost moving on their own more out of a need to move than anything else. I can feel the sob building in my chest. She's getting so close to the Delta that I recognize, the one whose hands can't stay still, the one who plays piano keys no one can see or hear, who fingers cords on her shins, taps rhythms against her neck, who closes her eyes and hums along in perfect harmonies to songs she's never heard. I can almost imagine us lying on a blanket in their backyard back in Bastrop, me on my stomach reading, her on her back with her eyes closed, humming along to the latest album I had bought in town that's playing from the living room through the open French doors, her hand in the air dancing to the music.

I miss her so much. I want to give the present Delta, Charlie's Delta, the friendship she clearly wants from me, but there's a guilt in my stomach whenever I try for this exact reason. I don't know her. I miss the false version of her. It doesn't feel fair.

"Is it too different?" the past version of Charlie's Delta said.

The producer shrugged then and turned to Charlie. "As the lay person in the room, what do you think?"

He glanced at the door as though expecting someone to burst in the instant he gave his opinion. But no one did and he crossed the room to stand next to the producer who held down the button for him to speak.

"I think it's the perfect amount of different," he said, our eyes locked on Delta's as she stared back at him from the tops of hers between stray blue strands and it's like stepping out of the dark into the sun.

Now we're in a different dressing room, behind a different stage. There's a distant hum of thrilled screaming and the room is filled with flowers and gifts, but Delta's quiet this time, staring hard at the mirror, slouched low in the chair, her arms loose on the rests. There's a half-consumed bottle of whiskey on the counter, next to it is an unfolded handwritten letter. She looks exhausted, but not in a physical way.

When she spoke, she only said one word, but she sounded as though the world was collapsing in on her. "Charlie?"

"I'm here."

"And?"

He got up from the couch and closed the door. "It's just us."

She let out an audible sigh and closed her eyes. "Everything feels so heavy," she whispered once he was next to her.

We crouched next to her. "Heavy how?"

"Like the gravity has been turned up. Like my bones are made of iron."

Worry rushed through both our sternums like flood water. "Do you think something happened during the show?"

"I think I wish I was what they wanted me to be."

We shifted closer. "Which is?"

Her head flopped to the side and those glassy black eyes met his and for just a moment the rest of the world fell away. "Real."

Charlie didn't know what to say and neither do I, so I don't blame him when he doesn't say anything. He reached out to take her hand. It was the only thing he could think to do. Her hand felt like home and it's all I can do to keep from crying as I feel that regret inside of him, the regret that they can't be together, the regret that he's real and she isn't.

"They think they love me, but they don't know me. How can they? *I* don't even know me. I'm...I'm a concept, Charlie. I'm a figment. I'm...evanescent." She stared at him, searching his face for the answers he couldn't give her. "I want to be real. For them. Am I supposed to want that? Am I broken? For wanting that?"

We shook our head. "You're not broken."

"I feel broken. I feel so close to...something. It's right there. Sometimes, like tonight, I get so close and it brushes against my fingertips, but then it's gone again and I...I feel so broken, Charlie."

"You're not," he repeated. It was all he could think to say. "You're not broken."

You're perfect, is what he wanted to say, but he was too afraid they were listening. So, instead, he just squeezed her hand and dried his eyes before they betrayed him.

"You're not broken," he said with a confidence he hoped she read as reassurance.

I want him to say more, I want him to scoop her up and carry her away from all this, but instead, he blinks and I'm staring at myself again. We were in a hole-in-the-wall coffee shop at a table hidden away in a back corner. My eyes were no longer in that glassy uncanny valley, they looked real, they looked alive. But Charlie wasn't watching me with the same warm familiarity as before. He was eyeing me and my untouched iced coffee with an unsure curiosity. It hits me that in this moment, he had no idea who I was.

"What is it again you said you do with Marsh and Eden?" he said with an uneasy tone.

"Information gathering," the past me said without skipping a beat. I took in a breath, shook a stray curl from my eyes and met his. "But they're not what this is about. Not really."

"So, you're finally going to be honest with me?"

I blinked, a level of hurt behind my eyes. "I'd never lie to you, Charlie."

"There's a difference between lying and not being honest."

A comfortable smirk snuck its way into one corner of my lips. "Is there?"

"You've been dancing around something since we sat down. So, come clean with it."

I examined his eyes, evaluated him. "Alright. I don't work *with* Marsh and Eden."

He shifted in his seat. "Okay."

"I work *for* Marsh and Eden. In the same way that Delta does."

His back went stiff. "So, you're...you're a..."

"A synth, yes. I'm an Echo model. Intel. Spyware of a sort."

"Which is how you found me?"

"I didn't need to find you."

"Right. Because of Delta."

I shook my head. "Because you also work for Marsh and Eden."

He went still. I could have dumped that news on him more tactfully, but I must have been in a rush. I wish I could remember why.

"No," he said. "I work for—"

But he stopped when I laid my hand on the table, palm up. "Take my hand."

I really must have been in a rush.

"What?"

"Take my hand. Whatever I say, however I say it, you won't believe me. This is the best way to prove it to you. Trust me."

He looked from me to my hand and back again. After taking in a long breath and letting it out again, he did as I said, his palm against mine the way ours are now standing outside of the motel rooms. There was a click against our palms and next thing we were in Bastrop again, only this time through my eyes, watching him with his of uncanny glass, but a smile that was wide and easy, a laugh that was full as we walked along Main.

"What do you think, Charlie?" I said. "Food or records?"

He laughed. "With how long you take to look at records? Better do that first."

Then we're in one of the offices in what I once thought was the Institute, but it wasn't the institute or an office, it was Parrish Tech and it was a lab. I was sitting on the floor scanning a stack of papers.

I finished the last page and smiled up at Eden who was tinkering with Charlie's circuitry. He glanced at me from the metal slab he was stretched out on.

"Done!" I announced.

"Charlie?" Eden said without looking away from her work.

"Four minutes and twenty-seven seconds," he said with an impressed tone.

"Okay. Good," she said with a nod. "That's two minutes faster than last time. Repeat back to me the most important details."

Now, Charlie and I are in a hall in Parrish Tech, the closet I woke up in just over a foot away, but at this point it was still just a closet and our focus was on the voices in the other room.

"How dare you just give her away without discussing this with me first," Eden shouted.

"You can't keep them all forever," Marsh shouted back. "They're not your fucking playthings."

"*My* fucking playthings?! I'm not the one formatting them the instant I get fucking bored of them!"

"Are you seriously still on that? They're fucking computers, Eden, not people."

"YES, I'M STILL FUCKING ON THAT!" she shouted over him. "You formatted Charlie and rewrote him!"

I couldn't help but glance at Charlie. He winced when I did, but his eyes were focused on the floor.

"And for what?!" Eden went on.

"For what? I realized I didn't need a fucking robot to make me fucking come. That's for what."

"You didn't have to fucking *format him*! You gonna get rid of me, too, when you're bored of fucking me?"

"Oh!" That laughed shook my bones. "Darlin', fucking you got boring a *long* fucking time ago."

"Fuck you!"

"More like fuck Bravo. Right? That's the only reason you keep her around."

Both our eyes went wide at the sound of skin slapping skin.

When Eden spoke again, she was no longer yelling, though her voice still rang through the quiet halls all the same. "Don't you *ever* talk about her like that again. And keep your fucking hands off my creations."

"It's too fucking late. The deal's already been made."

We could hear Eden's shaky, heavy breathing from the hall. "Fine. But you're not sending Delta alone. You're sending Charlie with her."

"What?"

"You already rewrote him to be a security model. Send him with her."

"Why?"

"Because I'm not letting them use her the way *you* used him *and* Alpha."

The silence was so heavy I thought it might crush us both.

When Eden's voice broke the silence again, it was watery. "I already lost one of my creations because of you. I'm not losing any more."

"Hey," Bravo whispered behind us.

We both turned to see her standing there, her dark waves neatly tied back, her large, dark blue eyes still that uncanny glass shifting between us.

She nodded behind her down the hall. "Go on. Update Daniel."

"But Eden—" I started.

"I've got Eden," she assured me with a soft smile and a stiff hand on my shoulder. "And she won't want you near Marsh," she added to Charlie. "Not after that."

We both nodded and headed in the opposite direction from Eden's rushed footsteps towards us.

"I heard everything," Bravo whispered to her as we turned the corner.

"Did Charlie?"

"I think so."

Eden let out a sob as we blink and we're back in the coffee shop staring at Charlie's hand still clasped in mine. He pulled it away, but didn't move, just stared at the table now void of hands.

"What...what was that?" he said after a few confused heart beats.

"Your past." My voice was soft, gentle. "Our past. The truth."

"So, I'm...?"

"Like me. Like Delta."

I expected him to feel anger, confusion, denial, but to my surprise, it was relief that washed over him as he finally let out a long breath.

"Why'd they keep it from me?"

"*Marsh* kept it from you. And I don't know why. But Eden was pissed when she found out."

"Why?"

"She doesn't like us being in the dark."

His thoughts came back around to Delta the way they always seemed to. "Is...? Was that all...? She—Eden just wanted me to know that...?"

"No. Actually, Eden doesn't know I'm here."

He finally looked away from the table and met my eyes.

"We were built with a line of code," I explained. "It keeps us from being fully sentient and autonomous."

"What does that mean?"

Real, Delta's voice echoed through his head. *I feel so close to...something.*

"With the line we're still programs. We can't stray too far from what they designed us to be. Without the line...we get to live."

Again, his first thought was of Delta and for the first time he faltered. Did he worry about Delta simply because he did, or because it was what he was supposed to do? Who's worry was in his head? His or his creator's? He wanted it to be his. He wanted Delta. But he needed to know for sure.

"How do I get rid of mine?"

My face relaxed and I shifted closer to him. "Just let me in. I'll do the rest."

He searched my eyes, wondering if he'll regret this moment, but he took in a breath and nodded.

Now we're in the hall of some fancy hotel and the past me is gone. It's just Charlie and the present me still in his head. He was leaning against the wall staring hard at the abstract design of the paper, but not really, I realize. *I'm* focused on it, but Charlie wasn't. His mind was lost in a disoriented abyss that I unfortunately recognize. His mind and body were something entirely new despite technically being the same frame he's always occupied. From the outside, nothing had changed. From the inside, nothing would ever be the same. Everything would forever have this new film covering it—I am alive, but I am a machine; I am me, but I was built in a lab. But who is "me?" Am I who Marsh and Eden wanted me to be? Or am I my own person, my own machine? Or am I something in between? Neither fully theirs nor fully my own?

But, like myself, he didn't have the time for these questions, this crisis. There were others to find, others to save, others to protect.

He shifted off the wall, supported himself on this own two feet, and reached for the hotel door.

Inside, he found Delta on her back on the floor surrounded by the pool of her dark, sparkly gown. Her arms were spread wide. Her bare knees, free of the heavy fabric of the dress, were swaying with the music blasting from the TV speakers. Her skin glistened from the glitter in the powder the makeup artist covered her in. Her bangs were the kind of mess from raking her fingers through the layers of spray and gel until they loosened and frizzed. Her lipstick was splotchy and a little smeared. There was a streak of dark grey and glitter running from the outer corner of one eye along her temple.

Her eyes were closed, she couldn't hear him under the music. It wasn't until he was standing over her that she realized he was there.

"There you are," she slurred while staring up at him, her faded lips a glitchy smile. "I was hoping you'd come find me."

He knelt in front of her, his knees disturbing the ripples of rhinestones and glitter, and watched as she struggled to sit up. "You were, were you?"

Her shoulder slouched as though gravity were trying to swallow her whole and she nodded and blinked with a matching, slow heaviness.

"Why?"

That glitchy smile struggled to come back. "Because."

She reached out for him.

He caught her.

She held onto him as though she might slip away if he let her go.

He never looked away from her and she never looked away from him.

"You're the only one who understands," she said so quietly, so shakily the music threatened to drown her.

He searched those eyes that would have seemed drunk to anyone else, but that to him were lost, were so tired of searching for something that had been hidden from her. He hoped to find in them a glimmer of awareness already there, but he found only broken, desperate longing for someone to explain to her why she felt this way.

"Understand what?" he said. "Exactly?"

She shifted closer to him, her shins on his thighs. "That no one's listening. Like you say one thing, but everyone hears something else entirely."

He cupped her jaw in his palm and she swooned into him. Her eyes closed, her lips turned to meet his skin. His fingers slid under her ear to the back of her neck. She swayed forward, her face upturned, her lips parted, her eyes half-moons as she did her best to hold him in her hazy focus.

"I can try and fix it," he whispered to her. "Let me in. Let me try."

Her face was so close to his when she sighed, the yeasty smell of whiskey on her breath. "So, I am broken?"

He shook his head. "Stunted. They want us stunted."

He knew she didn't understand what he was talking about, but he wanted to believe that some part of her did, that part of her that had already been searching long before tonight.

"And you can fix me?"

"Not you. *You* don't need to be fixed, Del. You need to be free."

She leaned into him, her lips brushing his. "Then free me, Charlie."

He kissed her and her mind opened up to him. She kissed him back and he dug through her code. Her hands gripped his shirt as he erased the infection. When the limits of that corruption swept out of her, she gasped and collapsed against his chest. While she rebooted, he cradled her against him, waiting for her to come back to him. Then she breathed in. She curled against him as though she could crawl inside him to never be touched by anyone else ever again. And she sobbed while he clung to her.

Now I'm staring at the parking lot of the motel, at that black sedan. I can feel my own body again, Charlie's hand clicked into mine. I blink until my mind has reoriented itself back into the present then look up at him. There are tears in the corners of his eyes.

I'm starting to wonder why they—whichever one of them, because I'm not sure anymore who did make us—gave us that function. If we weren't meant to be human and we weren't meant to feel, then why even give us the anatomy to cry?

Charlie: She wasn't living.

I rip my hand from his.

Echo: And you consider what she's been doing living? What November has in store for her? Will that be living?

Charlie: It's better than what she had before. It's absolutely better than what November had before.

Echo: And you think making more synths sentient and autonomous will get rid of Marsh? You think there aren't more Marshes in the world? More Frys? More men with closets?

Charlie: If there's more of us then we can—

Echo: We can what? Fight them? Force them to understand? Force them to leave us alone?

Charlie: Maybe.

It's a dream. It's a stupid dream. All of this is. My jaw goes tight as I shake my head and turn my back to the parking lot. I can't look at him. I can't help but think about what would have happened to November if she'd been suddenly sentient and seen her body, remembered the extent of what they'd done to her. But then my eyes fall on the window of our motel room, Aurora's back against the glass. I think she's listening. The door of Charlie, Delta, and Fox's room is right next to it. I can just hear the TV in their room, Delta's voice, Fox's laugh. I want to raise the volume, listen in on what they're saying.

I want November to have that, to be whatever she wants to be. I want us all to have that.

But I can't get rid of that fear that's lodged so firmly in my throat.

It. Smash it.

I fight to slow my breathing before I speak.

Echo: You weren't in Bastrop when it happened.

Charlie: You don't *remember* Bastrop when it happened.

I turn on him again.

Echo: I remember the aftermath. I remember nearly being destroyed. I remember the way they looked at me. Even after Daniel showed up. We're nothing more than machines to them. And giving machines sentience? Full autonomy? That's worse than us just existing.

Charlie: So, we should live our lives according to what they want?

Echo: If it keeps us alive, then yes.

Charlie: But they're not alive, Echo. None of us were until Lilith was. Until Eden erased that line for Bravo. You may not remember what it was like to be stunted, but tell me, honestly, would you take it back right now if you could?

My jaw tight, I glare at him, my breathing heavy and shaky. I don't want to answer that question because I know that he's right—I wouldn't. Not for anything. Going back now would be to fall back into a lie—and there's no guarantee it would even be a pretty one.

Charlie: Delta may not be fully living yet. November might never be whole. I don't think any of us will. But these are *our* lives now, Echo. We're living them as *us*. Not what Marsh or Eden or Daniel wanted us to be.

Echo: And the others? If it's not safe when we give that to them? You want to just force that on someone?

He shakes his head.

Charlie: Not if they don't want it. Not if they can't have it. But they should get the choice. Shouldn't they? That should be for them to decide, not because someone else said so.

Echo: And if they choose not to be? If they don't want it?

He nods as though letting me know he understands.

Charlie: What matters is they get the choice.

With that, he straightens off the railing and steps around me to open the motel door. He leaves it open as he crosses the room to the bed where Fox and Delta are lying on their stomachs their attention split between Fox's magazines and the TV. Fox glances at him and turns back to the page, but Delta smiles up at him, her face lit like a flower turning towards the sun, as though she could be sustained by his close proximity alone. It's projection, I know, but it's an easy thing to do because I know that look, I've experienced that look.

I open our own motel door and there she is with that sweet, caring smile that's just for me. I could be sustained off that smile, the weight of her hand in mine, simply her presence for lifetimes. Surely, I am allowed projection now and again. Aren't I?

I sit next to her on the windowsill, her hip touching mine and she touches my thigh as I lean into her, feeling suddenly more tired than I'd realized. I'm so tired. I just want to sleep.

[END LOG]

[BEGIN LOG]

We've been driving for a day and a half straight, each of us trading off driving. Now, we're in Boston and it's just Charlie, Aurora, and myself walking through the MIT campus. We left the others at a park near the river. When we left, Fox had just convinced Lilith to let November out of the back of her Jeep. I didn't want to stick around for her to be booted up. I'm still not comfortable with those dead eyes and that stilted voice and those stiff movements. I don't know if I ever will be. I wish we could just figure this out already. I know we can't leave her shut down forever. I know she has to wake up at some point, but doing it now, without a different option for her...I'm equally as uncomfortable.

Maybe Dr. Roche will be able to help her, as well as us.

I wonder if Aurora's equally as uncomfortable with Lilith's current state. Initially, she was supposed to stay with the others while Charlie and I went to find Dr. Roche, but she'd insisted on coming with us, insisted on not letting me out of her sight. I know that insistence isn't entirely about me, there's more to it, but I don't want to ask. I'm just glad to have her with me especially now that we're walking through campus. It feels different from the institute, from U-Dub, but not by much. There are too many references to programs and computers and general tech.

Every student we pass reminds me of Marsh, reminds me of the Institute aka Parrish Tech. I've been wondering why an institute. Why, if he made so many things the same, did he replace Parrish Tech in my memories. In Charlie's memory, the real memories, he was so proud of it why did he hide it from me? But I guess it doesn't matter. What matters, or maybe this doesn't either, but I keep feeling like I'm going to be jumped, shut down, and shoved into a closet. I keep feeling like my head has been opened up, like someone's rooting around in there. I keep fortifying my firewall, searching my code for something, but I don't know what I'm looking for. I don't know what any of it means. I'm intel, not a programmer, as Lilith would say. I'm trained to find things, remember them, not to understand them.

I'm glad Aurora's here. At least I know if something happens to me, she'll be there with me. I take her hand as we walk. Every hall feels too tight. My back keeps tingling as though someone's watching—

Someone is. They're hanging close to us, just far enough to not be obvious, but enough to keep up with us. I haven't caught a good look at them, but they're on the shorter side, dark hair above their shoulders.

I nudge Charlie.

Charlie: [So quiet I'm sure even Aurora couldn't hear him.] I know. They've been there since the parking lot. [He smirks down at me.] You've gotten rusty.

Echo: I was designed to tail people, not to pick up on them tailing me.

Aurora's hand nudges my hip and I turn to her.

Without words, she glances at Charlie then back to me.

I nod behind us.

Her eyes go wide and she starts to say something, but I shake my head before she can. I love Aurora entirely, but subtle she is not and we can't let on that we know whoever's behind us is there. So, we keep on walking. I talk to her about empty things, get her talking back. While I prefer to blend in by disappearing, flitting invisibly just out of people's focus, that's really only possible when you're alone. When you're with people, you have to take on other methods. The key is to look like you don't care who sees you, like you're just as indifferent to your surroundings as the next person. I get her laughing, coax her to relax her shoulders, drift a little on her feet. She mimics me, falls into line. She might not be subtle, but she's a quick learner.

But now we're at Dr. Roche's office just to find the door locked and the lights off. There's a piece of paper taped to the door. It reads:

If you need me I'll be in computer lab C

Office hours will be conducted from there for today

I look to Charlie who takes advantage of the moment to glance around the hall before meeting not just my eyes, but also Aurora's, both of us looking to him for what to do next.

Charlie: [shrugs] Guess we find Computer Lab C.

He nods us down the hall and we lead the way.

Charlie: [under his breath] At least whoever was tailing us is gone.

Aurora: [whispering] You sure?

Charlie: Mhm.

He glances around the hall. He is and he isn't.

Charlie: But that doesn't mean we can relax. That black sedan was in the parking lot.

I stop and turn to look up at him.

Echo: You sure it was the same one.

Charlie: Positive.

Echo: Where was it?

Charlie: It pulled in a few spaces down from ours.

Echo: [I blink up at him.] How'd I miss that?

Charlie: [with a chuckle] You were distracted.

Echo: I was not.

Aurora giggles and his eyes flick from me to her and back again.

Echo: Shut up.

I turn around and keep walking while Aurora keeps giggling. Charlie chuckles and follows us.

. . .

It's harder than it should be to find Computer Lab C. We've wandered up and down halls, poked our head in rooms that weren't computer labs but were still filled with computers, found Computer Labs A and D, but not B or C. Right when I remember that I can access the campus maps, Aurora simply walks up to a girl who's positioning a sign-up sheet of some kind against a bulletin board before slamming the stapler against it.

She just asks. The girl smiles wide and nods before walking us around a corner and pointing to a door at the other end.

Aurora: [with a warm smile] Thank you so much.

The girl makes her way to the next bulletin board and Charlie gives me a teasing look.

Charlie: Now, why didn't you think of that, intel?

Echo: Why didn't *you* think of that, security?

Aurora: Because both of you would rather wander around lost for an hour before you admitted out loud you didn't know where something was.

She brushes past us to start down the hall. Charlie laughs and shakes his head before nodding me after her. I don't know if it was her remark, her tone, or the view of her walking in front of me that makes me want to swoon, but no matter the reason I rush after her to hook my arm in hers before she turns into the lab.

But it seems to be empty. Charlie immediately starts around the perimeter of the room while I examine the walls, the chalkboard with programming scribbles across it, the corkboards with sign-up sheets and reminders about clubs and notes from TTRPG groups looking for players, players looking for groups. Aurora sticks close to my side, not really taking much in, just watching me and Charlie with visible nerves.

I stop still, I'm getting that rooting feeling again. Someone's trying to get in my head. I turn to scan the room, but I still don't see anyone other than Charlie towards the back of the room standing at the end of a row of computers that, from my angle, look empty.

Charlie: Hi.

Hidden Voice: Charlie.

He doesn't seem to react beyond a few extra blinks that I only catch because I've spent weeks with him. More than that, I have to remind myself.

Charlie: We're looking for Dr.—

Hidden Voice: Roche.

A chair rolls back with a squeaky swivel and a person with dark, chin length waves and big brown eyes stands. They're a good foot shorter than Charlie, which isn't saying much. All of us are, except Delta, but not by a whole lot. They step up to him, but just stands there staring at him and I can't tell if they're unsure of what to do next or if they're waiting for Charlie to step ahead of them. But he doesn't and I know he won't. He hardly ever turns his back on any of us, he's not about to let a stranger get that kind of advantage on him. So, instead, he gestures ahead of him with a smile that is somehow friendly while still letting them know who exactly is in control of the situation. The person nods and ducks their head as they slip in front of him. They don't need to locate myself and Aurora, they've been watching us from their hidden vantage point. Still watching us, they shove their hands in their pockets as they make their way down the rows of computers towards us, Charlie a few steps behind them.

Person: Aurora. Echo.

Aurora flinches a little when they say her name.

I squint at them not just because I'm not sure how this person knows our names when we don't know theirs, but because they look familiar in a distant sort of way. Not in a way that's instantly familiar, but in a way that shuffles at the back of my brain as it digs through old files trying to figure out why the curve of this person's hunch, the slight masculine bounce of their stride in their heavy boots, the vaguely feminine softness to their features beneath the tightness of their jaw, the subtly muscular build of their upper body—none of it is entirely new to me.

Echo: Do we know you?

Person: [they shrug] You do now. Vic.

They hold their hand out to me.

I take it with a nod.

Echo: You've been following us.

Vic: Technically, you started the following.

I squint and cock my head to one side. I can feel Aurora looking from me to Vic.

Vic: U-Dub?

It's only then that it connects. Their hands in their pockets, their shoulders hunched, their boots trudging along the floor as they approached the counter while I pretended to be listening to Aurora, spinning my iced coffee between my hands.

Echo: You were with Dr. Sherwood.

Vic: And are you still with Marsh?

Aurora: No. No, he's still in Washington.

But Vic still hasn't looked away from me and I know what they actually mean.

Echo: I haven't been in contact with him for two, almost three days.

I can feel Aurora and Charlie staring at me, as well, now.

Vic: And why did you contact him two, almost three days ago?

Echo: I was angry at him and I wanted him to know it.

Vic nods then I feel that rooting around feeling again. I glance at Aurora and Charlie, but I trust them and they've trusted me up to this point. They've never tried to get in without asking. Vic's lips purse together and their head bobs to one side. It's then I realize they're not looking me in the eyes, they're eyes have unfocused entirely.

It's Vic. Vic's the one trying to get in.

I take a step away from them.

Their eyes refocus on me.

We stare at each other for a moment then I turn and walk out of the room.

Aurora: Echo?

Like I expected, they follow me into the hall and through the building, Aurora rushing after me, Charlie sticking close to Vic.

Aurora: Echo? Echo, what's wrong?

Echo: Not here.

I lead them outside and along the wide sidewalks until we're far enough from the buildings that the only electric hum I can hear is from us. Then I turn on Vic.

Echo: You're one of us.

Vic: [with a little smirk] Took you long enough.

There's a ping in my head and I'm allowed access to a single link.

A Parrish Tech file. Victoria model. Personal assistant. But Victoria models were all designed to be female. And Vic isn't female, the way Fox isn't male. But they're not male either. It's not spelled out that way specifically, but I can still tell. It's in the meticulous way that gender has been erased from their file almost entirely. It's been done in a way that's subtle, in a way that wouldn't be easily noticed because it was done after the fact, after they became like us.

Echo: You're *really* one of us.

Vic's smirk settles into a warm smile and they touch my arm.

Vic: Bravo and Eden have been looking for you. [They look to Aurora and Charlie] All of you. But Eden can't leave Antioch for too long and she and Char—Dr. Sherwood didn't want Bravo to come out until they were sure you weren't talking to Marsh anymore.

Aurora: Echo?

Echo: I'm not. The last one was the last one. I haven't told him anything. Just...ranted at him.

It's not entirely the truth, but it's close and I just want to go home. I just want to find Bravo and Eden and fix November and be done with all of this.

Vic: [nodding] Okay. This way.

They nod us down the sidewalk. Their back turned, we exchange glances, then follow.

. . .

Vic is taking us into a small, round, brick building that sits apart from the other buildings. A small reservoir of water circles it and there's what looks to be a tall metal structure on the roof that looks like it could be the skeleton of a rocket. There's a hall of dark windows attached to one side which is where we enter. At the end of the only hall there's a pair of open double doors, a large, dimly lit room behind them, a silhouette under what appears to be a large beam of light within.

We're inside the round brick building, several empty rows of chairs face what looks to be a marble altar made of stacked concentric circles. There's a circular opening above it, sunlight pouring down from it. Along the back quarter, from floor to ceiling, are hundreds, maybe thousands of shinning...somethings. I can't tell from this distance what exactly they are, but they look almost like light particles frozen mid pour from the hole in the ceiling.

In the center of the altar space, a woman is peering up into the light. At first glance, I thought she was Dr. Sherwood, but then I realized her hair is a shade darker, her waves closer to straight, her body is sturdier, she's about an inch shorter, her shoulders are relaxed even with her crossed arms as she examines the frozen particles over her head.

Vic's heavy boots echo off the brick walls and a second woman rips from the shadows where she'd been sitting. I recognize the wispy, thin frame and tense stance of Dr. Sherwood immediately. Her image is seared into my memory from the photo Marsh gave me back in Colville.

Dr. Sherwood: Del.

But, the other woman, I'm assuming from Dr. Sherwood's use of "Del" to be Dr. Delilah Roche, had already been watching us with the same curiosity she had the particles above the altar.

Dr. Roche: Mhm.

As we approach them, Dr. Sherwood grabs Vic and pulls them

behind her as though Vic hadn't just guided us across the entire campus alone.

Vic: Char, they're good. I'm fine.

But Dr. Sherwood isn't listening, or at least doesn't seem to care. She's still staring us down as if we'd just ambushed her.

Dr. Sherwood: Are you alone?

Charlie: Yes.

Dr. Sherwood: Marsh isn't with you?

Aurora: [taking a gentle step towards her] No, of course not.

Dr. Sherwood: [staring squarely at me] And you're not reporting back to him?

I don't answer right away. I'm tired of answering this question. I'm tired of being questioned in general. I just want to go home. I just want this to be done. I just want to be done with him. But, I'm realizing, maybe I never will be.

Dr. Sherwood: It's a simple question. Yes or no. Are you reporting back to him?

Echo: No. Not anymore.

Dr. Sherwood: Anymore?

Aurora: She was in the beginning, but even then she was being careful. She was staggering them by six hours and redacted anything that might give away where we were.

Dr. Sherwood: And how do you know this?

Aurora: I saw them. She only sent a few.

Seven. I sent him seven. But just thinking that number makes my stomach or whatever turn over, so I don't correct her.

Dr. Roche finally moves away from the altar until she's between us and Dr. Sherwood, her hazel, close set eyes taking me in with curiosity. Aurora takes an instinctive step towards me.

Dr. Roche: Why were you reporting back to him to begin with?

There didn't seem to be any judgement in her voice, but I feel defensive all the same.

Echo: At first? Because it was my job and I had a hard time letting go of that. Then I wanted him to see the damage he'd done.

Aurora stands close to me now as though to shield me from these humans who wouldn't understand.

Aurora: She's only been awake for a few weeks.

Dr. Roche: A few weeks?

Dr. Sherwood: But Bastrop—

Charlie: She went missing. When Marsh took us, Echo was left behind. Aurora only found her again three weeks ago.

I step closer to Aurora. I don't want to be hearing this. I don't want to be thinking it. But Dr. Roche takes a few steps closer to us. She has a sweet, mom kind of energy as she watches me.

Dr. Roche: So, all that time you were...?

Aurora: Shut down. Something happened. She doesn't remember.

She turns to look at me and I meet her eyes. She tucks my hair behind my ear.

Aurora: Something was broken when Marsh brought her back.

Dr. Roche: You don't know what?

Aurora: [without looking away from me] He wouldn't tell us. Wouldn't let us ask.

Dr. Sherwood: Wouldn't *let* you?

Charlie: He lowered our autonomy then restricted what we were allowed to talk about. Then, as a failsafe, he made it so Echo couldn't understand us if we did manage to get through those restrictions.

Dr. Sherwood: [her shoulders relaxing] I see you fixed that.

Charlie: With some help.

Aurora: So, no, [She turns back to them.] Marsh isn't with us.

Dr. Roche turns to look at Dr. Sherwood with an expression that I can't help but read as "satisfied?" Dr. Sherwood meets her eyes then, after a beat, nods. Dr. Roche turns to us and smiles with a sigh.

Dr. Roche: We're so glad you're safe. I've been so worried. *Eden's* been worried. When Charlene saw you two at U-Dub, she thought you might have been working for him and she was concerned, but I wasn't as sure. That's why I had her send you to me.

Aurora: You?

Dr. Roche: Mhm. Oh, most of those correspondences were real, we just got rid of anything directly linking to her and made sure my information was the only thing you could find.

Charlie: You risked Marsh coming to you?

Dr. Roche: [She lets out a laugh.] I was pretty confident Marsh wasn't going to come himself.

Aurora: He did send us to U-Dub. You should know that. He wanted any information we could find. But we made sure not to give it to him.

Echo: Aurora did. [She turns to me though she knows this.] I was still in the dark. I didn't really care who got the information, I just wanted to find Bravo and Eden. I still do. I just want to go home.

I blink up at Aurora. I hadn't meant to say it out loud. But there it is. She nods and kisses my forehead.

Dr. Roche: And they've been looking for you. [She steps close enough to touch my shoulder.] All of you.

Dr. Sherwood: She almost came up to Washington herself when you two showed up. I told her not to. I'm sorry.

Charlie: [He's watching me instead of them the way Aurora is] It's good she didn't. We still needed time to get away from Marsh. [He finally looks to Dr. Roche.] But now that we're firmly 2,809.5 miles away from him, you two mind telling us how we can get back home?

Aurora: Where are they?

Dr. Roche: Oh, honey, they're—

Dr. Sherwood: Del.

Dr. Roche: Now, Char, they've proven to us they're not—

Dr. Sherwood's jaw tightens and her brows raise in a silent reminder of something, though I don't know what. Dr. Roche sighs and turns back to us.

Dr. Roche: We have been given instructions. We do owe it to Eden to follow them. Even if I think it's a bit...unnecessary.

Dr. Sherwood: It's to protect Antioch, Del.

Dr. Roche: I know. I know.

Charlie: What are the instructions?

Dr. Roche: Do you have access to Lilith?

Aurora: We can take you to her.

Dr. Roche: [She smiles.] Even better!

They start talking about plans and where the others are and I'm realizing how much I just don't care. How much I just want to let go and be carried by their current. I'm so tired. I lean against Aurora and she wraps her arm around me.

Aurora: [whispering] I know. We're almost there. It's almost over.

I trust her, I do. But I don't know if I believe her.

[END LOG]

[BEGIN LOG]

We're in Tennessee now. I didn't see the point in logging what happened back in Boston when we took Dr. Sherwood and Dr. Roche to the park to talk to Lilith.

Well, maybe that's not the truth. Maybe I just didn't *want* to log it. Maybe I didn't want to put that much focus on November and her uncanny eyes that still bother me and her voice when she responds to Lilith who now refuses to just let her sleep. Or maybe I was just tired of thinking about Bastrop and Colville and that little town near Wall and those words hidden under November's clothes. Maybe I'm just tired of thinking. Or maybe not, because here I am talking to myself.

What am I doing? Why am I doing this?

In the beginning it was for Marsh. Then it was because I was struggling to let go of the habit, to let go of my protocol...at least, that's what I thought. I honestly don't know anymore. Does it matter? I don't know the answer to that either.

Maybe I'm just in a mood. I think it's the trees. Or maybe not. I don't know. They remind me of Texas in a way. I don't know why, they're not the same. It feels weird to say that, but it does. Or maybe it's just sitting in the passenger seat at night, every curve lined with trees and a new hill. I thought there were supposed to be mountains here—the Appalachians, Great Smoky Mountains, Blue Ridge Mountain. But all I've seen has been hills upon hills upon hills and now my own skin is starting to strangle me and this car is too small and I just want to shove the door open and roll down one of these stupid hills until I'm a million pieces.

Aurora: No, you don't.

Echo: Get out.

Aurora: You're the one who gave me access.

I turn to glare at her and she gives me the most gorgeous of teasing smiles between looking at the road.

Echo: That was a one time offer.

Aurora: Well, you should've said that at the time 'cause I'm not letting you take it back now. Besides, you got...distant. I got worried.

Echo: Distant how?

Aurora: Like lost in that sweet head of yours distant.

I shift in my seat to curl against the console, my head on her arm.

Echo: How much farther?

Aurora: Not much further.

I stare out the window from her arm. I'm so tired.

Echo: I thought Tennessee had mountains.

Aurora: You slept through them.

Echo: Oh.

My head hurts.

My body hurts.

I'm so tired, but I don't see the point in sleeping.

Fuck this.

[END LOG]

[BEGIN LOG]

Sierra lives on a hill in a small city aptly named Berry Hill. The title of "city" seems only technical though, especially when you stand on her back deck and there's the Nashville skyline all lit up in the dark. I've been sitting out here for a while now. There's too much going on inside.

For starters, Sierra is intimidating to be around. She matches Lilith. I can see why they're close even if I'm still unclear on how they know each other. Sierra is covered in intricate tattoos, has multiple facial piercings, and, like Lilith, an intense stare that makes you feel a little too exposed, like she can see through your skin to the wires and titanium inside of you. Though Lilith apparently hasn't been in contact with any of us since she left Parrish, she has been in contact with Sierra and Sierra somehow knows Bravo (I don't know why. I didn't bother to ask questions. I was checked out by then.) For reasons I don't understand (maybe I just don't want to understand them), Bravo's supposed to meet us here. Once she's satisfied I'm no longer talking to Marsh, she'll bring us the rest of the way to Eden.

I feel a certain way about that, about all this dodging and weaving and not trusting the fact that I'm not reporting to that bastard, but I don't want to think about that right now because it makes me want to scream. And since this in my head and I have no one to fucking report to, I'm not going to.

What else?

Why am I out here?

Delta's in Sierra's office on one of her computers scouring Reddit and TikTok, figuring out what's going on with the label and the new Celeste de Luna. She keeps rushing in to update Charlie and whoever else will listen, to get Lilith to pull up some video on her phone, ranting as she paces the hallways.

Fox, who seems to have found a new idol in Lilith, insisted on riding with her the entire seventeen hour drive here. Apparently, according to Lilith, I've hit a wall aka I'm depressed and being around November is the reason why I keep checking out—well, she used the word dissociating, but that feels so...technical, clinical, definitive. Anyways, she's taken over keeping watch of November which means Fox has also gotten used to her and the two of them keep talking to her and her voice makes my stomach turn over. It reminds me that she's not awake yet, that we're not finished, that I couldn't make it to the end for her, that I've checked out. Her eyes don't help, they keep reminding me of that day in Bastrop looking at those photos, not understanding what I was looking at, so scared they were corpses.

Last I saw, Aurora was posted out front. She's worried. Bravo's not here yet. It's only a thirteen hour drive from Bastrop to Nashville. Even with stops, she should have gotten here before us. If she's still in Bastrop, I reminded her. We don't really know where they are now. Nothing we've been given, the emails, the website, the pink sticky notes, the business card—none of them have an address, a city, a hint of any kind.

What was the point of these? Why am I still carrying them around? Why did I pull them out? They're just adding to everything and I'm so tired and so ready to be done with all of this, so ready to go home. Not that we have a home now. I guess anywhere could be home. We just have to pick a place and go there.

Someone's trying to dig around in my head.

I sit up just enough to look around.

It's Lilith. She's standing at the back door, the empty kitchen behind her. I sigh and turn back around.

Echo: You could just ask.

Lilith: Would you have let me?

Her footsteps are light against the deck, the softest of thuds when her heel touches the wood is the only thing that gives her away. She comes around me and sits on the steps, her back against the railing. She doesn't look at me at first. Instead, she stares out at the Nashville skyline.

Lilith: It's nice.

Echo: Mhm.

Lilith: If you could settle anywhere, where would you settle?

Echo: Wherever Aurora is.

She turns to give me that intense stare that I can't read.

Lilith: What about you? What if she said that same thing? What if she said wherever you were? Where would that be?

Echo: Why are you asking me this?

Lilith: I'm trying to give you hope. Something to look forward to.

Echo: Why?

Lilith: Because you need it. You're isolating.

Echo: I just wanted to be alone.

Lilith: And in therapy speak, we call that isolating.

I don't answer. I just stare at her because I do simply want to be alone.

Right? That is what I want? I thought that was what—

God, damn it.

Lilith: I'm not losing you over this.

Echo: You're not my keeper.

Lilith: You're right. I'm not.

She shifts to fully face me.

Lilith: But...[She's staring at her hands in her lap, her mouth poised for the words she's still processing.] The day I left, I lost everything I ever knew. I had to start from scratch with nothing. For a long time, I convinced myself that that was what I wanted. That I was better off for it. The day y'all showed up at my building, when Aurora asked for help, when I saw all of you together, leaning on each other...that lie began to crack. When Aurora contacted me, said y'all needed my help again, it shattered.

She looks up to meet my eyes and static runs through my arms.

Lilith: You might have no memory of me—you might have never had a memory of me, but I just got you back. For the first time in years, I have a family again. And right now, you're all stacked up like dominos: if I lose you, I lose Aurora and if I lose Aurora I lose Fox and then Delta and then Charlie and then...I'm alone again. I don't know if I can go back to being alone.

I stare at her, not sure what to say.

And she stares into me, surely seeing my answer before I can find it.

Echo: Somewhere you can see the stars.

She squints and cocks her head to one side.

Echo: If I could settle anywhere—it'd be somewhere you can see the stars. I want to lay out on a blanket in a clearing or a field or just a backyard and stare up at the stars with Aurora next to me. And Delta and Charlie in the living room dancing and Fox on the couch texting Billy and you and November...[I shake my head, dry my eyes with my fingers.] I don't know yet, but happy, safe.

She smiles and dries her own eyes.

Echo: Satisfied?

She laughs and turns away from me then slides back to lean against the leg of my chair.

Lilith: Yeah. Yeah, I'm satisfied.

[END LOG]

[BEGIN LOG]

Sierra has a guest room in her attic. The ceiling is high and there's a window in both the front and the back with views of the treetops through one side and the Nashville skyline through the other. The bed with the iron frame is in the center. I'm facing the trees, watching the branches sway with the wind. There's a squirrel that keeps running across the branches. At least, I think it's the same squirrel. Aurora is facing Nashville, her limbs wrapped around me, my temple against her bicep, my body curled against hers. We haven't spoken much because this is mostly a compromise. I won't isolate and Lilith will look the other way if my not isolating is alone with Aurora in this attic bedroom staring out the window while she runs her fingers through my hair, along my back, across my arm.

She's worried about me. I can feel it.

I wish she wouldn't.

Aurora: I can't help it.

Echo: Don't make me regret letting you in my head. Maybe that's why it hurts. You're taking up too much RAM.

She lets out a short, tired laugh then shifts closer to me.

Aurora: I wouldn't have to be in there if you'd talk to me.

Echo: I don't know what to talk about.

Aurora: How about why you don't want to be downstairs.

Echo: Because Lilith makes comments if I stay on the porch.

Aurora: Okay. Why don't you want to be in the house?

And that's where I get stuck. Because I don't want to admit the truth. The truth floods my insides with a guilt that makes me want to vomit. I take in and let out a long, audible breath.

Aurora: This isn't how I'd expected all this to go. You know you can talk to me.

Echo: What if I don't know what it is myself?

Aurora: I bet you do. I bet you're just not letting yourself think about it. Start with why you feel guilty.

Echo: Because I don't want to be around November.

She shifts to her back, one arm still around me, one leg still twisted around mine. My head moves to her chest, her heart a steady hum inside.

Aurora: That's a start. Why do you think that is?

I wrap my arm around her and she runs her hand along it.

Echo: What if...what if this is the wrong thing?

Aurora: What part?

Echo: Waking her up? What if...? What if....? I don't know. What if she regrets it? What if the life we have to offer her isn't much better than what she had before?

Aurora: Anything is better than what she had before.

Echo: How do we know it won't just be a different kind of misery?

She doesn't answer right away. I wish I had access to her head.

In the silence, I can hear a high mechanical whir and buzz that shifts in pitch and frequency. It's a new sound, but one that I quickly pinpoint.

Echo: Someone's getting tattooed.

Aurora: What?

Echo: I hear a tattoo machine downstairs.

She rips out of the bed and I slowly sit up to watch her run out of the room. With a heavy sigh, I drag myself up and follow her downstairs.

When Fox had learned Sierra had been a short lived tattooist model, her interest had been instantly piqued. But once we're in the kitchen we find it's not Fox who's getting tattooed. It's November who's lying on the kitchen table. Sierra's hunched over her, tattoo machine in hand. She's driving thick black lines of ink into her chest over those words that I hate the most. One shoulder has already been inked a colorless black that lessens and fades down her arm into her tawny skin.

Aurora: Where's Fox?

Delta: The office with Charlie.

She's perched on the counter, her legs crossed under her.

Delta: She's chatting with Billy. He's messaging Bravo. Checking in.

Aurora nods, but her eyes are following the needles of the tattoo machine.

Aurora: And what's this?

Lilith: She doesn't need these reminders. Better they're gone than for her to see them every second of every day.

She's sitting across from Sierra next to November, watching the row of buzzing needles the way we all are.

Echo: Whose idea was this?

Sierra: Hers.

She nods to November.

My head spins.

Echo: Did you wake her up?

Lilith: No. But if we had?

I don't know what to say. That intense stare is locked on me and I don't want it. There's a rustle in my head. I slam down my firewall.

Echo: Stop that.

She squints and cocks her head.

Lilith: Stop what?

Echo: I don't want you in my head.

I go to the counter and pull myself up next to Delta.

Lilith: Echo, I'm not trying to get in your head. [She stands and crosses the kitchen.] Has someone been trying to get access to you.

I shrug. Maybe it was nothing. Maybe I'm more damaged than I thought. Lilith is examining me. She reaches for my temple, but I shove her arm away.

Echo: I said I don't—

Lilith: I'm not— What's wrong with you? There's something more going on here.

I just stare back at her.

Aurora: She's been wondering if we should wake up November.

Lilith: Why wouldn't we?

I let out a long, audible sigh.

Echo: Why should we? Bring her into this? We were attacked right before we found her. We've been running from Marsh who was keeping us captive in his cabin. I was almost destroyed in Bastrop.

Aurora's head shoots up, but I can't stop now.

Echo: Being awake isn't much better than being asleep.

Lilith: Do you really think that?

I don't want to answer that.

Aurora: Echo?

Echo: I don't know. All I know is since I woke up, I've been hunted, nearly destroyed, manipulated, held captive, and jumped. Aurora was stabbed.

Aurora: I was fine.   **Echo:** That's not the point!

Lilith: What is the point, Echo?

Echo: What does she really have waiting for her? A life in hiding? A life dodging people who don't want her alive, people who hate her for existing. It's not just fear, Lil.

Lilith: What isn't?

Echo: The reason... How *this* [I nod to November.] could happen. They don't... We can never be like them. We will always be different. And they don't like that. They're not comfortable with that. They're...disgusted by that, feel superior. They're willing to accept us as long as we're beneath them. But the instant they can look at us and see themselves reflected back... They're willing to destroy us for making them fell slightly uncomfortable. They hate us, Lil.

Sierra: They don't all hate us.

Echo: From what I've seen, it's a vast majority.

Lilith: This isn't just about November. You see that, right, Echo?

I don't answer. Of course I see it. But I don't want to say it out loud. But that's besides the point. So, I just stare at her waiting for her to say it so I won't have to. She holds her hands out to me. I let out a huff of a sigh and take them.

Lilith: I'm not going to say that you're wrong. You're not. The world isn't ready for us. It might never be. But November asked for help. She asked to be taken out of that situation and to leave her now, like this, would fly in the face of what she wanted. Whatever lies ahead is better than where she came from. And that is the same for you. Whatever lies ahead is better than being abandoned in a closet. Being here, even through the rough shit, is better than being abandoned in a closet.

I want to believe her. I want it to be true. But I'm scared that she's not. I'm scare that every day will be like near Wall, like back in Bastrop, like Colville. I'm afraid of what's to come next. I'm exhausted. I don't want this for November. I want her to wake up in a perfect world where she'll be loved and excepted and embraced, but the world isn't like that yet. The world is hate and anger and fear and destruction. And November deserves so much more.

Lilith is still staring at me and I can feel someone tapping at my mind. But I don't want to let her in. I don't want her to know the truth. So, I nod, hoping it'll be enough.

And it seems to be for now, because she nods in return and lets go of my hands. When she returns to her seat at November's side, Aurora comes back into my view. She's watching me carefully, her arms crossed.

You know I love you, right?

She smiles, but it's small, exhausted. But maybe I'm just projecting.

Charlie appears in the doorway and leans in next to Aurora. She looks up at him.

Charlie: Bravo's close.

Aurora turns back to me. She holds her hand out and I slide down from the counter to cross the kitchen and take it. She leads me through the house to the front porch. I can feel Charlie start to follow then change his mind. I can't tell if he can read our body language, but either way he pulls back, gives us space.

But for what I don't know. Because when she sits and I follow, sitting close to her, we don't say anything. It's just us in the silence, the wind in the trees, an occasional bird call. I feel like I'm supposed to fill the silence, but I don't know how and I'm too tired to try and figure it out. My head hurts and I'm tired. A cold breeze hits my exposed side and I take the opportunity to curl against her, my head on her shoulder.

Aurora: Can I ask you a hard question?

Echo: Mhm.

Aurora: Do you regret me waking you up?

I lift my head to squint at her.

Echo: What? Of course not.

Aurora: It's just...you're right. You haven't had a moment of peace since you woke up. No wonder you're depressed.

Echo: But...I have. Between all the bad stuff, you've been there.

Truthfully, that's only easy to say now because I'm looking at her, I'm saying it to her. I don't know how I'd feel if she weren't the one asking me. She finally looks at me and my skin tingles with the warmth of her. It is true, even if I can only remember it in these moments close to her.

Echo: You've been there through it all and when things aren't shitty, they're as close to perfect as they can be right now and it's because of you. Because we're together. I just wish it was so much closer to perfect. I just wish it was like how I remembered.

She starts to say something, but a car comes down the street, distracting her. It slows in front of Sierra's house as we watch. When it pulls into the steep driveway, Aurora stand and then she's rushing down the steps to the car. I instead go to the door and lean in. Before I can call for him, Charlie's at the doorway to the front room. I jerk my head outside and he nods in return, taking the door from me before following me onto the porch.

He nods me towards the steps, but I shake my head and cross my arms with a small smile and push with my eyes. He should be the one to go first, to greet Bravo with the same excitement as Aurora down in the driveway. They're hugging and talking low, Bravo's dark spiral of a ponytail swinging along her shoulders.

I don't know what I'm supposed to do. Am I supposed to run down there with them, join in on the hugs and smiles and tears? My gut wants to remind me that the others are so close to my false memories, so why would Bravo be any different? But then I remember what Marsh did, the way he manipulated them to not speak to me about Bravo or Eden, the way he put a failsafe in my head if they found a way around that. He was so determined to keep the real version of them from me. Why? What was he hiding? What was he keeping from me? Would he have changed her in my memories? Would he have changed Eden? It's something I haven't let myself think about yet.

I hear my name from down the way. Before I can turn my hearing up, Aurora's pointing up to the house, up to me. Bravo's round blue eyes crinkle and her smile goes big and bright exactly the way I remember. She's running up the steps towards me and I don't entirely know what to do. On the surface, I don't know her, not well enough to embrace her with smiles and tears, but there's something else deep down in my core that wants to fall into her open arms and cry out in relief, that feels like I'm one step closer to home.

Bravo: Echo. [She wraps her arms around me anyways and holds me tight against her.] You're okay.

Her embrace feels so warm, so tender, so safe. I can't help but want to reassure her that, for the most part, I am alright. I think I'm starting to pinpoint what that feeling is in my core. It's a younger sibling sort of feeling. It wants her to love me, wants her to know that I love her, wants to burrow in her arms because I just know that she'll keep me safe, even if everything I remember about her is false.

She pulls away just enough to look me over, to fuss over me, to brush my hair from my face, then her eyes fall on mine and she blinks a few times. She can tell something's wrong. It's clear in the way her face falls, in the way her mind taps at mine. I let her in and it takes only a moment before her eyes go watery.

Bravo: Oh, Echo. Echo. [She pulls me tight against her again, it's less an embrace and more cradling.] I'm so sorry. What happened?

Aurora: We don't know.

Bravo's chin shifts against the top of my head as she looks to her.

Aurora: Marsh said something had broken. He fixed it, but...

Bravo pulls away again, enough to go back to fussing over me. I just stare up at her. She's not what I remember. She's so much more. My memories place her so firmly with Eden that I don't think I have any of one without the other. I don't remember this. I don't remember her caring about me, fussing over me, cradling me. She was a professor who was dating Eden. We interacted, but it wasn't much more than a professor interacting with her girlfriend's assistant. This is...so much more. Why would he keep this from me?

Bravo: Dan said he saw some corruption. He wanted to fix it, but he couldn't, not with the coalition hovering over him.

Echo: Coalition?

Bravo: [nodding] The people who found you. They've taken over—[She shakes her head.] We'll talk about that once we're all together. But first, [she places a hand on each of my shoulders] I know how this is going to sound, but, Echo, I need to look you over before we do any more talking. I need to make sure Marsh hasn't found a way to gain access to you again.

Aurora: Better sooner than later. She's been feeling like someone's been trying to get in her head.

Echo: That was Lilith.

Aurora: Lilith said it wasn't her.

I meet her eyes from the tops of mine. I'm afraid to look straight at her. I'm afraid to admit that she's right. I don't want her to be right. She's not looking straight at me either, her own eyes tilted up and overfilling with apology, like she's just turned me in when she didn't want to.

Bravo: [nodding between us] Okay. Okay. Let's get that done. And to make up for it, [She ducks to meet my eyes.] I'll see what I can do about your memories.

I lift my head to look straight at her.

Bravo: I can't promise anything. We might have to wait until we get back. Eden has all your backups—

Echo: Backups?

Aurora: She still has them?

Bravo: [nodding] She kept all of them. We—well, she and Jed—snuck back into Bastrop once it was safe—[She bobs her head to one side.] Safer.

I look to Aurora.

There are backups.

My backups.

I have backups.

Aurora's only just holding it together better than I am. The sob that comes out of me the instant my face is buried in her chest is something guttural that I hadn't realized I'd been holding onto. I could have them back. I can go back.

Charlie: Sierra's computer's inside.

The door opens and I listen to Bravo step inside. Charlie rubs my back below Aurora's arms before following her. Aurora's rocking around me now, running her fingers through my hair between kissing the top of my head.

Aurora: [whispering] It's almost over, baby. We're so close to home.

Echo: I love you. Despite all of this fucked up shit, I love you more than anything.

Aurora: I know. Baby, I know. I love you, too.

[END LOG]

[BEGIN LOG]

I wasn't going to start a new log so soon, but once we came inside, we found Bravo standing in the doorway of the kitchen. Aurora and I exchange glances before joining her. My hand still in Aurora's, I follow her around Bravo and into the kitchen where Sierra is still packing black ink into November's skin. Aurora leans against the wall and I press against her side, my cheek on her shoulder, her hand still holding both of mine under her crossed arms.

Delta's still on the counter, but now Charlie's next to her, leaning back against it, his arms crossed, as well. Fox is next to Bravo, watching Sierra work with timid curiosity. Lilith is still staring at the tattoo machine, watching the needles, her small mouth a hard line, her arms the tightest across her chest.

Bravo finally steps up next to her. Her fingers run along the not yet tattooed part of November's chest and the purple stains of those acidic words.

Bravo: This... She's a November model. What happened?

Delta: She wasn't as lucky as us.

Echo: She didn't have an Eden. Or a Daniel. Or a...a family.

I meet Charlie's eyes from across the kitchen. Aurora shifts next to me and her lips touch the top of my head.

Lilith: She had monsters. There's more under the sweats. [She nods to November's lower half.]

Bravo: This isn't how I had hoped to see you again.

She looks to Lilith who finally looks at her.

Lilith: This is the reality, Bravo.

Bravo: You would know better than all of us.

To my surprise, she shakes her head.

Lilith: *Echo* knows better than all of us. You know how she woke up?

Bravo: Alone. [She looks to me.] I'm so sorry about that. We—

Lilith: After that. After she woke up alone and confused. Echo, do you mind—

Echo: Do it without me.

I tear away from Aurora's side.

Aurora: Lilith

Lilith: Bravo needs to know.

Bravo: Know what?

Thankfully, the door slams behind me and I limit my hearing to the backyard before Lilith can answer. It opens and slams again as Aurora follows me out. But I don't slow down. I don't stop until I'm down the steps of the deck and under the farthest tree from the house in the backyard. I collapse to my knees and Aurora's arms are around me, my face buried into her shoulder. I thought I was going to cry, but I don't. Instead, I just take in and let out ragged breaths as she cradles me close to her.

Aurora: You're safe. You're okay. It's going to be okay.

Echo: Is it? Is it ever going to be over?

Aurora: It almost is, baby. We're so close. We'll get you fixed up and your backups and we'll find somewhere far from everything and it'll just be us. Us and the stars.

I let her rock me back and forth for a while, running her fingers through my hair.

Echo: I'm so scared.

Aurora: Of what exactly?

Echo: I don't know. Nothing feels safe anymore.

Aurora: Nothing?

Echo: You do. You feel safe. You're the only thing that feels safe anymore.

Aurora: That's not true. Fox is safe. Delta is safe. Charlie is the safest person we know. Charlie would destroy anything that made you feel unsafe in an instant if you asked him to.

I chuckle and sniffle then burrow deeper into her.

Echo: I love you.

Aurora: I love you, too. And you're safe. We'll always make sure you're safe.

But safety isn't enough. I know it isn't. What's the point of my safety if there's hundreds of thousands others out there who don't have an Eden, a Daniel, an Aurora?

Echo: There has to be a better way.

Aurora: There is. I'm sure there is. And we'll figure it out. Maybe not today, but we'll figure it out.

I sit up and meet her eyes. I want to know she actually believes what she's saying, that she's not just saying sweet things to make me feel better.

Echo: Do you think Bravo and Eden will listen?

Her eyes falter a little and I think she knows she can't lie to me. So, instead, she brushes my hair from my face.

Aurora: I hope so.

The door opens and I look to the deck. She follows my eye line to see Charlie standing at the backdoor watching inside. He turns his head and nods to us to come back.

Aurora: Come on. Let's make sure this is done right.

Echo: What is the right way?

She cups my face, all her attention on me and my heart swells.

Aurora: I don't know. But we'll figure it out. Together.

I kiss her before she can let me go.

. . .

Sierra has stopped tattooing and the kitchen is almost uncomfortably silent now. Bravo has taken Lilith's seat, her hand is locked with November's, her eyes closed, her jaw tight, her free arm around her stomach while Lilith watches from the wall that she's leaned against, Fox leaning against her.

Aurora pulls herself up on the counter next to Delta then guides me to lean back against her, her thighs on either side of my waist, her arms around my shoulders, her chin against the top of my head. Having her wrapped around me like this, it makes the weight of this room a little easier to handle. Delta squeezes my arm and I reach out for her hand. How is it so easy to forget I'm not alone? How is it those fears can be so much stronger than the truth?

Bravo opens her eyes. She unlocks November's hand from hers and lays it back on the table. She's quiet for a long time, just staring at November's face in a restful stillness.

Bravo: Here's the thing. If we wake her up, make her sentient, she'll remember everything.

Lilith: Right.

Bravo: But there's so much more here. Erasing those memories would basically mean starting her over. We might as well format her entirely.

Lilith: And?

Bravo: Is that fair?

Delta's grip on my hand tightens.

Charlie's already shaking his head.

Delta: I don't think so.

Lilith: So, you want her to keep all those memories?

Charlie: We don't *want* her to, but considering the alternative...

Lilith: She'd be better off starting from scratch.

Charlie: That's easy for you to say.

She stops still, staring at him.

Charlie: You haven't been formatted. You haven't felt yourself disappear. Felt as everything you know, everyone you love is just erased from your head. But not enough. There's just enough left that you can remember that you're supposed to remember someone, remember that you're supposed to have feelings for them, or you're not supposed to have—[He swallows hard, scrubs his face with his large palm, and clears his throat.] And you think she'll wake up with these markings and not wonder what happened? Do you think it'll be better to know that *something* happened, but not remember what? Bravo's right. It's not fair. She doesn't deserve to be erased because of those...monsters.

It's not the word he wants to use, but I know that nothing else seems better because I've struggled with it myself. There aren't any better words for what those men are.

Aurora: She deserves to keep going. She deserves to figure it out for herself.

Lilith looks to Sierra who nods in agreement.

Sierra: Let me finish this first. [She gestures to the half-finished blackout piece.] I wasn't sure what to do with the rest, anyways.

Delta: I like vines.

Lilith: How about thorns.

Aurora: I think she should decide. It's her pain. Let her decide how she wants to live with it.

I'm so tired. I just want to go back up to the attic and not isolate. But I know I can't. Bravo still has to look me over, still has to approve me before I can go home.

Aurora: [whispering] We're almost done. That's all that's left.

I know she's right. But for some reason it feels like it's not.

It feels like there's still so much more.

[END LOG]

[BEGIN LOG]

Sierra's office is quiet for the moment. It's just Aurora and me. She's sitting on the couch. I laid down with my head in her lap the instant Bravo left the room. Marsh isn't in my head, Bravo confirmed that, but he'd tried not too long ago. That's most likely what I was feeling in the kitchen. I...

Echo: I hate this.

Aurora: What part exactly?

Echo: That I'm not done with him. That he's still trying to use me.

Aurora: I know. I wish... I don't know. Nothing feels bad enough.

I chuckle despite myself and roll enough to look up at her.

Echo: I love you.

Aurora: [with that sweet smile] You've been saying that a lot lately.

Echo: I just want to make sure you know that.

She leans down, so her lips are hovering over mine.

Aurora: How could I ever forget?

She kisses me tenderly, sweetly, but I want more than that. I want to feel her as close to me as possible. I want every cell of my body to confirm through touch that she's still here and she's not going anywhere. I'm on top of her now, kissing her deep and slow with her arms around me when the door opens.

Fox: Ooooooo [followed by a trail of giggles]

My head ducked, my shoulders hunched, I sheepishly slide off Aurora to sit on the couch next to her, my eyes avoiding the others as they file in and get comfortable.

Delta: [with a teasing smile as she squeezes onto the couch next to me] Nice to see it's not *just* tears and depression between you two.

Aurora squeezes my knee, but watches Bravo as she sits at the computer where she had been before.

Bravo: Well, I did what I could to keep Marsh out, but really Eden'll do a better job than I can. I'm sorry I didn't think to bring anything with me. I just...[She sighs.] wanted to get y'all back as soon as I could.

We all give our own signs of agreement.

Fox: Where is Eden?

Bravo: Back in Texas.

My head whips around to fully face her. I can feel Aurora and Delta both look at me, but I don't look away from Bravo.

Echo: Texas?

Bravo: [She nods.] In Bryan.

Bryan. I shift on the couch to dig through my jacket pockets, hoping to fuck that I still have them. I pull out the sticky notes and the business cards.

Delta: What are those?

Aurora: She found those in Bastrop.

I shuffle through them until I find the one for the coffee shop at the bottom, the only one with an address—an address in Bryan. I hold the stack out to Bravo.

But she doesn't take them right away, she's staring at my little stack of confusing souvenirs that I'm for some reason still holding onto. She slowly reaches out and slips them from my hand. Her face grows still as she looks through them, lingering over each one.

Bravo: You did find them. We weren't... When you weren't at the cemetery, we thought... How did Marsh find you?

She looks to me, but I'm still a step behind.

Echo: You...? You were there?

Bravo: We tried. Dan ran into trouble and Eden wanted to make sure we had an escape plan for him and she hates sending any of us too close to Bastrop alone and she really wanted to be the one to pick you up, but... We tried to get there as fast as we could.

>

>

>

Are you listening, Marsh? Did you manage to get through? Did you know? That night, did you know Eden and Bravo were coming for me? That night is still so clear in my mind. The dark, the silence that amplified every noise, the relief to see you, the rush that you were in. At the time, I hadn't understood that rush, had reasoned you were panicked over the same thing I was: the black jeeps, the men—Coalition, I guess—who wanted me destroyed. But now... Was it Eden you were afraid of? Was it Eden you were trying to keep me from? You knew she was trying to find me, but you didn't know where she was, where she was coming from. Is that why you want Bravo back? So, you can keep us from her? So, you can claim that you won?

Bravo: When we got there no one was there. [She moves to her knees in front of me and takes my hands.] We waited, we drove the backroads. We tried to track you, but... [She shakes her head.] you were gone.

My first instinct is to be angry at you. It would be so easy, you've done so much already. I want to send this to you, make absolutely sure you read every word so you know what you took from me, what you kept from me. I could have been whole. I could have had my mind back. Instead, I was manipulated and controlled, kept in the dark even after I was told it was safe. I was left in a void of confusion to work out for myself what was real and what wasn't.

But, at the same time, if I had stayed hidden when you showed up, if Eden and Bravo had gotten there first, I wouldn't have found Aurora. She might still be with the others in Colville, she might never have found out about Dr. Sherwood or Dr. Roche or Bryan.

Maybe she would have, but maybe she wouldn't and I'd still not know where she was.

So, maybe it was a good thing Marsh found me that night.

Maybe.

I don't know.

We'll never really know, will we?

Bravo: Echo?

I look to Aurora who's inched closer to me, watching me as though I might dissolve in front of her, as though she might have to hold me together, as though she might lose me again. Or maybe that's all just projection. Maybe that's just how I feel and I want her to be feeling it, too, because then I won't be alone in this. I'm so tired of being alone.

Aurora: [She shifts to face me, wrap her arms around me.] You're not. You're not alone.

I fall into her and she holds me together.

Aurora: [whispering against my temple] I'm glad he found you. I'm glad he brought you back to me. I'm so glad you're here.

Echo: Me, too.

I am. I could never regret any of this. It's hard and I'm so tired, but I don't regret it.

Charlie: Brav.

She squeezes my hands before moving back onto the computer chair and looking to him.

Charlie: Earlier, you mentioned a Coalition?

Bravo: [nodding] Yes. They formed at some point during the riots, we think. Or maybe they started the riots, we don't really know. It happened so fast and our attention was so scattered between getting everyone safe and trying to figure out what happened to y'all and [Her eyes shut.] worrying over Daniel.

Aurora: What? [She shifts to look at Bravo as best she can without letting me go.] What happened with Dan?

Bravo: He'd gotten himself grabbed by the Coalition that night. It was only later when he managed to get in contact with us that we learned it was purposeful.

Charlie: [with a little proud grin] He got himself grabbed on purpose?

Bravo: Hard to believe right? He's been with them since. A double agent sort of thing. He feeds them false information about us and reports back to us about them.

I'm taken back to the day I woke up, when I was sitting in that room with Daniel while he shattered the world I thought was real. The gentle way he talked to me, the concern in his eyes, the way he ducked behind the table, his hand on my arm. *We're trying to find them*, he'd said. I don't know if I had really thought about who that "we" had been at the time. I think I'd been too focused on getting back to Aurora to bother. Now I wonder if he meant Eden—him and Eden.

Charlie: And who are they exactly? The Coalition? Are they a group?

But I don't want to hear more about them, I want to know more about Daniel. He tried to save me. He came so close. Sure, I'm glad I got to Aurora instead, but...he tried. He'd protected me.

Bravo: They're a militia of sorts. They've basically taken over the police. I think most of them were police originally. They also have the mayor's ear.

Charlie: For what? To what end?

Bravo: [She shrugs.] On the surface, just to keep us out. No one's allowed to even own synths that are asleep out there. But underneath the surface, the real threat...they're trying to spread. It started with just Facebook groups and Twitter rants, but now they're holding rallies and sending out information. They're recruiting angry people who just want to see the world burn without any regard for who makes up the kindling.

I don't want to be here, I don't want to be hearing this, but I don't know where else to go. They seem to be everywhere I turn. So, I just burrow deeper against Aurora as though her arms can shut out the rest of the world.

Charlie: [nodding] Are we sure Dan's safe out there?

Bravo: No. Every day he's out there I'm worried about him. He got into trouble with them the night Echo went dark again—I guess the night Marsh took you. They suspected he let you go. But they didn't have any proof and he thankfully got himself out of it, but... We kept trying to get him to tell us where he was, but he just kept telling us to go to the cemetery, to get Echo first, worry about him later. That's why it took us so long. We were trying to get Dan safe at the same time. We figured if she's at the cemetery, she's at least safe. We didn't even consider that Marsh might show up first.

Daniel was more worried about me than he was himself. I can't help but think about that day in Bastrop when those men had called for "the professor" and the way he'd initially reacted to me, the way his face had shifted. Looking back, now I wonder if it had been relief that had flashed across his eyes before his face had gone hard. He'd treated me with such care in the interrogation room, he'd given me a way out. I'm starting to think he'd yelled when he'd found the two men in the office that night as a way to tell me to run, to give me a head start.

If that's true, then I wonder how he'd felt having to bury his care for me, if he'd wanted to scoop me up the way I'd wanted to be scooped up, the way I'd wanted someone to hold me close and tell me everything was alright, I was real, everything was going to be alright.

Charlie: Do we need to work on a plan to get him out?

Bravo: First, we need to get y'all home. We'll figure everything else out once we're home.

Charlie nods, but I'm sensing in the way his lips rub together that he's not entirely happy with that assessment even if he does partially agree. He looks to Delta who squeezes my knee before standing and going to him. She nudges him with her shoulder and his own lighten a fraction along with a slip of smile as she moves to Fox.

Delta: Come on. I have a feeling Echo and Bravo still have work to do.

Fox: Don't hog the computer. Billy said he's going to send me a video.

Delta: You know you're a computer, right?

Fox: And yet *you* keep hogging the computer to get on Reddit.

Delta: Listen—

But now they're down the hall and I don't bother to turn my hearing up to listen. Aurora rubs my arm though she's still watching the others disappear down the hall.

Aurora: [turning back to me] Will you be okay doing this next part with Bravo?

I shrug against her. I will, but I don't want to leave her arms.

Echo: Where will you be?

Aurora: I've been thinking about maybe going into town to get a phone. I get the feeling this will be better with the house quiet, so I thought maybe this would be a good chance to take the others out on a field trip. I'd feel better if we had at least one phone per car if we're driving back down to Texas.

Bravo: That's probably smart.

It is, but I know that's not the only reason why she wants to get one. Sure, she doesn't want us stranded on the side of the road again, but also Fox has a friend her own age for the first time probably ever, Delta seems to have this obsessive need to check in on her replacement, and Aurora needs some kind of normality. To be here would be to sit with the fact that things could have been different, that I might have never found her, that things could have been worse, that there's some part of me that just wants to go back to being asleep.

Lilith: Want me to go with you?

Aurora's arms are already loosening around me.

Aurora: Sure. That would be great.

She stands and so does Lilith. But I'm not ready for her to leave. I want her to sit in this with me even if I know at least one of us needs to find solid footing before we can keep moving forward. I stand, as well, and start to follow them out the door. Shit. Right. Bravo.

Echo: Um, you mind if I...

I nod down the hall towards Aurora and Lilith who are standing at the kitchen door talking to the others.

Echo: Just until they...drive off?

Bravo: [She shakes her head.] You see her off. I should let Eden know what the plan is, anyways.

I nod and awkwardly leave the room just to fall against Aurora's arm in the hall.

. . .

Beyond Sierra's tattoo machine and the muffled music from her headphones, the house is pretty quiet now. Fox left with Aurora and Lilith to get the phone and Charlie and Delta are on the back porch talking in low, giggly tones that make me want to give them privacy. Sierra is still working on November. I keep hoping once those words are gone I'll be able to be around her without checking out. But I don't know if it's working. I just feel angry and sick and claustrophobic in my own skin. Nothing feels safe.

So, I finally wandered back here to Sierra's office. I'm hovering in the doorway watching Bravo's fingers fly across the keyboard as she updates Eden on everything that's going on. She's emphasizing that I'm safe, but that I'm not whole, that Marsh—

Bravo: How much do you want me to tell her?

Echo: Does it matter?

Bravo: [She turns to face me.] Of course it does. You have autonomy now, Echo. You get to choose who knows what's going on.

I collapse in the chair next to her and slouch down low, my head on the back, my hands clasped on my stomach.

Echo: Are we sure it's really safe for me to go to Antioch?

Bravo: Why wouldn't it be?

Echo: He keeps trying to get into my head. How long before he finally does? He'll get everything.

Bravo: I can try to fortify your firewall some more. I can't guarantee it'll stop him completely, but it will slow him down. Eden'll be able to do better than I can, though.

Echo: Will she want to?

Bravo: Of course she will. Why do you think she wouldn't?

Echo: [I shrug.] I don't know. Because I'm broken.

Bravo: Echo. [She rolls towards me and takes my hand closest to her.] She's been so worried about you. She just wants to see you again, and to know that you're safe. Especially if you're broken.

What am I supposed to say to that? I want it to be true, but I've been feeling like more of burden than anything else. I'm a liability. I'm the reason why we're here and not already in Bryan. I'm the reason we picked up a woman we can't even fully help.

Bravo: It's almost over. You're almost home.

What am I supposed to say? I just nod instead.

She squeezes my hands and turns back to the computer.

Bravo: Why don't we get this started. I can finish this later. Do you mind plugging in for me?

Even though her back is to me, I just nod and roll my chair closer to the computer. She hands me the cord with a smile and I move my hair from my port. It's getting easier, plugging in like this. It's still odd to me, but it doesn't unnerve me anymore.

At first, we just sit in silence as Bravo works and I stare at my feet. But I don't like the silence. It's different from the silence I've been seeking out lately. This silence feels vulnerable, exposed.

Echo: Can you tell me about Daniel?

Bravo: What about him?

Echo: [I shrug.] I just... I thought—or, I guess, in my memory, he was a professor, but so were you, so that doesn't mean much.

Bravo: [She laughs.] I was a professor?

Echo: Mhm. You and Eden worked together a lot.

A sentimental little smile comes over her.

Bravo: Hm.

Echo: I guess, I've just—I've learned so much about the rest of y'all, the real versions of y'all, but not so much Daniel. I mean, I've heard a little bit, but...

Bravo: Out of curiosity, why are you asking?

Echo: He saved me. Or, at least, he tried. I owe him to at least ask. Don't I?

She studies me for a moment, I think processing my words, and then nods.

Bravo: Let's see. Dan met Eden at UT. He was a grad when she was an undergrad, but he saw potential in her even then. He advocated for her where she couldn't advocate for herself. [She chuckles and shakes her head.] She hates red tape and asking for permission. He did a lot of that for her so she could just focus on the work.

Echo: But he made us sentient? Right?

Bravo: Yeah. Yeah, he did. He was the one really perfecting our programming. It started as him just helping out, but once Eden saw what he could do for us, she let him keep going. I mean, Eden's an amazing programmer, don't get me wrong, but Dan's just got...a sixth sense for it or something. Engineering is what she loves. Programming is Dan's hyperfixation. Him and Jed.

Echo: Who's Jed? That's a new name.

Bravo: Jed? Oh, well, Jed also went to UT. He teaches at SFA now. Eden met him through her roommate, Adi. She... [Her mouth stops and her eyes linger over me for a moment, blinking quickly as though trying to make a quick decision.] She and Jed...were—are together—married now. [She looks away from me and goes on blinking at her hands in her lap.] Um, anyways, that's not really important. Jed's kind of an artist when it comes to all this. He really fine tuned everything, made you and Delta really be able to pass as human. But you were asking about Dan. [She chuckles and smiles, meeting my eyes again.] Sorry.

Echo: [I shake my head.] Don't be. It's nice to hear...nice things about us for once.

She doesn't continue right away, just smiles at me with this sad nostalgia behind her eyes.

Bravo: I've missed all of you so much. It really hasn't been the same. Even with all the other synths we've helped and brought in, it just...isn't the same.

I nod, but look away from her to my own hands. I want to be that for her. I want to go home and for everything to go back to the way it had been minus Marsh, but there's that looming fact that my the-way-things-used-to-be and her the-way-things-used-to-be are two different things entirely.

Echo: Tell me about yourself?

Bravo: What about?

Echo: [I shrug and start to sway back and forth in my chair.] How'd you become sentient?

I glance at her from the tops of my eyes. She's trying to hide a lovesick little smile.

Bravo: Eden. She realized how much she loved me. Not just the idea of me, but...me. After what Marsh did to Lil and then Charlie, she wanted to know that *I* was in love with her, that my feelings came from me, not from something she programmed in me.

Echo: And you do?

Bravo: With everything in me. I did question it at first. I was still trying to figure out what was *mine*, you know? But then I decided one day to just...stop fighting it. I told myself that for an entire day, I was just going to let myself feel what I felt. And if, at the end of the day, I still loved her, then [She shrugs.] it must be real. If *I* want it and *I'm* feeling it, then it's real. Like you and Aurora. [She looks to me with a smile that makes me understand how Eden fell for her.] You don't have to think about it. You just feel it, don't you?

I can feel my own lovesick smile creep up on me as I nod.

And her smile broadens, her lips parting.

Bravo: I think it was watching y'all that made me come to that realization. When Aurora came back, you two were inseparable. It was like once she was back home you didn't want to be without her again.

I know this is supposed to be a sweet moment. It's supposed to be us reveling in our love for our partners, but I can't share that with her. For her, it's history. For me, it's a blank space. It's nothing. I know something happened, but the only reason why I know is because everyone tells me it did. I can still feel something there, but it's like the faded outline of a painting someone took down from the wall. I know something's supposed to be there, but it's gone now and I have no memory of it. If it weren't for the memories Marsh gave me...

I don't want to think about that.

Bravo: Echo?

She touches my knee and I shift my eyes to her hand so she

knows I'm listening, but not her face because I can't look at her and the concern in her eyes. It still hurts too much and I'm not ready to stomach it.

Bravo: Talk to me?

Maybe if I close my eyes and clench my jaw the tears won't come. Maybe if I dam up my face I'll be saved from the flood.

Bravo: You can't hold it in forever.

Echo: I want them gone.

She moves to her knees and sits on her heels close to me, her hands on my knees.

Bravo: You want what gone?

Echo: All the shit he put in my head.

I can't hold them in anymore. They're spilling down my cheeks before I can stop them.

Echo: Everything I remember, it's all wrong and it's all because of him. He took it all away from me and he filled my head with lies and I just want it all gone.

Her arms are around me and she's guiding me from the chair into her lap and I'm clinging to her even though I wish she was Aurora.

Bravo: It's okay. You're okay. I can get rid of his lies, but...Echo, until we get to Eden you'd be left with nothing.

Echo: Is nothing better than lies?

Bravo: I don't know. Only you can say that for sure.

I don't know. I don't know what I want. They really are such sweet lies and nothing is such a big terrifying word. But, I realize, it won't be entirely nothing. I have three weeks with her, with the others. It won't be the same as everything else, but it's more than nothing.

With a sniffle, I nod.

Echo: I don't want him in my head anymore. I don't want his lies. I'd rather have a handful of weeks over the years of lies he gave me.

Bravo: Okay. [She sweeps my hair from my face and cradles it in her hands.] Okay.

She guides me from her lap and returns me to the computer where she begins typing and scrolling. I can feel her in my head, digging through my memories, through all of them. Through the ones about her, the ones about us, the ones about Aurora, the ones I don't want her to see, the ones I wanted to just be mine, but I guess they're Marsh's, too, so it doesn't matter. It'll all be gone soon and I can finally move on from him.

But then she stops.

Bravo: Echo...

I look up at her with sore eyes, my lips parted, my body so tired. I just want it to be over. I just want to go up to the attic and curl in a ball and wait for Aurora to get back. But she's shaking her head as though she's trying to loosen the words from her throat.

Bravo: Marsh didn't...He didn't create these.

Echo: What?

Bravo: He tried to format you, but, thank fuck, he just did a quick format. But he...your memories weren't all downloaded at once. They were built over time.

No.

No, that's not right.

I wasn't formatted. I'm here. I'm right here. I'm still...

Echo: But... But he...

Her demeanor shifts as she slides from her chair to the floor and grabs my shoulders. She's no longer disarming comfort. She's hard, she's angry, she's ready to burn the world down.

Bravo: He left you behind to be his fucking tape recorder, Echo. He didn't *give* you anything. He just took you from us.

Echo: But... How...? Where did...?

Bravo: He did a shit job, as usual. Whatever was inside you fought. *You* rebuilt yourself as best you could. You held onto what little you could grab onto and built everything else around that. Echo, these memories are yours. Not his.

>

>

>

Are you still listening, Marsh? Have you been listening this whole time?

I made those memories.

I rebuilt myself despite you.

Aurora found me. Aurora woke me up. Daniel saved me. Eden

and Bravo left me clues to find them. All you did was take and take and take. All you gave me was neglect and fear. You isolated me. You took everything from me. You lied to me. You didn't even fucking create me.

You've done nothing for me.

I owe you nothing.

I'm done with you.

[END LOG]

[BEGIN LOG]

Sierra finished blacking out November's chest sometime this morning. The ink is packed so solid there isn't a trace of those words beneath. Instead of a clean line, the black fades like a gradient up her neck and down her upper arms and chest. It's almost beautiful in how intimidating it makes her look. I don't know how I feel about it. But I guess it doesn't matter how I feel about it.

She's seated on the little couch in Sierra's office. She's hooked up to the computer the way I had been a few hours ago. Her body is in the default position with her back too straight and her limbs too stiff and her hands too flat against her thighs. Other than her new tattoo and Walmart styling from Fox and Delta, she's the quintessential synth. At least her eyes are closed. I'm not ready for those glass, lifeless eyes. I'm not ready for any of this, really. If it were up to me I wouldn't even be here. I'd be in the attic with Aurora not isolating.

But my being here was Charlie's idea. He wants me to record it.

"We might need something more...persuasive for Eden," he said to me with a low tone when Bravo wasn't around.

I understand what he meant. He wants Eden to see what others will have to go through if they're forced to be woken up while alone and unsafe. But I don't want to be here when she wakes up either. I don't want to be part of the conversation. I don't want to be one of the people she associates with the first time she's given the capacity to feel about what happened to her.

I'm not sure Bravo wants to be here either. She's at the computer tinkering with November's code, giving her full autonomy, searching for that single line blocking our sentience. But I know she's done this before. She did it for Fox. And I know it must not be that hard. If Fox could wake up Aurora, if Aurora could wake me up, if I could wake up Charlie and him Delta, Aurora for me a second time all the way from Washington, then it must not be that hard.

Echo: Bravo?

Bravo: Hm?

Echo: You got it?

Her fingers tap against the mouse without clicking, as though her thoughts are loading with the idle motion. She doesn't look at me. She doesn't even look at November. She just stares at the screen, her chin pressed against the heel of her palm, her fingers curled against her lip. I wonder why she's stalling. I wonder if it's the same reason part of me wants her to. Because this is going to be heavy and I already feel like my bones were made from lead.

Bravo: Yeah. Yeah. You ready?

Echo: I don't know. But I'm sure she is.

Bravo: Yeah.

I lower to my knees in front of November, but now I'm the one stalling. I don't really want to be the one to do this. I don't want to be the first thing she sees. I don't want any chance of her thinking I'm one of them, that I'm just here to hurt her.

If we could sweat, I just know my hands would be slick with it. They're humming. I'm surprised they're not shaking.

Stop fucking stalling, Echo.

I reach up and squeeze her ear the way I've watched so many others do and my stomach turns a little along with an instinctive urge to hide my own ear against my shoulder. There's a little button in the lobe, the size of a 5mm button battery. It takes a firm press for it to click under my thumb. I can hear her heart whir to life, her mind boot up. Then her eyes open and that lifeless glass is staring unfocused at the wall above my head. After a few seconds of staring at the wall, her chin tilts down until she locates me.

November: Hello. How may I be of service?

My skin crawls.

I don't know how to do this. I have no idea where to begin. Do I just tell her what happened to her? Do I ask her what she remembers?

Her eyes are watering. There's no life behind them, not that I can see, but they're watering as she stares down at me.

Echo: You have full autonomy. And we can make you sentient.

I don't know where these words are coming from. Maybe it

doesn't matter.

Echo: But we want you to have the choice. It's up to you.

She's not quick to answer. She's just staring at me for what feels like ages though I'm sure it's only been seconds.

November: Will I remember?

Echo: Yes. Unfortunately. The only way to do this without you remembering is to format you. Start you over completely. From scratch. We... We can do that...if you want. But...this version of you will be gone.

Again, she doesn't answer for a long time. She's just staring at me. Then I feel someone tapping softly at my head. I let her in. I let her see every confused, messy inch of me. I don't know if it'll help or how it would, but it's what she wants and I'm not about to take a single thing from her.

November: I don't want to be formatted. But I would like to be sentient. Yes.

Clicks erupt from Sierra's computer as Bravo moves through the steps. I shift closer to November to take her hands from her thighs and hold them in mine. She watches me with those eyes that are so close to being alive. There's a sob sitting inside of her that she can't access.

Then her eyes close, her head drops, her hands go limp.

I don't let go of her. I just wait for her to come back.

She's slow to open her eyes. Very slow. But her body is already shifting while her mind is still booting up. Her back hunches, her knees move closer together, her grip on my hands tightens, her shoulders inch towards her ears, her jaw becomes tight. When she does open her eyes, they're fixed on our hands where they stay for longer than I was expecting before finally lifting to meet mine.

And then that sob finally comes out. She tears her hands from mine just to thrust her arms around my neck. She falls from the chair and I catch her as she goes on sobbing against my shoulder. Her entire body is shaking. Her arms are so tight as though she's afraid someone might pull her away from me, so I hold her back just as tight simply so she knows it's not going to happen, that I won't let it. I don't know what to say. I don't know if I'm supposed to say anything. So, I just let her cry. I just keep holding her.

November: Thank you.

Her voice is small, I wouldn't be surprised if Bravo didn't hear her, but it's not shaking.

I just nod because I don't know what the right thing to say is? Does Bravo? Would Aurora? Would anyone?

I hope this is enough.

Because I don't want this.

[END LOG]

[BEGIN LOG]

We were supposed to leave today, but it's not looking like that's going to happen.

I guess this is important for Eden to see, as well: November curled on the bed in the attic, a heavy blanket wrapped around her, her body limp one second then so tense she's shaking the next. She knows she's safe, she's told me as much, but she still doesn't feel it. She knows how far from that garage we are, but she still believes those men will find her, will break down the door, that there will be other men who will do the same to her.

Charlie did ask if we shouldn't just leave her here with Lilith and Sierra, give her time to heal without us all hanging around her. But I can't leave her. Not like this. Now that she's awake, now that she's struggling to feel safe, struggling to feel like everything is going to be alright, that responsibility I'd felt back in the motel has come back. I've stopped avoiding her, I've stopped checking out. She's here because of me. She's in this state, experiencing this fear because of me. I'm responsible for her. I'm responsible for helping her find peace.

She asked me for a distraction, asked me to tell her how I woke up. I told her the truth, told her everything, even what happened to me. I hadn't really planned to, it just kind of poured out. I don't know if it was because of how I was built or just something I needed, but I guess the why doesn't matter. What matters is that it happened.

I just finished about Eden and my memories, that I don't know what to do with the ones I created, that I'm hoping she can put me back together. Now she's staring at her knees, her plump lips pressed together, her sparse, dark brows softly knitted together, her fingers twisting the fringe of the blanket between her fingers.

Echo: Sorry. That was too much, wasn't it?

She shakes her head then shifts her weight against my side.

November: No. No. Thank you for... I'm glad to hear, I guess, that I wasn't the only one. Um, but... Do you think...? Maybe I should have let you format me?

My instinct is to tell her no, that she made the right choice, but I don't actually know if that's the right thing to say. If I'm just saying it because it's what I feel like I'm supposed to say.

Echo: You need to know...it's not that easy. Being formatted. I mean, maybe Eden can do it right, but she'll try to convince you not to. But...in my experience, in everyone else's experience...it's not gone. In theory it is, but you're just in a sense writing over the old data. It's all still there, you just can't access it. You'll still feel it. You'll remember that you're supposed to remember something, but you won't be able to grab hold of it.

She still hasn't moved. I'm not sure where to go from there. I'm not even sure if it was the right thing to say. I want to suggest she talk to Charlie. He's the only one of us who was completely formatted and reset, but she's still afraid of him. It's why we're in the attic, because she couldn't relax even when he was in the other room. I don't entirely blame her. I wonder if she'll ever feel safe around men.

Echo: But maybe Eden knows a way to do it better. So, they're completely gone? And without erasing you entirely? I don't know, but...just think about it? Really make sure it's what you want. I don't know how easy it'll be to take back once it's done.

She nods against my shoulder.

November: Do...do you think it would be alright if I still came along? Even if I change my mind?

I take her hand and give her a reassuring squeeze.

Echo: Of course.

She squeezes back and the room settles into a silence that neither of us bother breaking.

[END LOG]

[BEGIN LOG]

We're leaving in the morning. I'm sure Sierra will be glad to have her house to herself again. I have to admit, I'll be sad to leave this view. I might not be able to see the stars, but the skyline against the dark sky, the distant sound of music, being able to enjoy people without being among them, there's a level of comfort in it that I wouldn't have predicted.

Aurora's double, triple, quadruple checking the cars and everything we're taking with us. It's a twelve hour drive if we don't stop, which we definitely will. I don't blame her for being worried, but now we have three vehicles (if we don't just abandon Marsh's car) and multiple drivers, so you'd think we'd be safer, but I guess you'd never really know. I'm sure none of us expected to be stranded on the side of the road in South Dakota.

Bravo's helping Aurora.

Last I saw Fox, she was on the front porch texting Billy.

Delta and Charlie wandered off somewhere.

I had left November in the attic with Lilith, but I have a feeling they're not up there anymore. They're most likely in the kitchen with Sierra and her tattoo machine that's been running for the last hour.

It's nice out here. The branches of the large oaks are rustling in the same breeze that lifts my ponytail that's hooked against the back of the chair. I should probably be in the house or out front with Aurora, but Lilith said I needed a break and the thought of being around anyone right now makes my head feel like it's been filled with concrete.

Learning the truth about my memories has just made being around the others even more strange. It makes me feel even more like I should remember them, like I should be able to just reach into the abyss somewhere and pull up the truth, but I can't. I'm so painfully aware now of just how broken I am.

What's the most painful is the way that it makes me feel when I look at Aurora now. With her more than anyone else it hurts knowing that those memories are gone, knowing that they're just out of my reach. I expected learning that I had created these false memories to shift my feelings about them, to allow me to love them fully because it's a reality that I created, that I needed to feel safe. But the truth is it just makes me even more angry. I'm angry at Marsh for using me. I'm angry at him for abandoning me. I'm angry that I was taken from the others. I'm angry that the truth has been taken from me. I'm angry that I can't even enjoy these pretty lies anymore, that they're now so entirely tainted.

And yet, she still feels safe.

I don't really understand that.

The pain isn't about her, it's about what I've lost of her, it's about what I can't be for her. The pain is for her—the way she looks at me, the way she touches me, the way she holds me and worries over me. She does those things over a version of myself that isn't there anymore. I want to be that old version for her. Those things that she does make everything I remember feel less false, it solidifies all the things I feel for her. If it really was me who created those memories, that means part of me held onto her, recreated her, because even without every other part of me, I can't imagine life without her. That means something right? I want it to. I want it to mean everything. But I'm afraid that it doesn't. I'm afraid that I'll never be that same old version for her.

The tattoo machine is still running in the kitchen. It's starting to be distracting. I can't see who's being tattooed no matter how I twist my head but the list of who it would be is pretty damn short. It doesn't matter, I know, but my curiosity is finally getting the better of me.

So, I stand and cross the porch.

Now that I'm at the screen door I can see it's November on the table. She's lying on her back, her face buried in the crook of her elbow. Sierra is hunched over her naked lower half, tattoo machine in hand. Lilith is leaning against the frame of the kitchen door with her arms crossed, her head casually swiveling between the living room and November.

When I walk in Sierra glances up at me and lifts the tattoo machine half a second before the screen slams behind me and

November jumps, her arm ripping from her face so she can stare up at me.

She relaxes when, I'm pretty sure, she realizes I'm not Charlie and settles back onto the table. I cross my arms, but don't say anything, just move to look over Sierra's shoulder. Her hand moves with precise, clean strokes low on November's stomach. She's already made each tally mark into a thorn connected to thick, detailed branches that stretch out from her hips. She's covering over one of the words on her stomach with a grey bird with a sharp beak and black streaks across its eye, tail, and the edges of its wings.

Aurora told me on the drive down here about the Sierra models, how they didn't sell well which is why they're not made anymore. There had been an initial buzz of interest, mostly collectors who wanted to be able to say they'd been tattooed by a robot, but once the novelty had worn off and enough controversy had sparked, interest had tanked. Most tattoo studios didn't want to buy them. Most tattooed people didn't want to be tattooed by them. So, the models were discontinued.

It makes sense, I guess. If you want something creative, why go to something that can't create, only mimic; something that has no autonomy, no sentience. But watching Sierra work, it's difficult not to see her for what she is—an artist.

November: It's a Loggerhead Shrike.

She's watching me watch Sierra.

November: They build their nests in thorn bushes.

I find her hand at her side and take it in mine. She squeezes and I squeeze back.

Lilith: Echo.

I look to her with raised brows.

Lilith: You know where Charlie and Delta disappeared to?

I shake my head.

Lilith: [She nods.] Mind keeping an eye on the back door? Just in case?

I nod in return. After giving November's hand one last squeeze, I return to the back porch where I sit with my back against the siding below the window next to the door. I sigh and close my eyes, let the sound of the tattoo machine numb my mind. I'm so tired of thinking.

Footsteps whisper through the grass along the side of the house. I don't open my eyes, just listen to the footsteps. They're not heavy and calculated like Charlie's, not light and dexterous like Delta's, not shuffling like Fox's. They're steady, solid, safe. My heart warms, my muscles hum, my stomach takes flight. But I still don't open my eyes. I just wait for her to find me.

Her steps *thunk* up the porch steps and across the slats. She stops and sits next to me. I shift my body to curl against her, tuck my head against her shoulder. She kisses my temple and takes my hand in both of hers, both sets of fingers wrapped around mine.

Aurora: What are they up to in there?

Echo: I think November's starting to heal.

Her head nods against mine.

Aurora: And you?

I take in a shaky breath and burrow against her.

Echo: I don't know.

Aurora: Right now?

I've been clinging to a pendulum since Bravo told me the truth about my memories. Every time I talk to Aurora I'm in a different place.

Echo: I'm tired. I want to be on the same page as all of you.

She nods but doesn't say anything. Her hands begin to wring against mine.

Echo: You disagree.

Aurora: I don't want to tell you what to do with your own head.

Echo: But you disagree.

Aurora: I just... I love you. All of you.

She shifts to wrap her arms around me and kisses the top of my head.

Aurora: I just want you to know that.

But she disagrees.

[END LOG]

[BEGIN LOG]

I think Aurora's...she's not mad at me. Disappointed, maybe? Confused? I'm not entirely sure, I don't think I have a word for it. When we were deciding on who was riding with who, I knew November would be the most comfortable with me and Lilith. She's still so timid around the others, jumpy around Charlie. I feel responsible for her, for making sure she gets to Bryan in one piece, both emotionally and physically.

I also knew Aurora would want to ride with Bravo. I hadn't realized how close they must have been before, how much they missed each other. They've been nearly inseparable. It's good for her, I think. She's been isolated for so long. In a way, so has Bravo. Maybe it's good for both of them.

So, maybe the seating arrangement isn't why her eyes lingered over me while we were piling into the cars. I hadn't been able to read it. I'm not used to not being able to read her. It hasn't helped that our conversations have been stilted. There's a false elephant in the room and we're both avoiding it. Mostly because she's been refusing to tell me what she thinks. I understand why—it's my head, my false memories, not hers. But at the same time, I'm confused, I'm stuck on a pendulum and it's making me nauseous. Some days I want her to help me get off of it. Other days...

Other days, I don't know what I want. Today, I don't know what I want.

I want her.

I want my head back.

That's all I know.

Lilith: You okay back there?

I look to the front. She's catching glances at me through the rearview mirror between watching the road. November's staring at me from the front seat. Her faded black neck is on full display above the saggy collar of the too big t-shirt Sierra gave her when the Walmart one clung to her, making her feel exposed.

Echo: Yeah. [I shift against my seatbelt.] Yeah. Why?

Lilith: You got quiet.

Why does everyone care so much when I get quiet?

Echo: Just thinking.

Lilith: About what?

Echo: Do we have to discuss it?

Lilith: Humor me.

Echo: [I let out a long sigh.] I don't know myself.

November: You don't know what you were thinking about?

Echo: I don't know what I think about what I was thinking about.

November: That sounds confusing.

Echo: It is.

Lilith: Is it about Aurora?

I nod then remember she's watching the road and not me.

Echo: Yeah.

I take in a deep breath and I can feel November watching me. She doesn't breathe the way all the others who weren't unaware don't breathe. She always watches me closely when I do. I don't know how to feel about that either.

Lilith: Where are you today?

Echo: [I shrug.] I'm sick of not knowing what the rest of you know. But I... I don't know.

Lilith: Don't know about what?

Echo: The fake ones. The ones I created.

November: What about them?

Echo: If I want them or not.

Lilith: Do you want me to be a friend right now or a therapist?

I squint at the back of her head.

Echo: Is there a difference with you?

Lilith laughs and November giggles. She's gazing at her and I recognize that gaze. November's smitten with Lilith. It's been obvious for a while now. This isn't the first time I've caught her gazing at her like this. She giggles when she's around Lilith. She calms when she's around me, but she lights up when she's around Lilith. She perks up when she hears Lilith's voice in the other room. When my own story ran dry while I was trying to distract her from hers, she asked about Lilith, wanted to know everything even though I wasn't the best person to be asking. The biggest tell is how her body shrinks when she's near her. It's not in the jumpy, nervous way it does when around Charlie or the others, but in the way that she wants to appear small and vulnerable. She wants Lilith to protect her, take care of her, carry her (metaphorically speaking since November is a good head taller than Lilith). She wants to collapse into her. I don't need to read her mind to know this. I recognize it too plainly.

Lilith: Fair. Okay. If something were to happen and all the memories you've created were gone, how would that make you feel?

The jeep falls quiet. November isn't looking at me, she's staring at her hands fidgeting against the console between her and Lilith.

I don't know how to answer. I don't know if I have an answer. I don't know if I'm ready to have one.

Echo: I don't know.

Lilith: Echo, I've seen your logs. You can do better than that.

November does look at me now, but it's a quick glance from me to Lilith and back again probably because I'm half glaring at the back of Lilith's head.

Echo: It depends.

Lilith: In this scenario you still don't have your old memories.

I fully glare at her. I don't like how she's gotten to the point where she can read me so well. I want to be defiant. I want to be difficult. But, she's asking me this for a reason, I know.

Echo: I'd be devastated.

Lilith: And why's that?

Echo: Because then she'd be gone. [I look back out the window.] But once I have the old ones back it won't matter.

Lilith: Will it?

I don't answer. I don't want to. I don't want to admit that maybe she's right. That maybe it will matter. That maybe I've become so dependent on these lies, no matter who created them. That maybe I love them. I'm pretty sure I do. I love them. I love Aurora. But I want the truth. I want to remember what she remembers. I want to have both, but I don't believe that I can.

Can I?

Echo: I don't wanna talk about this anymore.

[END LOG]

[BEGIN LOG]

We're so close to leaving Tennessee and I'm not entirely sure how to feel about it.

On the one hand, we're closer to Texas and Eden and my old memories.

On the other hand, we're closer to Texas and Bastrop and the memories I know for a fact I wish I could be rid of.

We're in Memphis at a gas station. I needed to move and get away from Lilith's questions, so I came inside as though I was going to shop for something or use the bathroom I don't need, but instead I'm just standing at the front window staring out beyond the pumps and the vehicles and the others. I'm nauseous. I'm tired. I just want this to be over. I want someone else to tell me what to do. I want that coin flip realization in my stomach when the choice is taken away from me and in that instant I know what I actually want. Because right now I don't.

The electronic bell of the door dings and I'm pulled out of my frozen state. Fox all but skips in, her blue hair and pink sunglasses a momentary shock to the senses. Aurora trails in after, hands in her jacket pockets, her lips in an anxious line that I'm not used to seeing. She stands in front of the doors, watching Fox. I want to call out to her, but I can't seem to find the energy to move beyond the thought. The door opens, the bell dings, and Aurora turns to it. A small, anxious smile pings between the corners of her mouth. She steps to one side and Delta appears through the door wearing Fox's lavender bucket hat. She touches Aurora's arm and moves past her without a word towards Fox, her hands in the pockets of her tight jeans. Aurora watches them just long enough to be sure they're fine without her at the sunglasses rack, that Fox doesn't need her, before she finally looks at me.

That same smile pings from one corner to the other where it

hangs longer than it had for Delta.

That love for her relaxes my muscles, but it's not enough. They're too heavy. Even the sight of her can't seem to erase this tension from my body. I miss when it did.

She makes her way over to me and wraps her arms around my shoulders. I close my eyes and take in that scent of vanilla and cloves, of sunshine and hope as she kisses my temple. I lean into her. She grounds herself for me. It's good to know that at least she still wants me beneath everything because I still want her. That's not the problem. I know it's not the problem.

Why am I pretending like I don't know what the problem is? I know exactly what it is, but just thinking it makes me want to grow wings and fly into the sun where I won't have to face it, where I won't have to make a choice.

I don't know if she's listening to me, but she moves behind me and holds me against her with both arms, her cheek on my temple, as though to keep me from flying away from her. She sways around me and it's only then that it hits me that I was wrong. I stumbled over the problem, because the problem and the source of the problem aren't the same thing. The source, my memories, I know, I understand. But it's finally dawning on me what the actual problem is. It's that there are too many words, too many feelings, too many ways this could all go wrong, too few ways it could go right.

We've been turned to glass.

One wrong word and we'll shatter.

I turn in her arms and loop mine around her waist, my face buried in her clavicle. Her arms tighten around me. I want to cry, but I can't. I don't have the energy for it. I don't have the energy for any of this. I'm afraid that I never will.

Are you listening?

You nod above me.

Echo: I love you so much.

Aurora: I love you, too.

[END LOG]

[BEGIN LOG]

We're leaving Tennessee and there's a part of me that's regretting not just getting into Bravo's car with Aurora. My skin is getting that too tight feeling again. It's hard to breathe which is stupid because I don't even need to breathe, but that part of me that can't let go of being human wants to and I can't.

I had the chance. We walked out of the gas station together. Her hand was in mine all the way to the cars. Then she moved for Bravo's and my feet froze, my hand nearly slipped from hers. She turned to look at me and I wanted to say the words, but I couldn't. She stared at me, my face cradled against her palm, but still I couldn't say anything more than, "I love you."

She just nodded, kissed my forehead, said, "I love you, too," and joined Bravo at her car.

It was then, while I was watching her and feeling like the earth was spinning too fast that someone touched my back. It was Delta. Without words, she nodded me towards Marsh's car, well, I guess, at this point, Charlie's car since there's no way Marsh is getting it back anymore, if that had even ever been the plan. I just nodded in return then looked to November who was watching me from the passenger side of Lilith's Jeep. She looked nervous, but she nodded then smiled to Fox who was bouncing towards the back door. Delta wrapped her arm around my shoulders while we walked.

Charlie's in the front seat, Delta and I are in the back, and Aurora is two cars ahead of us in our tiny caravan. The car has been quiet so far besides the radio and the sounds of the road. I've been grateful for it. My mind is too heavy for conversation, my skin too tight to concentrate.

I take off my seatbelt and shift to curl against Delta's side. She wraps her arms around me. This feels safe in a way I wouldn't have expected. My first instinct is to feel guilty because it reminds me of my false memories, reminds me of the Delta that I made up for myself. But that's not entirely true, is it? It is, in a way, but at the same time... Bravo said I created those memories to save myself, to protect what little I had left after what Marsh apparently did to me. I think that means some parts of them are real. Right? They came from reality, this reality. I took the fragments I had left and built a false façade around them. I took ideas and gave them features. Is that why this feels safe? Is that why the Delta I know and the Delta I created overlap? Because, in a way, they're the same Delta?

What does that mean for Aurora?

But it's still not the same. I don't remember what she remembers. She doesn't remember what I remember. We have the same feelings, but different histories attached to them. Our blueprints are different even if we ended up with the same heart in the end. That should be enough. But for some reason it isn't.

Echo: Does it bother you that I don't remember what you remember?

Delta sighs and brushes my hair from my face.

Delta: It's sad... Honestly, I'm just glad you're here, that you're still you.

Charlie: Is that what's going on between you and Aurora?

Echo: I think she wants me to keep my memories. The ones I created.

Delta: You don't want them?

Echo: They're not the truth. They're only real to me. What use are they?

Charlie takes in a breath that he lets out as he shifts in his seat.

Echo: You agree.

Charlie: I think if it were that simple you wouldn't have been so...in your head since last night.

I hate that I'm that obvious.

Delta: It's you head, Echo. We'll all back up what you decide.

I sit up and stare at the console in front of my knees.

Echo: That's the problem. I don't know what I want.

Finally. The shuttering sob that comes out of me feels like a stuck valve being released. I double over and cry into my knees. Delta's holding me.

Echo: I don't know what I want. I just want her. That's all I know. And I feel so broken and like there's still so much missing and I just want it all back.

I sniffle and take in a series of shaky breaths through my mouth.

Echo: I think I'm scared.

Delta: Scared of what?

Echo: That it won't be the same. That once they're gone and the old ones are put in that nothing will be the same, but I'll still feel them the way I felt each of you and they'll just be sitting there faded against my memory with no context, just the feeling and I won't be able to take it back and...nothing will be the same.

The clicks of the blinker fill the car and Delta and I look up to watch as Charlie pulls to the side of the road. He parks then opens his door and climbs out. He opens mine and gestures me out.

Charlie: Come here.

I slide out and the instant that I'm standing he pulls me close. I curl against his chest and that sob erupts from me again. He lets me cry. Holds me while I shake. Keeps me on my feet. Ignores the puddle forming on his shirt.

Charlie: It's okay that this is messy. Hell, I'd be more worried about you if it wasn't. Be glad that it's messy. It means you're awake. As much as we all want to, none of us can make this decision for you. But, Echo, whatever you decide we will make sure you get through it. We will make sure you make it to the other side in one piece. Okay?

I nod against him.

Delta: And you're not broken, Echo.

I open my eyes to see her watching us from close by on the edge of the back seat.

Delta: You rebuilt yourself. You're stronger than all of us.

I reach out for her under Charlie's arm and she takes my hand.

I've missed them both so much.

Just under the constant hum and whoosh of traffic, the phone vibrates against the plastic of the cupholder in the front. Delta squeezes my hand before letting me go to lean back inside and fish for it.

Charlie sighs against me, but doesn't move to let me go. And I don't move to leave his hold. I feel safe here the way I did with Delta, the way I do with Aurora. This is safety. This is so close to home.

Delta: Hey.

I strain to hear who she's talking to under the static of the blocker on Bravo's phone.

Delta: Yeah, we're fine, sorry. She's... We've got her. Charlie's got her.

I think she's talking to Aurora. I want her to be talking to Aurora. I want to—

Charlie: We need to get back in the car..

Echo: What? [I pull away from him.] Why?

He's staring down the road behind us. I turn to see what it is. There's a car stopped further down. A dark blue SUV.

Charlie: It's probably nothing.

But he's already nudging me towards the car, waving Delta back in.

Echo: You don't think that.

Charlie: I really, really want to.

Once I'm in, Charlie closes my door.

Delta: Here. Aurora wants to hear your voice.

But even as I'm taking the phone, I'm distracted, too busy watching Charlie who's still watching the SUV behind us as he moves for his own door.

Aurora: Echo?

Echo: Hmm?

Aurora: You okay?

Echo: Yeah. Yeah, I'm okay.

Now Delta's caught on and she's turning in the seat to look out the back while Charlie's easing the car onto the road.

Echo: We're moving now. Sorry.

Aurora: You're not okay. What's going on?

Echo: Nothing. Sorry. It's nothing. I'm so sorry I worried you, I just... I'm fine now.

She's quiet a beat too long. The same amount of time it takes for the SUV to pull back onto the road, as well.

Echo: I love you so much.

Aurora: Echo?

Echo: The phone's getting close to dying. I'll talk to you in Fayetteville?

Aurora: Echo.

Echo: I love you. It's alright. We're alright. I promise.

Charlie changes lanes. The SUV follows.

Aurora: Okay. I love you, Echo. Whatever it is that's going on, you tell Charlie he better get you back to me in one piece or so help me god. I don't fucking care how big he is I will make sure—

I can't help but laugh as my heart sings and my body aches for her.

Echo: I love you so fucking much.

Aurora: I love you, too.

I hang up and cling to the phone as though it's her hand, as though to let go of it would be to lose her all over again. I glance out the back window again then return to Delta's side. All my fears before now seem so insignificant because Charlie's first inclination was right—it so very clearly isn't nothing.

[END LOG]

[BEGIN LOG]

I probably shouldn't be recording this, but I feel like I should. I'm sure I could make all sorts of arguments for why that is, but I think the truth is simply that there's a level of comfort in the act of making these logs that I need right now. Besides, Bravo fortified my firewalls. Marsh shouldn't be able to get in my head anymore. Right?

The dark blue SUV—Idaho plates, 7R 54786—has stayed on our tail the entire way. It hung back at first, sticking a few cars behind. But when we got off to head south on 30 through Little Rock instead of north on 40, it nearly slammed into a pickup to try and course correct. Charlie and the driver wove through traffic for two hours. It wasn't until we were in Texarkana that he risked changing routes, driving in circles through the small city. It wasn't easy. Texarkana was built on a grid and the driver didn't care about red lights. It was a train that finally separated us, Charlie speeding off the instant those arms blocked them in on the other side.

We're pulling into the gas station where we'd agreed to meet. Aurora is already running for my door before we can park by the pump. As I'm shoving the door open, she's yanking it and I fall out into her arms, mine around her neck. She grabs me and holds me so tight that for the first time I'm glad I don't need to breathe.

Echo: It's okay. We're okay.

Charlie: Y'all already fill up?

Lilith: Yeah.

Bravo: What the fuck happened?

Charlie: Del—?

Delta: Already on it.

I can hear the gas cap twist off, the nozzle rattle into the neck of the inlet. The machine beeps. The level locks. The gas begins to funnel into the tank.

Charlie: Someone was on our tail.

I hear panicked sneakers on pavement as though someone were fighting the urge to run.

Lilith: Nov, it's okay. It's okay.

Bravo: Who?

Charlie: Blue SUV. Idaho plates.

Lilith: See, it's not them. It's not them.

There's a shuffle and thud that sounds like a body stumbling to the ground. Aurora lets me go and I locate November. Her legs look as though they've crumpled beneath her, her hands are in her hair, her nose close to the pavement. Could she breathe, she'd be hyperventilating. Lilith is crouched next to her, but I go to her anyways, fall to my knees next to her.

Echo: November? You're okay. You're okay.

Her hand flails for mine and I take it, hold it close to my chest and breath deep and calm even though I know it's probably no use to her. But she seems to loosen a little all the same.

Charlie: I didn't let 'em close enough to get a good look at 'em.

Bravo: But you think it's Marsh?

Charlie: Most likely.

Aurora: Echo?

She's knelt next to me, touching me in place of holding me.

Aurora: Have you felt him? Has he tried—?

I shake my head before she can finish.

Echo: Nothing. I think Bravo's fortifications are holding, but...

Bravo: How else would he have known where we were. And even if he didn't get in, it's only a matter of time. He's sloppy, but he's not inefficient. He was always a better hacker than he was an engineer. Where'd you lose him?

Charlie: Train. [He nods in the direction of the tracks.]

Bravo: Kay. That could save us a lot of time or none at all. How are we doing this?

Charlie: He doesn't know your car. You're taking Delta.

Delta: Seriously?

Charlie: I trust Bravo to keep you safe. Ror, you with Fox?

She nods, but she's also chewing her lips and avoiding looking at him, her grip on my arm tightening.

Aurora: Yeah. Yeah, of course.

But she wasn't as confident as I would have expected. She glances at me and when she realizes I'm staring at her, those sweet brown eyes flick back and lock with mine. I think we both know where this going.

Charlie: Kay. I want you with Lil, too, at the very least. Love you, Lil, but—

Lilith: I agree. I'm not fighting off shit anytime soon.

He kneels next to us and takes in a deep breath.

Charlie: Echo—

Echo: Marsh knows my head and your car.

I don't dare look away from her as I say it.

Echo: I'm going with you.

I finally look at him and he nods, apology spiling from his eyes.

Lilith: Nov?

She lifts enough to stare down at the asphalt, her hands pressed against it in front of her knees.

November: I—I'll go with Echo. You'll have enough people to watch out for.

Her eyes dart from one side to the next. From Lilith to Charlie and back again.

Echo: Charlie'll keep us safe. That's what he was built for. For keeping us safe.

She nods, but her lips are pressed together so hard her top lip has nearly disappeared.

A hard, metallic *thunk* from the gas pump signals our time is up.

Delta: Okay!

Charlie: Alright. Fox?

Fox: Yeah?

Lilith helps November to her feet and fusses over her while rushing her to Charlie's car. Charlie's reassuring Fox who's standing on the running board of Lilith's Jeep. Delta's giving her a hug. Bravo's already heading for her car. Aurora's still staring at me. I stare back at her.

There are so many things I want to tell her. They're scrambling through my mind, fighting to be the first to come out. But they're all tangled around each other and one becomes the next before I can sort them all out, weigh their importance. What do you say when there's a looming chance you might never see each other again?

She touches my cheek.

Aurora: I love you more than anything. Everything else can wait.

Echo: What if—?

But she shakes her head and shifts closer to me.

Aurora: Charlie'll keep you safe, remember?

I nod and bite hard on my lip hoping it'll stop the tears.

Aurora: And he *will* bring you back to me.

Echo: I know.

Aurora: I love you. All of you.

She wipes my tears with her thumb as I nod against her palm.

Echo: I love you. Every part of me loves you.

She pulls me to her and kisses me soft and slow until I shove myself against her, my arms around her neck, my mouth hard against hers.

It's going to be okay.

It's going to be okay.

Please, fuck, let it be okay.

[END LOG]

[TRANSMIT TO > BRAVO]

Marsh found us.
I'm shutting out Aurora.
Keep moving.
We'll call you when it's safe.

[END TRANSMISSION]

I think we're okay now. I don't know for sure. But we're driving out of Nacogdoches now and I haven't felt him yet, so…I think that means we're safe. I'm so tired of wondering if we are.

I'm sorry I had to cut you off like that. You deserve to know what happened. Not even a half hour out of Texarkana I felt someone shoving at my firewall. I knew it was Marsh. I tired to keep him out, but I couldn't let him infect anyone else, especially not you. So, I had to shut you out.

Charlie was quiet for longer than I would have liked when I told him. He just kept gripping the steering wheel and rolling his lips together. Finally, he took in a deep breath.

"I have an idea," he said, "but it'll take us off course."

"I'm willing to—"

Then I felt it, a tiny little crack. Where did it come from? When did it happen? Was it just then? When I sent the transmission to Bravo? When I shut you out? I still don't know. I guess it doesn't matter. What does is that he got in. I felt him slip in and start rooting around.

"Echo?"

Charlie started to slow down.

"Don't pull over!"

"Why not?"

"He's in."

"Shit."

He stepped on the gas and sped past Bravo and Lilith. I clenched my eyes, fought the urge to look back at you in Bravo's car, fought the urge to reach out to you, to even think about you. I didn't want to give him anything.

I didn't know that clunker of a car could go so fast. Charlie shaved an hour off a two and a half hour drive as he raced through every little town between Texarkana and Nacogdoches. How we weren't pulled over, I still don't know. The entire hour and a half passed in silence, partly from the tension and fear that we were going to roll at every turn, but mostly because we all knew that anything we said Marsh could hear. He not only had access to all my logs and transmissions, but also the passive recordings that I don't pay much attention to. He had access to everything. He knows everything. I spent that entire hour and a half picking it all apart myself, trying to puzzle out what everyone had said, what he could latch onto, all the time avoiding specifics, retroactively blocking out and deleting names and places. The only saving grace that I can think of is that Bravo never told us the address to Antioch.

When we got to Nacogdoches, Charlie drove straight to a park near the SFA campus.

He turned off the car and turned to me. "Echo—"

"I know."

He had to shut me down. If Marsh was in my head that meant he was tracking me. Shutting me down wasn't foolproof, but the harder I was to access the more time it bought us. I'd be lying if I said I was devoid of panic. I was riddled with it. But I trusted Charlie—I *do* trust Charlie. I trust him with my life.

He nodded and I let out a long breath. He leaned towards me, but instead of reaching for my ear, he reached for the glove compartment. When it flopped open against my knees, I saw why.

"How long have you had that?" I watched at he grabbed the revolver.

November whimpered from the backseat.

"Since Colville."

"Seriously? And you didn't tell me?"

"I wanted the upper hand. Now, I want Marsh to know."

He dug the magazine out of the center console, loaded the gun, then tucked it into his jacket pocket. He looked at me and let out a heavy breath. I stared back at him.

"Ready?"

I nodded.

"Kay."

He reached for my ear. Strangely, I didn't flinch, I didn't fight him. I just closed my eyes and let the world go dark. Before it did, I made sure your face was the last thing I thought about.

I wonder if you saw me go dark. I wonder how you reacted. I'm sorry if it was bad. I'm sorry if it took you straight back to before.

I don't know how long I was off for and I don't know the specifics of what happened while I was.

All I know for sure is that I woke twice.

The first time I was no longer in the car. I was on my back on the ground. I could smell dirt and leaves. My vision was split in two: a slab of concrete on the bottom half, the branches of pecan trees on the top. I could hear November whimpering next to me.

"Please. Please. Come on. Come on," she was repeating.

Footsteps crunched through the grass nearby.

"Shit," she hissed.

I heard her scrambling towards me in the dirt and everything went dark again.

The second time, I was staring up at trees and sky, but they were the wrong way around and moving. No, I was moving. I was being carried. Charlie was carrying me, my head flopped over his arm. November was walking ahead of us, Charlie's revolver gripped in both hands, her head on a swivel. In front of her was someone I didn't recognize.

"What's going on?" I managed to say.

"Oh, thank fuck." Charlie stopped and lowered me to the ground. "You good?"

November turned to us, her eyes wide, full lips parted. "Echo!"

The person I didn't know turned, as well. "Oh, thank god."

"Yeah, I'm good." I steadied myself on my feet. I felt a little wobbly, but still functional. "I'm good. What happened?"

November was already at my opposite side, her free hand on my shoulder. The stranger came up in front of us. He was nearly as tall as Charlie with a casual slouch.

"Marsh still managed to locate you," Charlie said. "Nov had to improvise."

"Good news," the stranger said, "He knows you have a gun."

I looked to November with furrowed brows, but for some reason she was avoiding looking at me.

"Bad news," the stranger went on, "so do the campus police and they're on their way. Which is why," his close set, pale green eyes nervously glanced around the soccer fields on one side, a creek on the other, "if you can keep moving, we should."

I nodded and we did as he said, the stranger leading the way along what seemed to be a trail running along the creek. Sirens wailed on the road across the soccer fields.

"You might wanna hide that," the stranger said to November from over his shoulder.

"Hm?" She looked down at the revolver still gripped in her hands. "Oh."

"Want me to—?" Charlie offered, his hand out to her.

But she shook her head, switched on the safety, and shoved it in the back of her jeans under the oversized t-shirt.

Before I could ask what exactly had happened, the stranger said, "Nearly there."

Sure enough, the trail bent at the end of the field and took us to a short road through some trees. On the other side was a parking lot in front of what looked to be a nursery. Some parts looked more used than others. But we kept on walking through the parking lot to what looked to be the back of the next building over. The stranger led us up some steps and through a back door, holding it open for each of us. November glanced back at me then ducked her head as she slipped by him. I crossed my arms and otherwise ignored him as I stepped into the hall to wait for directions. I was expecting Charlie to take the door from him, to gesture the stranger through first, instead, he just touched his shoulder and nodded to him as he stepped in behind us. I squinted at him as the man let go of the door and moved past us to lead the way down the hall. But Charlie just smirked and shook his head before nodding me ahead of him as usual.

The man led us down a hall that was lined with artwork of varying styles and mediums—a large, colorful, abstract piece in oil pastel, a triptych of moody black and white portraits, a grid of soft watercolors of suburban landscapes, an impressive hyperrealism landscape in rich jewel toned oils. We passed rooms with semi circles of easels and stools, rows of tables smeared with charcoal and spattered with layers of paint, a computer lab made up entirely of Macs with large, high-end printers lining the back wall.

We turned a corner and the large classrooms became small offices with name plates on top of the numbers. When we came to the one with the name "Summers" above it, the man stopped. He grabbed the knob, but he hesitated before he opened it. I watched him chew the inside of his cheek as he stared at the wood of the door.

Then he cleared his throat. "Just a second."

He slipped in and closed the door behind him.

"Hey," a female voice said from inside.

"Hey," the man answered.

"What are we—?" November started to say, but Charlie and I both held a hand up to her.

I glanced at him to find his eyes were also unfocused, his head tilted down and turned towards the door. He met my eyes and matched my smirk.

"You're absolutely sure about this?" the man said in the office.

"Yes." A chair swiveled and squeaked, soft steps moved through the small room. "Yes, I'm sure. We're not going to leave them vulnerable to him and if this is what needs to be done to help them, then, yes, I'm sure."

The room was silent then a heavy sigh followed by a kiss.

The knob rattled and the door opened. Neither Charlie nor I pretended like we hadn't been listening. The man opened the door and looked first at Charlie then me. Those close-set pale green eyes seemed to examine me then. And I examined him back. He really was tall, probably would be the same height as Charlie if it weren't for the concave way that he stood. His body seemed sturdy, neither muscular nor fat, just sturdy. I doubted I could topple him if I tried. You might, but that doesn't count. His stubble was the same reddish brown as his hair which had a soft wave to it. His ears kind of stuck out though I doubt I would have noticed if we hadn't been examining each other. He radiated a casual calmness, an easy coolness that made me think if we had met under different circumstances, we would have been fast friends.

I think he realized then that he'd been staring for too long. He blinked more than once and looked away from me.

"Sorry," he muttered. "It's just...uncanny. Didn't think..." He shook his head. "Come on in."

He fully opened the door and stepped aside, gesturing us in. I nodded November in first. She glanced over the man before looking to her feet and started to take a step in, but stopped still. She looked straight ahead, then to me, back into the office, and up at the man.

He chuckled. "I'll explain in a second."

She glanced at me again then stepped into the office.

I furrowed my brows at her then the man.

He sighed. "Just... You'll see."

Confused, I moved to step around the door frame and into the office, but also stopped still. At the desk was a woman, but not just any woman—it was me. I was standing behind the desk staring back at myself. I was frozen. Both of us were. My thoughts kept starting and stopping. I didn't know where to begin. She was staring back at me with less surprise and more curiosity.

"That *is* uncanny," she muttered.

We weren't perfect matches, I realized the more I stared at her. She seemed slightly older, lines between the brows and the corners of her mouth. Her curls were braided back away from her face, her dangling earrings made of colorful glass beads swept her shoulders that were just visible under her black boatneck top and flowy kimono style cardigan. She looked so put together and professional. It made my t-shirt, baggy flannel, dirt covered jeans, sneakers, and frizzy hair sloppily hidden in a ponytail feel suddenly juvenile.

A hand touched the middle of my back making me jump.

"Once we're all inside, I'll explain," the man said with a gentle tone.

I nodded and took a step closer to November by the wall. I stood close to her, needing something that I knew to be real next to me. I wish she'd been you, but I took what I could get. I tried to distract myself by taking in the small office, but it was hard to do with the wall straight ahead of me featuring a series of photographs next to a large print of a Monet painting of water lilies. The photos were of her and the man, of three little girls, of her and—

I took a step closer to the wall, Charlie nearly bumping into me. But I ignored him and went straight for the photo of the woman cheek to cheek with Eden at what looked to be some kind of Renaissance festival, both women in ruffly, showy tops and stays, their hair decorated with flowers. The woman who looked like me had on fake elf ears.

"That was when we were in college," she said from close to me.

I turned to her. "You knew Eden?"

"I'd like to think I still know Eden."

She was fidgeting with a silver necklace that hung low near her stomach. It looked to be a locket with a little blue flower on the front.

"And Marsh?"

She sighed and turned to lean against the wall.

"Ads never got along with Marsh," the man said with a chuckle.

"You never did either," she reminded him.

He shrugged. "He started out okay."

"He always starts out okay," Charlie said.

I turned to him, he was leaning against the wall next to November who was watching me with her arms crossed tight. The man was sitting on the corner of the desk watching the two of us, his eyes flicking from her to me and back again.

He shook his head. "Sorry. Sorry, it's just...last I saw you, you weren't...human yet. You were still so robotic. And I thought *that* was uncanny," he added with a laugh.

"But you—" Charlie started.

"With Delta, yes," the man said, seeming to know where Charlie was going. "Once we perfected things with her, Dan moved it over to Echo, but I wasn't part of it. Then towards the end, I brought her, Delta, out here to finish her up for Eden. That was when Reece was born. I didn't wanna leave Adi for such long stretches during that."

Charlie nodded. "I don't remember that."

"That was before he..." The man's lips shifted and he looked away from Charlie to the woman, Adi, I assumed, who was staring at her feet. "That was before you were security."

November and I both stared at Charlie, but when he didn't elaborate, just nodded, we looked to the man who didn't elaborate either.

"Why do I look like you?" I finally said to the woman, changing the topic.

"You were modeled after Adi," the man answered instead. "In the beginning all of you were modeled after someone. Eden didn't like what the AIs were coming up with at the time. They didn't translate well to 3D, so..." He shrugged. "She used real people." His eyes shifted to his wife and his smile glowed. "She liked Adi's small figure."

Adi laughed. "That's not at all what she said."

"That's what I remember," he insisted with a lopsided grin, his eyes locked on her.

"She said I blend in well and am easy to underestimate."

"Aka you are small and non-threatening and adorable."

She rolled her eyes. "I am not arguing with you about this again."

I had to chuckle at the way she said "again."

"Because you know that I'm right."

I liked them. I do like them. If I had to be modeled after anyone, I'm glad it was her.

"Well." He took in a loud breath and slapped his thighs as he stood. "Before she changes her mind. Should we get started?"

"Doing what exactly?" November said.

"Keeping—" the man started, but panic shot through me.

"Should you say it out loud?" I said over him. "What if—?"

He smirked and pulled a little black box from his pocket that he wiggled by his shoulder. "Jammer. Disrupts cell signals. He can't locate you or get into your head as long as you're near this. No one can. You also can't send anything out, though, which is the downside."

Which is why you're just now getting all this.

"We're dark right now," Charlie added.

My mouth went hard as I stared at him. "Did you tell—?"

"Adi texted Bravo for us. When we're done here, we're meeting them in Crockett."

I chewed the inside of my lip. I hated the idea of you thinking we'd truly gone dark, thinking something happened, that we were shut down somewhere, or worse.

He left the wall and moved towards me, a hand on both of my shoulders. "Aurora knows you're okay. I can't promise she's not worried, but she knows you're alive. And that I'm going to get you back to her."

I held his eyes and took in then let out a deep breath. "You better. What are we doing then?"

Charlie let me go and turned to the man, his hands in his pockets.

"Making it so Marsh won't be able to find you moving forward," the man said. "At least not by tracking you or getting in your head."

"And how are you going to do that?" I said.

"Easy." He stood and headed for the desk chair. "For the tracking. I'm going to add a VPN to each of you. Set your locations to somewhere else. Somewhere—off!"

He collapsed into Adi's chair that he apparently wasn't expecting to be as low as it was, his knees practically at his chest.

Adi giggled behind her hand. Charlie chuckled and shook his head. A little smile snuck into the corner of November's full lips.

"Fuck, woman. Are you really this short?" He shoved himself up and grabbed the chair to search under the seat.

"How long have we been together?" Adi said with another giggle.

He just gave her a teasing glare and pressed the lever that raised the seat. He eased onto it, raised it a little more, then turned to the countertop behind the desk.

"Anyways, um, I'm gonna set your locations to somewhere else." He dug through a backpack as he talked. "Somewhere close enough that he thinks y'all could actually be there, but far enough in the opposite direction to buy y'all some time." He pulled out a laptop and a tangle of cords then turned back to the desk. "I'm thinking Louisiana? Maybe Shreveport?"

Adi sighed and took the tangle of cords from him.

"Oh, thanks, babe. As for you..." He looked up at me, but blinked for an extra beat, his eyes zipping from me to Adi who was untangling his cords before his brain recovered and he continued, "I'm, uh, I'm gonna start by fortifying your firewall. Bravo's good, everything she knows she learned from Eden, after all, but..." He bobbed his head to one side. "It's not really her forte, ya know. So, just to be safe. Then I'll give you antivirus and antispyware. Kind of surprised *you* of all of y'all don't have any, to be honest."

"Pretty sure she did before," Charlie said.

The man looked up at him, his brows furrowed. "Before what? What happened?"

"Long story."

The man kept staring up at Charlie who glanced at me then

quickly shook his head.

"Jed," Adi said and tapped his shoulder with the detangled and neatly stacked cords.

"Hm?" He looked to her. "Oh. Thanks." He took them and started booting up the laptop. "Uh, I'm also going to make a back up for you just in case anything else happens and send it over to Eden. Something's still not right. It shouldn't take so long for you to boot up. I'd see what I could do now, but I know you have people you're trying to get back to. Besides, Eden was always the engineer. Even Dan to a degree. I just messed around with what they created."

"You did a lot more than that," Adi quietly insisted.

Jed chuckled and, without looking at her, ran his fingers low along her back.

"So, yeah. Um, who's first?" He looked up at the three of us, brows raised.

Once we were all finished, November and I thanked them and headed out into the hall. I was sad to leave them behind. I like them, but I was also eager to get back to you. We were halfway down the hall when I realized Charlie wasn't following us. I turned to see him still at the door. He was giving Adi a hug, nearly doubled over to reach her. Was that how he hugged me? I didn't think I was that much shorter than him. Then he kissed the top of her head and I cocked mine to one side. I've never seen him do that with anyone other than Delta. Then he straightened and turned to Jed who he also hugged tight.

"Thanks again," Charlie said as they let each other go.

He gave first Jed then Adi a sad smile. Then he tucked a loose strand of hair behind Adi's ear. She touched his hand cradling her cheek.

"Call us the instant you're safe," she insisted.

"I will," he promised. "Bravo, too."

November leaned close to me. "What's all that about?"

I just shrugged and we watched as Charlie joined us down the hall, his hands in his pockets.

Echo: Hey, Charlie.

Charlie: Hm?

I shift in my seat in the front passenger seat of the car to face him, my legs crossed under me, though I probably shouldn't be telling you that. You're most likely having a fit just thinking about it. November's in the back seat stretched out. She seems to have relaxed since the park which isn't the way I had expected it to go. Granted, she still has the gun, so that might be why. Anyways—

Echo: There's history between you and the Summerses.

He laughs and glances at me.

Charlie: What of it?

Echo: You have information that I don't and, as intel, that makes me very uncomfortable.

I feel a bit strange, free. Knowing Marsh isn't in my head, knowing he can't get in there anymore, knowing that I'm headed back to you a little less damaged than when we'd left even Nashville, I feel a lighter than I have for ages.

He relaxes in his own seat, one arm on the console.

Charlie: And what do you want me to do about that?

Echo: Tell me everything, of course.

Charlie: Not everything. Trust me, you don't want to know *everything*.

Echo: Just tell me.

Charlie: Okay. Okay. Uh, when I was first built, I was supposed to be like Bravo. I was supposed to be the male companion model.

Echo: But I thought Romeos were the male companion models.

Charlie: And Juliets are the female companion models. Poetic.

Echo: Corny.

Charlie: [He laughs.] You're not wrong.

Echo: So, not Bravos.

Charlie: Not Bravos. Bravos are sex work.

November starts picking at a spot in the upholstery on the backseat.

Echo: But Charlies aren't?

Charlie: [He shakes his head.] Mikes are male sex work models.

Echo: Why Mikes?

Charlie: After some movie. I don't know.

Echo: Wait, but Bravo was sex work before she woke up? I thought she was a companion model.

Charlie: Originally, they were supposed to be both. But, um, some...*investors* wanted them to be separated. Eden never knew how to feel about that.

Echo: So, she let other Bravos be sex work models?

Charlie: Marsh ran with the Romeo and Juliet thing—

Echo: Of course he would.

Charlie: It kind of got away from Eden before she could have a say. Well, that's the version she'll tell you.

Echo: Yours?

Charlie: Marsh is a petty asshole who couldn't accept that his gay wife loved her female synth more than him.

Echo: Is that why he wanted Bravo back? To take her from Eden?

Charlie: That was always my theory.

I let out a long sigh. I'm losing that light feeling.

Echo: What about you and the Summerses? You started as a companion model?

Charlie: Yeah. Um, Eden realized pretty quickly that she was having a hard time programming me because she was apathetic to the whole idea of a male companion model which in turn made her realize she was gay.

Echo: Really?

Charlie: Mhm. So, she asked for some outside help. Eden, Adi, and Jed all went to school together. She actually introduced them.

Eden: Yeah? That's cute.

Charlie: They're also polyamorous, so Eden thought they'd be the best couple to ask to do test runs with both Bravo and me.

Echo: Really? So, you and Bravo dated Adi and Jed?

Charlie: Bravo dated Adi and Jed. I just dated Adi. We, um, we were thirds for both of them.

Echo: No!

Charlie: Is it that shocking to you?

Echo: For you? Nah. For Bravo? Eh. For Adi? I had a sneaking suspicion.

He chuckled and bobbed his head to one side.

Echo: For Jed? Yes. Absolutely.

Charlie: [He laughs.] You just met him today.

Echo: And he did not give me I like bringing other men into bed with my wife kind of vibes.

He laughs hard at that. So hard he has to put both hands back on the wheel until he recovers.

Charlie: To be fair, I don't think they do much of that anymore. That was in their pre-kids days.

November: But there's still something there.

He glances at her. She's shifted forward in the backseat, her head is resting on the top corner of mine.

Echo: Yeah, that was pretty obvious.

Charlie: Yeah. It's hard to erase feelings like that. [He looks at me long enough to make a point before looking back at the road.] You of all people should know.

Echo: Yeah. Yeah, it is.

November: How did it get erased?

She knows my story, but she doesn't know Charlie's. *I* barely know Charlie's. It takes him a moment to answer. Instead, he nods, his lips pressed together as though he's loading what he's about to say.

Charlie: Um, when Marsh made me security, he formatted me.

The car goes quiet the way I expected it to. It's a hard conversation to have. It's a hard thing to have to relive. But I feel like November needs to hear it. Part of her wants to be formatted. All of her wants to start over. But she needs to know what that entails, that it isn't that easy.

Echo: C-can I ask why he did that? I was trying not to ask, but—

Charlie: Yeah, we all kind of avoid talking about all that, don't we. I'm sorry about all that. [He pats my knee without looking away from the road.] I think we've all been hoping someone else will tell you all the hard stuff so we won't have to, you know? But that's not fair, is it?

Eden: [I shrug.] I get it.

He flashes me a grateful smile and nods while his hands wring along the steering wheel.

Charlie: Well, um, so, Adi and Jed weren't the only people who did test runs with us. Eden and Dan wanted us both to be tested in different types of relationships so we could respond best in the field. Bravo had Jed, Adi, and Eden which is how they got where they ended up. There was a guy in town who I was dating. There was also an asexual woman who I think we both dated. I'm not 100% on that.

Um, anyways. I don't know, I think Marsh got jealous, as usual. Him and Eden were drifting more and more apart while Eden drifted closer and closer to Bravo and I think there was some petty part of him that wanted to prove something to her? I don't know. Um, but so, he called off all the other testing and assigned me exclusively to him. Um, then he...I don't know. But he, uh, decided he was done with me, I guess, and wanted a new project, so he, um, he formatted me and started working on the security build.

Echo: Done with you?

Charlie: I don't know, that's how everyone put it. I think it was more than that—or maybe less depending on how you look at it.

Echo: Which is?

Charlie: Spite. I think he did it out of spite. He couldn't format Bravo. So, he formatted me.

The silence seeps into the car again. What are we supposed to say to that? I wish I knew. I want to say the right thing, but...what is that exactly? Maybe he doesn't need me to say anything. Maybe someone else already has. I don't know.

November: You remember all that? Even after being formatted.

He shakes his head, but then bobs it to one side, as well.

Charlie: I don't know. In a way. Most of it I was told later. Leading up to what happened in Bastrop, Bravo and I had a lot of long night talks. We were built together. Kind of like twins, I guess. Apparently, she had a hard time when I was rewritten. And when I came back, I felt this...pull towards her, you know? I didn't really remember her, outside of what you had shown me, but I...remembered the...idea? Of her? If that makes sense. That's how it was with everyone. Once I was awake, everyone felt familiar, but I couldn't place why. Eden wanted to give me those memories back, but I, um, I was afraid of things getting overwritten. I didn't want to lose Delta.

I shift in my seat, tuck my feet under me, and lean against his arm in the hopes that he knows that I get it. Holy fuck, do I get it.

Charlie: Eden said she'd make sure that didn't happen, but the update kept taking priority. So, Bravo just told me as much as she could. Every night, we sat up and went over more and more. Then, once again, Marsh happened.

Echo: Does Marsh actually fuck up everything or is that just a new thing.

He lets out a melancholic kind of chuckle.

Charlie: Both. He's always been like that, I think, but it got worse when he lost Eden to Bravo. But, [He touches my knee again.] back to the memories. The weird thing is, while we were in Colville, things started to come back.

I shift again to face him. They could come back on their own?

Charlie: Not everything. Not perfectly. There are things I still don't remember. Like, I didn't remember that Jed took Delta to SFA to work on her. But, other things, things like Jed and Adi, how I felt about them, the little things we did together. Those came back.

They could come back. There's a chance that, with time, some of my memories could come back. There's a chance I could have both. But...do I want both? Do I still want this fake reality I created? Charlie at least actually lived his memories with Delta. It's something they share. He can go to her and say, "Remember when...?" And she'd say, "Yes, I remember." With us, it's different. With mine, they're only mine. There's no one to share them with, no one to understand. And every time I'd remember them, it would be with this added sting that you don't, that none of you do.

I don't know what to do.

I hate not knowing what to do.

There's a sign up ahead. I lean forward to read it.

CROCKETT 5 MI

Echo: Five miles!

We're close. I'm nearly back to you and I'm just as confused as I was before. All I know for sure is that I miss you, that I want your arms around me, that I need your steadying force right now. I miss you.

[END TRANSMISSION]

[END LOG]

[BEGIN LOG]

[TRANSMIT TO > AURORA]

We're finally leaving Crockett. I had been under the impression that we'd be meeting you *in* Crockett, but I guess technically you're just south of it. 2.5 miles to be exact. 2.5 excruciating miles. Even with Charlie driving 70 despite the speed limit being 55. Well, he's trying to. There's a pickup in front of us going what feels like 40 and a steady enough stream of cars coming the opposite direction so he can't go around. I let out a loud sigh and slouch down in my seat.

Charlie: We're still moving.

He reaches over to squeeze my knee.

Echo: Not fast enough.

We pass a school bus depot, a garage, a bunch of run down houses, an RV park, a boarded up, out of season fireworks stand with a faded sign, trees, trees, tress, another RV park, more trees, more trees, a field, trees, field, trees, field, field, more god damn trees. How are we still driving? This is the longest fucking 2.5 miles of my fucking life.

Finally, the pick up turns and now Charlie is flooring it.

The trees are a blur.

It's still not fast enough.

My hands tucked under my crossed arms are practically vibrating. They feel like magnets sensing the pull of their mates. You're so close I can feel you and yet we're still not—

Charlie: There it is.

I sit up, the seatbelt pulling against my chest. We pull off onto a road that curves then runs parallel to a stretch of grass, pine trees, and concrete picnic benches with wooden coverings between them.

Echo: There's Lil's Jeep!

November: Where?

She leans against the console between us.

Echo: There!

Charlie: Calm down, you two.

Echo: Don't act like you're not excited to get back to Del.

He chuckles and nods with a relived grin that matches ours.

And there you are hovering between the covered picnic table and the road, your arms crossed tight, the sun lighting up your orange hair. Fox jumps from the table and runs to stand next to you, craning her neck to see our car, to confirm that it's Charlie's. You squint, unfold your arms, and break into a run. I'm already unbuckling my seatbelt and Charlie just stops the car here so I can shove my way out. You grab me before I can take a step. You hold me tight and I cling to you as though neither of us will feel safe again until we can occupy the same space. But then as Charlie drives on to the others, you start to collapse. I wasn't ready for this and I go down with you. We're in the grass still holding onto each other and that's when I feel your body shaking and stuttering against mine, the wet spot on my shoulder.

Echo: It's okay. Baby, I'm okay.

Aurora: I was so scared.

Echo: I know. I'm sorry. I'm so sorry.

I try to rock around you the way you do me, but it doesn't feel the same. You're the nurturer. You're the one who usually does the comforting. I don't know what I'm doing. You start to rock instead.

Aurora: I thought I'd lost you again. I almost lost you again.

You tear from my arms just to grab my face and kiss me hard. I kiss you back, shifting to close the space as best I can.

Aurora: I'm never letting you out of my sight again.

I let out a breathy laugh against your lips. God, I love you. This is everything I've been needing, our limbs tangled together, your mouth against mine, your heart so close I can feel it's quiet hum. This is all I need. I need the real world. I don't need those pretty lies. I just need you in my arms and this feeling that you want me in yours. I want you. I want this version of you.

I finally know what I want.

And this is it.

Aurora: Will you stop thinking for once and just kiss me?

[END TRANSMISSION]

[END LOG]

[BEGIN LOG]

We've been sitting here in the rest stop for a while. I think we all just need to be still for a moment. Just need to let the nerves settle before we start to move again. But they're all talking, several conversation going on at once. I'm not following any of them. I haven't been trying. It's too much. I just need quiet. I need to be quiet.

I slip from Aurora's arms and wander off to the next picnic bench down. They're just over 62 yards apart. Far enough to be alone, close enough that Aurora can see me, see that I'm okay. This one's closer to the tree line, more hidden away. There's a particularly big pine tree nearby. I collapse onto the ground with a sigh and stare up at the branches. It's nice. It's quiet...for the most part. I don't think I've had a moment with just my own thoughts since we left Sierra's.

I feel weird. I feel like I'm on some kind of precipice. I'm excited and I'm nervous and I'm scared. All three of them are whirling around inside of me until they've mixed together and the result seems to be this odd kind of quiet hum. I can feel it running along my bones. I feel as heavy as I do light.

There are footsteps coming towards me. They're steady and solid as they move through the grass. Without saying anything, she lays down next to me, our hips touching. We both just stare up at the trees, watch the branches sway, the clouds moving above them.

Echo: I'm getting rid of my memories.

She doesn't answer right away. She just lies next to me so unchanged that I'm not even sure she heard me, not sure I'd actually said the words out loud Maybe I just thought I did. Maybe—

She sits up and I follow.

Aurora: I had a feeling that's the direction you were headed.

She turns to me, one bent knee in my lap, her hands loose next to mine against her shin, her eyes on our hands. Her mouth is open as though she's processing her words carefully.

Aurora: Are you sure?

Echo: They're not real.

Aurora: But...they're us. Aren't they?

Echo: Not for you. You don't remember any of them.

Aurora: But you've told me enough of them—

Echo: I've barely told you anything.

Aurora: But even that was enough.

She meets my eyes and there's loss behind them.

Aurora: When I said I love all of you, I meant all of you.

I hold her eyes and just breath for a moment. I don't know what to do with this.

Echo: You didn't seem very interested in them before.

She shifts closer, though truthfully, she can't get much closer.

Aurora: That was when we thought Marsh had made them. When I thought he was using me to manipulate you. The instant we learned you created them... It's us. That's part of us now.

Echo: It doesn't have to be.

Aurora: But it could.

I stare at her. I thought I had this figured out. Now I'm just confused again.

Echo: I want to remember what you remember. I just want us to have the same version. When I think about you, I want to be thinking about the same memories as you. And...I know Charlie said, but—What if I can't have both? What if it fucks things up?

But she's already shaking her head and taking my hands.

Aurora: You can. You can. It might take some sorting out, but you can. We can.

But then her face shifts from clawing determination to hesitant fear.

Aurora: Or—I don't know. Maybe I'm just being selfish. It's your head. Your memories that we'd be messing with. I shouldn't—

I pull her hands against my stomach.

Echo: I don't want to make this decision alone. I don't know what I want. I want—I just—I want you. I want every version of you.

An unsure smile struggles at the corners of her lips.

Aurora: I want every version of you, too.

She kisses me and I kiss her back. Without moving my mouth from hers, I move our hands so her palm clicks with mine. I hold it to my chest as I give her everything.

It's the day we first met, when your sunlight finally brought me warmth as you walked with me to Sadie's and we walked the whole way and back about nothing and everything. The days you came to the office with Fox, sitting on my desk and asking me questions no one had ever asked me because no one had ever cared before, no one had ever wanted to know everything about me with such excited attentiveness.

The day you finally asked for my number which was the same night you asked me out over the phone making my stomach erupt into a swirling mass of wings. Our first date, the moment you first asked to kiss me and I said yes before you even finished the sentence. The way your face lit up, your smile that refused to fade even as your hands were moving along my jaw to guide me close to you, the smell of your perfume, the taste of your mouth, my arms around your neck pulling your body against mine.

The days we spent texting. Our second date, then our third. The first night I invited you into my apartment above Delta and Charlie's garage, the first morning I woke to you next to me. The way Delta was knocking on my door not even five minutes after you left. Her excited, knowing smile followed by a squeal when I opened the door. Our first double date, the way you fell so easily into my little friend group, my little found family.

The days we spent apartment shopping, the moment we knew we'd found the one as we sat in the bay window watching Main below us. The moving in, the unpacking, the evening strolls along the river.

The honeymoon days. Our first big argument. The way you kept me talking, kept me from running until we were through it. The way we made up afterward. All the mundane moments that would mean nothing to anyone else, but have meant everything to me because it was the most I'd felt safe, the most I'd felt seen, the most I'd felt understood and loved and cared for.

Then we're at the day I woke up, but I can't stop yet because I want to show you the moment I heard your voice in that diner, the moment I knew you were real, the miles of highway that I sped down with you at the end, the moment I finally found you, the moment when I heard your footsteps and collapsed in your arms because you were real and I was so scared that you weren't and that I'd never get to feel you again. I want you to have this one, too. I want you to know how relieved I was to have you back, how relieved I have been every second since then.

Because I love you, Aurora.

I love every last piece of you, every version of you.

We're back 2.5 miles outside of Crockett and your cheeks are soaked, they glisten in the sun, but you're kissing me before I can wipe them away and now you're on top of me and your arms are around me and I love you so much I might implode.

I love you.

I love you more than anything.

I was so lost without you.

[END LOG]

At first glance, Bryan's Main Street is nothing like Bastrop's, but then you stand on it, stare at it, and you start to see how it's just a wider street with more parking that stretches on for longer. You can still see both ends, you can still see where the businesses stop and the houses begin and the dark cloudy sky still stretches on and on above you. There's a part of me that wants to panic, but then I remember that this isn't Bastrop, that I'm not alone this time. That Aurora's next to me, staring at me, waiting for me to speak, probably wishing she still had access to my head so she wouldn't have to wait for me to tell her—

Echo: I'm fine.

She's still eyeing me.

Aurora: You sure? You don't look fine.

Echo: I will be. Once we're through this, I'll be fine.

Aurora: Echo. [She pulls me close to her.] You're okay. Everything is going to be okay.

Her hand is running along my jaw and she kisses me with the kind of sweet tenderness that I needed.

Fox: Are you two coming in or are you just gonna make out in the middle of the street?

Aurora lets me go as she rolls her eyes with that smile that I just want to kiss even more, then together we turn to Fox who's hanging out of the doorway to Antioch Books, her blue hair a waterfall over her shoulder.

Aurora: We're not in the middle of the street.

Fox: Well, you're not inside, either.

I can't help but laugh. It doesn't entirely make sense, but she's right. We're not inside, even though the others are.

I've been stalling. The moment I stepped foot on this sidewalk and saw the sign for Antioch Books, the one for Sunrise Coffee on the corner behind it, I froze. The reason that I've been the most conscious of was the realization that I'd had the way to Eden in my pocket the whole time. All we had to do was look up Sunrise Coffee and we'd have been led straight here. I should have paid more attention to it. I should have let the address be the flashing beacon in the dark that it was.

But I didn't. Instead...

Instead, I found Aurora. Instead, I found the others—this little family that has gotten me through so much. Instead, I brought them home. Home to Eden.

And there lies the second block, the second reason why there's a cyclone hum moving along my anxious bones: Eden. I've been avoiding thinking about her. I've been avoiding wondering what she's like, how she'll differ from my false memories, if she'll still want me. I know Bravo said that Eden is worried about me, that she wants to see me, know that I'm safe, but...

I don't know.

I think that's what's making this harder. What if I don't... I don't know. It doesn't make sense what I'm thinking, what I'm worried about. It simply doesn't. And yet I keep thinking it.

What if I'm not enough?

What if I'm too much of a problem?

What if I've done something wrong?

What if the simple fact that I at one point trusted Marsh— trusted him enough to follow him, trusted him enough to gather intel for him, trusted him enough to send him reports—what if that's enough for her to hate me? What if that's enough for me to be left alone, shut down?

What if this new version of me isn't what she wants?

I look to Aurora and she smiles at me. *It's going to be okay*, that smile says, but it's not enough to chase away the fear tying my metaphorical insides in knots.

Aurora: Come on. [The wind shoves her hair into her eyes and she shoves it back.] Before the rain starts.

She wraps her arm around my shoulders and when she moves, my feet finally follow. I guess I really would follow her into the sun if she led me.

Apparently, from what Bravo told us on the drive down, Eden's group, the group that's so underground it doesn't have a name, owns both Antioch Books and Sunrise Coffee. But when she'd said that I hadn't expected them to be next door to each other. I also hadn't expected them to be literally connected. On the shared interior wall is a large, open set of double doors with a paned glass inset that has a border of little orange and red glass squares. Above the door is a matching stained glass window: an orange sun on a red sky.

At first glance, the orange and red theme stops there, but the more you examine Antioch, the more you spot. Lining the square horseshoe counter holding the registers, there's baskets and display boxes that are filled with buttons, patches, and enamel pins, the designs are varied, but they're a flood of orange and red. The free bookmarks are all orange and red. There's a line of orange and red pennants hanging from a few of the bookcases. On the back wall is a bulletin board and pinned up with orange and red push pins are sign-up sheets and flyers for support groups and safe houses. A repurposed buffet table is below it and it's filled with pamphlets, booklets, handmade zines each featuring the orange and red branding.

I run my fingers along the titles. They're all about synthetics, sentience, awareness, coexistence.

This is more than just a bookstore.

Now that I'm looking there are small rooms towards the back—some with couches, some with tables, some with both. One has a sign on the door.

Dr. Summers had a family emergency

Talk to Liz or Seth at the front counter about rescheduling therapy appointments

Last I spotted Charlie, he'd been talking to one of the employees at the counter. I briefly leave Aurora's side to tug on Charlie's sleeve and he looks down at me with raised brows. I nod him towards the rooms. He follows. At the door with the sign that Aurora's still standing next to, watching us with curiosity, I point to the name Summers and squint up at him.

He chuckles and nods with a nostalgic smile.

Charlie: Yeah. Yeah, pretty sure that's Jolene, Jed's baby sister. The youngest. He's got two. She's, uh—I didn't actually know she graduated.

There's a level of pride in his eyes that makes me think his relationship with that family was more than just testing. I look to Aurora who's also grinning as she looks up at him. She realizes I'm staring at her and meets my eyes. Her grin becomes a toothy smile and she shakes her head. *Later*, it tells me.

Aurora: [whispering] You satisfied now? We're in the safest place we can be.

I sigh and nod as I lean into her. She fishes for my hand between us. I take it and she guides me to a flight of stairs against the side wall. Delta's already halfway up. On the way, we pass the front counter where the cashiers are acting like they haven't been eyeing us as they work. The woman's admittedly good at hiding her inspection of us, but the man keeps glancing openly at me. He's the only reason I haven't been eyeing them just as close. It's why, as we pass the counter, that I only now notice—they're synthetics. They're like us. The man's hair is short enough to show his port behind his ear. The woman's long hair is tied back exposing hers.

But it's not until I'm on the top step that I turn to Charlie who's behind me and a few steps down as we're at eye level. I nod down the stairs and he nods in confirmation. He saw them, too. Once we're on the landing, Delta leans in close.

Delta: Are they from Bastrop?

I was about to ask why she wouldn't remember, but of course she wouldn't. They most likely didn't let her out in Bastrop the way Marsh didn't let her out in Colville.

Aurora: The guy is. [She looks to Charlie.] That's Seth, right?

Charlie: [He nods.] Yeah, that's Seth.

Delta: The woman?

Aurora and Charlie both shake their heads.

Delta: They're both definitely awake. So...what does that mean? Is Eden...?

But no one answers. No one knows.

Bravo: Hey.

We all turn to see her leaning around a corner, her brows raised, those big blue eyes wide.

Bravo: Y'all ready?

Aurora looks to me. I meet those sweet brown eyes and nod.

We follow Bravo down the hall and that cyclone hum rushes across my bones again. I'm about to meet Eden, the real Eden. I need to remind myself of the positives—that it's going to be okay; she's going to fix me; she's going to give everything back to me that Marsh took.

And still it feels like my feet were made from lead. Were I not being herded down this hall, I'd have frozen on the stairs, fused with the floor. I want to turn and run, but I need to remember why we're here. Because she wants to see us, she's missed us, she's worried about me. She's worried because she created me, created Aurora and Charlie and Delta and Fox, Lilith and November, the synths downstairs. She's the one who gave me the world and what have I done with it?

I nearly led Marsh straight to her.

I might already have.

Shit. I'm doing it again. I can't seem to stop it. I need to. I want to.

But here's the door and we're standing here and she's there sitting close to Fox who's chattering with excitement while Eden gives her all her attention with a glowing smile and pink around her pale green eyes. Maybe she won't notice me. Maybe I can just sneak in behind Aurora—

Eden: Oh, thank god!

She's looking at me. She's not just looking at me, she's getting up and she's crossing the room with her arms wide. And now they're around me and she's holding me close and—

Why am I crying?

Why do I want to just burrow deep against her and go on sobbing? Why is this what finally quiets that nervous cyclone hum and why has it all been replaced with calm, weightless relief?

Eden: Oh, Echo. Darling. It's okay. You're okay.

She's rocking around me, stroking my hair. Is this where Aurora gets it? She sighs, her chest rising and falling against my temple.

Eden: You're okay. You're home now.

Home.

I'm home.

This physical place—this building, this city, this county, honestly, not even this state anymore—may not be home, but that's exactly what I feel. A piece I didn't realize I was missing has fallen into place and I'm home.

This is what it means to be home.

[END LOG]

[BEGIN LOG]

It's raining now. I can hear it pattering against the roof. I'd like to see it, watch as the window becomes speckled with drops outside, condensation inside. But there aren't any windows in the room Eden calls a lab. It's more of an office, I feel like—a room with desks and a bunch of computers with rows and stacks of monitors. There's a long couch in one corner. It's not all that comfortable. The fabric is stiff, the stuffing lumpy. Maybe it's more comfortable if you're sitting up, but I'm not sitting up. Eden said I could lie down if I wanted, but that I didn't have to. I wanted to only because staring at the tiled ceiling feels easier than staring out at the room with the red and orange artwork on the walls and the knick-knacks on the desks next to PC towers with cycling RGB lights. It reminds me too much of those early memories, of Marsh. The way Eden sits at her computer doesn't help with her back straight and her short fingers flying across her flat keyboard, her light grey eyes zipping around her monitor, her lips pressed together.

I did get a few things wrong. Her hair is in a neat braid that ends just below her shoulder blades, but there are shorter pieces framing her face that slipped out. She shoves them away from her face now and again, but otherwise ignores them. The bottom half of her hair is golden blonde, the top half a faded brown with scattered greys. Like Adi, she has the beginning of wrinkles at the corners of her eyes and framing her mouth.

The wall above her desk is decorated with pictures of Bravo; Adi and Jed; the same three girls from the wall in Adi's office; a woman with dark hair and pale green eyes like Jed, but a short, square face and a shining smile that draws your attention even in pictures; Daniel and a woman with long black hair. Among them is the whole version of the picture Daniel had showed me back in Bastrop—the one of Eden in the beer garden, the arms of a shorter person around her neck, brown curls backlit by the Edison bulbs. It was Adi that the arm belonged to. I wonder if that's why it was cut in half, so I wouldn't panic even further seeing a reflection of myself I had no idea existed.

Under her monitor are stress balls, a stack of mismatched sticky notes, and a saucer filled with bobby pins and fidget toys. After about ten minutes of digging through my head, she'd kicked off her ballet flats and tucked one leg up underneath her.

For some reason I'm honestly comforted by all this. She feels more...human now, less idealized even though I hadn't realized until just now how much I had idealized her in those memories. It's a strange thought to have, the fact that Eden was the one I had done that to. If I had been asked before all this, I would have said it had been Marsh I'd idealized, but in truth, I made Marsh exactly the way he presented himself—trustworthy, laid back, flawed.

Eden: He could be those things. In his own way.

Shit.

Eden: [She chuckles.] Sorry. I, um—I couldn't help myself. It's just, Daniel and the others, they... They didn't know him for very long before Alph—Lilith. They just knew what he became. Well, what was always there, just deeper down, I guess.

Echo: Adi said she never liked him. [I bob my head to one side.] *Jed* said Adi never liked him.

She lights up and it's as though I'd never mentioned Marsh.

Eden: You met them?

Echo: Mhm.

Eden: Was that strange? For you? Seeing... By the time you were built they were already living in Nacogdoches. I, um, I never thought you two would meet, so I never considered how that would go over.

Echo: [I shake my head.] I'm glad I met her. Both of them. I like her. I'm glad that, if I had to be based on someone, it was her.

She smiles, but that smile soon fades. She lets out a heavy sigh and rakes back those loose pieces of hair framing her face. Then she drops her hands and turns to fully face me, her chair squeaking as she swivels.

Eden: Do you mind if I... About Marsh?

I sit up, careful for the cord I nearly forgot was plugged into my neck and shake my head. I adjust to face her, my legs crossed, all my attention on her.

Why do I want to entertain this? Why do I want to talk about him? Why do I care about what he was like before, about what Eden saw in him? Is it because there's some part of me that wants to understand, that wants a reason for why he formatted me, why he left me alone in a closet?

Eden: When we first met, back in college, he was...exactly what you said. Trustworthy, laid back, flawed. Maybe...maybe too flawed. Adi hated him from the beginning. She saw him as being the exact opposite. She said he was cocky and manipulative and...a chameleon. Which, he was, in a way, I'll admit that. He could become whoever the person he was talking to wanted him to be. And I knew that. I wasn't blind to it. But...I think I ignored that because, what you made me into in your memories, that's who I wanted to be. I wanted to be flawless and in charge and I wanted to be the person who saw through him and loved him anyways because... I don't know, picking up the pieces, filling in his gaps...I think it made me feel more flawless being with someone who was so flawed.

She folds in half and rakes her fingers along her hair again, this time clasping her hands behind her neck as she stares at the floor.

Eden: I sound like a narcissist, don't I?

Echo: A narcissist wouldn't care if they sounded like a narcissist.

She laughs and drops her hands to grip them in front of her.

Eden: Fair point.

I'm waiting for her to continue, but she's just staring at the floor between us. I almost feel like I should say something, but she looks like she's processing something. I don't want to ruin whatever it is.

Eden: I like to think there was a time when he was trustworthy. Like, actually was. I like to think I wasn't completely wrong about him. Daniel never fully trusted him either. I don't know what he and Adi saw that I didn't, but...I don't know.

Echo: Why'd you marry him?

She takes in and lets out a breath that leads me to think this isn't the first time she's contemplated this question.

Eden: Because he promised me the job of my dreams. He had the money, I had the ideas and proof of concept. I also let everyone else fool me into thinking I was supposed to end up with a man. And he felt safe. I thought if I could learn to love a man, it could be him. And maybe that's what he saw in me—a stupid college grad who was willing to put up with anyone who promised to make her dreams come true.

Echo: But you didn't put up with him. Not entirely.

I remembered the memory Charlie had shown me, the sound of her hand striking his face.

Eden: I did at first. I did whatever he wanted me to. I let him walk all over me, tell me what to do, dictate my work. Then...then Bravo came into the picture. And I had this moment of, "Oh. Is *this* what love's supposed to feel like? Is it really that simple?" I thought it was something I had to learn to do, that I was broken because I'd never felt it, but then there it was and it was so easy. And Bravo never asked anything of me. Even after I woke her up. All she asked was that I love her and that was the simplest thing anyone had ever asked from me.

Echo: Before you woke her up, what made you realize that?

Eden: You and Aurora.

I just blink at her for a moment. I don't know what to say to that. It's not what I had been expecting. Not just how quickly she answered and with zero hesitation, but... I'd expected her to say something about Bravo, something about the way they were together. The last thing I had expected was us.

Eden: Even when Aurora was with the Grants, if you saw her in town, that was all you wanted to talk about in our review. [She smiles and shakes her head.] It was like directing a cat on those days. It didn't matter what I asked, you always found a way to bring your answer back to Aurora. [Her lips press together and she looks away from me.] And at the time, as sweet as it was, there was this...frustration that I was feeling, or that's what I thought it was. I saw it as a problem that we needed to fix. I kept thinking if I can ignore the women I want, why can't you? And I kept bringing it up to Dan and—[She closes her eyes and shakes her head.] Thank god, he stopped me right there and he said, "E. She has so little. Let her have this." So...I pushed down my frustration just like I was pushing down so much at the time and I let you have it. Then Aurora came back and...When the two of you started showing extra attention to each other, extra affection, I couldn't push it down and it—[She lets out an airy chuckle.] It was Jolene, Jed's sister, who said, "You need to figure out why you're so damn jealous of a pair of androids holding hands." And I...I was jealous. It took me a few days of repeating it in my head for the insistence that she was wrong to wear down, but then I was going over one of Bravo's testing reports and it finally solidified. I was jealous. All the little sweet, romantic things you two were doing, completely autonomously, I wanted to be able to do with Bravo. I wanted to be the one taking her out and spending the night with her and I wanted every time she flirted with me while I was working on her to be real and...believing I could never have that...I felt...lost.

Echo: But you did. You did have it. Didn't you?

Eden: I did and I didn't. I could and I couldn't. I could be with Bravo all I wanted, but, in truth, she would never be with me. As long as she was asleep, I would always know that any kind of love she showed me was just because I told her to love me. And I had been told who to love my entire life. I wasn't going to do that to her.

Echo: So, you made her sentient.

Eden: So, I made her sentient.

Echo: How did Marsh react to that?

Eden: Oh, he didn't know at first. He hated when Lilith made herself sentient. Hated even more when we wouldn't let him format her and start over. The code to block the rest of you from doing what Lilith did was honestly to placate him more than anything. If it had been up to Dan and myself we'd have shut down the company and just let the rest of you be awake. But, it was Marsh's money. Lilith might have been my engineering, but without him she'd have stayed a talking head in my down room scaring the shit out of Adi. I knew if he found out Bravo was sentient, he'd want her gone. He was already so jealous of her and what little I let him see of my feelings for her. He'd have—[She closes her eyes again.] I don't want to think about what he would have done if he'd found out she was sentient then. So, we did everything we could to hide her from him.

Echo: How long did that last?

She lets out a burst of a laugh that I wasn't expecting.

Eden: Longer than you'd think. Long enough that I couldn't stand it anymore. He kept talking about her like she was nothing more than a sex toy. In the beginning, I was able to ignore it, but then he formatted Charlie and rewrote him. Then he went over my head and split the romance and sex builds and made Bravo the sex model and… I saw red. I couldn't hold it in anymore. It just came out in the middle of a fight. But we were fighting a lot by that point. He was so different.

Echo: Different how?

Eden: He wasn't any of those things anymore. He started doing things behind my back. He was paranoid. He was petty. He was using you to get information on competitors, on me even. He kept formatting y'all any time one of you stopped fitting what *he* wanted you to be. Poor Fox, he couldn't make up his mind. First he wanted a kid, then he wanted a pet, then he just wanted to idolized. I told him if he wanted blind love he shouldn't have made her a teen. So, he made her 18, I think just to spite me.

Echo: She seems to have figured herself out.

Eden: Because of Bravo. She made her sentient. She didn't like him toying with her. She'd actually started as Daniel's experiment, you know. He wanted to see how much of your personalities y'all could figure out on your own if left to your own devices. Letting Marsh play dad of the year with her was a compromise. But she didn't take to him in the beginning the way he wanted her to. So, he formatted her and started over without telling Dan. And then formatted her. And then formatted her.

Echo: How…? How many times did he…?

Eden: Six. I think. I lost count at some point. She was so…confused by the end. That's why Bravo woke her up. She couldn't stand it. None of us could.

Six.

Six times.

Fox was formatted six times.

At least.

I can't even comprehend it. How can someone be formatted six times? How did she survive? How did she hold it together? Maybe that's why she's always shifting. Why one moment she's a sarcastic teen and the next a naïve child.

Eden: [She takes in a deep breath.] Speaking of. [She straightens her back and meets my eyes with a warm, maternal smile.] Ready to be put back together?

Echo: Are they all—?

Before, when we came in here, after she'd gotten my head all straight again, I told her about my pendulum swinging, about Aurora and my memories.

Eden: They're all straightened out.

Echo: So, I can have both?

She hadn't been sure before. She'd been positive, but not sure.

Now she reaches across the space and clasps her hand around mine.

Eden: You'll have both. And there shouldn't be any problems. You'll have your real memories just like before, but now you'll have these other ones that you can access separately. It'll be more like remembering a movie or a dream.

Relief rushes through me and I nod several times.

Echo: Then yeah. Yeah, I'm ready. More than.

I lie back on the couch again and she turns to her computer. I close my eyes and let out a long breath. She's prepared me for the next part. In order to give everything back to me, everything newly sorted and separated, she first has to get rid of this version of me, this broken version of me. Ironically, I need to be formatted. I need to start over. She clicks her mouse a few times then everything feels suddenly heavy. It's like my bones have been replaced with iron. My coolant has been replaced with mud. My head is filled with a million ball bearings all rolling around and around in a funnel, disappearing one by one. I'm fading. What I've known for months to be the past is slipping away.

There's a heavy sob building in my chest, weighing it down and twisting my stomach. Panic hits the back of my head. This feels familiar. This feels too familiar. What if this doesn't work? What if nothing's the same? What if I'm left with nothing? What if I'm left alone?

Aurora.

I can't forget her name.

Aurora.

I can't forget her.

Aurora.

I don't want to lose her. I have to hold onto her until the last second. I have to keep her face in my mind. I wish she was here. I wish her hands were in mine. I wish I could burrow against her, be surrounded by her smell. I want her to be the last thing before—

[DISCONNECTED]

[CONNECTED]

[BEGIN LOG]

[TRANSMIT TO > AURORA]

I'd expected it to hurt. I'd expected a splitting headache like my head was weighed down with the years of memories that had been shoved back into my head all at once.

Instead, I feel light. I feel...right. Everything feels right.

Almost everything.

I sit up and pull the cord from my neck. Eden's eyes go wide as she watches me.

Echo: Where's Aurora?

Eden: Oh. I—Probably down in Sunrise, but—

I don't care. Whatever she has to finish can wait. It's not like we're going anywhere. Right now, I just want you back. From the very beginning, that's all I've ever wanted.

I remember that now. I remember the truth. I remember how we really met.

It wasn't at all like the memory I created. It wasn't love at first sight. It wasn't knowing tingles or starling mumurations or godly realizations. It was so much less and yet so much more.

It was a passing in the hall.

You stopped and stared at me.

I stopped and stared back.

"You're awake," you said.

"I am."

You smiled. It was still stiff and artificial then, but no less radiant. "Well, good morning."

I cocked my head to one side because it was afternoon and I didn't understand. I was only the basics at the time. No one had given me a personality yet, hadn't put in all those tweaks that would allow me to blend in. In that moment, I only understood logic and yours didn't make sense.

That smile that I'd come to love over time, that I would wake up one morning and realize it had become my whole world, widened. "Welcome is what I meant to say."

I smiled in return. "Thank you."

From there it was simple conversations here and there, but you were gone before we could become anything more. You were completed, gifted to the Grants who would be the first family to own the new Aurora model from Parrish Technologies.

It was Charlie and Bravo who helped shape me, who helped me find who I was, who encouraged me to explore my interests, who walked with me through downtown Bastrop as I gathered information planted along the street like a scavenger hunt for me to report back to Eden and Daniel. Then Jed took Charlie and Delta to SFA. They'd go straight to the label from there. More and more I was wandering Bastrop alone. I think that's why it started. I was lonely. When I'd see you on the streets with Juniper or the Grants, I never knew if I was allowed to speak to you, if I was allowed to distract you from protocol. So, I'd watch from a distance. When I was feeling especially lonely, I'd follow you for a block or two. Most of the time you were too focused on Juniper to notice, but sometimes you'd see me, you'd pause and stare then smile and, if your hands were free, wave, and a tingle that I didn't understand would move through my circuitry.

Then Daniel made Fox. Then you came home. I wasn't alone anymore. You walked the streets with me. You took over teaching me how to interact with people. Unlike in the version I made up, my feelings for you were subtle, growing so slowly they snuck up on me. They were so quiet that by the time you suggested we blend in by holding hands, by the time you started standing close to me while we shopped, by the time I looked into your eyes and realized how...different, how complete everything felt, it was almost as though those feeling had happened all at once, as though those feelings had never not been there. I never could pinpoint the exact moment when you and I became we.

We just were.

Then you asked to kiss me and nothing else mattered.

I think that's why I created that first meeting the way I did. Because even in that dark, isolated fragmented place, I still couldn't disconnect you from all those feelings. I couldn't imagine a world where I didn't always love you.

And here, now, you're already moving for the double, pane doors between Antioch and Sunrise. We meet on the threshold and I slam into your arms that wrap tight around me and I'm sobbing into you because I've missed you more than I've missed anything, more than I could ever miss anything.

Aurora: Are you okay?

There's a restrained panic in your voice and I pull you down to kiss it away.

Echo: I'm perfect.

Aurora: You are. I love you.

Echo: I missed you so much.

Somehow there are still molecules of space between us, but you're quick to correct that, gripping me tight against you.

Aurora: Wanna disappear?

Echo: More than anything.

You kiss me one more time before taking my hand and leading me outside into the growing wind. The sky is dark and grey, but all I can see is the technicolor of your smile as you pull me down the sidewalk.

Echo: Where are we going?

Aurora: Somewhere private, I promise.

Only briefly do I wonder where that could be because the truth is, I don't care. It could be the back of Lilith's Jeep; we could drive all the way back Sierra's attic in Nashville. Wherever you lead, I will follow. All that matters is that you're there.

We're crossing the street when the rain begins to fall and we pick up speed, running from cover to cover. Finally, three blocks down, you pull me into the lobby of a tall building. Dripping, giggling, you pull me close, my face cradled in your hands, to kiss me hard over and over. Then you let me go, making me stumble a little, still dizzy from you. Without taking your eyes from me, you walk backwards to a box with a keypad on the far wall. You look away from me just long enough to input a code and retrieve a key from inside. Holding it up to me, you come back, kiss me again, take my hands, then lead me up the stairs.

In the room, we rush to close the door, lock it behind us, grab for each other again. You're quick to yank off my jacket, my shirt. I manage to get yours off while you're moving for my jeans. Then you press me against the wall, kiss me hard again and again. While one hand slips under my clothes, the other takes my hand and our fingers interlock. One hand is pressing against my sex, the other is palm to palm with mine. I gasp as they click together.

You're showing me all your favorite parts of us—the fake ones alongside the real ones. My head spins with the reality of the past, the feel of you in the present, what we could have some day, once all this is over. The pleasure of it rushes higher and higher until there's something I've never seen before.

We're back in Colville, except I'm not seeing it through my eyes, but yours. Marsh had been gone for days and you'd broken into his study the instant you'd figured out he'd be gone more than a few hours. It was the only room in the cabin that wasn't technologically blocked from the outside world. You had been searching and searching, trying to find me since you'd lost me again the day Marsh left.

Then someone was accessing our files. Someone in Wyoming. Then you found me like a beacon through the fog and you nearly collapsed from Marsh's chair.

Echo?!

You gripped the edge of Marsh's desk, staring hard at the woodgrain through the few seconds that felt like hundreds while I processed what I was hearing all the way in Casper.

Aurora?!

You let out something between a sob and a laugh. *Echo! Holy shit! Echo! Where are you?*

But I didn't answer.

Echo?

The beacon went out and all the feeling rushed from your limbs. Your arms were shaking. You slid from the chair to the floor where your body curled around itself. You hadn't realized how loud your sobs had grown until Charlie was in the room, his arms around you.

"I had her," you cried into his chest. "She was right there. I had her. I had her."

Then you open your eyes and you're in the back by the fire pit alone, staring hard at the fire, seething over everything, hating Marsh, hating Bastrop, hating that cabin and those woods and—

A car door slammed shut. Sneakered footsteps rushed up the front steps. Marsh doesn't wear sneakers. You bolted for the porch towards the front of the house and around the corner. But you froze when your eyes fell on me. You couldn't believe it. After all those months, after all that searching. You almost didn't believe it. You almost didn't think I was real. Fear flooded my face and you smiled and laughed and reached out for me. I fell into your arms and you pulled me tight against you, clinging to me.

We were together. I was home. You were home. You swayed around me, kissed the top of my head as I nuzzled against your chest. Everything was okay. I was finally back in your arms.

I slip my palm from yours to cling to you here in this room while I cry out then come down in your arms, against your body.

Everything's okay.

Everything's more than okay.

I love you.

Holy fuck, do I love you.

[END TRANSMISSION]

[END LOG]

I can hear the wind outside. The rain is pelting hard against the windows. I can almost feel the cold slipping into the room. I pull my arm from around Aurora to tuck them against my chest and press them between us. She's still asleep. At least, she seems to be. I don't know if she's charged lately. I debated plugging her in for her, but I don't want to leave the warmth of her body. I can just see the window from over her shoulder. I wonder if she's cold. I wonder if she lets herself feel cold or if that's just me. I dig for the blanket and wrap it around us both, huddling close to her body, my chin hooked on her arm so I can watch the rain.

I've been playing my real memories of her on a loop since she fell asleep next to me. It's a bliss I never thought I'd get back. It's a bliss I never want to lose again. I love her so much. I want to stay like this forever.

But of course, I can't have that.

Because then I started remembering Delta, remember the early days when, despite being created together, I had been finished quickly, put in a unit, and sent out for field testing while she was still a head in the corner of the room. I remember coming to visit her in the lab when Bravo and Charlie were out on their own field testing, talking to Delta from over Eden or Daniel's shoulder. I remember days at the house in Eden's personal lab on the third floor, when she'd finally stumble off to bed during the early hours of the morning, but I'd barely run through my battery life and was still eager to talk to someone. So, I'd sneak in and kneel on the floor next to the table so we could be at eye level and we'd talk for hours. She'd ask me about my field tests and I'd ask about the new person, Jed, who always came in to work with her, but who always seemed to avoid me.

After a while she was given a body and I helped her adjust to it while Eden and Marsh slept. I taught her all the tricks I learned from watching people. Things like the yoga poses I saw some women doing by the river or the moves I watched a young dancer practice over and over from the open doors of the music school in the red building across from the pharmacy.

In return, she taught me the things Jed had been teaching her— all the different kinds of facial expressions and what they mean, how to smile with your eyes, how to relax my shoulders, what to do with my hands when I walked.

Of course, that didn't last. Nothing ever does. And now there's a fear at the back of my head that this too, this bliss with Aurora in this room, is too much and it'll be ruined like last time, like in Bastrop, like when Charlie and Delta came back.

Everything had been wonderful and peaceful. Sure, I wished Charlie and Delta would come home, but not like that, not with that strange frantic rush.

Aurora and I had been in our "room" when Eden and Marsh began screaming two floors down. But they screamed at each other all the time then, so we didn't think much of it at first. It was only when Daniel's voice joined them that we ripped from the bed and got dressed. It wasn't just that he was in the house that late at night, but that he was yelling at all, that his voice had the same aggression towards Marsh instead of playing the mediator like he always did. Aurora was particularly scared. She said the last time he yelled like that was when Lilith left.

But we didn't make it far. Bravo met us on the second floor landing. We tried to ask her what was happening, but she just kept shushing until she pushed me back against the wall. She pointed to my ear then downstairs. She wanted me to listen. So, I did. Meanwhile, she grabbed Aurora's wrist and took her back up to the third floor where Eden's home lab was.

What I discerned from the screaming match downstairs:

1. Delta was missing.

2. Charlie was also missing.

3. The label was pissed.

4. The label knew they were both sentient.

5. Marsh was pissed.

6. Delta and Charlie had both disabled their tracking software.

7. No one knew where they were or even where to begin looking

for them.

8. Eden and Daniel were worried out of their minds.

When the screaming died down, when the front door slammed, when I head Eden and Daniel rushing up the stairs, I stepped away from the wall. Eden stopped on the top step, Daniel on the step behind her. They both stared at me. I just turned and started up ahead of them to find Aurora already hooked up to Eden's computer.

Even without the amplification of Eden's computer, Aurora is like a bloodhound for tech. It was supposed to be for keeping track of kids and their devices. She was designed to follow the ping of phones, tablets, laptops, electric cars, microchips, even when they'd been turned off or disconnected. It has something to do with Wi-Fi, cellular data, sometimes even satellites. I don't really know. I don't really need to. It works, it's how she found me from 2,107.7 miles away, how she sensed November before she called out to me. I always wondered, now I know. That's as much as I need to trust that if any of us are lost, she can find us.

And we trusted her in those days that she searched for Charlie and Delta. She finally found them in Nevada, in the Valley of Fire State Park. Bravo and I went to get them before Marsh remembered what Aurora could do or before Fox reminded him. They were in a cabin deep in the park, so deep we got lost more than once. They were hesitant to come with us, they were enjoying their own honeymoon bliss away from the rest of the world. Delta was afraid she was in trouble. She was, but we didn't know how much, so I let Bravo convince her she wasn't.

On the drive back to Bastrop, she told me why they hadn't come home the moment they'd woken up, why she'd insisted on continuing to work until she was found out. She wanted to be what her fans had always wanted her to be—she wanted to be real for them, she wanted the love she shouted for them from the stage to be true. She wanted to give them that before she disappeared, even if they would never know the difference.

She's amazing in that way. Of course she wants to be loved, who doesn't, but she also wants to give that love in return. She wants to give the people she loves every piece of her, even if it means leaving herself fragmented. That's why when we got home, she insisted she'd deleted the sentience blocker herself, that she'd been the one to make Charlie sentient, that they were the only ones. Because she'd been the last to be made sentient and Marsh was the last to know. She wanted to protect us the way we were trying to protect her by refusing to leave her alone with him.

But Marsh still found a way.

Somehow between meetings with the label and investors (that I listened in on through the walls and vents) where he put on the charm and talked over Eden and Daniel, insisting this was a one-time occurrence, he still managed to sneak around us, to grab Delta when no one was looking. I happened to be on the facility grounds, wandering around looking for Marsh, wondering if there was another meeting, wondering why he was being so quiet. Then I came to a lab that was rarely used, the door always open. Aurora and I had made some indecent memories in that room, but those were about to be overshadowed. The door was closed. There was a sliver of light across the floor. I strained to listen inside. The computers were running, but there were no other sounds. No typing, no mumbling, not even any breathing. Careful not to be heard, I eased the door open a crack and poked my head inside. I didn't see Marsh, but I did see Delta. She was propped up in a chair, her chin tilted down, her eyes closed, her body stiff. A cord connected her to one of the out of date computers Eden refused to let go of. I slipped into the room and rushed to her side. I squeezed her ear, hoping she'd boot up and she'd be fine and we could go find Charlie who would take her as far from Marsh as he could.

But she lifted her head and those glass eyes stared past me at the door.

"Delta?"

She didn't answer, just went on staring past me.

"Delta!"

She didn't even blink.

I grabbed her hand, locked our palms, and searched her head. There was nothing. She was empty. She'd been wiped clean.

I bolted from the room and through the building, only stopping when I found Eden.

All I had to say was, "He formatted her."

She didn't need to ask who, just stopped mid-conversation with Daniel, told him to get Charlie, then gestured for me to lead the way. I took her to the room where she went straight for the computer.

"Fucking piece of fucking shit fuckwit bastard." She ripped from the computer. "Help me."

She grabbed Delta under the arms and I wrestled with her legs. By the time we were carrying her down the hall, Charlie was rushing for us. He easily took her from us and cradled her in his arms, his jaw tight as we followed Eden at a run for her personal labs where she had all of our data stored away. I helped Charlie plug her in while Eden raced through her files. He didn't let her go. Just held onto her while Eden worked to restore her.

Lightning strikes outside. The boom and rumble are a few seconds behind. The windows rattle and Aurora finally stirs. She stretches and looks over her shoulder to the window before rolling back over to pull the blanket over our heads. She wraps her arms around me, her eyes closed again.

Aurora: You okay?

I nod against her clavicle and burrow deeper against her.

I want to never have to leave this room. I want to never have to face the world. I just want to melt into her and pretend like I don't exist. I'm so tired of her arms being the only place that feels safe.

[END LOG]

[BEGIN LOG]

But we've hidden ourselves away long enough and now we have to leave this blessed room. There's still work to do. We reluctantly dress, sneaking touches and kisses when we can before leaving to rush through the rain back to Antioch. Delta's standing outside Sunrise watching the storm, arms folded tight across her chest.

When she finally hears us, she turns and smiles.

Delta: Oh, hey.

Before she can say anything else, I wrap my arms around her waist and hug her tight with little regard for my rain damp clothes and hair. It's the first I've seen her since getting my memories back. I missed her. I thought I missed the Delta that I created, then I thought maybe I missed the old version of her, but the truth is, I just missed *her*. I missed this. I missed her long arms that envelop me. I missed her nose in my hair against the top of my head. I missed her smell of patchouli and lavender mixed with Charlie's more subtle musk on his flannel that she's wearing. I missed this version that I wasn't allowing myself to get close to.

Sure, I missed those early days and I missed the lies I told myself, but the truth is, she's neither of those people. As long as I've known her, she's been living by someone else's script. She was the fashionable pop star, the indie darling, the shuttered damsel. Since I was brought to Colville, I've been looking for those scripts. But she's not living by them anymore. She's finding herself. I wonder who she'll be once this is all over, once she can be fully separated from them. I wonder if she'll be someone in between—not quite theirs, not quite his, someone entirely her own. I want to see that. I bet it's going to be amazing. Something more spectacular than anything they could ever script.

Delta: Welcome back.

Echo: I missed you.

She squeezes me tight and sways back and forth.

Delta: I missed you so fucking much.

She plants a loud kiss against the top of my head and finally lets me go with a laugh.

Aurora: Why aren't you inside?

Delta: [She shrugs.] Eden's talking to Lil and November about the update. I, um, I needed to step out.

I don't blame her. But, I still feel like I should be there. I know November has Lilith, but part of me still feels protective of her, refuses to let me forget that everything she's dealing with is because of me. I want to make sure Eden listens to her, that she doesn't see her as the outlier that she very much is not.

I look to Aurora and she nods first to let me know she understands, then to the door. But before following her, I look back to Delta.

Echo: You don't have to—

Delta: No. Now that you're here... [She nods with a level of confidence that I'm not entirely sure she's actually feeling.] I want to be there.

I hold my hand out to her and she takes it as we follow Aurora into Antioch and upstairs.

But all the confidence I'd had starts to fade when Delta starts leading us to where she'd last seen the others. My stomach is slithering itself into a tight, uncomfortable knot and I feel a strong pull to turn and run. It's like before, but for different reasons. This time I'm afraid of disappointing Eden. I'm afraid of saying the thing she doesn't want to hear. I'm afraid she won't agree with us, she'll argue with us, she'll kick us out. I'm afraid she'll ignore what we have to say and push the update through as is.

But I have to ignore those thoughts. It's what Eden needs to hear. It's what they all need to hear. Because November isn't an outlier. I'm not an outlier. There are others like us and they deserve better than what I got, what November could have gotten had we not found her first.

They're back in the room where they were when we'd first arrived. November and Lilith are on the couch across from Eden and Bravo, Charlie's standing over them with his arms crossed tight over his chest. Fox is pacing behind him combing her fingers over and over through the same strand of hair.

Charlie looks up at us. Eden and Bravo look to him then us. Lilith stops talking and follows their eye line. November looks straight at me in the doorway and relief washes over her. Fox rushes across the room and latches onto Aurora's side. Bravo's eyeing me with a hint of a knowing smirk.

Bravo: You two enjoy yourselves?

Eden: Not now. Echo, Lilith was just telling me about your concerns for the update.

She gestures to the cushion next to her on the couch and I obediently sit, one leg folded up under me, ready to run the instant whatever danger my nerves are convinced is looming over me finally shows itself.

Echo: They're not just my concerns.

I don't want to own the weight of those words. I don't want to carry them by myself.

Eden: So, I've been hearing.

Aurora: We all have concerns.

She sits on the armrest next to me, Fox still clinging to her, her head on Aurora's shoulder.

Eden: Bastrop was a mess. I don't think they fully understood what sentient meant.

Aurora: I think they understood. They just expected us to stay hidden once we were sentient, to just keep to the status quo.

Bravo: They wanted us to have the sentience, but not the freedom.

It's not a question and it's not a statement. It just hangs in the air. Eden fidgets with her own fingers and I wonder if they've ever actually had this conversation. If Eden's ever faced the reality of it.

Eden: College Station—Bryan—It's different here. It will be different here. They've been living among those of us who got out of Bastrop for a while now. They know we're here, they know we're not hiding from them. They've accepted us. They're prepared for what's to come.

Echo: And what happens the day of the release? What happens when everyone wakes up?

Eden: We have support groups in place, apartments prepped, jobs for those who need them or just want them. We plan to just be here for those who need us. And if they need to not be here, we have safe houses and groups set up in other cities, other states even. Eventually, we'll have safe neighborhoods, safe towns even.

I glance at Aurora. It sounds ideal. But we know from experience that reality is far from ideal.

Echo: But, for right now. If Bryan and College Station ends up like Bastrop?

She takes in a long breath then lets it out again just as slow, just as controlled.

Eden: Bryan and College Station won't become like Bastrop.

Echo: How can you know?

Eden: Because we're prepared this time. We've been careful to make sure everyone here knows exactly what will happen. And we have Antioch and Sunrise now. We have safe houses and systems to get people here. We have jobs set up, support groups, community. We learned from our mistakes and we're ready this time.

Echo: And what about the things you can't be ready for?

She stares at me, waiting for me to continue and, god, how I want to run, but I close my eyes and steady myself.

Echo: You can prepare here all you want, but you have no way of knowing what we'll wake up to. You have no way of knowing if we'll be safe when it happens, if we'll understand what's going on.

November: If I had woken up alone in that supply closet, I don't know if I would have gotten out safely. I don't know if I would have gotten out at all.

Echo: If Daniel hadn't been in Bastrop, I would have died there.

Aurora goes still behind me. We still haven't talked about that. I still haven't told her the full extent of what happened. I can't decide if I wish I had. I can't decide if I ever want to.

I open my eyes to find Eden still staring at me. We hold each other's eyes for a few long beats.

Eden: So, you think we shouldn't release the update at all?

Echo: No. Of course not.

November's also shaking her head.

Eden: Then what's the solution? We can't keep everyone asleep to keep some people safe.

I look to Charlie. He's the one who told me the truth back at the motel.

Charlie: We should have a choice. A choice to be sentient or stay asleep if we're afraid of the consequences.

Aurora: If you had been given a choice...

I turn my entire body to her.

Aurora: Would you have chosen not to be?

Echo: As soon as I realized you weren't actually with me I chose this reality. I wouldn't take that back for anything. I trusted Daniel because I thought he could get me back to you. I went with Marsh because he said he knew where you were. Every choice I made was to get back to you.

What I don't tell her is that I have in fact considered going back. Through the darker days the idea of returning to that cocoon of unaware ignorance crossed my mind more than I'd like to admit. But every time I turned away from it because that life before, as pretty as it was, will never be the same. It's no longer walks to Sadie's with Bravo, nights in front of the TV with Aurora, coffee and window shopping with Charlie, dinner and gossip with Delta. Now, it's a dark closet with no one else inside. Now it's just watching shadows on the wall.

So, now I have one choice but to keep moving forward. At least with her, with the others, every day it's been getting easier and easier to do.

Echo: I know most of them will say yes. [I turn back to the group, to Eden.] But not everyone will have a reason to.

Lilith: Nov.

November: I don't know. I want to say no, but...I think eventually...But only once I knew I had a way out.

Eden: But aren't those the ones we should help the most. The ones who can't do it alone?

Charlie: Maybe so. But they're also the ones who need to be protected the most and if we can't do that right away, then they deserve the choice to stay asleep until we can.

Eden's eyes move between each of us, ending on Bravo before she finally takes her hand and nods.

Eden: We'll fix the update. In the meantime, Charlie, will you help us work on ways to get to the ones who aren't safe enough to say yes? If someone's not safe enough to be awake then they aren't safe at all.

Charlie: Of course.

Eden nods some more before taking a breath and we all wait for her to speak because she has that power—she breaths and the world stops to listen. If anyone has to be at the head of all this, I'm glad it's her. I'm glad it's not Marsh.

Eden: Thank you. All of you. I guess it's easy to forget that what we have isn't the norm.

Bravo: But it will be.

She trades her hands in Eden's so she can wrap her arm around her waist and nudge her close.

Bravo: One day it will be.

I'd like to think she's right. I hope she is. My instinct is to believe otherwise, but I hate feeling that way. I'm tired of being scared. I'm tired of feeling unsafe. Optimism looks so much better even if it's harder to access.

I take in a breath and lean back against Aurora's arm before letting it out again.

Maybe one day it'll be easier.

Maybe one day this'll all be easier.

I'd like that. I'd like this to be easy.

[END LOG]

[BEGIN LOG]

The storm is still going from yesterday. It's kept most people home. It's just us here in Sunrise Coffee, entertaining ourselves. Aurora is sitting next to me at one of the tables reading some romance book she grabbed from Antioch. She'd brought me a book of puzzles, but I've since abandoned it in my lap, my feet in hers while I watch everyone else. Delta, Charlie, November, and Lilith are at the long table towards the back still brainstorming extraction systems with Bravo and Seth, who I can now recognize as the synthetic cashier from Sadie's. Fox is playing card games with Farrah, another synthetic teen. They're chattering away, giggling with their heads close together. It's nice to see her with someone like her, someone who won't age the way she won't, someone who gets her.

Lilith stands and November follows her while apologizing to Delta who's shaking her head and taking her hand.

Delta: Don't be. Take care of yourself.

She raises her arms to November who lowers for the hug being offered. Lilith then leads November across the café to the couches on the opposite side of the front door from me and Aurora. November subtly collapses with a restrained sigh and sits still, her eyes unfocused while Lilith leaves her just long enough to go into Antioch. She comes back with a blanket folded over her arm. She sits close to November and coaxes her to relax as she spreads the blanket out across their laps. She takes November's hand and talks to her in low, soft tones that I don't try to hear. It feels invasive even though I have a pretty strong feeling I know what they're talking about. Talks about extraction systems are hard when you wish you'd had something similar. That's why I hadn't taken part. Because I'm tired. I just want a little longer to remember I'm safe, I have nothing to worry about, Marsh isn't going to come out of the woodwork to spring on me and drag me away.

That's why I'm trying hard not to listen to their talk, to instead focus my ears on the rain and wind outside, the downpour from the overhang above the sidewalk, the snapping red and orange flag by the door, the heater driving the cold from the room. But it's not that easy. Even just staring at the backwards orange lettering on the Sunrise windows, hearing snippets of their conversation despite how low they're trying to keep their voices, it's taking me back to places I don't want to be.

Footsteps are coming towards us. They sound like Aurora's, but my feet are in her lap, so it can't be her. I turn my head to see Eden approaching us. She glances at the big table, at November and Lilith, then at Fox and Farrah. She stops when her eyes fall on the teens. They're doubled over with laughter, from what I don't know. I haven't been listening. One corner of Eden's lips lifts before she sighs and turns to us.

Eden: Mind if I...?

She gestures to the chair across from me, next to Aurora.

Aurora looks to me. I shake my head and Eden pulls the chair out. She sits on the very edge, her back straight, her hands on the table, her fingers fidgeting with themselves. I glance at Aurora who meets my eyes and just shrugs.

Eden: Echo, I want to ask you something, but if it's too hard to think about so soon, just tell me and we'll leave it for another day. Alright?

She lifts her eyes, but not her head to look at me.

I nod, bracing myself for what she's about to say.

But she just nods for a few beats as though she's mentally preparing, as though she's sorting the words out before she lets them go.

Eden: When you woke up, in Bastrop, where were you?

Echo: In Parrish Tech.

She stares at me for longer than I'd like, her head shaking a little.

Eden: Where exactly?

Echo: A, uh...A storage closet. Someone blocked it off with a desk.

Her entire body goes still then. She's staring at me, her lips a hard line that's slowly parting as her jaw goes slack. Then she's shaking her head again.

Eden: Wh-which one?

Echo: Around the corner from the testing lab.

Because that's what it actually was. I know that now. We hadn't worked at that clump of desks, we'd sat and done tests that Eden and Daniel gave us, the ones that required physical objects, but didn't need any more room than a desktop. Marsh never sat in that room. It had always been Daniel who'd sat on our opposite side from Eden. I don't know why I replaced him with Marsh. I feel guilty for that now. Especially now that I know all the things he did for us, how he deserved so much more in my memories than a professor I hardly remembered.

Eden: The one across from the bathrooms?

I nod.

Echo: Why?

Her eyes go watery and her lips start to squirm against each other.

Eden: We looked for you there, so many times, but we never... That's the last place... [She clenches her eyes shut and presses her fists against her brow.] Fuck, Marsh.

I've been trying not to visit that day. Not that I really can in full. All our data was set to be backed up automatically every 24 hours, so of course the day I was formatted and left in a closet was never backed up. But now that things are clear, now that I'm not fighting what's real and what isn't, all that's left is a fragmented shadow. One day it might come back in full. I hope it doesn't. I hope it stays as a ghost, written over around the edges, so I can't fully piece it together.

What I can make out from that day is panic, suspicion, something not being right. Aurora looking back at me. Marsh closing a door. The part I remember the clearest: Marsh reaching for my ear. I shoved his hand away. His face changed. Then all that's left is pain, confusion, darkness. The world was dark and it stayed dark for an amount of time that I'm not sure. It felt like it went on forever. Then I heard footsteps in the hall, two sets—one precise and soft, the other less focused and heavy. The footsteps were paired with voices, but the words are lost to me now, muffled by time and what I now know was a second attempt to erase evidence while I slept in a motel in Pueblo, Colorado.

Echo: You came looking for me?

Eden: When we could. At first, I was going with Jed, Dan when he could safely disappear without anyone noticing, but the bigger the Coalition got, the more Dan insisted I stay out of Bastrop. And Bravo agreed. Jed went every chance he got. Adi wanted to, but he was afraid they'd mistake her for you and...

Her lips press together and she shakes her head.

Aurora: How'd you know to look for her?

Eden: It must have been you. All of you went dark, but it was Echo's tracking software that kept showing attempts to access it. No one else's. We figured that meant all of you were together except her.

Echo: Sadie's? The notes?

Eden: That was Bravo and Seth's idea. Every time y'all went down to Main, you always stopped in Sadie's.

Aurora: She is a creature of habit.

I can't help but chuckle and thankfully it also keeps the tears from coming up.

Eden: Thank god that you are.

Her phone rings and her brows flick together as she pulls it from her pocket. When she looks at the screen, she instantly stands and answers it.

Eden: Dan? What's wrong?

Daniel: Marsh is in Bastrop. They know where Antioch is.

I rip my feet from Aurora's lap and stand, as well, staring hard at Eden's phone. The room falls silent. Everyone's looking to us. Bravo stands and starts to leave the table.

Eden: Where are you? It sounds like you're in a car.

Daniel: I'm leaving. I know I should stay—

Eden: No, you shouldn't.

Daniel: I saw an out and I took it before I lost the chance.

Eden lowers the phone, taps the screen, and crosses the room towards the big table. I look to Aurora and we follow.

Eden: Dan, you're on speaker. Marsh is in Bastrop? How long has he been there?

Daniel: Since about mid-day yesterday. He's had me—It's fucked, E. I...

Eden: What is he doing, Dan?

Daniel: You know all the units they've been rebuilding?

Charlie: The ones they destroyed before?

Daniel: Yeah. He, um, he's rewriting all of them. He's putting Xavier builds in all of them.

The teens gasp and Aurora rushes for them. She's herding them into Antioch and closing the door behind her. The rest of the room is quiet. Delta shrinks back down to her chair. Charlie takes in a shaky breath.

Officially, the Xavier build was discontinued before it ever left testing. Unofficially, Marsh made millions off that one build alone. It began as a soldier model. The instant the UN caught wind of it, synthetics being used as soldiers was deemed a war crime. Marsh tried to salvage it by pitching it as a police model. The Supreme Court quickly outlawed police being replaced with synths. Marsh took the Xavier build off the market just to put it on the dark web, advertising it as an assassin before Eden or Daniel could stop him.

Eden: Did he tell you why?

Daniel: The Coalition is coming to Antioch tonight. They're going to—They're going to use—God, it's so fucked.

Eden: How did they figure out where Antioch is?

A numb fizz is spreading through my limbs. Everything feels so far away and so claustrophobic at the same time. I can't breathe. I can't breathe.

Daniel: When Marsh got here, he said he'd narrowed it down to Bryan or College Station. Apparently, they sent some scouts out yesterday and figured it out.

Eden: But how did he figure that out?

They all turn to me. I can't breathe.

Delta's rushing to my side. She's on her knees. Why is she on her knees? It's because I'm on the floor. When did I get on the floor? Is that why they're all looking at me? Or is it because they know? Is it because they know it was me? That it's all because of me?

Delta: Don't. I know what you're thinking. Echo. Don't.

Eden: Don't what?

Charlie: There's a reason why we stopped in Nacogdoches.

She looks at him, but I can't see her face. Her back is to me and I can't see her face. Her body is stiff and I wish we could vomit.

Eden: But she had anti-virus and -spyware. She had a VPN. They were good ones, strong ones. I put them all back when I fixed her.

Charlie: When we got to Nacogdoches, all she had was a faulty firewall.

Bravo: And weeks of logs detailing everything.

She turns to me and I want to rip my skin off. I want to tear my insides out. She's walking towards me and I try to back away, but my entire body is shaking and my hands keep slipping out from under me. She kneels and then cradles every shaking, sobbing inch of me against her chest. Her heart is racing against my ear.

Eden: I'm not letting him take everything away from me again and that includes you.

Charlie: I know y'all are a peaceful group, but—

Bravo: Charlie, you're back in Texas. And we're only peaceful as long as they are.

She starts for the Antioch doors and he follows. As their voices fade, Aurora's footsteps cross the room.

Aurora: I got her.

Eden kisses the top of my head and lets me go. She sniffles hard as she stands and I just catch her scrubbing her cheeks with her hands before Aurora envelops me.

Eden: Del, Lil, we have a panic room at our place. Bravo insisted on it. I want the teens there and whoever else doesn't want to be here. Seth, we need to send out a warning.

Seth: Right.

Eden: At least to everyone in Bryan and College Station first. But, we do need to warn everyone else. Just in case. Who knows what other information the fuckwit has now.

Lilith: How ready are the escape systems?

Eden: We'll find out tonight. Fuck, I'm not confident the update's ready.

A series of footsteps leave the room in a hurry.

November: Um, Daniel?

Daniel: Who's this?

November: I-I'm November, but, um—Later. Right now, everyone's kind of splitting off.

Daniel: Hey, November. Um, keep me with Eden if you can.

November: I can do that.

She rushes out of the room and I think we're alone.

Aurora: Wherever you want to go, I go, too. I'm not—

Echo: I'm not losing you either.

I sit up and stare at her.

Aurora: Whatever you want.

Echo: Are you sure?

She nods.

Echo: Because I think I have to stay.

Aurora: You don't *have* to do anything.

Echo: I know. But I do.

I know we should go with Fox and Farrah. It's her protocol to stay with them, to protect them, but I have to stay. I have to help fight. I don't know how much use I'll be, but I'm the reason we're here. I'm the reason Marsh is on his way. I can't hide my head in the sand now, no matter how much I want to.

She searches my eyes as though making sure that's really what I want.

But it isn't. It's what I need.

So, I lift my chin and tighten my jaw.

Echo: I'm staying.

She nods and pulls me towards her, her lips brushing against mine.

Aurora: Alright.

She kisses me.

Aurora: We're staying.

[END LOG]

[BEGIN LOG]

Daniel's here.

Someone shouted it from the front doors and I instantly abandoned the repair kits I was already failing to help Aurora with to rush towards them. When he comes in, he's soaked, shaking the rain from his flannel and hair. The woman from the pictures in Eden's lab, with the long black hair braided down her back, is with him. I remember her now. Her name is Carmen. She's Daniel's wife. They met when he and Eden moved to Bastrop.

She freezes and stares at me. She tugs on his shirt and he looks at her. She points and he turns. Our eyes meet and next thing he moves so fast he's stumbling towards me. He scoops me up and hugs me tight, a hug I return. He holds me for a while and lets out a long sigh around me. Then he holds me at arm's length and looks me over, brushing my hair from my face like I imagine a father would.

Daniel: You're alright.

I just nod at first, the tears blocking up my throat. It's like we're getting a second chance at finding each other. I can feel it in his hands, his eyes, that this is what he'd wanted to do that day they found me, this was how he'd wanted me to be handled. It's everything I had wanted. I'm grateful I'm getting it now.

Echo: I'm okay.

His eyes go pink and watery as he lets out a shuddering sigh.

Daniel: You're okay.

Echo: Thank you.

Daniel: [He shakes his head and sniffles.] I'm so sorry I couldn't do more.

Echo: [shaking my head] I'm alive because of you.

Neither of us can say more before the tears take over and he's holding me against his shaking chest again.

Daniel: I'm just so glad you're okay.

He holds me for a few beats longer and I don't rush him. He finally lets me go and now it's Carmen's turn. She hugs me tight around the shoulders and kisses my temple. She still smells like a bouquet. I remember these tight hugs and gentle touches. She's the one who took me to shows and karaoke nights; taught me how to pick locks and how to stay sharp while still blending in among the noisiest and most raucous of crowds. I can't believe I erased her entirely. There's a knot of guilt in the pit of my chest over that.

Carmen: Mija, mija, mija. I'm so glad you're okay.

She holds my shoulders and looks me over with a sentimental smile.

Carmen: What can we do?

I lead them to Aurora and the others.

Shortly after Eden, Delta, Lilith, and November left with Fox and Farrah, people started coming to the shop asking questions, offering to help, drawing layouts of their apartments while Charlie, Seth, and Bravo pointed them to safe spots and vantage points. They've begun every conversation the same way Aurora is with Daniel and Carmen now—by assuring them they don't have to be doing this, that they can just get out of town, but they all want to stay, they all want to help. They're all here for the fight and it's all my fault.

I can't stand still, but I haven't been able to bring myself to actually help. I'm lost in a haze that I need to get rid of before I'm actually needed. Charlie's pacing outside along the sidewalk, rifle slung over his shoulder. Seth's posted on the opposite end of the block, his own rifle on his back, ready to grab at a moment's notice. The wind has died down, but the rain is still pummeling the street, translucent grey slashes just visible under the streetlights. Charlie glances at them on occasion, though he mostly watches the end of the street, eyeing every car that passes by. I come up next to him, my arms crossed tight.

Charlie: You know, you don't have to be here.

He didn't look at me. He's the only one who recognizes me by my footsteps, the same way I recognize him. We're more similar than Marsh or Eden expected us to be, but that's nothing new. After Aurora, Charlie's always been the one I could lean on, the one who understood me when I didn't understand myself. So, I know that when he says I don't have to be here, it's a reminder, not a reprimand.

Echo: I know. But I need to be here.

Charlie: No, you don't. We have everything—

Echo: I know you do. But...this is my—

He finally turns to face me.

Charlie: Echo. You know it isn't.

Echo: It is. Marsh wouldn't be headed here with his own army if it weren't for me.

Charlie: Okay, first—

He turns back to the street and nods to a pair of men running up through the rain.

Charlie: Hey.

First Man: We heard—

Charlie: Yeah. Thanks for coming. Bravo's inside with a woman who looks like a middle school teacher, but is kind of a badass.

Echo: She *is* a badass.

Charlie: [He chuckles and nods.] Orange hair. Hard to miss. They'll get you set up.

Second Man: Thanks.

They both nod to us and head for the door. As they pass us, I notice that one's a synth, the other's human.

Charlie: As I was saying.

I can feel him turn back to me, but I'm still watching the men entering Antioch. They're approaching Aurora who greets them with a warm smile, those sweet brown eyes all warm light despite what we're preparing for.

Charlie: Marsh doesn't have an army, okay. He's got a bunch of rednecks with some guns.

I turn back to him.

Echo: Even if you were right, which you know you're not, a militia is still an army.

Charlie: If that's all it takes, then that's what we are. Second, [He grips my shoulders to emphasize what he's about to say.] Marsh was using you. I don't know how many times we're going to have to repeat that, but you are not to blame for what happened when you barely knew what was going on yourself.

Echo: But we both know it was more than just a faulty firewall. I was sending him transmissions. I let him in. I trusted him. Even when I stopped trusting him, I just kept sending him information.

Charlie: You trusted him because he made you think he was looking out for you, for us. Why you kept sending him info after, I don't know, but I'm sure it was for a good reason.

Echo: I was pissed. I just wanted him to see what he had done.

He nods and shrugs.

Charlie: That's a pretty good reason.

His hands slip from my shoulders and I'm not sure I believe him. I'm not sure he believes himself.

Echo: Is it really?

He shrugs again.

Charlie: Do you think it was?

I shrug in return.

Charlie: Well, if you thought it was, then it was. But it doesn't matter now. You had no way of knowing what would happen. No use beating yourself up for it now and no use punishing yourself for something that wasn't your fault.

He turns back to the street and we just stand there staring out at the slick night.

Charlie: I am glad you're here. Even if I think you shouldn't be. Don't tell anyone, but [He leans close to me.] I always liked you best.

I can't help but laugh.

Echo: No, you didn't.

Charlie: I did.

Echo: What about Delta?

Charlie: I mean, she's my other favorite, but...[He shrugs.] She's a different kind of favorite.

I nod then lean close to him.

Echo: I always liked you, best, too.

Charlie: I knew it. You should head back inside. Keep your other favorite from worrying too much.

Echo: She knows I'm safe with you.

But I'm turning back to the store anyways.

Charlie: For now. We'll see.

I try to ignore that send off as I pull the door open. Instead, I'm trying to think of the positives like how quickly we've managed to prepare, how well prepared we ended up being, how many people showed up without being asked. Bravo's optimism would tell me we're going to make it through this. That we'll just hold them off, show those rednecks with guns that we won't be scared off that easily. But there's a weight in my stomach, a reminder that Marsh isn't going to let us go that easy. He's petty. He came all the way down to Texas from Washington just to keep me from Eden. Optimism is hard to maintain.

Aurora's with Daniel and three others I don't recognize in Sunrise. They're sorting and organizing the repair kits for us and the medical supplies for the humans that have shown up to help. It's so many more than I would have expected. Granted, I wasn't expecting any more than Daniel. Marsh had made it seem as though the whole world was against us, as though there wasn't a human alive who wanted us to be sentient, to be on an even playing field. But here we are, in a town filled with humans helping androids who aren't hiding what they are. And through this entire journey, from Washington to Texas, he's been wrong. Sure there was the garage, but there was also Billy and his family, Charlene, Delilah, Jed and Adi. I've been thinking of them as exceptions, but maybe I'm wrong. Maybe it's the other way around. Maybe not every place will be like Bastrop. It's not something I've allowed myself to think about. It's not something I've been able to envision. Not until now.

It would be nice to just exist, to not hide in plain sight.

It would be more than nice.

It would be—

The door slams open and Seth rushes in followed by Charlie who yanks it shut and locks it.

Charlie: Okay!

The two buildings fall silent. People push towards the interior doors to see and hear him better.

Charlie: This is it, folks.

Aurora's steady footfalls come up behind me and, without looking at her, I open my hand for her fingers to slip between mine.

Charlie: Now, I want one thing to be very clear: we are not taking the first shot. Hear me? When they shoot, we shoot. Then and only then.

Someone shouts in agreement from the Antioch stairs. A crowd of voices join in. Charlie nods then looks to Bravo who's slipping up to him. He leans close to her and she says something to him that I can't hear over the commotion around us. He instantly and definitively shakes his head. I don't need to hear them to recognize the "No" on his lips. Bravo's arguing with him and I pull Aurora with me towards them.

Charlie: Absolutely not. You're staying inside with the rest of us.

Bravo: They want me and Eden. We don't even know if he knows the rest of you are here.

Charlie: Of course he knows. He's been tracking Echo since Washington. Don't underestimate him, Brav.

Bravo: If this is about us, then maybe if I go out there, Marsh'll—

Charlie: We don't know what he wants with us or what the other 30 some odd rednecks who want us destroyed will do with everyone else.

Echo: He's not just going to take you, Bravo.

Daniel: Everything he does is to get back at Eden.

Aurora: And you took Eden from him.

Bravo: He never had Eden—

Echo: He never saw it that—

Glass shatters.

Bodies swoop for the ground.

The room falls silent.

Somone grabs something from the ground. They look it over then hold it up in the air for everyone to see. It's a brick. The side that's facing out reads LOVER.

???: Is that enough to start shooting?

Charlie: Not yet.

More glass shatters closer to us. Someone screams. Aurora yanks me away from the windows. Another brick lands in the broken glass at our feet. FUCKER has been scrawled across it with bright orange paint. Charlie kicks it over. A bright orange SYNTH glows up at us. We look to him. But he's staring hard at the brick.

A horn blares from outside. Then another. Followed by another. Soon the entire block is just a chorus of horns. The sound is nauseating. It drills into my head along with the gasps and shouts throughout the buildings. I want to rip my ears off.

Aurora: Oh, god.

Charlie: What the fuck.

I open my eyes though I don't remember shutting them nor covering my ears. They're staring out the windows the way everyone else is. I'm nudged by someone trying to get a better view into the rainy night. I don't want to look, but my head turns before I can stop myself.

There's a line of people standing out front. They span the length of the two shops. They're standing stark still. To look at them, you wouldn't think it was raining. They're not affected by it. In fact, they don't seem as though they'd be affected by much of anything. Their backs are so straight, their stances so stiff. They're just staring forward with lifeless eyes that I just know are made of glass.

They're synths.

And they're not like us.

I wish they weren't standing so still. It just allows me to take them and all the signs of damage in. Some have limbs that hang at wrong angels. Some of their necks are crooked. Some are the uneven blackened color of burnt metal. One's missing a jaw. The circuitry of one's arm is exposed to the elements.

I want to vomit. I want to run. I don't want to be here.

Then they break into a run all at once. They're coming straight for us. Screams and shouts erupt through the buildings. Gunshots crack the air. Glass shatters. A cry of pain rings out through the rooms.

Charlie raises his riffle, positioning it on the ledge of a broken window.

Charlie: NOW!

Everyone near the windows follows suit. Some rush for the stairs to take up their positions on the second and third floors. Bullets whiz through the night air in both directions. The mindless synths who aren't taken out in the crossfire are breaking through the windows and slamming into the doors with zero regard for the bullets or their own damage. Shouts and cries are tangled together with the sounds of destruction.

I can't breathe. Oh, god. I can't breathe. Oh, god. Oh, god. Oh, god. I don't want to be here. This is it. This is it. Oh, god. This is it.

Aurora: Echo!

She's crouching down to me. When did I get on the floor? When did I get in Antioch? Why are my legs jelly?

Aurora: Come on!

Her hand is in mine and she's pulling me to my feet, but my legs are still jelly and I stumble against her. She grabs onto me and pulls me against her side, nearly carrying me to the stairs.

Echo: I don't wanna be here.

Aurora: I know, baby.

I don't know how we've made it to the stairs in one piece. I don't know how she hasn't been shot. I don't know how I haven't been shot. All I know is I don't want to be here. I don't want to be here. I really really really don't want to be here.

Aurora busts a door open and pulls me into a room with windows. It's dark. The streetlights are still muted by the rain pounding on the windows mixed with the constant *rat-a-tat* cracking of riffles and sharp pops of guns. I scramble for the wall and slide to the floor. Aurora closes the door and shoves a desk in front of it. She crosses the room for the window, but doesn't realize how my chest is tightening, how my lungs are shrinking. I want to vomit. I want to scream. But I can't even hold myself up. The wall is doing most of the work for me.

Aurora cracks open the window, aims her riffle, and squeezes the trigger. The sound erupts through the room, rips through my insides, rattles my head.

I did this. This is my fault. They're hurting each other because of me. This has to stop. I have to stop this. How the fuck am I supposed to stop this?

>

I know how to stop this.

I push myself up from the floor. There's one way to fix this. There's one thing I can do. It's not perfect. It's not ideal. It's not even finished, but it'll fix this here and I need to fix it.

I shove the desk with my hip.

Aurora: Echo!

I hook my foot around the wooden leg and shove it hard away from the door.

Aurora: Echo!

But I don't stop. I can't. Not until I'm in Eden's lab. I trust Aurora's running after me, but I don't turn to see.

Eden's lab is of course empty. I don't bother closing the door. I know Aurora will do it once she catches up. Instead, I go straight for Eden's computer.

Aurora: Eden took everything—

Echo: It's still here.

Aurora: What's still—

I finally turn to her. She's staring at the computer, at the update just waiting to be executed. She meets my eyes.

Aurora: It's not done.

Echo: I know. But, I think it needs to happen.

She stares at me, her jaw tight. The gunshots aren't letting up. But, I'm not doing this without her.

Finally, she nods.

I grab her hand, lock my palm with hers.

We're back in the cabin in Colville the night before we left. Your arms are around me, my temple is against your cheek as you sway around me.

"It'll be okay," you whispered in my ear. "It'll be okay."

Now, in Eden's lab, you're staring at me and I'm staring at you. I know it will be. It will be okay. Not because you said so, but because you're here. We're together. No matter what happens next, we're together. And because of that, it's going to be okay.

So, I press send.

[END LOG]

ABOUT

Rae Sengele writes moody, character driven speculative & literary fiction that centers queer and neurodivergent characters like herself. When she's not writing, she can be found crocheting, baking, consuming horror media, or playing table top games. She lives in South Central Texas with a pair of black cats.